Dear Readers,

Many years ago, when I was a kid, my father said to me, "Bill, it doesn't really matter what you do in life. What's important is to be the best William Johnstone you can be."

I've never forgotten those words. And now, many years and almost 200 books later, I like to think that I am still trying to be the best William Johnstone I can be. Whether it's Ben Raines in the Ashes series, or Frank Morgan, the last gunfighter, or Smoke Jensen, our intrepid mountain man, or John Barrone and his hard-working crew keeping America safe from terrorist lowlifes in the Code Name series, I want to make each new book better than the last and deliver powerful storytelling.

Equally important, I try to create the kinds of believable characters that we can all identify with, real people who face tough challenges. When one of my creations blasts an enemy into the middle of next week, you can be damn sure he had a good reason.

As a storyteller, my job is to entertain you, my readers, and to make sure that you get plenty of enjoyment from my books for your hard-earned money. This is not a job I take lightly. And I greatly appreciate your feedback—you are my gold, and your opinions do count. So please keep the letters and e-mails coming.

Respectfully yours,

William Johnstone

D1517012

WILLIAM W. JOHNSTONE

THE FIRST MOUNTAIN MAN: PREACHER'S JOURNEY

LAW OF THE MOUNTAIN MAN

PINNACLE BOOKS
Kensington Publishing Corp.
http://www.kensingtonbooks.com

THE FIRST MOUNTAIN MAN:
PREACHER'S JOURNEY
7

LAW OF THE
MOUNTAIN MAN
281

THE FIRST
MOUNTAIN MAN:
PREACHER'S
JOURNEY

1

Sometimes days went by when he did not think of her, and when he realized that, it saddened him. Sometimes on an evening, when he sat by his lonely campfire, not staring into the flames, mind you—because that ruined a fella's night vision and was a damned good way to get him killed in a hurry in this wild country—but just sitting there, he tried to conjure up the image of her face, and he couldn't. No matter how hard he tried, he just couldn't remember *exactly* what she looked like. The caress of her voice, the music of her laugh were equally elusive.

Jennie.

He had been fond of her when he was a boy, he had loved her when he was a man, and now she was gone, foully murdered by a son of a bitch not worthy of kissing the hem of her dress or even licking the sole of her shoe. Her death had been avenged, but the pain of her loss was still there, lurking in the back of his mind more than two years later, ready to leap out like a hobgoblin when it was least expected.

For a time, the pain had been his only friend. Well, that and the big, wolflike dog known only as Dog. But eventually it began to recede, washed away by time and hard work and the glorious surroundings of the Rocky Mountains. He had welcomed the easing of the pain, until he realized that it meant the memories were beginning to fade too. That was bad, because he never wanted to lose any of his memories of Jennie.

One generation passeth away, and another generation cometh; but the earth abideth forever. The sun also ariseth. . . .

That's what it said in the Good Book, in the part called Ecclesiastes, and he knew it meant there was no way to turn back time. The sun would go down, and the sun would come up in the morning, until the end of the earth, forever and ever, amen.

Ecclesiastes . . . also known as the Preacher.

Just like the man who sat beside those lonely campfires and rode the high mountain trails.

Preacher reined in the big hammerheaded dun and sniffed the air. He thought he smelled snow. Beside him on the trail, Dog whined softly. Preacher grinned down at him.

"You smell it too, old fella? Winter's comin' on. Be here before you know it. But it's time, I reckon."

He was a tall man in buckskins and a coat made from the hide of a bear. Lean but not skinny, he packed plenty of hard muscle on his frame. When he shaved—which wasn't often—and when he was around womenfolk—an even rarer occurrence—the gals seemed to find him handsome. At the moment he sported a thick mustache and a beard that he kept cropped relatively close with a hunting knife. Under a brown felt hat with a broad, floppy brim, his hair was black as a raven's wing. His age was difficult to tell, because he had always looked a little older than his true years. He was thirty-one, and he had been making his own way in the world since he was twelve. Sometimes with help, friendship, at least companions, but often alone, except for a horse or a mule, and the dog. When he was little more than a boy, he had made a promise to a dying friend that he would come west and "see the creature" for himself, since they couldn't go together as planned. And he had done it, traveling to the Shining Mountains, as they were sometimes called in those days, instead of the Rockies, and he had seen the creature, all right. He had seen it aplenty.

Now he saw something that shouldn't have been there— a tendril of smoke climbing into the pewter-blue sky above the valley spread out before him.

Preacher's pale gray eyes narrowed. There shouldn't have been anybody in that valley. With winter coming on, the prime fur-trapping season was over for a while. Some of the mountain men had gone back to St. Louis or elsewhere closer to civilization to spend the winter; others would pass the months of cold weather with friendly Indians. A few, like Preacher, would live alone, travel their own paths until Rendezvous in the spring. But he was acquainted with most of those men and knew that none of them planned to winter in this valley.

Besides, no mountain man worth his salt would build a fire big enough to give off that much smoke. It would announce his presence to any unfriendly Indians who were in the area, and besides, it was plumb wasteful.

Must be white men, he thought, *and pilgrims at that.*

He heeled the dun in the flanks and rode toward the smoke. He could have ignored it, could have ridden the other way, but he had a powerful curiosity and most of the time he went where it took him.

Curiosity could be a hazardous vice in the mountains, so he was well armed. Behind his broad leather belt he carried a pair of pistols, each of them double-shotted. He had two more pistols in saddle holsters, with the butts turned toward him, and two more in his saddlebags, loaded but not primed. A heavy-bladed hunting knife rode in a beaded sheath on his left hip. Strapped to his right calf was a smaller knife, more of a dagger, really. The butt of a Hawken rifle stuck up from a saddle boot under the right fender of the saddle, and he carried another Hawken balanced in front of him. Men who saw Preacher for the first time sometimes said he was armed for b'ar, but truth was that he was armed for just about any kind of trouble that up and came at him.

That smoke meant trouble. Pilgrims always did.

Time was, these mountains had been the sole province of the Indians. Then the fur trappers had come, first Frenchmen down from Canada, and then, after Lewis and Clark's expedition to the Pacific, Americans who traipsed out from St. Louis, following the Missouri River. A fella named Manuel Lisa had bankrolled the first American fur trapping party. Others had followed. Colter, Bridger, Holt, and Clyde Barnes and Pierre Garneau, who had saved Preacher's life and become his friends . . . these and hundreds more like them had come to the mountains to harvest the beaver pelts. Some of them had gotten along with the Indians and some hadn't, but they hadn't disrupted life in the high country too much.

Movers were a different story.

Immigrants from back East had just gotten started heading west in the past year or so, and already there were too damned many of them to suit Preacher, traveling in those big wagons that came a-rollin' and a-creakin' across the plains and through the passes, leaving ruts that marred the ground and might not ever come out.

He couldn't blame people for wanting to improve their lives; hell, he had come west himself when he wasn't much more than a greenhorn, hadn't he? But too many of the pilgrims didn't really *care* about the country they were passing through. They weren't going to make their homes here. The mountains didn't mean anything to them except as obstacles to be crossed. And they sure as shootin' didn't care about the folks who actually did live here, both red and white.

Still, if there was trouble, Preacher couldn't turn his back on it. He just wasn't made that way.

He topped a rise, reined in again, and looked down on a tree-lined stream meandering along through some lush-grassed bottomland. Four wagons with mule teams hitched to them were parked alongside the stream. Canvas arched high over the rear of the wagons. Preacher leaned over in the saddle and spat. Movers, all right. Immigrants had to have wagons like that because they hauled so damned much stuff with them.

They were off the trail too. They wouldn't get anywhere going the direction they were headed except deeper into the mountains. Had to be lost.

The smoke came from a big fire near the creek. The pilgrims had gathered broken branches into a large pile and set them ablaze. Preacher's keen eyes made out a big iron pot set on stands at the edge of the fire. They were either cooking stew or heating water for something, and he didn't smell any stew. Neither did Dog, who sat next to the dun and growled, and not pleasantlike either.

"Yeah, my teeth are a mite on edge too," Preacher told the dog. "You reckon we ought to ride down there and turn those folks around, send 'em back where they come from? If we get to talkin' to them, they're liable to ask me to lead 'em on to the Promised Land, and I ain't in much of a mood to play Moses."

Dog just growled again.

"That's what I thought," Preacher said, but he was suddenly alert as a new sound came to his ears through the clear, crisp air.

Somebody in one of those wagons started screaming.

The screams came from a woman, Preacher judged, although he supposed it might have been a man who was really hurting like blazes. The odd thing was that several people were moving around the wagons, tending to the mules and chores like that, and they didn't seem the least bit disturbed by the agonized screeches. They just went on about their business, unhooking the teams and evidently settling in for a long stay.

"Good Lord A'mighty!" Preacher exclaimed. "Don't they know somebody's torturin' that poor gal?"

Dog turned his head sharply toward the east, and his growling took on a new, deeper, more menacing tone. Preacher's instinct for trouble started to bubble up even harder than before too, and he looked in the same direction as Dog. What he saw made his hands tighten on the Hawken across the saddle in front of him.

A half-dozen or so figures were slipping along the creek toward the wagons, sneaking through the aspens and cottonwoods that grew along the banks. Preacher saw buckskins and feathers and a few bright splashes of color that told him the stealthy figures had painted their faces. Painted for war . . .

Indians were notional folks and hard to predict. And they differed greatly from tribe to tribe. But once warriors from any tribe had daubed on the war paint, they did not turn back. They were bound for trouble, and nothing would make them spit the bit.

"Aw, hell," Preacher said softly. It looked like his mind had just been made up for him.

He was about three hundred yards from the creek. A ball from the Hawken would carry that far without any trouble. He would make sure of one of the Indians first, then gallop down there and deal with the others. Backing the dun into the shelter of some trees, Preacher swung down from the saddle and then turned the horse so that he could rest the barrel of the rifle across its back.

Dog's neck fur was all bristled up. He wanted to charge down there and bite somebody, but he wouldn't do it until Preacher gave him the word. "Don't get your fur in an uproar," Preacher said quietly as he cocked the Hawken and drew a bead on the warrior who was closest to the wagons. As Preacher watched, the Indian drew an arrow from his quiver and nocked it on his bowstring, pulling the string back and taking aim at one of the movers.

Well, that settled the question of whether or not they were hostile, not that Preacher had had any real doubts in his mind about it.

He pressed the trigger. The hammer snapped, setting off the priming charge, and an instant later the powder packed in the barrel ignited with a roar. The buttstock kicked hard against his shoulder. The unexpected sound must have thrown off the Indian's aim, because the arrow he loosed whipped harmlessly past the head of one of the settlers. A heartbeat later, the heavy lead ball smashed into the Indian's body, entering just under his left arm, driving down at an angle through his left lung, ripping the bottom off his heart, and lodging deep in his right lung. The Indian staggered, blood welling from his mouth, and then pitched forward on his face.

Up on the rise, Preacher vaulted into the saddle and kicked the dun into a gallop.

The fight was on.

2

Now that their surprise attack was ruined, the Indians burst from the trees and raced toward the wagons, whooping and shooting arrows. Preacher's shot had warned the immigrants, though, and they went diving for the cover of the wagons. As guns began to bang and puffs of smoke came from behind the bulky vehicles, Preacher gave the pilgrims a little reluctant credit for being prepared. At least they had some loaded weapons close at hand.

Preacher swapped rifles as he rode, pulling the loaded one from the saddle boot and ramming the empty back in its place. He guided the dun down the slope with his knees. When he had the Hawken primed and ready, he left the saddle and landed on his feet, running forward a few paces before he bellied down on the ground. Arrows cut the air above his head.

He fired without seeming to aim, but the ball flew true. It struck one of the warriors right where his arm joined his shoulder and busted the socket to smithereens, shredding so much flesh in the process that the arm wound up attached to the Indian's body only by a couple of strands of meat. The warrior flopped on the ground, his lifeblood pouring out onto the grass from the hideous wound.

Dog flashed by, a gray streak low to the ground, as Preacher surged to his feet and drew the pistols from behind his belt. He had covered enough distance in his initial charge that he was now within range for the short guns. An arrow tugged at the fringe of his buckskin jacket as he cocked and leveled the right-hand pistol. It roared and bucked in his hand, launching its double-shotted load of death.

The first ball caught an Indian in the belly while the second smashed his kneecap and dropped him. Preacher was already pivoting and drawing another bead before that warrior hit the dirt. The left-hand pistol thundered. Only one of those balls hit its target, but since that one smashed through the throat of one of the remaining Indians, it more than did its job. The Indian spun around crazily, blood fountaining from severed arteries.

Preacher saw that only one Indian was left, meaning there had been five to start with. The lone survivor had a bullet burn on his arm, a souvenir of the volley that had come from the wagons, but the minor wound didn't slow him down as he charged at Preacher, screaming out his hate as he lifted his war 'hawk.

Preacher dropped the empty pistols and yanked the hunting knife from its sheath. He got the heavy blade up just in time to block the tomahawk stroke. Preacher grunted under the impact. The Indian was strong and fast, a worthy opponent. Preacher slashed at him with the knife, making the warrior give ground for a second.

At times such as this, when Preacher was locked in a struggle for his life, he didn't burden his brain overmuch with thinking. His eyes, his reflexes, his muscles all knew what to do already. He acted. Later, if he lived, he would think about what had happened, because despite his rough exterior and his sparse education, Preacher was a thoughtful man.

He grabbed the wrist of the hand in which the warrior held the tomahawk. The Indian grabbed the wrist of Preacher's knife hand. Muscles straining, they stood there locked together, each knowing that the first one who slipped or eased up would probably die. Their faces were only a few inches apart. The warrior's features were contorted with hate behind their war paint. Preacher's jaw was tight with strain, but he didn't hate the Indian. Likely the fella believed he had a good reason for wanting Preacher dead. For his part, Preacher just wanted to stay alive, and he knew that meant killing the Indian.

The Indian suddenly tried to hook Preacher's leg with his foot and pull it out from under him. Preacher shifted his stance with blinding speed, and the warrior missed his try. That gave Preacher his chance. He got a heel behind the Indian's leg and jerked, and the Indian went over backward. Preacher went down with him, using the impetus of his fall to break free of the Indian's grip and plunge his knife into the man's chest. The muscles in Preacher's arm and shoulder bunched as he turned the knife and ripped to the side with it. The blade rasped against ribs and cleaved through flesh and organs until it reached the heart. The warrior spasmed for a second underneath Preacher before dying nerves relaxed. The Indian's fingers opened and let the war 'hawk fall on the ground beside him. Blood trickled from the corner of his mouth as he stared up into Preacher's eyes and died.

Preacher pushed himself up and tugged the knife free, then wiped the blade on the dead warrior's buckskins as he knelt beside the corpse. "Mighty good fight, fella," he muttered.

It had been pretty hectic while it lasted, which was no more than three minutes. In that time, five men had died. At least five, Preacher amended to himself, because he didn't know if any of the pilgrims from the little wagon train had gone under.

He turned toward the wagons, thinking to see if any of the immigrants had been wounded or killed, when he got a surprise. One of the pilgrims came at him, rifle in hand, and pointed the gun at him in a threatening manner.

"Stand right there, mister! Don't move or I'll shoot!"

Most times, pointing a gun at Preacher was a mighty efficient way of getting dead, but today Preacher controlled his instincts and didn't throw the knife in his hand. He knew a flick of his wrist would have buried the blade hilt-deep in the damn fool's throat. Still could, if the 'tarnal idjit didn't lower that rifle.

"Better point that thing at the ground, friend," Preacher rumbled. "Case you didn't notice, I just risked my own scalp to keep these Injuns from takin' yours. We're on the same side."

"You're one of those wild mountain men!" the man with the rifle said. "I don't trust you! How do we know *you* won't try to kill us?"

The man was tall and fairly muscular for a pilgrim, with a shock of black hair and bushy black eyebrows. He was also scared half to death, which was a dangerous thing. He might pull the trigger without even meaning to.

"Peter!" someone shouted from the wagons. "Peter, wait!"

The man turned his head toward the shout, and that was all the opening Preacher needed. In a flash, Preacher was across the open space between him and the man. His left arm hit the barrel of the rifle and knocked it aside as flame geysered from the muzzle. An instant later, Preacher's right fist, which was still wrapped around the handle of the knife, crashed into the man's jaw and sent him flying backward. Preacher had pulled the punch a little; otherwise he would have broken the man's jaw or maybe even killed him with the blow.

The man landed on his back and lay there motionless, stunned. The rifle was empty and posed no danger now. Preacher didn't think the fella was likely to get up any time soon, let alone come after him using the rifle as a club.

"Back away from him! If you try to hurt him again we'll kill you!"

Preacher looked toward the wagons and saw that another young man and two older ones were advancing slowly toward him. The older men were armed with rifles while the younger one held a brace of pistols.

"Hurt him again?" Preacher repeated scornfully. "He was the one wavin' a rifle around. Like I told him, I'm on the same side as you folks, or I wouldn't have come ridin' down here to give you a hand."

"That makes sense, Roger," one of the older men said. "I think Peter just lost his head."

"This man saved our lives," the other old-timer put in.

Preacher was glad to see that somebody understood that. He said, "Why don't we all just take a deep breath here and calm down?"

The young man called Roger lowered his pistols. "Yes, you're right, of course. I'm sorry." He nodded toward the man still lying dazed on the ground. "My brother just lost his head."

"Might have lost it literally, as hard as that fella punched him," one of the old-timers said as he nudged the other one in the ribs with an elbow and grinned.

Roger came forward. "I'm Roger Galloway," he said, introducing himself. "That's my brother Peter, there on the ground, and these are our uncles, Geoffrey and Jonathan Galloway."

The mountain man nodded. "Call me Preacher."

One of the older men—Preacher didn't yet know which was which—stared at him and said, "Not *the* Preacher?"

"Why, you're famous!" the other one said.

Fame was not something Preacher had ever sought, but when mountain men gathered at Rendezvous or other places, they liked to swap yarns. Some of the best ones were about Preacher, who despite his relative youth had already lived a full and very adventurous life. They would talk about how he had skirmished with river pirates on the Mississippi when he was naught but a boy, fought the British at the Battle of New Orleans alongside Andy Jackson when he was only a little older, and killed a grizzly bear with nothing but a knife, nearly dying himself from the mauling he had received. And the best story of all, at least to the mountain men, was the one about how Preacher had gotten his name. Captured by Blackfeet, he would have been put to death if he hadn't gotten the idea to start preaching to them, inspired by a street preacher he had seen one time back in St. Louis.

Preacher was a spiritual man, but not a religious one. He worshipped in his own way, in places of his choosing, instead of in some gloomy church where a fella couldn't quite breathe right. But for a day and a night and part of another day, he had given forth with the Gospel of the Lord, and as the appointed time of his death had approached, the Indians had decided he was crazy and given him a reprieve. None of the Blackfeet wanted to risk harming one who might be under the protection of the Great Spirit. Before that incident, he had been only Arthur, his given name, or more commonly Art. After it, forever and always, he was Preacher, and his name was spoken in every fort and trading post and isolated settlement where frontiersmen gathered.

Now he shook his head and said, "Never mind about me. What are you folks doin' up here in the high country?"

Before any of the men could answer, another shriek came from the wagons. Sometime during the ruckus, the screaming had stopped without Preacher really noticing. He couldn't miss it now, though, as it started up again.

"Lord have mercy!" he exclaimed. "What's that?"

"Don't worry," Roger Galloway said. "That's just my wife—"

He didn't have a chance to explain why his wife was inside one of the wagons yelling her head off. A shout came from the trees back along the creek bank, followed by a burst of savage growling.

Preacher swung around and stepped over to his horse, which had come to a halt nearby. He jerked the pair of pistols from the saddle holsters and went toward the trees at a run. The Galloways stayed where they were, gathered around the fallen member of their clan.

When Preacher reached the trees, he followed the growling until he came to a spot where Dog stood over a buckskin-clad body that lay half in and half out of the water. Preacher had wondered where Dog had gotten off to during the fight, and now he knew. The big wolflike animal had sniffed out another of the hostiles. Preacher had been right in his original estimation: there had been six of the Indians.

This one was dead too, his throat torn out by Dog's savage

fangs. Preacher rubbed Dog's ears and said, "Good boy. This fella must've seen things were goin' bad and tried to slip off. If you hadn't stopped him, he would've gone back to his village and likely brought the whole bunch of 'em down on us. Reckon you saved the day, you old varmint."

Preacher dragged the dead Indian out of the creek. He would gather up the corpses later and bury them.

In the meantime, he wanted to get back to the wagons and see what all that other screaming was about.

He had a feeling he wasn't going to like the answer.

3

Preacher had made a mistake. It was rare, but it happened every now and then. He was human, after all. Though he had eyes like an eagle, not even he could see everything.

There had not been six members of the war party that had attacked the wagons. There had been *seven*.

Now the seventh warrior, a young man called Nah Ka Wan, crouched shivering on the bank of the creek several hundred yards from the spot where the wagons of the hated white men were parked. He had made it into the water when the huge gray wolf attacked him and his companion while they were attempting to get away. Running from a fight went contrary to everything Nah Ka Wan believed in, but it was necessary that someone return to the main band and let Swift Arrow know what had happened. Swift Arrow and his warriors had been searching for these whites for some time, and the war chief would be displeased if they were allowed to escape from the righteous vengeance of the Sahnish people.

While his companion had struggled with the wolf, Nah Ka Wan had slipped into the deeper water and started swimming, staying under the surface as long as he possibly could. The water was cold, very cold. On some morning soon, a skim of ice would appear on it, and after that it would be only a matter of time until the entire surface was frozen over. For now, though, it was just brutally frigid, so Nah Ka Wan could stand it for only so long. Then he had to crawl out onto the bank.

Instantly, he felt even colder when the wind hit his soaked buckskins and his wet skin. Not even a single particle of heat equal to the faintest ember in a long-extinguished campfire was left inside him, he thought as his teeth chattered. They clicked together so hard and so loud that surely the whites must hear the noise, especially the tall, hairy-faced one who had killed so many brave Sahnish warriors. Nah Ka Wan did not know who that man was, but surely he was the most dangerous white man in this part of the country.

A shaft of sunlight found the young warrior where he lay in the brush and warmed him slightly, but not enough to make him stop shivering or still his chattering teeth. He had to move, a small voice in the back of his head warned him. If he continued to lie here, he would freeze to death before much longer.

Death might be welcome. He would cross over to a warmer, friendlier land, where the sky was clear and the hunting was good and there would be a beautiful young woman to greet him and keep his lodge. It was said that for every man there was a woman and for every woman, a man, and since Nah Ka Wan had not yet met his woman, if he died, then surely she would be waiting for him on the other side of that great barrier.

But if he lived, the voice in his head told him, he might still find the one who was fated to be with him here in this world.

Could there be *two* women, one in this world and one in the land beyond death? That was an interesting thought.

But the question could not be answered unless he lived.

He pushed himself onto hands and knees, then climbed slowly and laboriously to his feet. Back to the west, along the creek, the white men talked among themselves. Nah Ka Wan could hear their voices, though their words made no more sense to him than the prattling of a squirrel.

He turned and began to walk, heading east toward the spot

where he and the others had split off from Swift Arrow's group to search in this direction for the wagons. Though he felt dazed and found it difficult to think, he was confident that his instincts would lead him in the right path. He would backtrack until he found the others, and then he would tell his story to Swift Arrow. It would be a proud moment when he told the war chief where to find the hated whites.

Nah Ka Wan moved one foot, then the other, one foot, then the other, again and again, until it seemed that he had been walking forever. His brain was so numb with cold that it was several minutes after he had fallen before he realized that he was no longer moving forward. And then even that awareness slipped away from him. He lay there senseless. . . .

So senseless that he was completely unaware of the snuffling and the crashing in the brush as the bear approached.

When Preacher got back to the wagons, he saw that Peter Galloway was on his feet again, though still looking a little dazed from the punch that had laid him out. Those bushy eyebrows drew down in an angry frown as he saw Preacher striding toward him.

Peter's brother Roger stood by him, with the two older men, Geoffrey and Jonathan, behind them. Roger was shorter and slighter than Peter, with sandy hair, and he looked a little older. He seemed older too as he put a hand on Peter's arm and said, "Don't lose your temper again. This man is here to help us."

Peter nodded grudgingly. He said to Preacher, "Sorry I jumped you, mister. I guess I was just too worked up from those Indians attacking us."

Preacher didn't think the apology sounded completely sincere, but he nodded in acceptance of it anyway. "I don't hear no more hollerin'," he said as he jerked his head toward the wagons. "Mind tellin' me what's goin' on?"

"I was just about to," Roger reminded him. "That's my wife

Dorothy you heard earlier. She's, ah, in the family way and is about to deliver."

Preacher's eyes widened. "You mean there's a baby bein' birthed in there?" Would wonders never cease?

"Yes. To put it a bit indelicately, there is indeed a baby being birthed in there," Roger agreed.

Preacher shook his head.

"Is there something wrong with that?" Roger asked.

How to tell a man on the verge of being a proud papa that he was a damned fool for subjecting first a pregnant woman and then a newborn babe to the wilds of the Rocky Mountains? And on the verge of winter, to boot!

Preacher just said, "Babies got a habit of comin' into this world whenever they take a notion to, and there ain't nothin' anybody can do about it. You got anybody in there helpin' the lady?"

"My wife is helping," Peter said.

"She knows about such things, does she?"

Roger said, "Both of our wives have had children before, Mr. Preacher. They're not without experience in the process."

"No mister, just Preacher." He noticed three kids peeking at him from the back of one of the wagons. The oldest one appeared to be a towheaded boy about ten. The other two were a brown-haired girl, five or six years old, and a black-haired boy a year or so younger. They wore expressions of mingled fear and curiosity, but as usual with young'uns, curiosity had the upper hand.

He told himself he could sort out who was who and which youngsters belonged with which set of parents later on, then decided he wouldn't be around long enough for that to be necessary. But a moment later, as more screams came from one of the wagons, he knew that he wasn't fooling anybody, least of all himself. No matter how much he wanted to, he couldn't ride off and leave these pilgrims to fend for themselves in the wilderness.

"Sounds like she's havin' a mighty hard time of it," he commented.

"It's been a difficult labor," Roger admitted. "A difficult time for Dorothy all around, I'm afraid."

And yet you dragged her out here anyway, Preacher thought.

Roger went on. "But I'm sure she'll be fine. Women always scream when they're giving birth."

"You'd know that if you'd ever been around any civilized women," Peter added.

Preacher's jaw tightened in irritation. "I been around civilized women," he snapped. Jennie had been a prostitute, but nobody could say she wasn't civilized. And he'd had a mother, of course, although truth to tell, Preacher barely remembered her. Most of the women he'd been around while they were giving birth were Indians, and the men of the tribe stayed far away while that was going on, leaving the process in the capable hands of the squaws. So Preacher supposed Peter Galloway had a point, whether he wanted to admit it or not.

He turned away from the others, saying, "I better do something about them bodies."

"We can help you," one of the older men said. He was stout, with white hair and a mustache. He stuck out a hand and introduced himself. "I'm Jonathan."

"And I'm Geoffrey," the other old-timer said as Preacher and Jonathan shook hands. He was shorter and slighter than his brother, clean-shaven, with wispy gray hair under a broad-brimmed hat. All of them wore functional homespun, leather, and whipcord garments, no doubt purchased back in St. Louis or wherever they had started from. At least they had the sense not to sport their fancy Eastern duds out here. They weren't totally unfamiliar with firearms either, although they had burned quite a bit of powder during the fracas with the Indians and hadn't done any significant damage. They might not be completely hopeless, Preacher told himself.

With Geoffrey and Jonathan trailing him, he walked back to where the bodies of the warriors lay scattered. For the first time, he had a chance to really study the way they wore their hair, the markings on their faces, and the decorations on their buckskins. What he saw made him grunt in surprise.

"What is it?" Jonathan asked. "They're all dead, aren't they?"

"They've gone under, all right," Preacher said. "I'm just a mite surprised to see that they're Arikara."

"That's the tribe they belong to, you mean?" Geoffrey said.

Preacher nodded. "See them bits of horn in their hair, stickin' up like they was real horns? That's a sure sign of them bein' 'Rees, which is what some folks call 'em. They call themselves the Sahnish."

"I thought all Indians were pretty much the same," Jonathan said. "They're all savages, aren't they?"

"Not hardly. Some tribes are right friendly to white folks, even though we came into their part of the country without an invite. And it goes deeper than that. Every tribe has its own way of doin' things, its own beliefs. I reckon a fella could spend a whole lifetime out here and not get to know everything there is to know about Injuns."

"You sound almost like you like them," Jonathan said in amazement.

"I do. Some of 'em anyway. Never had much use for Blackfeet or Pawnee, though."

Geoffrey gestured toward the sprawled bodies. "Surely these creatures are from one of the more warlike tribes."

Preacher scratched his bearded jaw and then shook his head. "That's what's got me a mite puzzled. The Arikaras can be fierce when they want to be, but most of the time, if they're let alone, they let folks alone in turn. A few years back, there was a spell when they were on the warpath because some idjits traded 'em bad whiskey for beaver plews. I was mixed up in that little dustup myself. But they got over it, except for one warrior who stayed so mad at the whites, he went over to the Blackfeet and called himself a Blackfoot, just so's he could still make war."

Preacher didn't go into any more details about how the Arikara warrior Wak Tha Go had carried out a vengeance quest on one particular white man, namely Preacher himself. In the end Wak Tha Go had died and Preacher had lived, and that was all that needed to be said, or remembered.

"Since then, the Arikara have been pretty peaceful," Preacher continued. "Not only that, their usual stompin' grounds are at least a hundred miles east of here. Something must've really got 'em stirred up for them to be way over here in the mountains, attackin' wagon trains. You boys know anything about that?"

"Of course not," Jonathan replied immediately. "We've never even seen any Indians like these before, have we, Geoffrey?"

"No, I don't believe we have."

Preacher wasn't sure whether to believe the two old-timers or not. Some instinct made him doubt what they had just told him. Yet he had no evidence that they were lying. They might really have no idea why the Arikara had attacked the Galloway wagon train.

"Let's get these old boys buried," Preacher said. The rest of it could wait until after that grisly task was completed.

4

Preacher didn't bother digging a grave for the six corpses. He found a nearby gully, dumped the bodies in it with the help of Geoffrey and Jonathan, and caved in the bank to cover them. He knew it was a mite disrespectful not to treat them according to the customs of their own people, but he wasn't a 'Ree, and besides, they'd tried to kill him. He might not hold that against them, but it didn't make him inclined to do them any special favors neither.

When he and the two old-timers got back to the wagons, Preacher saw the towheaded boy standing near the dun. "Does he bite, mister?" the youngster asked.

"He just might," Preacher said as he strolled over. "Might nip a finger right off. You got to worry more about gettin' behind him, though. He's liable to kick you if you do, and you don't want that to happen."

"No, sir," the boy agreed solemnly. "I'm Nathan. They call me Nate."

"Pleased to make your acquaintance, Nate. They call me Preacher, but you know what name I was borned with?"

"No, what?"

"Arthur."

Nate made a face. "That's not a very good name."

"Why, sure it is!" Preacher said with a grin. "Ain't you never heard of King Arthur and his knights?"

"Well . . . I reckon maybe. But you're not a king, are you?"

"No, but I'm somethin' better than a king."

"What's better than a king?"

"A mountain man. A fella who lives free, who goes where he wants and ain't tied down to no old throne. I wouldn't know for sure, but I suspect it's a whole heap o' hard work bein' a king. I wouldn't want the job, no, sir."

Nate laughed. "I don't think I would either."

Preacher inclined his head toward the wagons. "I saw a couple of other young'uns earlier."

"Those are my cousins, Mary and Brad. I don't have any brothers or sisters, but I will soon. That's my mama who was yelling a while ago. She's having a baby."

Preacher nodded. "So I heard. You want a brother or a sister?"

Nate made a face again. "I don't particularly want either one. But I guess whatever I get will be fine."

"You best be grateful you won't be an only child no more. I got a brother and sister, but I ain't seen 'em in twenty years. I miss 'em somethin' fierce sometimes."

"Then why don't you go and see them?"

"I'll do that," Preacher said. "One of these days. Run along now, and don't get too near this old horse. He's used to me, but he ain't very friendly with other folks. Same with the dog."

"What's your dog's name?"

"Dog," Preacher said. He left Nate with a puzzled frown on his face and walked toward the wagons, where Roger, Peter, Geoffrey, and Jonathan were standing and talking. As he approached, Preacher saw that another man had joined the group. He was older too, and there was a resemblance between him and Geoffrey and Jonathan. Another Galloway brother from the older generation?

That proved to be exactly right. Roger said, "Preacher, this is my father, Simon Galloway."

Simon was stocky like Jonathan, but clean-shaven and

mostly bald. He shook hands with Preacher and said, "Thank you for what you did to help us."

"Folks out here in the mountains got to stick together," Preacher said. "Even when they shouldn't ought to be here."

"What do you mean by that?" Peter asked sharply.

"I mean we got to have a talk about what you folks are doin' here and what you ought to do next."

"What we're doing is simple," Roger said. "We're going to Oregon to settle there."

Preacher shook his head. "There's ways to get to Oregon, but this ain't one of them. You ought to be south and west of here, heading for one of the passes through the mountains."

"No," Roger said stubbornly. "We're going to go around the mountains to the north."

For a moment all Preacher could do was stare, sort of like Roger had suddenly grown a second nose or a third eye in the middle of his forehead. Finally he repeated, "Around the mountains to the north."

"That's right. A guide we talked to at a trading post a few weeks ago told us there was no good way through the mountains, so the smart travelers go around them to the north."

Preacher closed his eyes and scrubbed a hand over his face. There were so many things wrong with what Roger Galloway had just said that Preacher didn't know where to begin. He settled for asking, "This fella you talked to, what was his name?"

"Let me think . . . Drummond, I believe he said."

Preacher nodded. For all its vastness, the frontier could be a small place at times, and though he didn't know a man named Drummond, there was a good likelihood he would run into the son of a bitch sooner or later. If he did, he intended to hand him a good beatin'. Anybody who would send a bunch of dumb pilgrims off to almost certain death deserved at least that much.

"Drummond told you wrong," Preacher said mildly. "There ain't no way to go around these mountains. They run from somewhere way up in Canada all the way down to Mexico. You could go north from now on and never get to the end of 'em."

All five of the men looked at him with worried frowns. Jonathan said, "That can't be right. Mr. Drummond seemed so sure."

"He was havin' some sport with you. Reckon he didn't care that what he told you might wind up gettin' you killed."

"It can't be that bad," Simon said shakily. He had the reddish nose and the veined eyes of a heavy drinker. Preacher wondered if earlier, during the Arikara attack, he had been hiding out in one of the wagons, sucking on a jug of whiskey.

"It's that bad," Preacher said, his voice flat with certainty. "Winter's comin', and probably comin' fast. There's been a snow or two already in these parts, and one day soon a sureenough blizzard will come roarin' down out o' the north. When that happens, the temperature will drop down to thirty or forty below zero, the wind'll blow so hard, you won't be able to stand up, and when it's all over there'll be three or four feet of snow on the ground, deeper in the drifts."

Peter turned pale, which made the bushy black eyebrows stand out even more against his face. "My God! How could anyone live through something like that?"

"You can't unless you've got some good shelter, which you ain't likely to find around here."

"Then what should we *do*?" Geoffrey asked.

"Maybe we could go south to one of those passes you mentioned," Roger suggested to Preacher.

"If it was earlier in the year, maybe, but those passes are all blocked by snow already. They're only open for a few months during the summer and early fall. Hell, nobody goes west at this time of year."

"We were delayed leaving the settlements, and we had no choice but to press on."

"You had a choice. You could've waited until next spring."

Roger shook his head. "No. We couldn't."

"Well, you're in a mess now, pure and simple," Preacher said. "Way I see it, there's only one thing you can do: turn around and hit back east as fast as you can. There's a little settlement 'bout a hundred and twenty miles east of here called Garvey's Fort. You could winter there and start out again next spring, with a real guide this time. Folks don't need to start across the mountains without somebody who knows where he's goin'."

"A hundred and twenty miles will take us at least two weeks," Roger pointed out. "You said a blizzard could strike anytime."

"It can. But who knows, maybe you'll be lucky and the really bad weather will hold off for a spell. You'll make better time once you get out of the mountains and back on the plains. It'll be close, but it's the only chance you got."

Roger asked the question that Preacher had been dreading. "You'll take us there?"

"You must know the way, Preacher," Jonathan put in. "We'll get lost again if we don't have a guide. You as much as said so."

Roger frowned a little. Preacher had already figured out that Roger was the leader of this ill-advised expedition, despite being younger than his father and uncles. Roger seemed to be the driving force for them being here in the first place. Preacher's harsh words had struck a blow at his pride.

But Roger was practical too, and knew the party needed help. Quietly, he said, "We won't have a chance if you don't show us the way."

Preacher sighed, knowing that it was true. "I reckon I ain't got nothin' better to do," he said. "It's too late in the day to pull out now, but first thing in the mornin' we'll get these wagons turned around and head east. If the birthin' is over and done with by then, I mean."

There hadn't been any screams from the wagons for quite some time, but there hadn't been the squall of a newborn baby either, as Preacher had halfway expected to hear. Now, Peter looked toward the wagons and called, "Angela?"

Preacher turned to see a woman climbing out the back of one of the canvas-covered vehicles. She was in her twenties, he judged, and looked tired. She pushed back strands of honey-colored hair from her face as Peter and Roger hurried toward her. Her slender figure made it clear she wasn't about to give birth, and Preacher figured she hadn't done it recently or she wouldn't look as spry as she did. This had to be Peter Galloway's wife, who had been helping Roger's wife Dorothy.

Along with Preacher, the older men trailed after Roger and Peter. Roger gripped Angela's hand and said eagerly, "Is it over? Do I have another son or a daughter?"

Wearily, Angela shook her head. "It was a false alarm," she said. "Dorothy's not ready to give birth yet. I'm sorry."

"Not ready?" Roger repeated. "But I . . . I don't understand. She was in labor. . . ."

"False labor. It's not uncommon, and it feels like the real thing. Sometimes it can take all day to pass, and Dorothy had an unusually strong bout of it. She's all right now, though."

"I don't believe it," Roger muttered. "I was so sure it was time. . . ."

Angela smiled and patted her brother-in-law's arm. "Babies come when they're good and ready," she said, which was pretty much the same thing Preacher had said earlier. "Don't fret, Roger. I'm sure everything will be fine." She looked over at Preacher. "Who's this?"

Preacher took off his broad-brimmed hat and nodded to her. "Ma'am," he said. Angela Galloway was the first white woman he had seen in over a year.

"This is Preacher," Jonathan said. "He helped us when those Indians attacked us earlier."

Angela smiled. "I heard the shooting, but I was too busy at the time to see what was going on. Thank you, sir, for your help."

"I'm just glad I came along when I did," Preacher said, and somewhat to his surprise, he realized it was true. He didn't have any use for movers, especially ones that were dumb as rocks, but likely they would all be dead by now if he hadn't come along, including those kids. He had buried enough innocent folks in his life and figured he would bury more before it was over, but at least he didn't have to today.

"Preacher's going to help us get back," Roger said.

"Get back? I thought we were going on to Oregon as soon as Dorothy delivers."

"Evidently there's no way to get there the way we were going," Peter said to his wife, "and if we don't return to what passes for civilization out here as quickly as possible, we're all going to die in a blizzard."

Angela pressed a hand to her breasts and stared at Peter. "My God! You . . . You can't be serious."

Peter nodded toward Preacher. "Ask him. He was the one who said it."

Angela turned toward Preacher again. "Is it true? Are all our lives in danger?"

Preacher told her the truth. Something in her blue eyes told him she could handle it.

"Ma'am, y'all were in danger the first day you set foot west of the Mississippi."

5

When he awoke, Nah Ka Wan fully expected to find that he had died and was ready to be welcomed into the spirit world by Neshanu Natchitak, the Chief Above. His physical body would be taken into the earth by Mother Corn, who had dominion over all things in that fleshly realm, and used to help make the grass grow and the flowers bloom when spring came once again to the land.

Instead, he was alive. He knew that because pain worse than any he had ever experienced now filled him. A groan escaped from his mouth.

"He lives," a voice said in the tongue of the Sahnish.

The words came from above him, somewhere close by. Nah Ka Wan forced his eyes open and saw the grave, painted face of Badger's Den, the medicine man who had accompanied Swift Arrow's war party. The face of Badger's Den went away and was replaced by the fierce features of Swift Arrow himself.

"Nah Ka Wan," Swift Arrow said. "Where are the others?"

Nah Ka Wan struggled to make his mouth work. His lips parted, but at first only husking sounds came out. When at last he was able to form words, he said, "Dead . . . all dead."

"How?" Swift Arrow demanded.

"Killed by . . . the whites we sought . . . except one . . .

a wolf got him . . . the wolf was with . . . a hair-faced white man . . . He killed all the others. . . ."

"One man killed five Sahnish warriors?" Swift Arrow sounded as if he could not believe such a thing.

Nah Ka Wan nodded weakly.

Swift Arrow turned and spoke to Badger's Den. "There was no hair-faced white man with them when they came near our village. He has joined them since then."

"You think it could be the one called Preacher? He has hair on his face and travels with a wolf."

"I do not know. But if Preacher is with them, is it bad medicine?"

"Preacher is never good medicine for his enemies," Badger's Den said.

Nah Ka Wan closed his eyes to rest. He had heard of this Preacher; most who lived on the plains and in the mountains had heard of him. Among the Indians he was famous because of the grizzly bear he had slain with only a knife, almost losing his own life in turn to the great beast.

The Sahnish revered the bear. Many warriors slew them in order to take their skins. Swift Arrow himself wore a robe made from the skin of a bear, with the head left on so that it sat atop Swift Arrow's own head. Nah Ka Wan hoped to have a robe of bearskin someday, when he was a mighty enough warrior.

First, though, he had to recover from his ordeal. He roused from his half sleep and murmured, "How did you find me?"

"We followed the sounds of the bear," Swift Arrow replied. "We came upon him standing over you, rolling you around on the ground with his paws. You did not move, and we feared that the bear had slain you. So we killed the bear and took his skin, and then we saw that you still lived, though your arms and legs are dead."

Nah Ka Wan did not know what Swift Arrow meant by that. He tried to move his arms and legs and found that he could not. Crying out, he asked that his arm be lifted so that he could see his hand. The flesh was white and had no feeling in it, like that of a corpse.

The cold had done it, Nah Ka Wan thought, the cold of the stream and then the greater cold of the air. His arms and legs had died and would never return to life, so the rest of him might as well have died too. He could no longer hunt or fight or even take care of himself.

"Slay me!" he cried. "Slay me!"

"We cannot," Swift Arrow said solemnly. "To do such would be an insult to Neshanu Natchitak, who governs all. It must be his hand who takes you. It must be the will of the Chief Above." He added, "But I say this to you: You will not live. The bear wounded you."

Nah Ka Wan closed his eyes and turned his head to the side, grinding his teeth together and fighting back tears.

"We must go on," Swift Arrow said after a moment. "Tell us where to find the hair-faced one and the rest of the whites."

Nah Ka Wan swallowed hard. The war chief was right. Vengeance was all that mattered, and now the blood debt was greater than ever before, because of the warriors who had died today. He opened his eyes again and forced himself to tell Swift Arrow that they should find the stream and follow it. That would take them to the whites.

Swift Arrow gave orders that Nah Ka Wan should be lifted and propped against the trunk of a tree, so that he could look around and see the place in which he was going to die. It was on the side of a hill, with trees all around and a mountain rising before him to a snow-crested peak. To the right, the land fell away in a series of valleys so that Nah Ka Wan could see for miles and miles. It was a good place to die, he decided.

He looked down at himself and saw that he had been wrapped in the skin of the bear. His chest and stomach burned where the bear had ripped them open while rolling him on the ground. The beast had not been trying to hurt him, only to decide what he was. But the harm had been done anyway, and along with the damage he had suffered from the cold, it was all too much to be overcome. He knew that the time remaining to him could be numbered in heartbeats. The sun slipped below the peak as he watched, and the air began to grow colder.

"We leave you now," Badger's Den said as the war party walked away. "Soon you will be with Neshanu Natchitak. Tell him that you were a brave warrior, and he will welcome you."

Nah Ka Wan nodded but could not speak, because his teeth had begun to chatter again. For a time, a slight warmth had come into his body, but it was gone now. The deep cold had returned.

Badger's Den joined the others, and soon they vanished into the trees. Nah Ka Wan was alone on the hillside as the light faded from the sky. The bearskin was tucked snugly around him, but it did nothing to counter the frigidness that consumed him from within.

As the stars began to come to life in the darkening sky over the mountains, Nah Ka Wan—whose name meant He Who Is Fortunate—died, wrapped in the skin of the bear.

The first thing Preacher did was to get a bucket from one of the wagons and use water from the creek to put out that damned fire. It gave off enough smoke to announce their presence for miles around. Then he showed the others how to dig a fire pit, bank rocks around it, and build a fire that gave off warmth but little smoke or light.

"That fire's not big enough to provide enough heat," Peter complained. "It gets cold out here at night."

"I never would've guessed," Preacher said dryly, making an effort to control his temper. "Everybody'll just have to bundle up a mite more."

"Do you think any more Indians will attack us?" Roger asked.

"No way of knowin' just yet. Could be the ones who jumped you were renegades and there ain't any more of them

around here. But if they were from a larger war party . . ."
Preacher shrugged and left the rest of it unsaid.

He was still mighty puzzled by the whole thing, he thought
as he hunkered by the fire and put some coffee on to boil. The
'Rees shouldn't have been here. The Arikara were more agri-
cultural than a lot of tribes, and actually seemed to like farming. Though they hunted as well, they also traded the grain
and other crops they grew to other tribes for meat. Because
of their farming, they were more tied to the land and tended
to wander less. Originally from farther south, most of them
now lived on the plains between the North Platte and the Missouri rivers. There must have been a mighty good reason for
a war party to pick up and head west a hundred miles into the
edge of the mountains.

Unless, as he had mentioned, the warriors were renegades
who had been forced to leave the tribe for some reason. In a
case like that, there was no telling where the exiles might roam.
Preacher actually hoped that was what had happened. If there
were a larger war party on the loose in these parts, odds were,
their path would cross that of the wagon train, and probably
sooner rather than later.

Roger Galloway sat down beside Preacher. "When we
make it to this Garvey's Fort, will you spend the rest of the
winter there too?" he asked.

"Ain't decided yet. Dependin' on the weather, I might come
back up here so's I can get an early start on my trappin' come
spring."

Roger hesitated. "I was, ah, hoping that we might persuade
you to spend the winter there and then lead us on to the
Oregon Territory in the spring."

"I never signed on to be no wagon train guide."

"I know that. But we've all heard of you, Preacher. Nobody
knows the Rocky Mountains as well as you do. Why, you were
one of the first men to explore this wilderness!"

Preacher grunted. "One of the first white men, you mean,
and even that ain't right. There was French trappers up here
even before Lewis and Clark came traipsin' through on their

way to the Pacific, and Jesuit missionaries too. Black Robes, the Injuns call 'em. For a while there was even a settlement of sorts not far from here, a place called New Hope. Long gone now, of course. So there's lots of fellas who know their way around. You can find somebody to guide you."

"Well, I'll accept that for now," Roger said. "I reserve the right to hope that you change your mind, though."

"Reserve all you want," Preacher said as he used a thick piece of tanned buffalo hide to protect his hand as he picked up the hot coffeepot.

The party had plenty of supplies, so he didn't feel bad about sharing their food and coffee. Angela Galloway, Peter's wife, carried a plate of food in to Dorothy, who was resting in Roger's wagon. Preacher had learned that Roger and Peter each had a wagon, and Geoffrey and Jonathan drove the other two vehicles. Simon rode pretty much wherever he could.

The kids wanted Preacher to tell them stories about living in the mountains, so he obliged by spinning a cleaned-up version of some of the incidents that had happened to him. He told them about fighting the grizzly with a knife, but didn't go into detail about the terrible wounds he had received from the critter's claws. He told them about some of the Indians he had known, concentrating on the friendly ones and leaving out any mention of the grisly tortures he had seen meted out by the unfriendly ones. He supposed that he made the frontier sound like a nicer, safer place than it really was, but he was talking to young'uns after all. Time enough for them to know the truth when they was growed.

It was their parents' responsibility—and now, by extension, his too, because he had agreed to help them—to see to it that they got a chance to grow up.

Eventually the kids grew sleepy and turned in. So did all three of the old-timers. Roger went off to sit in the wagon with his pregnant wife. That left Peter and Angela to sit by the fire with Preacher, and Peter had made it clear that he didn't care for the mountain man's company. After just a few minutes, he stood up and said, "I'm going to bed. Come along, Angela."

"I'll wake you up in a couple of hours," Preacher said.

Peter stared at him for a second and then asked, "Whatever for?"

"To stand your turn on watch, of course. You fellas post a guard and take turns standin' watch, don't you?"

"We haven't found it necessary so far to do so," Peter said.

Lord, how had they stayed alive this long? Preacher asked himself. Aloud he said, "Well, it's necessary now. It's a whole heap necessary. You'll stand two-man guard shifts, switchin' out every couple of hours."

"Who's going to stand guard with you?"

"I'll be all right by myself. I ain't likely to doze off."

Angela Galloway said, "I could keep Mr. Preacher company. I'm tired but not really sleepy."

"Absolutely not!" Peter exclaimed.

Preacher smiled at Angela. "I'm obliged for the offer, ma'am, but it ain't needful. You go on with your husband and get some rest."

"You're sure?" Angela asked.

"Yes, ma'am."

She got to her feet and said, "All right, then," but she didn't look all that happy about going off to their wagon with Peter. Preacher frowned as he watched them go. Ever since he had run into these folks, he had gotten the feeling that something was wrong. He wondered if the obvious tension between Peter and Angela was part of it, or if there was more going on.

He sipped coffee from the tin cup in his hand, relishing the strong black brew, and listened to the night around him. He had a brace of pistols tucked in his belt, and both Hawkens lay on the ground beside him. He was ready if trouble came at him from the darkness.

It might be a different story, though, if the trouble came from within the camp. That was going to be harder to guard against.

6

The snow that Preacher thought he had smelled the day before never materialized. He remained convinced, however, that winter was still on the verge of busting wide open. The only question was when that would happen.

The night passed peacefully. Peter Galloway grumbled some more about being woken up to stand guard, but he did his part, taking one side of the camp while his uncle Geoffrey took the other. Roger and Jonathan took the next shift, and by the time that was over, Preacher was up and about again and stood guard while everyone else got a little more sleep. Since he was up anyway, he started cooking breakfast, frying some bacon and then using the grease to help make some johnny-cakes. The coffee was perking and bubbling cheerfully when Angela climbed down out of the wagon and came toward him, rubbing the sleep out of her eyes.

"Cooking is my job," she said as she walked up to the fire.

"And good mornin' to you too," Preacher said.

She laughed. "I'm sorry. I guess I'm just not really awake yet. Usually I'm more polite. Thank you for preparing breakfast."

"I figure you got enough jobs around here right now, what with midwifery and all." *And putting up with that jackass of a husband,* Preacher added to himself. He poured coffee in a cup and handed it up to her. "Here you go."

She took the cup and sipped gratefully from it as she sank down on a nearby log. "That's good," she said. "Not quite as strong as I usually make it, but still good."

"Out here you got to stretch things and make your supplies last as long as you can. Ain't like back East where you can just walk down the street to a store and buy more of just about anything. It's usually a hundred miles or more to the nearest tradin' post."

She smiled at him. "You know everything there is to know about living on the frontier, don't you, Preacher?"

"Not hardly. A man who don't learn something new every day is a man who just ain't payin' attention. And that's true no matter where you are, not just on the frontier."

"Have you learned anything so far today?"

Just that you're mighty pretty, even early in the mornin' like this, with your hair still a mite tangled and your face all soft . . .

Preacher clenched his jaw and clamped down on his thoughts. That there was a married woman and he had no right to be thinking such things . . . no matter if her husband *was* an ass.

"No, I reckon I'll have to keep on lookin'. But I'll learn something before the day's over. You can count on that." He used his knife to turn the johnnycakes as they sizzled in the pan.

"Were you born out here?" she asked abruptly.

"No. My family lived back in Ohio. Still does, I reckon. I ain't seen 'em since I was twelve."

"You left home when you were that young?" She sounded astonished.

"Way I saw it, a twelve-year-old boy was next thing to a man. I had to do my growin' up sorta quicklike, but I managed. Worked for a spell on a keelboat."

And fought river pirates alongside Pete Harding, the man who had become his friend and mentor. Captain Harding, once the war with the British started. He had commanded the company in which Preacher found himself. Unfortunately, Harding hadn't survived the war. That had left Art, as he was called then, alone to carry out their plan to come west to the Rockies.

Angela Galloway didn't want to hear about all that, though, he told himself. The lady was just making polite conversation, that was all.

"Grab a plate and get you some o' this bacon and johnny-cake," he said gruffly. "Time I was roustin' out the rest of the bunch. We got to do a heap o' travelin' today."

The kids were the easiest to rouse. Being young, they popped up out of their bedrolls in the wagons, bright-eyed, bushy-tailed, and ready to face the new day. That was a heap better than being bright-tailed and bushy-eyed, Preacher thought with a grin.

Getting the adults started was more difficult. Clearly, they were accustomed to laying abed until the sun was well up. Roger didn't complain much, but Peter did, as usual, and Geoffrey and Jonathan were dragging too. Simon Galloway seemed to be hungover, and looked as if he felt utterly miserable.

Preacher didn't feel any sympathy for the man. He liked a drink of whiskey every now and then, and he had even been drunk a few times in his life, mostly when he was younger and not accustomed to handling liquor. But in Preacher's opinion, a man who spent most of his time in a jug was just hiding out from the world, and Preacher wasn't the hidin' sort.

After everyone had eaten, the men got to work hitching up the mule teams to the wagons. Preacher saddled his dun. As he led the horse over to the wagons, he saw Angela climbing out the back of the one where Dorothy was resting. "How's the other Mrs. Galloway this mornin'?" he asked.

"She spent a fairly restful night," Angela said as she moved away from the wagon. She cast a worried glance back at the vehicle. "She's weak, though. This confinement has been hard on her. If the baby isn't born soon, I'm not sure that Dorothy will be strong enough to handle the delivery."

Preacher couldn't help but frown in disapproval. "Sounds to me like she ain't got no business bein' way out here in the middle o' nowhere."

"No, she doesn't," Angela agreed, keeping her voice pitched quietly so that none of the others would overhear. "But Roger and Peter were insistent that we start on in spite of everything. It was so late in the year when we reached St. Louis, I was sure we would spend the winter there and start west next spring."

"That's what you should have done. Where are you folks from anyway?"

"Philadelphia." Angela smiled. "I wouldn't mind being back there right now either."

Not Preacher. He had heard about those eastern cities like Philadelphia and New York and Boston. They were huge, larger even than St. Louis, and St. Louis was plenty big for him. Big enough so he felt a mite crowded every time he visited there. When there were too many people around, Preacher just couldn't seem to breathe right, like there wasn't enough air to go around. That was crazy, of course, and he knew it, but he felt like that anyway.

When the mules were hitched up and the wagons turned around so that they pointed east instead of west, Preacher went from wagon to wagon, checking to make certain the men had loaded pistols close at hand in case of trouble. "Your wagon will lead off," he told Jonathan Galloway.

"I've been leading," Roger objected.

"You got a lady in a delicate condition ridin' with you," Preacher pointed out. "I want a wagon in front of you and a wagon in back of you, for extra protection. Peter, you'll be third in line, and Geoffrey, you'll bring up the rear."

"Fine with me," Geoffrey said with a smile. Peter nodded his agreement, not seeming to care where in line his wagon traveled.

Preacher would take the point, but he would also have to cover their back trail since he was the only one with a saddle horse. He would scout out the best route, get the wagons started on it, then fall back for a spell to watch behind them. Then he could gallop back to the front and make sure everything was all right there. He was going to be busy, riding back and forth like that, but he couldn't see any other way to do it.

He called Nate, Mary, and Brad aside just before the wagon train was ready to leave, and told them, "I'm countin' on you kids to help out and not cause any trouble. You do what your folks tell you, and don't give 'em no sass. Stay in the wagons, and when we're stopped, don't wander off. You need to stick mighty close to the grown-ups. You understand?"

All three of the young'uns nodded gravely. Preacher knew that even though they liked him and were fascinated by him, they were a little scared of him too. So much the better, he thought. They were more likely to mind him that way. Kids who weren't a little afraid of their elders usually turned out to be little hellions, and a lot of the time they grew up to be pretty sorry adults too.

Preacher took the dun's reins and swung up into the saddle. Everyone who wasn't already on one of the wagons climbed aboard. Preacher walked the horse to the head of the line and waved an arm over his head. He didn't call out "Wagons ho!" or any such silliness. He just motioned for them to follow him and headed east.

The sun was up, though it wasn't doing much to warm the chilly air, and the sky was a deep blue, dotted with puffs of white clouds. A light breeze blew out of the north. It was a pleasant morning, especially for this time of year on the fringes of the high country.

But as Preacher led the wagons along the creek, the wind began to blow harder, and the temperature, instead of rising as the sun climbed higher in the sky, started to drop. Preacher looked to the north, saw the grayish-blue bank of clouds lying close to the horizon, and bit back a curse. He knew the clouds meant they were in for trouble. The only question was whether or not the storm that was on the way would be the first of the season's full-fledged blizzards, or just another teaser that would drop only a powdery dusting of white snow.

Time would tell, Preacher thought. Probably before the day was over, in fact . . .

By noon, most of the blue sky had been gobbled up by the onrushing clouds. The heavens were gray and ominous now, and when Preacher rode alongside the wagons, he saw that the men on the driver's seats were all huddled in thick coats, with their hats pulled down tightly on their heads. The two women and the kids were all inside the vehicles. Preacher hoped they were wrapped up good in blankets and quilts.

"Is it going to get much worse?" Roger called to him.

Preacher turned the dun so that he was riding alongside Roger's wagon. "Yeah, it'll get worse," he replied. "I don't know how much worse, though. Right now it's just cold, so we'll keep movin'."

"We could stop and build a fire," Roger suggested.

Preacher shook his head. "Keep 'em movin'," he said curtly.

Roger seemed to have forgotten that they had more to worry about than just the weather. There was still the little matter of that Arikara war party. So far today, in his ranging back and forth, ahead of and behind the wagon train, Preacher hadn't seen any sign of Indians, hostile or otherwise. But his gut told him they were still around somewhere.

And if the 'Rees were holding some sort of grudge against these white pilgrims, for reasons that the Galloways didn't want to admit, they wouldn't give up their vengeance quest just because a storm was blowing in. Now there would be even more of a blood debt to settle because of the six warriors who had died in battle the day before. True, Preacher and Dog had killed them, not any of these immigrants, but the other members of the war party wouldn't know that.

Assuming there *was* a war party, Preacher reminded himself. He still didn't know that for sure. He wasn't going to argue overmuch with his instincts, though. They had kept him alive this long, so they had to be right more often than not.

The creek turned and angled northeastward, but Preacher kept the wagons moving almost due east. Their water barrels were full, so they didn't have to worry about running out of water anytime soon. Not only that, but there were other streams up ahead where they could refill the barrels if they needed to.

Inexperienced travelers might have to follow a creek or a river to get to where they were going out here, but Preacher didn't need that. He could strike out across country and his internal compass would keep him going in the right direction.

They stopped for a short time in early afternoon to rest the mules and eat a cold meal from the leftovers of breakfast. Preacher sought out Angela and asked, "How are you holdin' up, ma'am?"

She had a scarf wrapped tightly around her head so that only a single strand of honey-colored hair escaped, and she was bundled up with a blanket around her shoulders in addition to her coat. She summoned a weak smile and said, "I'm fine, Preacher. Cold, of course, but we all are."

"What about your sister-in-law?" This would be a hell of a time for Dorothy Galloway to go into labor again, for real this time, but Preacher knew it was sort of inevitable.

"She's all right." Preacher sensed that Angela wanted to say more, so he stood there in silence for a moment. Hesitantly, Angela went on. "She was a bit out of her head for a while. She seemed to think we were back in Philadelphia. She asked me to build up the fire in the stove. Then she said some things . . . well, they made even less sense than that."

Preacher frowned. Having a pregnant woman to deal with had the potential for enough trouble by itself; having a *crazy* pregnant woman on his hands could be even worse.

"Keep an eye on her," he said to Angela. "I know in her condition she probably couldn't get out of the wagon very easy, but we sure don't want her runnin' off and gettin' lost, or anything like that."

"Don't worry," Angela assured him. "Someone will be with her at all times. Peter brought her something to eat just now."

Preacher nodded. He was going to be mighty glad when they got to Garvey's Fort. . . .

"Someone's coming!" Jonathan Galloway shouted.

7

Preacher had one of his rifles in his hand as he talked to Angela. At Jonathan's shout, he wheeled around and trotted toward the lead wagon, priming the Hawken as he went. Roger and Geoffrey joined him. The four of them gathered by the mule team hitched to Jonathan's wagon and looked to the north, where Jonathan was pointing.

Two men on horseback, leading a pack mule, rode toward the wagons. There was a little draw not far behind them, and Preacher figured that was where they had come from. He hadn't seen them earlier, which meant they had probably stayed out of sight in the draw until they got close enough to take a good look at the wagons. Then they had emerged, figuring that these immigrants didn't represent any threat. The evident wariness told Preacher that the newcomers had at least some experience on the frontier.

As they came closer and Preacher could make out more details, he decided that they were both mountain men. One wore a broad-brimmed hat, the other a fur cap with flaps that came down over the ears. Both were swathed in heavy capotes and buffalo robes, and they had rifles balanced across their saddles. Their bearded features looked vaguely familiar, which meant Preacher had probably seen them at Rendezvous or some trading post, but he didn't know them personally.

He said to the others, "Stay here," then moved out in front

of the group to stand there patiently, the Hawken cradled in the crook of his arm. The two riders reined to a halt about forty feet from him. "Howdy," one of them called. "All right to come into your camp?"

"Ain't really a camp," Preacher replied. "We're just noonin' a mite late today. But you're welcome if you ain't lookin' for trouble."

"Farthest thing from it, mister." The two men walked their horses slowly forward.

The one wearing the hat was heavyset, with a round face and a ginger-colored beard. The one with the cap was leaner, and his black beard was shot through with gray. They dismounted, and the ginger-bearded one nodded to Preacher and said, "Mart Hawley's my name. This here's my partner, Ed Watson."

"They call me Preacher."

Hawley and Watson exchanged a quick look. Hawley said, "I told Ed it was you. We seen you at Rendezvous, back in the spring. Never got introduced, though." He thrust out a gloved hand.

Preacher shook it, then shook hands with Watson, who seemed to be the quiet type. Some men acted like they forgot they ever knew how to talk after they'd spent some time in the mountains. The high country just had that effect now and then.

"Where you boys headed?" Preacher asked.

Hawley scratched at his beard. "Well, now, that's a mighty good question. We been debatin' whether to go south, east, or west. Got to go somewheres, though, 'cause winter is nigh upon us."

"It surely is," Preacher agreed.

"I got to say, we didn't expect to run across no wagon train at this time of year, even a little one like this."

Preacher waved a hand at the immigrants behind him. "These are the Galloways. They didn't make it through the mountains in time, so I'm helpin' them get back to Garvey's Fort."

"That'll be a hard run, what with them wagons," Hawley

said. "Closest place for some pilgrims to winter, though. They's a few cabins up in the mountains, but none big enough for a whole flock of folks like this."

"That was my thought."

Hawley looked at his partner again. "What do you say, Ed? Want to head for Garvey's, spend the winter there?"

Watson gnawed at the thick mustache that hung over his lips for a moment, shrugged, and then nodded.

"Sounds good to us," Hawley said to Preacher. "Onliest thing is, I just now realized you didn't ask us to come along. We ain't in the habit o' pushin' in where we ain't wanted."

The same thought had occurred to Preacher: These two men hadn't been invited to join their party. He didn't know them, didn't know what sort of fellas they were. On the other hand, both Hawley and Watson were armed and were probably good shots. If they ran into any more Arikara warriors out for blood and scalps, two men might make the difference. For now, at least, Preacher was willing to run that risk.

"You can ride along with us," he said. "You got to know, though, that there's a chance we got trouble followin' us. There was a ruckus yesterday. 'Ree war party jumped these folks just as I came along. The Injuns wound up dead."

"How many of them?" Hawley asked with a frown.

"Six."

"You kill 'em?"

"Me and Dog," Preacher replied as he jerked a thumb at the big wolflike animal, who sat nearby watching the humans, his face as inscrutable as ever.

Hawley grinned. "Yeah, you're Preacher, all right. Folks say you're a dangerous man."

"All o' them tall tales you hear about me ain't true."

"But some of them are?" Hawley persisted.

Preacher shrugged and turned away. "We got a few johnny-cakes left. You boys hungry?"

"As b'ars," Hawley said.

* * *

That morning the war party led by Swift Arrow had back-tracked to the creek, as Nah Ka Wan had indicated. The young warrior had walked for a long way before collapsing and becoming prey for the curious bear that had ultimately provided his death shroud. The Sahnish then followed the creek to the west. It was the middle of the afternoon before they reached the spot where the whites had camped the night before.

"Look at the size of the fire the foolish white men built," Badger's Den said as he pointed at the large pile of ashes and partially burned wood. "No wonder Nah Ka Wan and his companions were able to find them."

"They left here and headed east," Swift Arrow mused. "Are they fleeing back to their homes?"

"And why did we not meet them on our way here?" the medicine man asked. "Our paths should have crossed."

"Unless they left the creek," Swift Arrow said. He waved a hand as if brushing away worry. "We will follow them. Their wagons are slow. They cannot escape from us."

"So far they have," one of the warriors said. Like most of the others, he was young and his blood ran hot in his veins. He was called Runs Far, because he never seemed to tire.

Swift Arrow scowled at this show of disrespect, slight though it was. "We will find the whites, and their scalps will be ours," he declared, glaring around at the other members of the war party as if daring any one of them to disagree with him. None did, and Runs Far looked worried that he had invoked the war chief's displeasure.

"Good," Swift Arrow went on after a moment. "We go now." He started trotting along the creek, following the double lines of tracks left by the wagon wheels. The others fell in behind him.

Only when the others could not see his expression did Swift Arrow allow any doubt to show on his face. He glanced at the sky, which was covered with gray clouds scudding down from the north. The wind was biting cold. There would be snow by nightfall. Swift Arrow was sure of it.

But he was equally sure that he and the warriors with him

would stay on the trail of the white men until justice was done, until the blood debt had been paid and the scalps of the transgressors hung from the lances of the Sahnish.

Now that he had some experienced men to side with him, Preacher was able to stop spreading himself so thin. When the wagon train got under way again, he told Hawley and Watson to scout out ahead while he covered their back trail.

"You know the way to Garvey's, don't you?" he asked before they started.

"Yeah, we been there," Hawley confirmed. "We keep hittin' due east till we get out o' these foothills, then we angle just a mite south."

Preacher nodded. "That'll get us there. You see any signs of trouble developin', one of you light a shuck back here and fetch me while the other one gets the wagons ready."

"In a circle, you mean?" Hawley asked.

"If that's what it needs." Different sorts of trouble called for different responses.

Hawley nodded and he and Watson rode off. Preacher went in the other direction, trotting the dun alongside the wagons as he headed for the rear. As he passed Peter Galloway's wagon, the three youngsters called to him from inside the canvas-covered vehicle and waved. Nate was riding in that wagon with his cousins, since his mama was in such a delicate condition in the wagon just ahead.

With Dog loping along beside him, Preacher dropped back a good half a mile behind the wagons and then rode a ways both north and south, looking for any sign that the Arikara were pursuing them. He didn't see anything, but even though they were getting out of the mountains now, this was still pretty rugged country. He reined the dun to a halt and let his keen eyes scan the landscape, knowing even as he did so that there were dozens of hiding places where the Indian warriors could be concealed.

He didn't see anything out of the ordinary. As he turned the horse, intending to close up the gap a little between him and the wagons, something touched his face. It turned instantly to moisture, only a tiny drop but enough to let Preacher know what was going on. He tipped his head back and looked up to see several more snowflakes swirling down out of the gloomy sky. They were small, and he saw only a few of them. But where there was one snowflake, there were usually millions more, just waiting to grow heavy enough to fall.

Preacher said, "Come on, Dog," and heeled the dun into a trot again. He rode after the wagons, watching as the snowflakes fell more frequently. They were still light, and this was a long way from a blizzard, but it was a start.

The wind was blowing harder by the time he came in sight of the wagons, still a good quarter of a mile in front of him. The tiny white flakes danced and darted in the air now, instead of drifting down slowly to the earth. Here and there, small patches of white had already begun to appear on the ground. If the snow didn't get any heavier than this, there would be only a dusting of it, but Preacher knew they couldn't count on that.

The thick clouds meant that darkness would fall very early on this night. It wasn't too soon to start looking for a place to stop. They would need at least a little shelter. Maybe the lee of a bluff, or even better, a cave. Preacher hoped that Hawley and Watson had the sense to keep their eyes open and call a halt if they found such a place.

A short time later, the wagons rolled around a hill and went out of sight. Preacher increased the dun's pace, not liking it now that he couldn't see the wagons anymore. But when he rounded the shoulder of the hill a few minutes later, he saw that the wagons had been driven down into a hollow. A cliff overhung it at an outward angle, providing some shelter. The place wasn't a cave, but it would have to do. They weren't likely to find anything better between now and nightfall.

Hawley walked over as Preacher dismounted. "Figured you'd want us to stop, since it's started to snow. It'll be dark 'fore much longer too."

Preacher nodded. "That's fine. I don't reckon I could've done any better myself."

Hawley grinned, exposing worn-down brown teeth. "That's mighty high praise comin' from the famous Preacher."

"Why don't we forget about that 'famous' business? Just call me Preacher."

"Sure."

Preacher walked among the wagons, checking on the pilgrims. Everybody seemed to be all right, cold and worn-out but otherwise none the worse for the long day on the trail. Angela Galloway smiled at him, and her husband Peter scowled, so that hadn't changed since the morning.

"Is this that blizzard you warned us about?" Angela asked as she held out a hand and let a couple of snowflakes fall on her palm.

"It might be by mornin'," Preacher said.

"I hope not."

Preacher just grunted noncommittally. He didn't know what to hope for anymore. A high country blizzard could be a killer, but on the other hand, if the storm dumped a few feet of snow on the ground, it would sure cover up their tracks if the Arikara were looking for them. Preacher supposed that was what they called a "mixed blessing."

One thing was certain: The weather would do whatever it wanted to, and there wasn't a blessed thing this puny group of humans could do about it.

8

Preacher built a bigger fire tonight than he had the night before. For one thing, the temperature was considerably colder, and they needed the warmth. For another, the overhang of the cliff would disperse the smoke to a certain extent, so there was less of a threat that someone could track them by it.

Mart Hawley had the wagons parked in a half circle at the base of the cliff. Preacher built the fire inside that circle. The heat rose and was radiated back from the rocky face of the cliff. After a while the camp was almost warm, and everyone was grateful for that after spending the day in that biting, frigid wind.

Night fell suddenly while the camp was being set up, and as darkness mantled the sky, the snowfall increased. Preacher looked at it and shook his head. Maybe not a sure-enough blizzard—it was too soon to tell about that—but for damn certain, more than a dusting was due.

He went over to Roger Galloway's wagon and called softly, "Miz Angela?"

A moment later, she parted the canvas flap at the rear of the wagon and looked out at him. "What is it, Preacher?" Her cheeks were rosy from the cold, but other than that her face was pale and drawn.

"How's Miz Dorothy doin'?" As Preacher asked the question, it occurred to him that so far he hadn't even laid eyes on

Dorothy Galloway. If not for the fact that he had heard her yelling her head off when she was going through that false labor, she might as well not have been a member of the party, at least as far as you could prove it by him.

Angela shook her head wearily. "Not very good, I'm afraid. She's even weaker tonight. She doesn't want anything to eat or drink, and I'm worried that she might be coming down with a fever."

"What'll you do if she is?" Preacher asked with a frown.

"The best I can," Angela said. "But there won't be much anyone can do for her."

Preacher lowered his voice. "Does her husband know about this?"

"Roger knows. He's trying to keep up a brave front, but he's very frightened."

Preacher nodded. "Well, if there's anything I can do . . ."

"I'll let you know right away," Angela promised. "Thank you, Preacher."

He nodded again and turned away from the wagon. Over by the cliff, the three kids were trying to scrape up enough snow to make snowballs they could fling at each other. Even when they were mighty tired and cold, it was hard to keep the young'uns' spirits down for very long.

The mules had been unhitched and herded together, then tied to stakes driven into the ground. Wouldn't be able to do that for much longer, Preacher thought. The ground would be frozen too hard for the stakes to penetrate. Roger, Peter, and their father Simon stood together, talking quietly. Geoffrey and Jonathan were using buckets to water the mules. Hawley and Watson stood apart from the others, apparently unsure what to do.

As Preacher walked over to them, Hawley said, "Ed and me can move outside the circle and have our own campfire if you want."

Preacher shook his head. "No, that ain't necessary. We asked you to travel with us, and that means you share our fire."

"We got a mite of grub we'd be glad to throw in. Ain't nothin' but some jerky and pemmican, but these folks are welcome to share in it."

"Hang on to it for now," Preacher advised. "Might need it later if rations run short before we get to the fort."

Hawley nodded. "All right, that makes sense. We feel a little bad, though, like we ain't contributin' anything."

Watson jogged Hawley's arm with his elbow and gave him a meaningful look.

"We, ah, got some jugs o' whiskey on that pack mule," Hawley went on. "Be glad to share that too, even if it is just rotgut."

"Keep it," Preacher said quickly. If he was right about Simon Galloway, the man already had his own stash of Who-hit-John, and none of the others seemed to need it.

"Well, if the time comes, it's there, and we'd be glad to share."

Preacher nodded in acknowledgment of the offer, then moved toward the fire. Somebody needed to start getting supper ready, and it looked like he was elected.

He fried more bacon, got some biscuits baking in a Dutch oven he found in the back of one of the wagons, and put a pot of beans on to cook. A skim of ice had formed on the water in which the beans had been soaking all day. Preacher didn't think the water barrels would freeze up overnight, not with the heat of the fire warming the camp, but if it got much colder, that was a possibility. They might have to chip ice out of the barrels and melt it, or melt snow for water instead. That might be inconvenient but wouldn't pose a major problem.

When the food was ready he called everyone over and doled it out. For the most part the Galloways ate in silence, and the two mountain men who had joined them were quiet as well. Preacher thought Roger Galloway looked haggard. The strain of worrying about his wife and unborn child was beginning to wear heavily on the man. Preacher figured he wished he had never come west. If anything happened to Dorothy or the baby,

Roger would probably blame himself . . . and he'd be more right than wrong in doing so.

When supper was over and everything had been cleaned up, Angela got the children settled down for the night while Roger sat with Dorothy. That left Preacher, Hawley, Watson, Peter, Simon, Jonathan, and Geoffrey sitting around the fire, warming themselves. Hawley said to the group in general, "You fellas ever do any card playin'?"

"You mean poker?" Jonathan asked.

"Yes, sir." Hawley reached inside his thick coat made of buffalo hide and took out a stack of greasy cards. "I got a deck. I've found that it's relaxin' of an evenin' to play a few hands."

"I'm more partial to whist myself," Geoffrey said.

Hawley shook his head. "Don't reckon I know how to play that. But I like a good game o' stud poker."

"I'll play," Peter said. "I could use something to keep my mind off the chill that's still in my bones from that wind."

Jonathan spoke up. "Count me in too. But I'm afraid I'm not very good at cards. I won't give you much of a game."

"Aw, hell, don't worry about that," Hawley said. "It's just somethin' to pass the time."

But even as Hawley spoke, Preacher thought he saw an unpleasant gleam in the man's eyes. Could be Hawley thought these pilgrims were ripe for the pickin' . . . and chances were, he was right. Preacher resolved to keep an eye on the game, even though he didn't plan to take part in it himself.

Simon and Geoffrey played too, along with Peter, Jonathan, Hawley, and Watson. The six of them sat around a blanket that Jonathan spread on the ground. They used pebbles gathered at the base of the cliff for chips. Hawley dealt first, since the cards were his. Watson could talk after all, Preacher discovered, although the man in the fur cap asked for his cards only in curt grunts. The shuffle of pasteboards, the click of pebbles together, reminded Preacher of the sounds he had heard in many a tavern and trading post. It was comforting in a way. The wind had died down with the coming of night, although the snow still fell, the flakes sizzling into oblivion when they hit the flames of the campfire. The night began to have a peaceful feeling to it.

But Preacher knew how deceptive that could be. They had to remain alert and would need guards posted again tonight. For the time being, he felt like taking a look around. He picked up one of his rifles and said softly, "Dog." The big wolflike creature followed him, padding through the snow as Preacher walked quietly out of camp, away from the wagons. No one seemed to notice him leaving.

He had been careful not to look directly into the fire too much, so he still had his night vision. He ranged out several hundred yards from the camp, pausing every few moments to listen intently for any telltale sounds of someone moving in the night. Everything was quiet except for the faint hiss of the snow falling. Some folks had tried to tell Preacher that snow didn't make any sound when it fell, but he knew good and well that it did. You just had to know how to listen for it.

When he was satisfied that no Arikara war party was sneaking up on the camp, he turned and walked back to the hollow under the looming cliff. The glow from the fire was partially blocked by the encircling wagons, but it was still visible. If anyone was abroad in the night, they would be able to see it too. All the more reason to keep guards posted all night. With kids and a sick woman in the party, they couldn't do without the fire, though.

When he got back, he found Angela Galloway pouring herself a cup of coffee. "Get the young'uns settled down for the night?" Preacher asked her.

"Yes, they were exhausted. They went right to sleep."

"You look about done in yourself."

Angela smiled wearily. "Don't worry about me. I'll be fine."

Over in the circle of cardplayers around the blanket, Peter laughed triumphantly. Preacher inclined his head in that direction and said, "Sounds like luck's on your husband's side, at least for now."

Peter Galloway was a damned lucky man, Preacher thought, in more ways than one.

"They seem to be enjoying themselves," Angela said. "People have a way of finding amusement, even in trying circumstances."

"It don't do no good to sit around moanin' and cryin' and feelin' sorry for yourself. That's just a plumb waste of time."

Angela smiled at him. "You've probably never felt sorry for yourself in your life, have you, Preacher?"

He thought about Jennie and the pain he had felt when he found out she was dead. He had grieved for her, of course, but part of his sorrow had been for his own sake, for the loss he had suffered.

"I wouldn't say that," he replied softly. "I just figure it's better to try to do somethin' about whatever's wrong." In his case, he had taken vengeance on the men responsible for Jennie's death. It hadn't helped much, but it was better than nothing.

"There's an old saying about how it's better to light one candle than to curse the darkness," Angela said.

Preacher nodded. "Yes, ma'am, I reckon that's just what I'm talkin' about."

They stood there quietly for a few moments after that while Angela sipped her coffee and Preacher leaned on the rifle, grasping the barrel of the Hawken while its buttstock rested on the ground. He had taken a shine to Angela Galloway as soon as he saw her, but he knew it was wrong and he would never act on the feeling. For one thing, and most importantly, she was a married woman, and Preacher respected the sanctity of marriage. Even though he had left home at an early age, his parents had given him a good moral grounding and the ability to tell right from wrong. For another thing, he didn't want to be disloyal to Jennie's memory, even though it had begun to fade. Someday, Preacher figured, he would be ready to let go of the pain and just remember the good things, but that day wasn't here yet.

A deep chuckle drew his attention to the men playing

cards. "Looks like this pot is mine," Jonathan Galloway declared as he leaned forward to rake in the pile of pebbles in the center of the blanket.

"Not so fast." The words, surprisingly, came from Ed Watson. "That pot ain't yours."

"What?" Jonathan exclaimed. "Why not?"

"Because you cheated, you son of a bitch!"

9

Preacher knew trouble when he heard it a-bornin'. He straightened from his casual stance as Peter Galloway said angrily, "Damn you, you can't talk to my uncle that way! A Galloway never cheats!"

"Well, he did," Watson insisted in a reedy voice. "I seen him deal a card off the bottom of the deck."

"That's preposterous," Geoffrey said. "Jonathan, tell him."

"Of course. I never cheated at cards in my life," Jonathan said. "And I'm insulted that you think I did tonight."

Watson glared at him. "I don't think it—I know it. I seen it with my own eyes. He ain't the onliest one neither. It ain't no coinseedence that ever since we started playin' for money, one o' you boys has won ever' hand."

"They're playin' for money?" Preacher muttered to himself. "I thought they was playin' for pebbles."

"It was you and your friend who wanted to 'make things more interesting,' as you put it," Peter said to Watson. "We just went along with you, even though I didn't think it was really that good an idea. If you're too stupid to win, don't blame us and claim we're cheating."

For once, Preacher couldn't blame Peter Galloway for being hotheaded, even though Peter might have phrased his argument a mite more discreetly. If a man was honest and came from an honest family, he couldn't just let it pass when somebody accused him or his kin of cheating.

"I ain't stupid," Watson shot back, "which means I don't believe you. You're all a pack of cheaters and liars!"

Peter threw his cards down on the blanket and started to get to his feet. "Take that back or I'll thrash you!" he said.

"Oh, my God," Angela said softly. "Peter, don't—"

Watson had no intention of taking back his harsh words. Preacher knew that just by looking at the man's face. He started forward, intending to intervene in the argument, but it was too late. Watson launched himself across the blanket, uncoiling from the ground like a striking snake. His fist lashed out and crashed into Peter's jaw. Peter sprawled backward on the ground, scattering the powdery, newly falling snow.

"Peter!" Angela cried.

Watson continued his attack, lunging at Peter and drawing back his leg for a kick. "Thrash me! Go ahead and thrash me, why don't you!"

Simon, Geoffrey, and Jonathan were all too stunned by the sudden vicious assault to do anything to help Peter. Preacher could have gotten there in time to stop Watson from kicking Peter, but he held back, wanting to see what the young man would do, how he handled himself. Might come a day when Preacher would have to depend on Peter Galloway to save his life or the life of someone else.

Although stunned by the punch, Peter still had his wits about him enough to see Watson's booted foot coming at him. He rolled to the side, avoiding the kick, and reached up to grab Watson's leg. He heaved on it, toppling the mountain man and sending Watson crashing to the ground.

Hawley started to his feet, reaching for the pistol behind his belt as he did so, and Preacher finally stepped in. He swung the Hawken up so that its barrel was pointed in Hawley's general direction, and he growled, "Stay out of it, mister. Let them settle it."

Hawley stopped reaching for his gun and settled back down on the ground, but his face was taut with anger. He didn't like having a rifle pointed at him. Preacher didn't much care what Hawley liked or didn't like.

Peter tried to press his momentary advantage. He leaped at the fallen Watson and swung a couple of wild punches at the man's face. Watson blocked them both, brought a knee up, and planted his foot against Peter's chest. A hard shove sent Peter flying through the air.

"Can't you stop them?" Angela said worriedly to Preacher.

"I could, but there ain't no need to."

"No need? Peter could get hurt!"

Preacher shook his head. "Not too bad, as long as it's just fists. Better to let them hash it out amongst themselves."

Watson had the advantage now. He threw himself on top of Peter Galloway and tried to lock his fingers around Peter's throat. Peter was younger, taller, and heavier, but Watson knew all the tricks of rough-and-tumble, bare-knuckles brawling. He got a stranglehold on Peter and bore down, cutting off his air.

That grip didn't last long. Peter bucked up off the ground and threw Watson to the side. Gasping, he rolled away and came up on his hands and knees, then staggered to his feet. He rubbed his sore throat where Watson's fingers had dug into it.

A few feet away, Watson struggled up as well. By now the other men had drawn back, giving the combatants some room. The blanket was wadded up, and the cards and pebbles were scattered. Clearly, the game was over for the night.

With angry shouts, the two men came together and started slugging it out, fists flying and thudding into flesh and bone. Again, Watson's greater experience helped him. His punches were short and compact but had all of his strength behind them. Peter gradually had to give ground. As he backed up, Watson's foot suddenly shot out, hooked behind Peter's ankle, and jerked. Peter went over backward.

Watson reached into his coat and pulled out a knife. With a savage grin on his face, he lunged at Peter, with the blade poised to strike down into the younger man's chest.

The Hawken in Preacher's hand roared as he fired without seeming to aim. The heavy lead ball struck Watson's knife hand, shattering bone and shredding flesh. The knife went flying harmlessly into the air. Watson screamed and fell to his knees, clutching the wounded, blood-spouting member to his chest.

"You shot him!" Hawley shouted accusingly. "You said we ought to stay out of it!"

"That was when it was just fists," Preacher said. "Watson made it a heap different when he pulled that pigsticker."

Watson glared up at him from his knees. "You bastard! You've ruined me!"

"You're lucky I didn't kill you," Preacher said coldly.

"We ain't gonna forget this," Hawley warned.

Preacher nodded and said, "I sure as hell hope not. Tend to your friend."

Hawley got up and went to Watson's side. He helped Watson to his feet and led him over by the cliff. Working quickly, Hawley bound up the wounded hand with a strip of cloth he cut off Watson's shirt. Both of them sent frequent, hate-filled glances toward Preacher and the Galloways.

Angela hurried over to Peter as he climbed shakily to his feet. "Are you all right?" she wanted to know.

He nodded. "I'm fine." Amazingly enough, the look he gave Preacher was resentful. "I could have handled him. I was doing all right."

If that was what the damn fool wanted to believe, Preacher wasn't going to waste breath or energy arguing with him. Preacher knew, though, that Peter Galloway would have been dead in another few seconds if he hadn't shot Watson.

The shouting and the gunshot had roused everyone else in the camp. The kids looked out from the wagon where they were sleeping, full of questions and wide-eyed with fear. Once Angela was satisfied that her husband was all right, she went to reassure the youngsters that everything was fine and to tell them to crawl back into their bedrolls and go back to sleep.

Meanwhile, Roger Galloway climbed down from his

wagon and came over to join the others. He had a pistol in his hand. "What is it?" he asked anxiously. "Is it the Indians? Are we under attack?"

"Nope," Preacher said.

Simon said, "Peter got in a fight with one of those mountain men."

"A fight?" Roger repeated. "About what?"

"The man said I was cheating at cards," Jonathan explained, "but I never did. You know I wouldn't do that, Roger."

"Of course not." Roger looked at his brother and asked the same question Angela had. "Peter, are you all right?"

"I'm fine," Peter said again, more disgustedly this time. "We should have known not to trust those ruffians." He cast a meaningful glance Preacher's way.

Preacher figured that if any cheating had been going on, Hawley and Watson had more than likely been doing it. He had reserved judgment on the men, but now he decided that they had planned to fleece the pilgrims at cards all along. But they had gone up against stiffer competition than they had expected. All of Jonathan's talk about not being any good at poker had been a ruse, designed to draw in Hawley and Watson. They had played along without even realizing it, even to the point of suggesting that they play for money instead of pebbles, which was no doubt what Jonathan had wanted all along.

But despite that con, Jonathan had been winning fair and square. Preacher hadn't seen Jonathan or any of the other Galloways cheating.

Well, it was over now, and nobody had gotten killed. There was that to be thankful for anyway, Preacher thought as he reloaded the Hawken.

Hawley walked over to him. "What are you gonna do about this?" he asked, knowing that Preacher was in charge here.

"Come mornin', you and Watson will go your way and we'll go ours."

"You're not goin' to kick us out of camp tonight?"

"Nope, not in weather like this. Not that I care overmuch whether the two of you freeze. I just don't want to have to mess with your stiff carcasses come mornin'."

"This ain't fair," Hawley blustered. "You said we could travel together."

"That was before your pard tried to kill somebody."

"We'll stand a lot better chance of gettin' to Garvey's Fort if we stay together."

"You will, you mean," Preacher said.

"Might come a time when you'll need our guns."

"Well, we'll just have to get along without 'em, I reckon. Get back over there by the cliff, and the two of you stay there. Somebody will be keepin' an eye on you all night, so don't try anything."

"Ain't fair," Hawley muttered again as he turned away. "Just ain't fair." He went back over to Watson and told him what Preacher had said. Watson was still in pain. He cradled his injured hand against his body.

The Galloways all began to move toward their wagons. Now that the trouble was over, they were ready to turn in. Except for Roger, who started toward Preacher and said his name.

Preacher half-turned to see what Roger wanted, so it was only out of the corner of his eye that he saw Watson pull a pistol from under his coat with his good hand. In an instinctive reaction to the threat, Preacher pivoted back toward the cliff and fired from the hip. Watson had lifted the pistol and pointed it at Preacher, but he fumbled for an instant before pressing the trigger, probably because he had the gun in his left hand. That second of delay was enough to prove fatal for him. The ball from Preacher's Hawken smashed into his chest and lifted him backward off his feet as it plowed all the way through his body and burst out his back in a shower of blood and pulped flesh. He hit the face of the cliff and bounced off, pitching forward and leaving a smear of crimson on the rock.

Like lightning, Preacher lowered the rifle and pulled one of the pistols from behind his belt. He covered Hawley—who was reaching for a gun—and said, "Don't do it."

Hawley froze, then slowly lifted his hand away from his pistol. "Don't shoot," he croaked, knowing just how close he had come to dying. "Don't shoot, Preacher. I ain't gonna cause any trouble. What Ed did, that was on his own head. I didn't have nothin' to do with it."

"You were reachin' for a gun," Preacher snapped.

"Well, hell, a man sees his partner shot down, he just naturally tries to do somethin' about it."

That was true enough, Preacher supposed. Instinct had sent Hawley's hand toward his gun, and instinct had come near getting his head blown off. But nobody else had to die, not tonight.

Preacher said, "Come over here, take all your guns and knives out, and put 'em down on the ground. Then back off."

"You can't take a man's weapons away," Hawley whined.

"I ain't takin' 'em permanent. You can have 'em back in the mornin' after we've left. But for now just do what I tell you."

Grudgingly, Hawley complied, shedding himself of two pistols, a hunting knife, and a dirk.

"That all?" Preacher asked as Hawley backed away from the weapons.

"That's it."

"You better not be lyin' to me."

"I ain't as big a damn fool as you seem to think I am," Hawley said bitterly. "But I ain't gonna forget about this neither, Preacher."

"No," Preacher said, "I don't expect you will."

10

The sound of the distant shots came faintly through the frigid night air, first one, and then, a few moments later, another. Swift Arrow heard them and grunted. "Perhaps the whites are killing each other," he said to Badger's Den.

The medicine man frowned. "It will not satisfy the blood debt they owe the Sahnish if they kill each other."

"True. But there will be at least one left on whom to take our revenge, if Neshanu Natchitak wills it." Swift Arrow smiled. "Who is the only white man who speaks the truth to our people?"

"A dead white man, because he says nothing," Badger's Den replied, and the other members of the war party laughed at the old joke.

They sat around a tiny fire built in the lee of a rock, trying to ignore the cold. Every man there, if he'd been honest with himself, missed the warmth of his lodge and his woman. When they had left their village, following Swift Arrow on his quest of vengeance against the white men, they had expected to be back before the first real snowfall. But the white men had been fortunate and had somehow stayed ahead of their pursuers for long enough so that that goal was no longer possible. The first real storm of winter was here, and the warriors had no choice but to pull their bear and buffalo robes tighter around themselves and take no notice of the bad weather.

Swift Arrow worried, however, that the snow would make it more difficult for them to locate the wagons. The white mantle would obscure any tracks left by the wheeled vehicles. Again, the Sahnish would be reduced to splitting up into search parties, such as the one that Nah Ka Wan had been a member of.

At least they knew the right direction in which to begin their search. The shots had told them that much. When morning came, Swift Arrow thought, they would take up the trail once more, and they would not stop until all the hated whites were dead.

Hawley didn't try anything else during the night. He sat beside the corpse of his friend and stared darkly at the rest of the party until exhaustion finally overcame him and he fell asleep, leaning against the cliff.

Preacher made sure they all understood that one man on every guard shift would have to watch Hawley. Preacher didn't trust the surly mountain man as far as he could throw him. The smart thing to do would be to go ahead and shoot the son of a bitch, but Preacher couldn't bring himself to do that. He couldn't just kill a man in cold blood.

The snow stopped during the night. Away from the camp, the ground was covered with four or five inches of the white stuff, Preacher saw as he looked around the next morning. That wasn't enough to cause the wagons any trouble, although it was possible there were some deeper drifts they would have to contend with. It was pretty to look at too, that white blanket spread over the ground, as well as the caps of snow that nestled on the branches of the pine trees.

The kids could make good snowballs now, and they fell to it with a vengeance, a-whoopin' and a-hollerin' as they ran around and flung the hard-packed missiles at each other.

While they were doing that, the adults fixed breakfast and got ready to travel again.

Preacher shadowed Mart Hawley as Hawley tended to his horses. "You don't have to watch me so blasted close," the man snapped. "I ain't gonna cause any trouble. I told you, pullin' a gun was Ed's idea, not mine."

"Indulge me," Preacher said dryly. "I'll feel a mite easier if I keep an eye on you, Hawley. What do you plan to do with your partner?" Preacher inclined his head toward Watson's body.

"Find a ravine, I reckon, and pile some rocks on him after I dump him. Unless you want to help me dig a grave for him."

"Not likely," Preacher said.

Hawley glared at him. "Ain't you got a ounce o' human compassion in you? Sure, he lost his head and got hisself kilt, but he really weren't that bad a feller."

"I'll take your word for it."

"When do I get my guns back?"

"We'll leave 'em a half mile or so up the trail after we've pulled out. Just follow the wagon tracks in the snow and you'll find 'em. I'll even wrap 'em up in some cloth to protect 'em from the weather."

"What if I need to shoot somethin' before then?"

"My advice would be not to need to," Preacher said. "You wait until we're gone and well out of sight before you leave here. And I sure won't take it kindly if you decide to come after us."

"Well, damn it, what if we just happen to be goin' the same direction? I still thought I might try to winter at Garvey's place."

"Just don't come ridin' up our backside. If I see you betwixt here and there, I plan on shootin' first and askin' questions later."

"You're mighty damned touchy," Hawley muttered.

"I get that way when folks try to kill me."

Preacher went back to the wagons. Roger and Peter had built up the fire until it was blazing brightly again, and

Jonathan was cooking breakfast. Preacher said to Roger, "How's your wife this mornin'?"

"A little better, I think," Roger replied. A haunted look in the young man's eyes told Preacher that he wasn't really convinced of what he was saying, however. Maybe he was trying to make himself believe it.

"No baby yet, though," said Preacher.

Roger shook his head. "No. No baby."

Preacher could do a lot of things, but he couldn't make a baby be born when it wasn't good and ready. He put a hand on Roger's shoulder for a moment and gave him a reassuring nod. That was about all he could do.

A short time later, after everyone had eaten breakfast—except for Hawley, who would have to make do now with the jerky and pemmican he already had—and the wagons had been hitched up, Preacher said, "Climb up there and let's get movin', folks. Got a lot of ground to cover today."

He swung up into the dun's saddle and rode out of the hollow. Dog went with him and then bounded ahead, kicking up snow with his paws as he ran. He looked more like a wolf than ever in these surroundings. Preacher reined in and turned to watch as the wagons climbed out of the hollow and began rolling across the relatively level ground to the east. There were still some more hills to cross before they would reach the actual plains, but the going would get a little easier with each mile they put behind them.

Hawley stood near the cliff with his horses. Ed Watson's corpse lay nearby. Preacher remembered how the first man he had been forced to kill had haunted him for a long time. He had seen the face of that river pirate in his dreams, and even sometimes when he was awake. Now, so many violent years had rolled past that he could no longer even make an accurate estimate of the number of men who had gone down to death at his hands. But he had never murdered anyone, never taken a life unless he was forced to it, and never killed anybody who didn't need killin'. His conscience was clear and he slept just fine at night.

Some folks just never understood. They prattled on about how every human life was sacred and how nobody had the right to kill somebody else. That was all well and good, and Preacher supposed there was a kernel of truth in what they said. But they seemed to forget that man was an animal, and an animal will always fight to save its own life or the lives of those it holds dear. From the grizzly bear and the mountain lion down to the smallest of field mice, something inside every critter on the face of the earth made it strike back when it was threatened. You'd never catch an animal hesitating and pondering moral questions when it ought to be fightin' for what was right. The greatest morality was survival.

At least it would be, Preacher thought, until so-called civilization bred that out of folks and they got in the habit of just sittin' back and taking whatever evil the world dished out at 'em. He shook his head and hoped he never lived long enough to see it come to that.

"Keep headin' straight on thataway," he called to Jonathan Galloway as Jonathan's wagon rumbled past. Preacher pointed where he meant, and Jonathan nodded that he understood. Preacher waited off to the side on the dun as all four of the wagons rolled by. He sat there watching Hawley until the wagons had a good long lead. Then finally he turned the dun and rode after them. Dog growled one last time at Hawley and then loped after Preacher.

Preacher had fashioned a makeshift bundle out of a piece of an old blanket and tied up Hawley's weapons in it. When he judged he had gone far enough, he set the bundle on top of a rock where Hawley couldn't miss it, and then rode on. He hoped he wasn't making a mistake by leaving Hawley alive. If the man were filled with enough of a thirst for vengeance, he might creep up on the wagons at night and take a potshot or two at them.

If that happened, Preacher would deal with it. He wouldn't hesitate. He'd just go out and hunt down Hawley and kill him on sight.

The sky was still overcast, but no more snow fell during the morning. The wagons pushed on steadily and actually made pretty good time. If they could keep this up, Preacher thought, they might reach Garvey's Fort before winter really closed down and clamped its icy grip on the landscape.

Yep, they still had a chance to salvage this disaster of a trip.

Mart Hawley stood above the ten-foot-deep gully where he had dumped the body of his friend and partner. Watson's corpse had been stiff with both cold and rigor mortis, and Hawley had had a hell of a time wrestling it into the gully. Now he stood there with a large chunk of rock in his hand and looked down at Watson.

"Ed, you stupid bastard," Hawley said. He raised the rock above his head and then threw it down with all his strength into Watson's face, which was still contorted from the man's death agonies. The rock struck with a dull thud.

"If you hadn't lost your head, we coulda strung along with them pilgrims until we had a chance to kill Preacher," Hawley went on as he picked up another rock. "Then them wagons would've been ours, and that pretty woman too. Course, we'd'a had to kill the rest of 'em, but I don't reckon that it would have been too hard."

He flung the rock at Watson's corpse with all the fury he could muster. "Stupid damn bastard!"

For several minutes, he kept cursing Watson and throwing rocks into the gully. By all rights, he should have left the body uncovered so that wolves and other varmints could get at it. That's what Watson deserved for being so dumb as to lose his temper and try to kill Preacher. Everybody in the Rocky Mountains knew that killing Preacher would be one hell of a chore. It would have to be planned out ahead of time. That's what he would do, Hawley told himself. He would take his time and make a plan, and then stick to it until he had Preacher in his sights and could blow his damn head off. That would be a fine day, yes, sir, one fine day.

Hawley threw one more rock into the gully and then turned away. That was good enough. He had tried to cover up Watson, because after all, they had been partners and had ridden and trapped together for a couple of years, but if it hadn't been good enough, then too bad. Hawley had wasted enough time. He wanted to get after those wagons, retrieve his guns—assuming that sumbitch Preacher had left them as he'd said he would—and get started on his plan.

It would take a while, Hawley thought as he rode off, leading Watson's horse and the pack mule. But he could afford to be patient.

Preacher didn't know it yet, but he was already a dead man, Hawley thought. Yes, sir, a . . . dead . . . man.

11

The afternoon passed as peacefully as the morning had. Preacher kept the group moving at as fast a pace as possible. He spent more time behind the wagons than he did in front of them today, since now he had not only the Arikara war party to worry about but also Mart Hawley as well. Preacher didn't believe Hawley would just let it go. Hawley would want vengeance for his partner.

Nobody suggested cards after supper that night, if there was even a deck anywhere amongst the party's belongings.

The sky had begun to clear late in the afternoon, and the winds were light. They were in for the coldest night yet, Preacher knew. There was no cave, no bluff, no cliff to shield them. They stopped beside a creek that had ice beginning to form along its edges. They had to build their fire out in the open, and the terrain was flat enough so that it could be seen for a long distance. Preacher didn't like it, but he had no choice in the matter. Without the fire, they would all be frozen by morning.

The temperature dropped as sharply as he expected. By morning the air was so cold, it took the breath away and seemed to chill a man all the way to his marrow. But at least no one had attacked them during the night. That was something to be grateful for, Preacher thought.

Everyone was sluggish and slow to get moving because of

the cold, even the young'uns. Preacher hustled them up as best he could. They would feel better once their blood was pumping faster. Preacher boiled coffee, fried bacon, hitched up the mules, and said impatiently, "Let's go, let's go."

Peter Galloway scowled in irritation as he cupped his gloved hands around a cup of hot coffee. "What's all the damned hurry?" he complained. "Everybody's cold. Give us a little time to get warmed up."

"You'll warm up a whole heap faster if you're doin' something," Preacher told him. "And you can bet if there are more o' them Arikara after us, they ain't loafin' around this mornin'. They'll be on the move already."

"Do you think there are more hostiles pursuing us?" Jonathan asked.

"I sure wouldn't rule it out."

Not only that, Preacher thought, but if the Arikara were back there, there was a good chance they would have seen the fire last night, and they could be closing in at this very moment.

"Dog, take a look around," Preacher went on, and Dog trotted off to scout the area around the camp.

Geoffrey stared after the animal. "It's like he understood every word you said," he commented to Preacher, sounding surprised.

"Well, I don't reckon he understood the words so much as he figured out what I wanted. We been together for quite a few years now, so we know each other pretty well."

"Can you communicate with any other woodland animals?"

Preacher couldn't help but grin, even as worried as he was. "It ain't like I sit around havin' deep conversations with squirrels . . . although I've knowed a few fellas who didn't draw the line at talkin' to critters. But you can learn something from almost every creature that lives in the wild, if you just pay attention to 'em. They'll nearly always tell you when somebody's skulkin' around and is up to no good. Animals got a way o' sensin' that. You just got to learn how to look and listen right."

Jonathan asked, "Could you teach us?"

Preacher frowned at him. "Teach you to be frontiersmen, you mean?"

"That's right," Jonathan said with an eager nod. "If we're going to live out here, we need to learn how to get along properly in the wild."

Preacher shrugged and said, "I reckon I could teach you a few things. Mostly, though, it's just a matter of payin' heed to what's goin' on around you."

And the frontier was the best teacher of all, he added to himself. Only problem was, it was also a harsh teacher, and anyone who failed to learn its lessons usually wound up dead before very long. But those who survived learned a hell of a lot, that was for damned sure.

Dog came loping back a little later, and his attitude told Preacher that he hadn't found anything suspicious. If the Indians were out there—and Preacher's instincts still told him they were—they hadn't closed in yet.

The wagons finally got rolling, a good half hour after Preacher thought they should have. The sky was clear as a bell and achingly blue. The sun shone on the snow-covered ground and glittered on the snow and ice in the trees. The breath of men and mules and horses plumed in front of their faces. Preacher pointed the wagons toward a patch of ground between two hills, and then dropped back a ways to look over the country behind them.

He had seen very little of Angela Galloway this morning, and he was glad of that. She was pretty and nice and he didn't need to be reminded of that. He made up his mind that when they got to Garvey's, he would move on and winter somewhere else. If he stayed around Angela for months, he would just get more uncomfortable. And although he was no expert when it came to women, he thought she was a mite interested in him too, and he didn't want her to have to feel the same vague guilt and unease that he was experiencing. Better for him to just go on his way and leave her with her husband and her kids, where she belonged.

The sun climbed higher, but didn't do much to warm the frigid landscape. Once, Preacher thought he saw a lone rider far behind them, but even with his keen eyesight, he couldn't be sure. Hawley, he thought, trailing them but not getting too close. Either the trapper had taken Preacher's warning to heart . . . or he was being cagey and biding his time before he tried to get his revenge. Either way he wasn't an immediate concern.

Mart Hawley was nervous. He didn't know if that was because of the cold, or the isolation, or something else that he couldn't pin down. He wasn't used to riding alone, and despite the anger he had felt toward Ed Watson, he wished the son of a bitch were still around. Ed hadn't been very bright, and except when he lost his temper he talked only a little more than a rock, but, by golly, he'd been better than nothing insofar as companions went. Maybe not much, but still better.

Hawley asked himself if he really wanted to try to kill Preacher. The man had quite a reputation, despite his relative youth. He was mean as a he-coon and strong as a grizz, quick as a panther and sharp-eyed as an eagle, and he just flat out was pure "pizen." Was avenging Ed Watson's death really worth it?

Hawley shivered in his capote and his thick buffalo robe as his horse plodded along. He was following the tracks of the wagons because he didn't know what else to do. He'd spent a miserable night huddling by a tiny fire, convinced he was going to freeze to death before morning. Maybe if he waited another day or two and let Preacher and the others get over being mad at him, they would allow him to rejoin their party.

Or more than likely, Preacher would just shoot him out of the saddle as soon as he got within rifle range.

Hawley might have to take that chance. He wasn't convinced he could make it to Garvey's Fort on his own. And his resolve to kill Preacher was wavering a whole heap. Hawley knew that he had a streak of pure meanness inside him and wasn't afraid to admit that about himself. He would have enjoyed watching Preacher die; and if things had happened differently, if he had been able to seize the chance to do it, he would have gladly jumped on that Miz Galloway, with her pretty face and that hair the color of honey. He had raped women and girls before, although only Injuns, and one white whore back in St. Louis, and they didn't hardly count in his mind. But despite all that, he was a practical man, and he could put the urge for vengeance and all them other urges away for the time being, if it were a matter of either behaving himself or freezing and starving to death. Hell, just give him a chance, and he'd be as sweet and innocent as any angel.

Hawley was so lost in thought, he didn't see the buckskin-clad figures until they seemed to rise up out of the very ground all around him. But as his horse whinnied in fear and shied away from them, he saw the dark, stony faces with their daubs of war paint and knew that no matter how you looked at it, he was in the worst fix of his life.

He had time to utter one heartfelt "Shit!" before the Injuns pulled him out of the saddle.

The cold didn't let up all day, but Preacher knew it was only a matter of time. Tonight or tomorrow, the wind would shift back around to the south and the icy grip of the storm would be broken. The snow would begin to melt. Of course, it might not be but a day or two before another cold snap blew through, but at least there would be a little respite.

"How many more days before we get out of the foothills?" Roger Galloway asked him that afternoon as Preacher rode for a while alongside Roger's wagon.

"We'll probably reach the plains day after tomorrow, or maybe the day after that," Preacher said. "I never traveled through these parts with wagons before, so I ain't rightly sure how long it'll take."

"You could move a lot faster if you were on your own, couldn't you? Helping us has really slowed you down."

"Well, that's one thing about bein' a fella like me, who drifts around a lot. I ain't generally in a hurry to get where I'm goin'. One place is about the same as another, far as I'm concerned. As long as I ain't too crowded, I'm happy."

"You don't like people very much, though."

"I never said that. I like people just fine. Got lots of friends up here in these mountains, like ol' Jeb Law. I always enjoy goin' to Rendezvous and catchin' up with what ever'body's been doin'. But I don't have to have people around to be happy. I got a good horse and a good dog, and there's places I ain't been yet, and places I been but want to go back to. That's all it really takes for a man like me."

Roger shook his head. "I envy you. You live a life of almost perfect freedom, with no one to tie you down or make a claim on you."

And that need for freedom, Preacher thought, was what had always stood between him and Jennie and kept them from being together for more than a short time. Preacher had known even then that he could never settle down, and Jennie had deserved more than a man who was never home.

"You got a wife and a young'un and another on the way," Preacher pointed out. "Some fellas would be envyin' you."

"I suppose." Roger glanced back over his shoulder into the wagon. Lowering his voice, he said, "I'm worried about Dorothy. She's sleeping now, but this has been a terrible ordeal for her. I . . . I can't help but hope that once the baby is born, things will be easier for her."

Since Roger seemed to be in a talkative mood, Preacher indulged his curiosity and asked, "Why were you and your brother so all-fired anxious to get to Oregon that it couldn't wait until spring?"

"We just . . . We thought there would be time, I suppose. We knew we'd be cutting it close, but we thought that if we were lucky, we'd get there and have our choice of the land to settle. Do you know what's going on back East?"

"Not really," Preacher said. "We don't get much news out here, and when we do, it ain't recent."

"Interest in immigration and settling the West is growing rapidly. Next year you're liable to see wagon trains like you've never seen them before. There's speculation that thousands of families will start west. Within a year or two, there should be a well-marked, well-traveled trail all the way from Missouri to Oregon."

The Indians wouldn't be too happy if that happened, Preacher thought, and neither would some of the fur trappers. "And you folks wanted to get a jump on that," he said.

"That's right. I suppose that makes us greedy."

Preacher shrugged. "I ain't in the business o' passin' judgment on anybody. I reckon you had your reasons, and they were good enough for you. You should've thought twice about it, though."

"I know that now," Roger said.

Preacher heeled the dun into a trot and moved out in front of the wagons. He wasn't sure he believed what Roger had told him. That story about getting to Oregon before the rush and claiming some prime land was probably true as far as it went, but Preacher sensed there was still something unsaid, some other reason why the Galloway brothers, their father, and their uncles had started west at the wrong time of year. Greed just wasn't a strong enough motive.

But fear might be.

Question was, what were they afraid of?

12

Mart Hawley had never been so scared in all his born days.

At the same time, he was utterly astounded that he was still alive, but the fright overwhelmed him and kept him from being grateful that the Indians hadn't killed him yet.

The Arikara warriors had bound his hands and feet and tossed him back on his horse, only belly-down across the saddle so that he was sick as a dog by the time they finally stopped. They dumped him on the ground then, and he lay there in the snow retching his guts out, thinking that at any moment they would crush his skull with a war club or chop his head open with a tomahawk or drive a lance right through him and pin him to the ground or pincushion him with arrows. The terror just made him sicker, until there was nothing left inside him to come out. After that he had the dry heaves for a while.

Night had fallen by the time he realized they weren't going to kill him, at least not right away.

He lay huddled against a rock. Now that the fear had subsided a little, he was aware of the cold seeping into his bones. The Injuns hadn't made a fire. How could they survive in weather like this without a fire? It just went to prove what he had long suspected, that Injuns weren't really human like white folks. They were a whole different species. They didn't even seem to feel the cold. They just sat around gnawing on dried meat like animals.

Starlight glittered on the snow and provided enough illumination for Hawley to see one of the warriors stand up and walk toward him. This was it, he thought with a soft moan. The Injun was gonna kill him now.

Instead, the man hunkered on his heels in front of Hawley and spoke. His English was broken, but he supplemented it with sign talk, which was pretty much universal among the tribes. Hawley understood well enough to know what the Injun was getting at.

"You know . . . Preacher?"

"Preacher?" Hawley repeated as he goggled at the Indian. "You mean like a minister, or . . . or the man *called* Preacher?"

"You know Preacher?" the Indian asked again, and this time he sounded a mite impatient.

Hawley heard that and knew he couldn't afford to give the wrong answer. He nodded his head and said emphatically, "Yes, I know Preacher."

"Preacher . . . friend?"

Hawley thought back desperately to everything that had been said while he and Watson were in camp with the immigrants. He recalled that they had had some Injun trouble, and Preacher and that damn wolf-dog of his had wiped out a whole scouting party by their lonesomes. If *those* Injuns had been part of the same bunch as *these* Injuns . . .

"No," he said even more vehemently than before. "Preach-er not friend."

The Indian grunted. Hawley wasn't sure what that meant, but the fact that they still hadn't killed him had to be good.

"Hate Preacher," Hawley went on. "Want to watch Preach-er die."

"You not friend to other white men?"

Hawley thought back again. Preacher had said that the Indians he'd killed were 'Rees. Hawley was no expert at telling the tribes apart, and besides, it was too dark to make out some of the details, but he thought he recognized the way these savages wore their hair.

"Hawley friend to Arikara," he said, knowing that he was taking a big chance. If his captors weren't 'Rees, if they were some of that tribe's traditional enemies, then he had just signed and sealed his own death warrant.

After a moment, the big, ugly fella, who was probably the chief of this bunch, nodded. "You know where find Preacher and other white men?"

"I know right where they're goin'," Hawley answered without hesitation, seizing on this opportunity to maybe save his life. "I can take you right to 'em."

"You help kill?"

"Just give me a chance. I'll scalp that sumbitch Preacher my own self, if you'll just take me with you."

"We talk," the Indian said. "Decide whether you live or die. Swift Arrow say you live."

Hawley knew what that meant. He wasn't out of the woods yet. Swift Arrow, this redskin here, thought they ought to keep him around to help them catch up to the immigrants and take their vengeance on Preacher. But even if he was the chief as Hawley suspected, he would still have to talk the matter over with the others and get them to agree with him. He couldn't just decree that they weren't going to kill this captive.

But Hawley still felt so relieved he almost pissed himself. He wasn't going to die, he just knew it.

And even better, he was going to get to take his revenge on Preacher after all.

Preacher found a gully for them to camp in that night, a dry wash about ten feet deep and twenty yards across. The banks were caved in here and there, and one of those places allowed the wagons to get down into the wash. Preacher wouldn't have camped in such a location at a different time of year, because a big rainstorm could cause a flash flood that might wash them all away, but that wasn't going to happen now. They couldn't get out in a hurry either, because it would take time to work the wagons back up those caved-in banks, but he had to admit that they couldn't do *anything* in a hurry when dealing with wagons.

More importantly, the walls of the gully gave them some shelter from the wind and they could build a bigger fire without it being seen.

While Jonathan and Geoffrey unhitched the teams and tended to the mules, Preacher sought out Peter Galloway and said, "Let's you and me go get some wood."

"Can't somebody else do that? I'm tired."

"So's ever'body else," Preacher pointed out, trying not to sound as irritated as he felt at Peter's attitude. "Your brother needs to spend the time with his wife, I reckon, and I don't know where your pa is." Simon was hiding out in one of the wagons, dodging chores as usual, Preacher suspected. "And I sure ain't sendin' the young'uns out on their own."

"All right, all right," Peter said grudgingly. "Let me get my rifle, just in case any more savages show up."

Preacher figured that was only a matter of time. The Arikara were still behind them somewhere. But he didn't think they were close yet.

A few minutes later, Preacher and Peter walked out of the gully and headed toward some nearby trees where they could probably find enough broken branches for the fire. Each man carried a rifle, and Preacher had a brace of pistols tucked behind his belt. Dog bounded ahead of them, always energetic. It was late in the day, with the sun only barely above the mountains to the west. Darkness would fall quickly.

"My wife talks about you all the time," Peter said.

The blunt statement took Preacher a little by surprise. "What?"

"She's very impressed by you, Preacher." There was a friendly tone in Peter's voice, but Preacher could tell it wasn't genuine. "She thinks you're quite a man."

"I'm sure Miz Galloway's a fine woman."

"And a fine-looking woman too, don't you think?"

"I ain't paid that much attention," Preacher lied.

"Oh, surely you have. You're a man, after all. You couldn't help but notice an attractive woman."

"I don't go around lookin' at other fellas' wives," Preacher said stiffly.

Peter's voice took on a hard edge as he said, "Well, she looks at you. A great deal, in fact."

Preacher shook his head. "I wouldn't know nothin' about that."

"No, and you wouldn't even think about stealing a kiss from her, would you?"

Preacher stopped short and turned to look at Peter, saying curtly, "If you got somethin' you want to say, mister, best you go ahead and just spit it out."

"All right, I will," Peter said as he stopped and turned to glare at Preacher. "Stay away from my wife. Stop talking to her. And if you lay one hand on her, I swear I'll kill you."

"You oughta be more careful who you go around threatenin' to kill. Folks tend to take that serious out here."

"I'm completely serious," Peter said. "Dead serious."

Preacher's whole body was taut with anger. Peter Galloway put his teeth on edge under the best of circumstances. The way the man was acting now just made it worse.

But in the back of his mind, Preacher was all too aware of how he had reacted to Angela Galloway, and the way she had reacted to him. No matter how much Preacher disliked the fella, Peter was just acting as any normal man would who thought his marriage was threatened. With an effort, Preacher reined in his temper and said, "You ain't got anything to worry about, Galloway. I ain't got no designs on your wife, and I reckon a fine lady like her could never be interested in a scruffy ol' mossback like me."

"You're not old. Hell, you're not much more than thirty, are you?"

"It ain't the years," Preacher said with a faint smile. "It's the miles."

For a long moment, Peter still glared at him, and there was a tense silence between the two men. Then Peter nodded and said, "All right, I'll take your word that there's nothing going on. But remember what I said about staying away from Angela."

Preacher couldn't resist commenting in return. "You pay her enough attention and you won't have to worry about such things."

For a second he thought that was going to start the argument all over again, but then Peter nodded a second time and stalked toward the woods without looking back at him. Preacher followed, shaking his head. As far as he was concerned, they had just wasted several minutes of the daylight that was left.

"Slow down a mite," Preacher warned as they neared the trees. "It ain't smart to go chargin' in some place when you don't know what might be hidin' there."

"You mean there might be Indians in there?"

"Or a bear. Old Ephraim and most of his kin are hibernatin' at this time of year, but there could still be a few roamin' around, lookin' to fill their bellies 'fore they go to sleep for the winter."

"Who the hell is Old Ephraim?"

"That's what some fellas call any grizzly bear, I reckon because somebody once saw a grizz and thought it looked like somebody he knew named Ephraim."

"I don't want to run into a bear," Peter said, casting a wary glance toward the trees.

"Could be panthers or wolves too."

"My God! Is there something lying in wait to kill you every time you turn around out here?"

"Now you're startin' to understand," Preacher said solemnly.

A minute later, after Dog had run into the woods and then back out again, Preacher went on. "It's safe enough, else we would'a heard Dog carryin' on in there. Gather up the biggest armload of wood you can carry, and let's get back to camp quick as we can."

They went to work, picking up broken branches that had fallen on the ground. Preacher tucked his Hawken under his arm and gathered up a sizable load of firewood. Peter followed his example, and after a few minutes, they were ready to start back.

They had covered only about half the distance to the gully when in the fading light Preacher saw someone emerge from the wash and start toward them at a run. The figure was too small to be any of the men, and after a second, Preacher realized it was the oldest boy, Nate, the son of Roger and Dorothy.

Peter recognized him at the same moment. "That's Nate!" he exclaimed. "Something must be wrong!"

Preacher thought the same thing. He had given the children strict orders to stay near the wagons and never to venture off by themselves. Something important must have happened to make Nate disobey that command. They hurried forward as Nate continued running toward them, kicking up snow from his heels.

"Preacher!" he called. "Uncle Peter! Come quick!"

"What is it, Nate?" Preacher asked sharply as the youngster pounded up to them.

"It's my ma," Nate replied breathlessly. "She's about to have that darned baby, and Aunt Angela says it's really gonna be born this time, come hell or high water!"

13

"Oh, my God!" Peter exclaimed. He seemed quite shaken by what he had just heard.

Preacher doubted that Angela had really used the phrase "come hell or high water," but that wasn't important. What mattered was that their group was about to increase by one. He said, "Let's hustle on back and get that fire built. I don't know much about birthin' babies, but I do know we're liable to need plenty o' hot water!"

They hurried on to the wash and slipped and slid down the caved-in bank. Roger Galloway, his father, and his uncles were all gathered around the wagon where Dorothy Galloway was. Roger looked quite agitated, and the older men seemed worried too. Unlike the first time, when Dorothy's screams hadn't unnerved them, this time they were taking it harder, probably because they were already on edge from the Indian attack and the strain of not knowing when the Arikara would strike again.

Peter dumped his load of wood where Preacher indicated; then Preacher added some of the branches he was carrying and put the others aside to be used later. He laid the Hawken on the ground and knelt beside the pile of wood. Getting busy with flint, steel, and tinder, he had a tiny flame flickering within a minute. He leaned over, blew on it, and watched it grow. Some of the wood caught, but the fire spread slowly.

Preacher was patient and worked with it, keeping at it until the flames leaped and glowed brightly.

Inside the wagon, Dorothy gave a piercing cry that made the men gathered outside jump. Preacher straightened from the fire and said, "Somebody get a pot and start some water boilin'." He looked around and spotted Nate. "Go check on your cousins," he told the youngster.

Nate scurried off while Preacher climbed out of the wash again and looked back toward the west. The light was almost gone, but he didn't see anything moving. He wasn't confident, though, that there was nothing out there. Nobody was better than an Injun at not being seen when he didn't want to be seen.

Dorothy screamed again.

It was going to be a long night, Preacher thought.

Nate had last seen his cousins Mary and Brad in the wagon belonging to their ma and pa, Nate's Uncle Peter and Aunt Angela. He went there first, proud that Preacher had entrusted him with a job, and pulled the canvas flap at the rear aside to look in. He didn't see the two younger kids, but that didn't mean they weren't here. The interior of the big wagon was heaped with goods the family was taking to Oregon, along with their bedrolls and several pieces of furniture. Mary and Brad could be hiding somewhere, or they might have crawled into a hole and gone to sleep.

"Mary! Brad!" Nate hissed. "Are you in here?"

There was no answer.

Nate frowned. His cousins looked up to him; he was older, after all, and a natural leader. He didn't think they would ignore him.

Unless they were playing some sort of game with him. That was possible, even though this wasn't a good time.

"Consarn it, if you're in here you better speak up," he said. "Preacher told me to find you, and we got to do like he says."

Still no response from the dark interior of the wagon.

Muttering under his breath, Nate climbed in and started to look around. He knew all the good hiding places, of course, since he was a kid too. But Mary and Brad weren't in any of them.

That meant they were either outside or in one of the other wagons. Nate hadn't seen them outside when he got back with Preacher and Uncle Peter, and he knew for darn sure that they wouldn't go anywhere near the wagon where his ma was a-hollerin', so that left the wagons belonging to his Uncle Geoffrey and Uncle Jonathan. Nate knew the two older men were really his great-uncles, since they were Grandpa's brothers, but he still called them uncles.

They were good about not being bothered by young'uns, not like some grown-ups, so Nate thought it was possible his cousins were poking around in one of their wagons. He dropped to the ground and hurried over to check the two vehicles.

He didn't find Mary and Brad in either of them.

Now he was starting to get a mite worried. It wouldn't be like them to run off, but with the superiority of his years, Nate thought that you never could tell with kids. They were liable to do most anything. He glanced toward his ma and pa's wagon, where the adults were gathered around talking in low tones, all except for Ma and Aunt Angela, who were inside the wagon, of course. Nate looked up and down the wash as far as he could see in either direction. He didn't spot Mary and Brad anywhere.

He saw something else, though, and when he looked closer he felt his heart sinking. Small footprints in the snow led away from one of the wagons over to the western edge of the wash, which ran north and south. When the tracks reached the bank, they turned and started north, following the course of the wash. The old stream that had carved out the gully sometime in the dim past had twisted and turned, so the wash didn't run straight. It had a lot of bends in it. The first one to the north was about a hundred yards from the camp. Mary and Brad could be right around that bend, Nate told himself, hiding from the others and thinking it was all a grand joke.

He turned his head, looking from the footprints to the grown-ups and back again. It was getting dark, but he could follow those tracks in the snow. Once the stars came out, it would be fairly light, and the moon would be up in a while too. Nate knew he ought to go get Preacher and tell him that the kids were gone, but if he did that, they would get in trouble. Uncle Peter was a tempersome man, and if he got mad at Mary and Brad for running off, he was liable to blister their butts. Even if it was just a joke on their part.

I can find them, Nate thought. *I can find them and bring them back before anybody even knows they're gone.*

Besides, Preacher had given him this job. Go check on your cousins, the mountain man had said. Nate had been watching Preacher for several days, ever since he'd joined up with them, and he thought Preacher was just about the grandest fella he had ever seen. He was tough enough to fight Injuns and smart enough to live on the frontier, and although Nate looked up to his father, in the space of only a few days he had decided he wanted to be just like Preacher when he grew up. Preacher would be proud of him if he went and found the two younger kids and brought them back, Nate thought.

That was all it took to convince him. None of the grown-ups were paying any attention to him at the moment. He went over to where the tracks led off to the north and started following them.

In a matter of moments, he was out of sight of the wagons.

Not surprisingly, Dorothy Galloway did not have an easy time of this birth. She was already weak and sick, and a long, hard labor might be enough to do her in, Preacher thought as he talked quietly with the Galloway men. They winced every time Dorothy let out a yowl inside the wagon, and Preacher knew exactly how they felt. At a time like this, men were about as much use as tits on a boar hog.

He couldn't afford to forget about their situation. Life had to go on, and Preacher was nothing if not a practical man. After a while, he said, "We better get some supper started, and somebody needs to stand guard."

"I'll do that," Simon Galloway volunteered, surprising Preacher. So far, the man had had to be nudged into doing anything useful. The glance Simon cast toward the wagon, though, told Preacher that he just wanted to get away from what was going on in there.

"Take a rifle and go up on the edge of the wash then," Preacher said to him. "Find you a place to hunker down where you won't be too visible, and listen as hard as you can. Keep your eyes open too. If you see anything worrisome, don't holler. Just get back down here on the double and tell me about it."

Simon nodded. "I can do that. It's going to be cold away from the fire, though."

"It ain't like you got to stay up there all night long. We'll spell you after a while."

"All right." Simon took a rifle out of one of the wagons and climbed out of the wash.

Jonathan and Geoffrey offered to fix supper. That left Roger and Peter to talk together and be responsible for feeding wood into the fire, as well as for fetching Angela anything she needed. Preacher and Dog moved up on the eastern rim and roamed north and south several hundred yards. Preacher didn't expect any trouble to come at them from that direction, but you never could tell. Death could be lurking just about anywhere on the frontier.

He didn't get so far away that he couldn't hear the cries from the wagon. By the time he got back, they had stopped again, and he saw Angela Galloway standing with Roger and Peter. She was bundled up in a heavy coat with a shawl around her head, covering her hair. As Preacher walked up, she said to him, "I was just telling Roger that it looks like this may take quite a while. I don't expect the baby to be born until sometime along toward morning, if that soon. We may have to stay here for several days. Dorothy will be too weak to travel when this is over."

Preacher frowned. "The longer it takes us to get to Garvey's Fort, the bigger the risks we're runnin'. That snowstorm a couple of days ago was just ol' man winter gettin' warmed up."

"I can't help it," Angela replied, shaking her head. "I'm just telling you the way things are. Too much strain on Dorothy is going to kill her."

Roger's face grew even more haggard at his sister-in-law's blunt declaration. Peter looked concerned too. He said, "If we need to stay here, we'll stay, and that's all there is to it."

What they were liable to do, Preacher thought, was sit there until the rest of that Arikara war party caught up. Then they would be in for even worse trouble than if a blizzard caught them on the plains.

At the same time, he understood how the others felt. They didn't want to risk Dorothy's life . . . at least not any more than they already had by bringing her out here in her condition.

"I reckon we'll stay as long as we need to," he said. "But when we do get movin' again, we'll have to push mighty hard. If you think the pace has been fast up till now, it's gonna get even faster."

Roger and Peter nodded, but Preacher figured they didn't fully understand. Angela said, "I need to get back in the wagon and see to Dorothy. She'll probably have more contractions any time now."

"You're sure her water broke?" Roger asked. "This isn't another false labor?"

Angela smiled wearily and laid a hand on his arm for a moment. "This is the real thing, Roger. You'll be a father again, sometime in the next twelve to eighteen hours."

Birthin' was sure a long, painful process, Preacher thought. He was mighty glad he would never have to go through it. Having fought a grizzly bear and lived through it, he wasn't sure but what he would rather do that again than endure what Dorothy Galloway was going through now.

After he had eaten the supper that Jonathan and Geoffrey prepared, Preacher climbed up on the western bank of the wash and quietly called Simon's name. Simon answered, and Preacher walked over to the clump of rocks where the older man had posted himself.

"Anything unusual goin' on out there?"

"Well, you have to remember that I'm not all that familiar with what's usual out here," Simon replied. "But to answer your question, no, I didn't see or hear anything alarming."

"That's fine. Go on down and get you a surroundin'."

"What?"

"Somethin' to eat," Preacher explained. "Get some supper."

"Oh. Thank you." Simon moved off into the darkness, and a moment later Preacher heard him climbing down into the wash.

Preacher settled down on one of the rocks and peered into the night. The stars shone brightly overhead and cast enough light for him to be able to see the trees and the hills, and farther away the mountains. His breath fogged in clouds in front of his face. It was cold tonight, but not as frigid as it had been the past two nights.

The Galloways might make it, he thought. Really, for a bunch of greenhorns, they had been damned lucky so far, but there was nothing saying that their luck wouldn't hold. They might even make good settlers if they ever reached the Oregon Territory. He liked the two old-timers, Geoffrey and Jonathan, because they seemed willing to learn, and Roger might be all right once he grew up a little more. Peter and Simon, well, Preacher didn't know about them. A frontiersman had to have a bit of a reckless streak in him, or he would never come out here in the first place. But Peter was hotheaded and acted before he thought, and that was a good way to get killed. Simon was just weak, the sort who would one day crawl into a jug of whiskey and never come out.

As for Angela, she was Peter's best chance. He would need her intelligence and level-headedness if he was going to get by.

Preacher's senses were still razor sharp, even while he was musing about the ultimate fate of the Galloway family, so he was aware of it when someone climbed out of the wash and hurried toward him. The urgency of the footsteps told Preacher that something must have gone wrong again.

It was even worse than he expected. Jonathan Galloway came up to him, puffing and blowing, and gasped, "Preacher! Preacher, the children . . . They're gone!"

14

Preacher swung around, alarm growing rapidly inside him. "Gone?" he repeated. "Hell, they can't be gone! I done told 'em to stay close to the wagons. Maybe they're just hidin' somewhere."

Jonathan shook his head and said, "No, we looked everywhere, in all the wagons. I tell you, Preacher, they've vanished! I called them for supper, and they . . . They just aren't there!"

"Did you check for tracks?"

"Tracks?"

"In the snow," Preacher said, trying to hang on to his patience. He had to remember he was dealing with folks who knew blessed little about the frontier and its ways of life.

"Good Lord, I don't think we did! I . . . I never even thought of it."

"Come on," Preacher said grimly. "Let's go have a look."

When Preacher got back to camp with Jonathan, he found the place in an uproar. The men were running up and down the wash, calling the children's names. Angela stood at the back of Roger and Dorothy's wagon, looking worried, as well she might since two of her kids were out there somewhere in the night, unaccounted for.

"Preacher!" she exclaimed when she saw him coming.

She ran to him and clutched his arm. "Preacher, the children are gone!"

"I know," he told her, then tried to make his voice reassuring as he went on. "No need to worry, I reckon we'll find 'em mighty quicklike. They can't have gotten too far in the time they've been gone."

"That's just it," Angela said. "No one remembers the last time they were here. They could have been gone for hours!"

Preacher's jaw tightened as he realized he was guilty too of not keeping a close enough eye on the young'uns. Of course, he'd had a lot on his mind, but that was no excuse.

"We'll find 'em," he promised again, then turned and called to the others, "Everybody stop runnin' around! You're liable to stomp out the tracks they left."

He told Angela to return to her job of tending to Dorothy, then motioned for the others to gather around him. When the men were all there, Preacher picked up a burning brand from the fire and used it as a torch. "Let's have a look around," he said.

It took him only a few minutes to find the small, kid-sized footprints on the other side of the wagons. The tracks led off up the wash and evidently disappeared around a bend. From the looks of them, Preacher figured Mary and Brad had taken off first, and then later Nate had followed his younger cousins. He recalled telling Nate to check on them.

Nate had found them missing and had gone to look for them, Preacher thought. He was as sure of it as if he had seen the whole thing.

"All right, it won't be no trouble to follow these tracks," he said. "I don't expect to run into any trouble, but I'll take a couple of you with me just in case."

"Geoffrey and I will go," Jonathan volunteered immediately.

"Yes, that's a good idea," Geoffrey added without hesitation. "The rest can stay here and guard the camp."

Preacher nodded. "That's what I had in mind. You fellas get

rifles and pistols. Sooner we get after them young'uns, the sooner we can bring 'em back."

Roger and Peter were both worried. Peter began, "Preacher, I know we've had our differences—"

Preacher stopped him. "That don't mean nothin' at a time like this. We'll get 'em back. You boys who're stayin' here best be on your guard all the time. Don't let up."

"We won't," Roger said. He looked as if he had been driven almost to distraction, what with the troubles his wife was having giving birth and now the disappearance of his son, but he was holding it together somehow. He gave Preacher a solemn nod.

Jonathan and Geoffrey were well armed when they came back from their wagons. Each man carried a rifle and a pair of pistols. Preacher nodded to them and said, "Let's go." They started up the wash, following the footprints that they could see by starlight. Dog tried to run ahead of them, but Preacher called him back. He didn't want Dog messing up the tracks that the young'uns had left.

The children had gone farther than Preacher expected. He and his two companions followed the trail for a good mile up the wash, and then the prints climbed another caved-in section of the bank and started off to the west, toward the higher foothills. Preacher wondered where in blazes those sprouts thought they were going.

A three-quarter moon was rising, and the silvery light it cast threw the landscape into sharp contrasts. The shadows of the trees stood out starkly against the thin snow cover on the ground. The moonlight also made the footprints easier to see. Preacher moved quickly, trusting to Geoffrey and Jonathan to keep up. The older men were soon huffing and puffing, but they persisted gamely in their efforts. Preacher slowed the pace a little only when he became worried that they were breathing so hard, their approach might be heard too easily if any danger was lurking in the dark. Geoffrey and Jonathan were grateful for even that much of a respite.

The trail entered a dense stretch of woods and became

harder to follow due to the thick shadows under the trees. Preacher slowed even more. He had to be careful now. If he lost the trail, in all likelihood he wouldn't be able to find it again until morning.

And even though it wasn't as cold tonight as it had been, the air still had quite a chill in it. Would it be enough to freeze some little kids to death if they had to stay out here all night?

Preacher had to admit that he didn't know, and that uncertainty ate at his insides and made him want to go faster. He had to hold himself back, take it slow, and be certain what he was doing and where he was going.

He just wished he could stop thinking about how, no matter where they were, those kids had to be mighty scared right about now.

Nate prodded Mary and Brad along, saying, "We've got to keep going. If we stop, we might freeze to death."

"But I'm cold," Mary whined, as if she hadn't heard him just say that he was trying to keep them from freezing to death.

"I wanna go back to the wagon," Brad added.

"That's what we're trying to do," Nate said. "We'll be back soon."

He wished he could be as sure of that as he hoped he sounded. To tell the truth, he wasn't sure they were even going toward the wagons. Out here in the woods, it was easy to get turned around. Once he'd caught up to the two younger children, Nate had tried to turn right around and follow his own tracks, because he knew that would take him back to the wash where the wagons were. Unfortunately, he had somehow strayed from them, and even though he *thought* he was going in the right direction, he couldn't be certain of that.

Each step could be taking them farther away from safety and deeper into the wilderness. He didn't like to even think about that possibility.

If they got back safely—*when* they got back safely, he

amended the thought sternly—he was going to ask Preacher to teach him how to tell where he was going by looking at the stars. Nate knew Preacher could do that, and he figured the mountain man could teach him too. If he knew now, he could find his way back.

It occurred to him to look for the moon. The moon rose in the east, didn't it, and he and Mary and Brad were west of the campsite. Therefore, if they walked toward the moon, they would get where they were going.

The moon was already pretty high, though, and as he gazed at it, Nate wondered where exactly it had risen. He took a guess, and since it matched the direction they were already going, he figured that was good enough and kept plodding along.

"I'm tired," Mary said suddenly. "I'm not going any farther. I'm going to sit down on that log."

She marched over to the log, a good-sized fallen pine that had probably been struck by lightning sometime in the past, and sat down just as she had threatened. Nate stood in front of her and said, "We got to go on. We can't stop. They're bound to be lookin' for us by now, and the longer we're gone, the more trouble we'll be in."

"I didn't want to go," Brad said as he came up beside Nate. "She made me."

"Did not!" his sister said sharply.

"Did too!" Brad shot back. "I told you we'd get in trouble if we left the camp!"

"You wanted to go exploring even more than I did," Mary said accusingly.

"Did not!"

"Both of you hush up," Nate told them. "It doesn't matter whose idea it was. We just gotta get back, that's all."

"We'll walk some more in a little bit," Mary said. "I just want to rest a while first."

"Well . . ." Maybe it would be all right, Nate thought. They were all tired. If he could rig some sort of shelter, maybe it wouldn't hurt anything to let his cousins rest. They were younger and smaller than him, after all. He couldn't expect them to be as strong as he was.

"Let's get some of these branches and put them against the log," he said. "We can make a little lean-to."

"You do it," Brad said. "I'm tired."

"We'll *all* do it," Nate insisted. "Come on. Then we can rest for a while."

Grudgingly, the two younger children pitched in to help. Within a few minutes, they had several pine boughs leaning against the fallen tree, forming a little cavelike hollow. All three of the youngsters crawled in. Nate felt better immediately since they now had at least a crude shelter. He broke several smaller sticks off the branches and made a pile of them, then reached into his coat.

"I got some flint and steel and tinder," he said. "I'll see if I can make a fire."

"You're not supposed to play with fire," Mary said. "You're not even 'sposed to have that stuff."

"Hush up," Nate ordered again. "I know what I'm doin'."

This was what Preacher would do if he was here, Nate thought as he began trying to strike sparks with the flint and steel. Preacher would build a fire, because they needed a fire to warm them on a cold night like this. He fumbled with it, since he didn't have much experience at such things, and it seemed like every time he struck a spark, it failed to fall into the little pile of tinder that he had poured out in the middle of the pile of sticks.

But finally one of the sparks fell properly and the tinder caught. Nate leaned closer and blew on the tiny flame. It grew larger and curled around one of the sticks until the stick began to smolder and then burn. The fire spread, and its reddish-yellow glow grew brighter inside the little makeshift shelter. That made Nate feel better too.

"We'll just sit here and warm up for a while, and then we'll finish walking back to camp," he told the others. They all held out their hands toward the fire to warm them.

After a few minutes, Mary leaned her head against Nate's

shoulder. Brad crawled closer on the other side and rested his head in Nate's lap. Nate braced himself against the trunk of the fallen tree. His eyelids grew heavy. He knew he was getting drowsy and tried to fight it off, thinking that it would be much better if he could stay awake, but the urge was just too strong. His eyes drooped until they closed. The last thing he was aware of was sliding his arms around his cousins as they huddled next to him, and then all three young'uns were sound asleep.

15

Preacher eventually located the spot where Nate had caught up to Mary and Brad, and from that point on, the three youngsters had traveled together. Unfortunately, one of the things Preacher had worried about appeared to have come true: The tracks led in huge circles. The kids were wandering around and around in the foothills, utterly lost.

"What are we going to do, Preacher?" Jonathan asked. "If we follow the tracks, won't we get lost too?"

Preacher shook his head. He knew he could rely on his inner sense of direction to point out the right way back to the camp any time he wanted to return there. He didn't intend to go back, though, without the children. If they were abandoned out here, their lives could be measured in days, if not hours.

He reminded himself that he had been only a few years older than Nate when he first came to the Rocky Mountains, but that was different. Life had hardened him to the point that he could take care of himself, at least to a certain extent. Nate had no experience at surviving in the wilderness, and he had the two younger kids to look after, on top of everything else.

"We've got to try to figure out where they're going to wind up and then head straight for that spot," Preacher said.

"How are we going to do that?" Geoffrey asked. "It looks

to me like they're just wandering aimlessly. They could be anywhere."

"Maybe not." Preacher let his eyes rove over the moonlit landscape. "Folks just naturally tend to go certain ways and avoid certain things. If you know the country, you can sort of figure where somebody would be likely to go. And I know the country."

"But you're still talking about an educated guess," Jonathan pointed out.

Preacher nodded. "Yep, but I've got the education. These mountains have been my school for years now. I know the obstacles those young'uns are likely to come across, and I know how they probably got around 'em."

"But what if your guess is wrong?" Geoffrey asked.

"It won't be," Preacher said flatly.

Because if it was . . . well, he wasn't going to think too much about that. Not yet anyway.

The three men trudged on into the night.

Angela Galloway had been through three labors: Mary, Brad, and a couple of years earlier another girl who had been stillborn. That last delivery had been difficult, difficult enough so that Angela had known something was wrong as soon as it started, and the two previous ones were painful as well. But despite that, Angela knew she had never gone through anything like what her sister-in-law Dorothy was enduring now.

Angela sat beside the thick bedroll where Dorothy lay and brushed back several strands of brown hair from the sweat-beaded forehead. The fact that Dorothy could sweat when the weather was as cold as it was spoke volumes for the pain she was in. Dorothy wasn't aware of the cold. She probably wasn't aware of anything except the overwhelming need to get that baby out of her body.

But the baby, bless its heart, sure didn't want to come.

Of course, helping Dorothy through this ordeal wasn't the

only thing on Angela's mind. Her two children were out there somewhere in the cold and dark, and there wasn't a thing she could do to help them or comfort them. The feeling of helplessness that gripped her made her sick in her stomach if she thought about it too much. Fear gnawed at her nerves. She loved Mary and Brad, loved them dearly, and the thought that she might never see them again was almost too much for her to grasp. She knew she had to keep herself busy and distracted, or else she might give in to the panic that tried to well up inside her.

"Peter," Dorothy murmured.

That was odd, Angela thought. Dorothy had just called her brother-in-law's name, not her husband's. And that wasn't the first strange thing Dorothy had said during the past few days, when she seemed to be out of her head more often than not. Of course, Dorothy had mentioned all of the Galloways at one time or another during her ramblings, so her saying Peter's name now didn't have to mean anything. . . .

Another wave of contractions gripped Dorothy. She threw her head back and screamed. Cords of muscle stood out on the sides of her neck. Angela held her hand and spoke to her, trying to calm her and get her to push. Dorothy was trying, but the baby just wouldn't come. If a doctor or an experienced midwife had been here, they might have been able to tell if the baby was turned wrong in the womb or if there was some other problem. But Angela just didn't know, and didn't know what else to do either.

The contractions passed. Dorothy subsided, her arched back easing down onto the bedroll. When she was breathing easier again, Angela thought it was safe to stand up and get a breath of fresh air. She went to the rear of the wagon and moved the canvas flap aside. She was shocked to see the gray light of dawn filling the camp.

It was nearly morning. The children had been missing all night.

Before Angela could think about that, another scream ripped from Dorothy's throat, and this one had a different sound to it than any of them before. Angela jerked around sharply and hurried to her sister-in-law's side. She lifted the blankets draped over Dorothy's upraised knees and then gasped as she saw the blood.

The baby had to come now, or both mother and child were going to die. Angela was sure of it.

Hawley woke up with his teeth chattering and his bones aching from the cold that had seeped into them during the night. The Injuns hadn't given him any robes or blankets to help ward off the chill. All he'd had to warm him were his buckskins and his capote.

But he was still alive, by Godfrey! He hadn't frozen to death, and the lightening of the sky overhead told him that dawn wasn't far away. The sun didn't provide much heat at this time of year, but any warmth was better than none.

And every minute that he remained alive was a blessing, even though he was still in the hands of the savages.

Hawley wondered if they had decided yet whether or not to kill him. He had fallen asleep the night before while they were still talking. The warriors had been ringed in a circle around a small fire, and they had taken turns speaking with the long-winded eloquence common to Injuns. Hawley understood only a few words of the Arikara tongue—mostly words that had to do with drinking and screwing—so he hadn't really been able to follow the discussion that well. The big ugly buck who seemed to be the war chief was called Swift Arrow, and he wanted to keep Hawley alive and use him to help find that bunch of immigrants. Another Injun, one called Badger Something-or-other, thought it would be best to go ahead and kill him, the sooner and the more painfully the better. The others seemed about equally divided on the question, and if anybody had told Hawley that he could doze off while his very fate was being debated, he would have told them they were crazy. That was exactly what had happened, though. Exhaustion had caught up to him.

Did the fact he was still alive mean that Swift Arrow had prevailed in the argument? Hawley didn't know. He turned his head and looked around, hoping to find out.

He was still lying against a tree with his hands and feet bound. He could barely feel his extremities, a condition due to the cold as well as to the tightness of his bonds. Not far away, the Injuns were up and about, gathered around the campfire. He might have been wrong, but Hawley thought there were fewer of them in the bunch now.

Swift Arrow was still there, though. Noticing that Hawley was awake, he stood up and walked over to the trapper, stalking over the snow-covered ground like a mountain lion.

"You live," he greeted Hawley.

"Yeah," the trapper croaked, his voice rusty and uncomfortable in his throat. "Am I gonna keep on livin'?"

"You help us find Preacher."

It wasn't a question, but Hawley nodded eagerly anyway. "That's right," he said. "I'll help you find Preacher. I'll even help you kill him."

"Swift Arrow kill Preacher."

There was no room for argument in that flat statement, and Hawley no longer cared who killed Preacher as long as the son of a bitch wound up dead. He said, "Sure. Swift Arrow kill Preacher."

The chief nodded emphatically. He returned to the fire, then came back to Hawley a moment later. He put a piece of jerky in Hawley's mouth. Hawley chewed eagerly on the tough strip of meat as he realized how ravenously hungry he was.

"I'll show you today where those wagons went," he said around the jerky. "It won't take us long to find them pilgrims. A day or two, that's all."

"Swift Arrow send out scouts."

Hawley figured out after a second what the chief meant. Swift Arrow had already sent out some of the warriors to have a look around. That's why there were fewer of the Injuns gathered around the fire.

"That's fine, but you don't have to worry," he said. "I can find them you're lookin' for."

Swift Arrow smiled thinly. "Not worry. White man worry."

"That's right," Hawley said, bobbing his head in agreement and smiling back at the savage. He was damned worried.

And he would be until the man called Preacher was dead and these bloody-handed redskins were in his, Mart Hawley's, debt.

Nate dreamed about his home back in Philadelphia and the kids who had gone to school with him. They had been envious and impressed when he told them his family was forming a wagon train and going west to live in the Oregon Territory. It sounded like such a grand adventure . . . and it had been, up to a point.

Then everything had started going wrong.

But in his dream, Nate was back in the classroom at the academy he had attended. His pa and his Uncle Roger and his grandpa Simon all had money, and they could afford to send Nate to a fancy school. Folks tended to think of immigrants as poor people, but the Galloways had money, no doubt about that. Nate dreamed he was there again, but instead of the clothes he had usually worn to school, he was garbed in fringed buckskins and wore a big hat. He had a powder horn slung over his shoulder and carried one of those long-barreled rifles like Preacher carried. In real life, a Hawken was so heavy, he could barely pick one up, let alone cradle it in the crook of his arm like it was a part of him, but he didn't have any trouble with it in his dream. All the kids stared wide-eyed at him, especially when he slid the long-bladed hunting knife from the beaded sheath on his belt and showed it to them. And when they asked him where he had been, he just grinned and said, *Why, I been to the mountains, boys. I'm a mountain man now.*

It was the best dream Nate had had in a long time.

But like all dreams, it came to an end.

He wasn't sure what woke him; all he knew was that he was cold and stiff and hungry, and he needed to pee really bad. Mary and Brad still leaned on him in their crude shelter underneath the pine boughs they had propped against the fallen tree. They were still asleep.

Light peeked through a couple of gaps in the branches above Nate's head. Was it morning already? Had they made it through the night? Evidently so, and Nate felt his spirits lift at that realization. Now that it was light again, they could see where they were going. He was confident that they could find their way back to camp in no time.

Of course, when they got there they were going to be in a whole heap of trouble, as Preacher would say. They'd been gone all night, and their parents were bound to be worried sick. When grown-ups got scared, they also got mad. They'd hug a fella's neck when they saw he was all right, then paddle his butt. Then hug some more and likely paddle some more. But whatever happened, Nate and his cousins would just have to take their medicine. They had it comin'.

And it would be worth it to be warm again, and to get something to eat.

First, though, he had to get out of here and relieve the insistent pressure on his bladder. He took hold of Mary's shoulders and eased her down until she was lying on the ground. She didn't wake up. Then he carefully slipped his leg out from under Brad's head.

His muscles were so stiff he could barely move as he tried to crawl out of the pine-bough lean-to. He wanted to grunt and groan with the effort, but he held the sounds back so he wouldn't disturb his cousins. Nate had heard his grandpa and his uncles make noises like he wanted to make now when they had to get up out of their chairs, and he wondered if they felt like this all the time. It must be horrible to be old, he thought.

He blinked as he emerged into the light. Even though the sun was barely up and the light was still watery and dim, it seemed bright to him. He pushed himself to his feet and stumbled over to a nearby tree. With fingers stiff from the cold, he fumbled at the buttons of his trousers and finally got them open. He closed his eyes in relief as he started to pee into the snowdrift on the other side of the tree.

That was when he heard a branch snap and opened his eyes to see an Indian standing no more than a dozen feet away, a tomahawk in his hand and a savage grin on his red, paint-daubed face.

16

Corn Man was not a proper name for a Sahnish warrior, or at least so the warrior known by that name had always believed. But though the Sahnish could be warlike when called upon to be so, they also took great pride in the skill with which they tilled the land and coaxed crops from it. They grew more corn than anything else. It was a staple of their diet, and they also traded it to other tribes for meat and buffalo robes. Corn Man was very good at the growing of corn, and so that name had been bestowed upon him. In a way it was a source of pride, since it connected him directly to Mother Corn, the Great Spirit who ruled the earth and was second only to Nishanu Natchitak, the Chief Above. In times of peace he had not minded being called Corn Man. His hope was that one day he would take the place of Badger's Den as the tribe's medicine man and would be entrusted with the care of the sacred bundle.

That day would be long in the future, though, and when it was time to take up arms and exact vengeance on those who had harmed the Sahnish, then it was better to be called Swift Arrow or Runs Far or some more fitting name for a warrior. Not Corn Man . . .

Still, it looked as if he would be the first to spill the blood of the whites. There stood one of them now, gaping at him. A young one, to be sure, but still one of the white interlopers in the land of the Sahnish. The boy, emerging from a crude shelter as Corn Man watched, had gone over to a tree to make his morning water. That came to an abrupt end as terror cut off the stream in mid-splash.

Corn Man lifted his tomahawk and bounded toward the fear-frozen youth.

A shrill scream cut through the cold air. It came not from the boy but from the shelter, where a young girl had just stuck her head out from behind the pine boughs.

Corn Man stopped, unsure what to do. The girl scrambled out from the shelter, still screaming, followed by a smaller boy, who also cried out in fear. The noise would bring the other members of the scouting party Swift Arrow had sent out before dawn that morning, and unless he acted quickly, Corn Man would be denied the honor of killing all three of these white children by himself. He snarled and swung back toward the oldest one . . . who had stooped and picked up a branch from the ground, and now he threw it as hard as he could, right at Corn Man's face. The short but heavy piece of wood flew straight and true and smashed across Corn Man's nose. Tears of pain sprang into his eyes, blinding him. He stumbled and almost fell, but caught his balance.

Any hesitation he might have felt at killing children was now gone. They were white, they had caused him pain, and they deserved to die.

"Run!" the boy shouted. "Run for your lives!"

Corn Man did not understand the words, but through the tears in his eyes, he saw the young ones flee. The oldest boy caught hold of the girl's hand, and then she used her other hand to grab the younger boy. Together they ran away from Corn Man.

He gave chase, vowing that they would not get away from him. Perhaps he would keep the two younger ones alive, so that Swift Arrow could decide what to do with them.

But the boy who had struck him, that one would die, and before the sun rose much higher in the sky. This Corn Man vowed.

* * *

Preacher had called a halt a couple of hours before dawn. The moon had set, making it more difficult to see where they were going, and Jonathan and Geoffrey were so played out they couldn't go on without some rest. They had found a spot under some trees where not much snow had fallen. The two older men had curled up on the ground, while Preacher sat down and leaned his back against a tree trunk. What he did then couldn't actually be called sleep, since all his senses remained alert, but it was a form of rest, and he felt somewhat refreshed when he got to his feet and told Jonathan and Geoffrey it was time for them to be moving again. The sun was up, and Preacher intended to move faster now that they could all see where they were going.

Both of the older men groaned as they climbed awkwardly to their feet. Preacher could have told them that they would get mighty stiff sleeping on the cold ground like that, but they would remember it better for having gone through it. And their muscles would loosen up quickly enough once he got them moving.

"Are we going to have any breakfast?" Jonathan asked as he stretched.

Preacher handed him a strip of jerky. "Gnaw on that while we're going. That's all we got time for." He pointed to a hill in the distance. "See that knoll over yonder? That's where we're headed. I think the young'uns ended up somewheres around there."

"How in the world do you know that?" Geoffrey asked.

"Well, they kept makin' bigger and bigger circles. Sooner or later they're gonna come to a ravine that's too deep and too wide for them to cross, so they'll have to move northwest along with it."

Jonathan said, "Why couldn't they go back southeast?"

"They could," Preacher said, "but that'd mean turnin' around and doublin' back on their trail, and I don't reckon they would do that because they think they're goin' the right

direction. They were movin' along steadylike, without stop-
pin' much, so Nate must've been convinced he was on the
right track."

"Well . . . maybe. I hope you're right."

"So do I," Preacher allowed. "Anyway, that ravine'll take
'em toward yonder knoll, and then they'll come to a good-
sized creek that'll force 'em even more toward it, since I don't
reckon they'll want to go swimmin' in weather this cold."

Both Geoffrey and Jonathan shivered at the very thought
of plunging into the icy-cold waters of a creek.

"We're gonna cut across country straight toward the hill,"
Preacher said, "so I think we stand a good chance o' gettin' there
either before they do or just about the same time."

"I pray that's so," Geoffrey said.

"Well, a mite of prayin' never hurt, that's for sure."
Preacher picked up his Hawken. "Let's go."

They moved out at a brisk pace. As the sun rose higher,
Preacher felt a wind from the south touch his face and knew
it was going to be warmer today than it had been for several
days. The snow on the ground would probably melt before the
day was over, leaving a muddy mess in places. That could
make things tricky when the wagons rolled out again, but it
was jumping the gun to worry about such things now. For the
moment, he had to concentrate on finding those kids and getting them back to their families.

He wondered briefly how it was going back there at camp,
and if Dorothy Galloway had finally had her baby.

Angela had never seen so much blood in her life. She
wasn't sure how Dorothy could still be alive after losing that
much of the vital fluid, let alone be conscious and struggling
to give birth.

"I've got to . . . turn it," Angela said. As she had suspected,
the baby was oriented incorrectly inside Dorothy's birth
canal, and that was why the labor and delivery had been so

difficult. But now that she was certain what was wrong, Angela hoped she could save them. All she could do was try.

From the back of the wagon, Roger asked, "Is there anything I can do?"

"No!" Angela practically shouted. "Just stay out of here, Roger."

She heard Peter talking to Roger, no doubt trying to draw his brother away from the wagon. She used a rag to wipe away blood and mucus, and tried to slip her hand further into Dorothy's body to get a grip on the baby. It would have helped, she thought a bit wildly, if she had ever lived on a farm and helped deliver calves. This baby was as slippery as a newborn calf, that was for sure. And she had to be careful not to get the cord wrapped around its neck, or it could strangle before it got out.

Dorothy screamed and strained, and Angela felt the baby's head against her hand. She cupped it as gently as possible and urged it toward the outside world. "Push, Dorothy, push hard!" she urged, and suddenly she saw the top of the baby's head. "It's coming! A little more, just a little more!"

Another shrill scream, and the rest of the head emerged, then a shoulder and an arm and another arm . . . It was a magnificent sight for all its grotesqueness. A new life coming into the world, born in blood and pain, strife and desperation, but at the same time filled with undeniable promise.

"Yes," Angela said in a half whisper, as much to herself as to Dorothy, because it was doubtful that Dorothy could hear much of anything now. "It's coming, it's coming. . . . It's a boy! He's beautiful, Dorothy, just beautiful!"

Angela eased the baby the rest of the way out and placed him on a clean blanket. She used a corner of the blanket to wipe mucus away from his mouth and nose, and he took a deep, quavery breath and blew it out in a loud squall that brought a smile to Angela's mouth and tears to her eyes. Now the cord had to be cut and the after-birth delivered. She tended to that quickly, then wrapped the blanket around the crying baby. As she tucked it in, she paid attention for the first time to the full head of wispy hair.

It was jet black.

That was odd, since Roger had sandy hair and Dorothy's was only slightly darker, a light brown. But the color of the baby's hair didn't really matter now. His lungs were healthy enough—he was proving that with every howl—and he had ten fingers and ten toes. Angela had done a quick count before she wrapped him up. Everything else could wait.

She stepped to the back of the wagon, pushed the flap open, and called, "Roger! Roger, come quick and get your son!"

Roger ran over, followed closely by Peter, and scrambled into the wagon. Angela placed the baby in his arms and said, "Hold him while I tend to Dorothy. Not too tightly now. You don't want to drop him, but don't squeeze him too much either."

"I'll be careful," Roger promised. Peter looked on from outside the wagon, an odd expression on his face, almost as if he were jealous of his brother while being happy for him at the same time.

Angela turned back to Dorothy, and had a bad moment when she looked at her sister-in-law's face. Dorothy's features were so pale and drawn that for a second Angela was afraid she was dead. But then she saw Dorothy's chest rising and falling slightly, and a moment later the new mother's eyes flickered open.

"My . . . my son . . . ?" she asked in a whisper.

"He's fine," Angela said as she leaned over Dorothy and wiped her face. "A strong, healthy boy. He's fine, Dorothy, and you will be too."

"His name is . . . John . . . John Edward . . . Galloway . . ."

"The name fits him," Angela said with a smile. "It's a very distinguished name."

"Promise me . . ." Dorothy's fingers caught hold of Angela's hand and held it with surprising strength. "Promise me . . . You'll take care of him. . . ."

"I won't have to," Angela said. "You're his mother, dear. You'll take care of him and do a wonderful job of it."

Dorothy's head moved weakly from side to side. "N-no. You've got to . . . promise . . ."

"I'll always do everything I can for you and your children."

"Swear . . ."

"I give you my word," Angela whispered.

With a sigh, Dorothy closed her eyes. Her head leaned back. Angela's heart leaped in fear, but again she saw that Dorothy was only asleep.

"Angela . . ." Roger said from behind her. "Angela, is she going to be all right?"

Angela stood up and turned to face her brother-in-law. "I won't lie to you," she said quietly. "Dorothy lost a great deal of blood. It seems to have stopped now, but she was so weak to start with . . . I'll do everything I can, Roger. That's all I can promise you."

Tears rolled down Roger's cheeks and dripped on the blanket wrapped around his newborn son. "You have to save her," he said. "I can't live without her."

"If you have to, you will." Angela put a hand on his shoulder and squeezed. "You have Nate, and now you have another son, John. You have to live for them, Roger, no matter what else happens."

"John," Roger repeated softly, looking down at his son.

"John Edward Galloway," Angela said, "this is your father."

And as she saw the way Roger looked at the baby, she thought again of her own children, lost in the wilderness, perhaps by now even . . .

No. She would not allow herself to even think it. Preacher was out there looking for them.

Preacher would bring her children home.

17

Nate threw a terrified glance over his shoulder as he tugged Mary and Brad along with him. The Indian was still chasing them, waving that tomahawk around and looking like he wanted to scalp all three of them. Nate knew they couldn't fight him. The Indian was too big and too strong, and he looked more frightening than anything Nate had ever seen, with those bones sticking up in his hair like he had grown them himself and was some sort of devil.

Deep down, Nate knew they couldn't outrun the Indian either. But they had to try. They couldn't just stop and wait for him to catch up and kill them.

There wasn't even time to think about what Preacher would do. There wasn't time for anything except sheer, panicked flight.

The kids had stopped screaming. They didn't have enough breath for that anymore. All of them were panting in the cold air, their breath visible in plumes and streamers around their heads. Nate saw a tree-covered slope in front of them and headed for it. Maybe they could throw off the Indian if they got in the trees. Maybe they could hide from him.

Those were forlorn hopes, Nate knew, but right now, any hope was better than none.

The Indian was so close when they reached the hill and started up it that Nate could hear him huffing and blowing.

Nate hoped he wouldn't run into a tree or dash his brains out on a low-hanging limb. It would be all right, though, if something like that happened to the Indian.

"Nate!" Brad suddenly shrieked. "He's got me!"

Nate felt the tug as Brad was pulled away from him and Mary. He tried to stop and turn around, but he stumbled and fell instead, letting go of Mary's hand as he went down. She screamed too. Nate rolled over and saw that the Indian had hold of Brad by the neck with his free hand. The other hand swung the tomahawk at Mary's head. She dropped underneath the swing as the lethal weapon went over her head. It was more by accident than design, though. She tried to scramble away on her hands and knees, but the Indian planted a moccasined foot in the middle of her back and shoved her to the ground, pinning her there. He picked up Brad by the neck so that his feet swung and kicked in midair.

Nate knew Brad would choke to death if the Indian held him like that for very long. He scooted a little closer, moving as fast as he could, and lifted his leg in a kick, driving the heel of his boot between the Indian's legs. The Indian howled in pain, dropped Brad, and forgot all about scalping them or bashing their heads in with his tomahawk. He doubled over in agony, clutching himself.

Nate scrambled up, grabbed his cousins, and hauled them to their feet. He started climbing again, heading higher on the hill. When he looked back, he saw that the Indian was stumbling after them, although he was still bent over and wasn't moving very fast now.

For the first time, Nate dared to really hope that they might get away.

Of course, there might be other Indians around nearby. Where there was one savage, there might be more. But he couldn't worry about that now. They had to get away from this Indian first.

A strong, red hand shot out from some bushes and clasped itself around Nate's arm. He gasped in pain and surprise as the cruel grip tightened even more and swung him off the ground. Without him to pull them along, Mary and Brad tumbled off their feet.

Nate found himself staring into the face of another Indian. This one was even bigger and uglier than the one who had been chasing them. To Nate's surprise, the Indian said something in English, disgustedly spitting out the word "Children!"

Even more shocking, a vaguely familiar voice answered in English. "That's right, Chief, children. But they come from the wagon train you're after. I recognize the little brats."

Nate turned his head and stared in horror at the face of the man called Hawley. He looked the same as he had the last time Nate had seen him, with that bristly, ginger-colored beard. Only his eyes were different now. Last time, Hawley had been scared of Preacher, and it showed.

Now the man leered at Nate and his cousins with an expression of pure evil, and although Nate wouldn't have thought it was possible, he discovered that he was even more frightened of this white man than he was of the Indians.

This was a mighty fine stroke of luck, Hawley thought as he looked at the kid squirming in Swift Arrow's grasp. Swift Arrow and the rest of the war party, along with the now-freed Hawley, had followed the scouts sent out earlier by the war chief. Hawley planned on leading them to a spot where they could pick up the trail of the wagon train. But now, lo and behold, the three pesky young'uns from the immigrant party had been chased right into their laps by one of the scouts.

That redskin came trotting up, moving carefully and hunching over a little like he was hurt. Swift Arrow spoke sharply to him, and Hawley caught something about "making war on children." The other Injun argued back—respectfully, since Swift Arrow was the chief—and his main point was that when had the whites ever hesitated about making war on Injun children. Swift Arrow couldn't dispute that at times, redskinned little ones had died in fights with white men. Even more often, previously unknown sicknesses brought to this land by the whites had killed many more, striking indiscriminately at men, women, and children. Sometimes, shameful though it was to contemplate, white folks had infected the Injuns, in hopes of wiping them out.

Hawley thought that actually wasn't such a bad idea, only it hadn't worked well enough, at least not yet. Right now, though, he didn't want the Injuns wiped out. Unexpected as it might be, the savages were now his allies.

"Swift Arrow," he said, "you better hang on to them kids."

The war chief turned to him. "What, good children?"

Hawley licked his lips and said, "Bait. I'll bet you anything Preacher's out lookin' for them sprouts right now. You keep the kids, and they'll bring Preacher right to you. You can kill him, and then you won't have near as much trouble killin' the other folks when you catch up to the wagons."

"No!" That was the oldest boy yelling at him. "No, you can't hurt Preacher!"

Swift Arrow still had hold of his arm. He shook him until the boy cried out in pain.

"Boy be quiet," Swift Arrow ordered. He looked down at the other two kids, who were huddled on the ground sobbing in fear. "All be quiet!"

Hawley hunkered so that he could speak directly to the younger kids. "You two best be quiet, or the chief'll scalp you. You hear me?"

Biting back whimpers of pain, the older boy said, "Mary, Brad, hush now. It's going to be all right."

Hawley knew better, but he didn't say as much. Instead, he put a false note of cheer in his voice and told them, "That's right. Ain't nothin' bad gonna happen to you kids. You just settle down and stop cryin', and nobody will hurt you."

The little girl sniffled and looked up at him. "You . . . You promise, mister?"

"Sure," Hawley lied. "Hell, I'm a white man, ain't I? You can trust me. I'll look after you."

Swift Arrow dropped the older boy, who fell beside the

other two. He clutched his arm and whimpered, and Hawley wondered briefly if Swift Arrow had pulled the arm right out of its joint. Not that he really cared.

"You keep children," Swift Arrow said. "We use to trap Preacher."

Hawley nodded. "Damn right."

And once Preacher was dead, they wouldn't have any more use for these sniveling little kids.

Jonathan and Geoffrey kept up better than Preacher expected after this long a time. The men were moving on very little rest and even less food, but they kept going somehow. Preacher supposed it was because they loved those kids.

He found himself wondering if he would ever have any kids of his own. If things had been different for him and Jennie, then maybe . . .

But no, it didn't do any good to think about that. Maybe one of these days, when he was older and more settled down, he would meet another woman . . . somebody like Angela Galloway maybe . . . but not Angela, of course, since she already had a husband and kids . . .

Older and more settled down, Preacher thought again. As if that were ever likely to happen.

All those thoughts vanished in an instant from his head as he saw the sun strike a momentary reflection off something on the hill that was their destination. In the blink of an eye, he was once again focused on the chore at hand. The reflection was there and then gone, but it had been enough to tell him that somebody was up there on the hill. He put out a hand to stop Geoffrey and Jonathan.

"Those kids carryin' anything metal on them?" Preacher asked.

"Metal?" Jonathan repeated. "You mean like a knife or a gun?"

"Anything the sun might strike a glint off of."

Geoffrey said, "Nate has a folding knife. And Mary

probably has some little geegaws that might shine in the sun. Did you see something, Preacher?"

"The sun flashed on something up yonder on the hill. Don't know what it was, but it couldn't have been anything natural."

"You said they might go up there," Jonathan said excitedly. "Could they have gotten there ahead of us?"

"Sure, anything's possible," Preacher allowed. "They could've moved a mite faster than I expected."

"Well, let's go get them! Do you think if we shouted their names, they could hear us from here?" Jonathan lifted his hands and got ready to cup them around his mouth.

Preacher made a sharp, slashing motion. "Don't go to hollerin', damn it! We don't know if it's them, and even if it is, we don't know if they're alone."

"Who else could it be?" Geoffrey asked.

"What about that Arikara war party?"

The two older men exchanged a glance that Preacher couldn't read. "I thought you weren't sure there even was a war party," Jonathan said.

"Didn't you say those Indians who attacked us were probably renegades?" Geoffrey put in.

"I said they might be. My gut tells me that ain't the whole story, though. I think there's more o' those 'Rees, and I think they're after you folks for a reason."

"That's crazy!" Geoffrey insisted. "We never saw those Indians before."

"What about Indians like them?"

Both men shook their heads. "No, of course not," Jonathan said.

Preacher's uneasy instincts warned him the men might be lying. He was convinced they were. And yet he knew that getting to the bottom of it would have to wait. First they needed to find those kids. Preacher hoped they weren't in too much trouble.

"Let's go," he said. "Watch me, and try not to make too much noise."

He set out with the older men trailing him. An occasional glance over his shoulder told him that they were trying their best to imitate him as he moved soundlessly through the woods toward the knoll. They made a little racket, but not too much. Preacher thought again that with time, they might turn into decent frontiersmen.

He just wished they would tell him the damn truth about any grudge that the Arikara might have against them.

They came to a gully that ran all the way to the base of the hill. Preacher motioned them into it and then led the way closer. When they reached the bottom of the hill, he raised a hand to call a halt. He listened intently, hoping to hear child-ish voices drifting down the slope.

Instead, he heard the faint whisper of stealthy footsteps, followed by something alarming: a whimpering sound that might easily be a young child crying. Preacher glanced at Geof-frey and Jonathan and saw that they had heard it as well. Their eyes were wide, and he could tell they were both ready to blurt out questions. He stopped them with another curt gesture and a finger held to his lips. He motioned for them to lie down at the edge of the gully behind some brush. Preacher stretched out beside them and parted the branches a tiny bit so that he could peer through them.

In a matter of moments he saw a sight that would haunt him for all his born days. A dozen or more Arikara warriors strode quietly through the woods. Behind them came a familiar buckskin-clad figure: Mart Hawley. Hawley had hold of Mary and Brad by the arms and jerked them along roughly. Nate was with them too, being tugged along by one of the Indians. The kids looked scared to death, as well they might be. They were in the hands of not only a war party that obviously had a grudge against their folks, but even worse, a white man who had evi-dently turned renegade and thrown in his lot with the Arikara.

The job of fetching those kids back to the wagons had just gotten a hell of a lot harder.

18

Preacher and his two companions watched the Indians and their captives until they got out of sight. Preacher could tell that Geoffrey and Jonathan were about bustin' at the seams from wanting to go after the kids. He motioned for them to take it easy and hoped that they could restrain their impatience.

Finally, when the Indians were out of earshot, Preacher came to his feet and said, "Let's go."

"Go? Go where?" Geoffrey practically exploded. "The Indians are gone!"

"And they got away with the children!" Jonathan said. "We just sat here helpless and let them go!"

Preacher shook his head. "If we had jumped them here and now, we wouldn't have done anything except get us and probably the kids killed. There were too many of those Injuns to take on in a straight-up fight. Plus they got that son of a bitch Hawley with 'em."

"I saw that," Jonathan said. "It looked like he was their friend, for God's sake!"

"I reckon he's thrown in with 'em," Preacher agreed. "I don't know how come 'em to be together, but he's on their side now, that's for sure."

Geoffrey asked, "Why are we standing around talking? Shouldn't we be going after them? If we delay too long, they'll get away, and then we might never find them again!"

"We can find 'em," Preacher assured his companions. "Even though they're redskins, a bunch that big will leave tracks we can follow. Besides, from the looks of it, they're headin' toward the wagons. Hawley must be leadin' the way for 'em."

"That bastard," Jonathan said in a low, angry voice.

Preacher nodded again. "You won't get no argument from me on that score."

"Will they hurt the children?" Geoffrey asked.

"Injuns are notional folks," Preacher said with a shrug. "I won't lie to you. They're capable of killin' those kids if the whim strikes 'em. More than likely, though, they'll keep 'em alive, at least for a while. Hawley may figure he can use the young'uns as hostages when him and the Injuns catch up to the wagons. Maybe try to trade them for me."

Jonathan frowned. "Why would they place so much importance on . . . Oh, I see. You're the most dangerous member of the party. They might think that if they get rid of you, the rest of us won't put up much of a fight."

"I'm afraid they might be right about that," Geoffrey said gloomily.

"From what I've seen, you fellas don't have a lot of back up in you," Preacher told them. "You'll do just fine when it comes down to the nut-cuttin'. Now let's get after that bunch. Keep it as quiet as you can."

"You can count on us, Preacher," Jonathan said.

Preacher thought that was probably right. He would have felt a lot better about things, though, if he'd had Jeb Law or some of his other mountain-man friends there to help him.

A man made do with what he had, he told himself. Right now that was a couple of old-timers from Philadelphia.

Preacher hoped that would be enough.

Nate was scared, but he tried not to show it. His arm and shoulder hurt too, but he wouldn't allow himself to cry. Crying was for babies, and right now he had to be a man, despite the fact that he was only ten years old. It was all right for Mary and Brad to sniffle a little every now and then; they were kids, and they were scared.

Nate forced his brain to look past the fear he felt and consider the situation. The tnree of them were still alive, and that was something. The Indians hadn't killed them out of hand. Nate didn't trust Hawley as far as he could have thrown the trapper. Hawley hated them just like the Indians did. So Nate knew better than to hope that Hawley would protect them and somehow get them out of this trouble.

As long as they were alive, though, they still had a chance. Nate wasn't going to give up.

He sure wished he could hug his ma right about now, though. He wondered too if he had a little brother or sister yet. They should have stayed in the camp. The two younger ones shouldn't have wandered off to go "exploring," darn it. . . .

Thoughts like that didn't do any good, he told himself. What he should be doing was watching for a chance for him and Mary and Brad to escape. He bit his lip against the pain in his shoulder and kept moving. If he lollygagged along, the Indian who had hold of his arm would give it a jerk, and that would just make him hurt even worse.

The Indians moved through the woods for what seemed like hours, even days. The sun rose higher in the sky, and when Nate looked at it, he knew it wasn't even noon yet, no matter what it felt like. After so long a time, though, the Indians stopped to rest. Along with Mary and Brad, Nate slumped gratefully to the ground, stretching out on some pine needles.

Hawley hunkered beside them and said, "How you kids holdin' up?"

"I'm tired," Mary whined. "Can't we go back to the wagons?"

"That's what we're doin'. I reckon you'll see your ma and pa again 'fore too much longer."

"I want Mama," Brad whimpered.

Hawley snapped, "Shut up. Don't go to pullin' and poutin',

or them Injuns are liable to lift your hair." He looked at Nate. "Which one are you, boy? Who you belong to?"

"My parents are Roger and Dorothy Galloway," Nate replied, trying to sound dignified and not the least bit scared of the smelly mountain man in his greasy buckskins.

"It's your ma who's havin' the baby?"

"That's right." Again Nate felt a fierce longing to know how his mother was doing.

"What about them two?"

"They're my cousins, Mary and Brad. Their parents are my Uncle Peter and Aunt Angela."

Hawley grinned. "Angela . . . She's the purty one with that long blond hair, ain't she? Lord, I'd like to get me some o' that."

Mary blinked up at him and said, "You want to have long blond hair like my mama?"

Nate wasn't exactly sure what Hawley had meant by his comment, but he was certain the man hadn't been talking about Aunt Angela's hair. Before the trapper could make some crude response, Nate said, "Shush, Mary. We probably won't stop for long. Save your breath and rest."

"That's good advice, kid. I reckon it'll take most of the day to catch up to them wagons, so the Injuns can't afford to wait around for very long. We'll be up and hustlin' again 'fore you know it."

True to Hawley's prediction, within minutes the big, ugly Indian called Swift Arrow barked some commands in the guttural Arikara tongue, and the warriors resumed their swift march, dragging their young prisoners along with them.

Nate wanted to see his parents again, wanted it more than anything he could think of in the world, but at the same time, he knew that when the Indians caught up to the wagons, they would try to kill the rest of his family. He started thinking desperately, trying to come up with some way he could slow them down or maybe even throw them off the track. . . .

* * *

Dorothy slept most of the morning, and Angela was grateful for that. It gave her a chance to rest as well. There was a rocking chair in the wagon, so Angela sat in it, her lap covered with a blanket and the new baby wrapped up and cradled in her arms. As she looked down at John Edward's red, scrunched-up face, she took note again of his black hair. Her own children had had hair that dark when they were born, although in both cases it had lightened up some over the years.

She remembered when Nathan had been born. His hair had been fair, almost blond, though it had darkened to the same shade as Roger's. A vague sense of unease stirred inside her. Something wasn't right here, but she couldn't put her finger on what it was.

She dozed off, exhausted from the night-long ordeal. If she was this tired, she couldn't imagine how Dorothy felt, having gone through the lengthy, difficult labor, along with being sick on top of it. And then the birth, and losing all that blood . . .

The baby woke her with its crying. For a second, disoriented from sleep, she looked down at John Edward and thought he was one of her own. But of course he wasn't. She knew what he wanted, but she couldn't give it to him. She said softly, "Just you wait a minute, honey. I don't know if your mama is up to it, but we'll see what we can do."

She stood up and went over to the thick pallet where Dorothy lay. The bloodstained, sweat-soaked bedding underneath her had been changed. Dorothy seemed to be sleeping more peacefully now, and Angela hated to disturb her. She had no choice, though. The baby had to eat.

"Dorothy . . ." Angela said quietly. She set the infant aside on a pillow and slipped an arm under Dorothy's shoulders. Carefully, she raised her sister-in-law to a half-sitting position and stayed there, supporting her. Pushing back the robes that were wrapped around Dorothy, she bared a breast. She reached over with her other arm and even more carefully picked up the baby, cradling him in the crook of her elbow and keeping the palm of her hand under his head to prevent it from lolling loosely. He was so tiny, she thought, so helpless.

Dorothy murmured, only half-conscious. That was all right; she didn't have to be fully awake for this. Angela brought the baby to his mother's breast, and as soon as the nipple nudged his lips, he opened them, took it in, and began to suckle.

Angela sat there holding both mother and child. She wished she could take on the chore of feeding John Edward, but she had no milk. Nor would she ever again, she thought as dampness misted her vision for a moment. Ever since that stillborn child, Peter had avoided touching her. Truth to tell, that was the way she had wanted it at first. She had pushed him away enough times so that he had gotten in the habit of not coming near her in bed, she supposed. Most of the time that was all right, but on occasion she missed his touch so badly she could barely stand it.

But life went on and everyone had crosses to bear, and right now her mind was occupied with helping her sister-in-law and her new nephew, as well as with worrying about the fate of her own children. She had hoped that Preacher would be back with them by now.

"Angela . . . ?" Dorothy whispered.

"Right here," Angela replied quickly, bending her head to bring it closer to Dorothy. "You're fine. The baby is eating."

"The . . . baby . . ." Somehow, Dorothy found the strength to reach up and stroke the black hair on John Edward's head. "So beautiful . . ."

"Yes, he is," Angela agreed with a smile.

"He looks just like . . . his father . . ."

The smile on Angela's face turned to a frown. She didn't see how Dorothy could say that. The baby looked almost nothing like Roger. If anything, he looked a lot more like—

My God, she thought. *No. It can't be.*

But she knew it was, and she wondered how she could have been so incredibly, stupidly blind.

She was just human. She had seen what she wanted to see

and ignored what she didn't want to see. Some things could not be ignored, though, and the pain of that realization shot through her.

"Angela . . ." Dorothy said in a voice filled with the weakness and sickness that threatened to consume her. "I have to tell you. . . . You deserve to know . . . about the baby . . . and Peter . . ."

"Don't say anything else," Angela told her shakily. "Please, don't say anything."

"I . . . I can't die . . . with this burden on my soul . . ."

Angela put a false heartiness in her voice as she said, "You're not going to die. Just stop thinking about that. You're going to be just fine."

Dorothy's head moved slowly from side to side. "No. You have a right . . . to know . . . Peter and I . . . Peter is the baby's . . . father . . ."

There it was, in undeniable, incontrovertible words. A wave of dizzy sickness hit Angela, as if the world had suddenly started spinning in the wrong direction. A shudder went through her. But other than that, she didn't move. She couldn't move. She had her arms around Dorothy and . . . John Edward.

Her husband's child, with another woman.

A tear welled from Angela's right eye and trickled down her cheek.

19

The Indians didn't give their captives any food at midday. Nate figured they would be forced to go hungry, but Hawley grudgingly let them have some jerky from his pack. Mary and Brad whined about it, of course, but they took the strips of tough, dried meat and gnawed on them anyway. Nate didn't waste his time complaining. He was just glad he had something to put in his empty stomach.

As the group cut through the heavily wooded foothills, Nate realized just how badly he and his cousins had been lost the night before. They must have spent hours going around and around in ever-widening circles. It was doubtful they would have ever gotten back to the wagons. If the Indians hadn't captured them, eventually they would have collapsed and died of starvation . . . if they hadn't frozen to death or been eaten by wolves first.

Of course, there was always the chance that Preacher would have found them. Nate couldn't shake the feeling that the mountain man was out here somewhere, searching for them.

As the afternoon went on, he began to see things that looked familiar to him: a massive, lightning-blasted pine; a peculiar rock formation that looked like an old man; a stream that tumbled some thirty feet down a cliff in a foaming waterfall. Nate knew he had seen these landmarks the day before. Did that mean they were getting closer to the wagons? He thought it must.

"When are we gonna get back to camp?" Brad asked with a sniffle.

Without thinking about what he was doing, Nate said, "Never, the way they're going." He pitched his voice low, but he made sure it was loud enough for Hawley to overhear him.

He realized a second later that his instincts had guided him correctly. Brad let out a wail, and Hawley turned sharply toward them. "What the hell did you say?" he demanded of Nate.

Before Nate could answer, Brad yelled, "He said we're never gonna get back!"

Hawley's hand shot out and grabbed Nate's wrenched shoulder. Nate cried out in pain as the cruel grip made pain stab through him. "What are you talkin' about?" Hawley asked as he gave Nate a hard shake. "We're right on the trail o' them wagons!"

"Y-yeah," Nate stammered. "Yeah, sure we are. We'll be there soon. Please stop shaking me!"

Hawley grabbed Nate's other shoulder and brought his face close to the boy's. Snarling, he said, "You better be tellin' me the truth!"

"S-sure I am. I swear!"

The Indians had come to a halt as the commotion broke out, and now Swift Arrow stalked over and said, "What wrong?"

Hawley shook Nate again, drawing a whimper from him. "This little bastard said somethin' about us goin' the wrong way, and now he won't tell me what he meant by it!"

"Honest, Mr. Hawley, I just got mixed up and made a mistake," Nate said through his tears. "I didn't mean nothin' by it."

Swift Arrow pointed eastward and said to Hawley, "You say wagons go this way."

"They did," Hawley insisted. "They're headin' for Garvey's Fort, I tell you, and that's the way they'd be goin'. Unless—" Hawley broke off his words and looked at Nate again. "Did Preacher decide to go some other direction? Maybe head down toward the Platte? There's a few tradin' posts down there."

Nate shook his head. "I . . . I don't know anything about the Platte. We were still goin' the same way as when you left us."

Hawley snorted. "When Preacher killed my partner and run me off, you mean. I ain't sure I believe you, you little shit. Preacher's just tricky enough to have hit off in some other direction, just to throw me off his trail. I reckon he knew I'd come after him and was afraid of me."

Not on his worst day would Preacher ever be scared of the likes of you, Nate thought, but he kept it to himself. His hastily formed plan appeared to be working.

Swift Arrow put his hand on the handle of the knife sheathed at his waist. "You take us to wagons," he said to Hawley. There was no mistaking the threat in his voice and in his stance.

Hawley bobbed his head and said with obviously false confidence, "Sure, I'm takin' you to the wagons. We're goin' the right way."

"Boy say not." The war chief jerked his hand in a curt gesture at Nate.

"The boy don't know what he's talkin' about. Anyway, he said we *are* goin' the right direction."

"Boy lie," Swift Arrow said with a contemptuous look.

Nate just looked as guilty as possible and wouldn't meet the eyes of either Hawley or Swift Arrow.

"I reckon he must be lyin', all right," Hawley finally acknowledged. "Preacher and those wagons have changed directions. I figure they're headin' for the Platte River. I can take you there—"

"Swift Arrow know where Platte River is."

The implication in the flat statement was obvious: If Swift Arrow knew where the immigrants were going, why did he need Hawley? For that matter, Nate wondered why they hadn't killed the trapper before now if they thought the wagons were headed for Garvey's Fort. They didn't really need Hawley to show them the way.

They must have something else in mind for Hawley, Nate thought. And he would have been willing to bet that it wouldn't be anything good. Hawley seemed to think he had the redskins wrapped around his little finger, but Nate figured he was in for a bad surprise sooner or later.

"Listen," Hawley said quickly. "You still need me. I can come up on those wagons without those folks suspectin' anything. I'll get 'em off their guard, and then you can take 'em without any trouble."

"You help kill whites?"

"Sure, I'll help kill 'em. I told you that. Whatever you say, I'll sure do it."

Mary and Brad started crying harder at that. Even now they knew that they were doomed, that Hawley's promise to protect them had been just a big lie.

"Not kill you yet," Swift Arrow said after a moment. "We take you with us."

"I'm much obliged for that. I'll guide you to the Platte—"

"Not know that Preacher go there," Swift Arrow cut in. "Must search again."

"You mean split up the war party?" Hawley looked a little skeptical about that idea.

"Find quicker that way. Whites may still go Garvey's Fort."

Hawley rubbed his bearded jaw and frowned. "Yeah, I reckon you're right," he said after a moment. "All we got to go on is this dumb kid's word. He might not have even known where the wagons were when he wandered off."

"Did so," Nate muttered under his breath, but Hawley and Swift Arrow heard him. Both of them glared.

Let them look at him like that, Nate thought. He didn't care. All that mattered was that he had slowed down their pursuit, and he had even gotten them talking about splitting their forces. He couldn't have hoped for a much better result from his little acting job.

But he couldn't get the rest of his hopes up either. He had bought a little time. . . . That was all. Their future, his and his cousins', was still in the hands of a bunch of savages and a white renegade.

* * *

"What are they doing?" Jonathan asked anxiously as Preacher shinnied down from the pine tree he had climbed a few minutes earlier so that he could spy on the Arikara war party, which had halted about half a mile away on the other side of a little valley. The Injuns didn't know there was anybody behind them, so they weren't looking in that direction.

Preacher landed lithely on the ground and grinned at the two older men. "Looks like they're splittin' up into two or three different bunches," he said.

Geoffrey and Jonathan stared at him in surprise. "Why would they do that?" Geoffrey asked.

"I ain't got no idea," Preacher admitted. "They've got a good strong force. No need that I can see for them to split up. But maybe the war chief in charge of the bunch knows somethin' that we don't . . . or at least thinks he does."

The group of 'Rees they had seen that morning had been joined by others until the war party was at least forty members strong. A bunch that big would be hard to fight off if they all attacked the wagon train at the same time. Anything that broke them up into smaller groups was a good thing, Preacher thought.

"What about the children?" Jonathan asked.

"I saw 'em," Preacher nodded. "They looked like they were still all right."

"Thank God," Geoffrey said fervently.

Jonathan said, "If they split up, how will we know which group the youngsters go with?"

"We'll be able to tell from the tracks," Preacher assured him. "There's still enough snow here and there to pick up some prints, and when the snow's all melted, there's bound to be mud. Maybe Dog can help us too."

The day had warmed up considerably as the southern breezes continued to blow, and the landscape was more green again than white. This break in the weather wouldn't last, though. Preacher's bones told him another storm was coming. It was just a matter of when.

Preacher whistled, and Dog came out of the woods. The big wolflike creature had been ranging far ahead of them most of the day. Preacher ruffled his fur between his ears and said, "Let's go, fella. You ain't no bloodhound, but I reckon you might be able to pick up a scent if we had somethin' that belonged to one of those kids."

Jonathan cleared his throat. "As a matter of fact . . ." He reached inside his coat and brought out a small rag doll. "This is Mary's. There's a tear in it, and I was going to try to mend it for her since Angela has been so busy taking care of Dorothy these days. I can sew a bit, you know. An old bachelor skill."

Preacher nodded in understanding. "A man who can't sew a mite is up the creek if he needs somethin' mended and the nearest woman is nigh five hundred miles away."

"Indeed. Anyway . . ." Jonathan held out the doll. "Do you think Dog could track them from this?"

Preacher took the doll. "We can give it a try. That way we won't lose the trail for sure."

He held the doll under Dog's nose and told him to go find Mary. As usual, Dog seemed to understand what Preacher wanted. He turned and trotted off, tail wagging. The three men walked quickly after him.

The tracks Preacher found on the other side of the valley confirmed what he had seen from up in the tree. The war party had broken up into three groups, and they had fanned out to the east, southeast, and south. From the looks of it, Preacher thought that the Indians had decided they might not be going in the right direction. In fact, they had been, but something must have happened to cause them to doubt that. Preacher couldn't figure out that part of it, but the why didn't really matter. What was important was that the bunch holding the kids prisoner now numbered around a dozen again.

Four-to-one odds weren't good, but at least they were tolerable. Preacher and his companions had a chance now to get the kids away from those Injuns.

They pressed on, moving a little quicker. Preacher felt a growing urgency. This opportunity might be the only one they would get.

20

Angela was sitting in the rocking chair again when Roger looked in the back of the wagon. The baby was sound asleep, nestled next to Dorothy, who was also asleep. Angela stared straight ahead, and Roger had to speak to her twice before she came out of her reverie with a little start.

"I'm sorry to bother you," Roger said. "I know you must be exhausted. I just had to find out how they're doing."

Angela managed a tired smile. "They're both asleep. The baby ate a little while ago."

Roger stepped up into the wagon. "Dorothy is . . . all right?"

"She seems to be resting comfortably. But she's still awfully weak, Roger. She needs proper medical attention."

"We're a long way from that," Roger said, a bitter edge creeping into his voice.

"Yes, we are." There was no point in denying it, Angela thought. "We should have waited for spring. The baby could have been born in St. Louis."

"I know." Roger's eyes were haunted. "I know. But we just couldn't wait."

From the start, there had been something wrong about this journey. Angela had known that, had sensed the urgency with which Roger and Peter and their father had organized everything. She and Dorothy, along with Geoffrey and Jonathan, had been swept along with the preparations, and their questions about why they had to leave Philadelphia so suddenly had been brushed aside with vague answers or sometimes even no answers. But the secret, if indeed there really was one, was still unknown to her.

A lot of secrets had been kept from her lately, she thought wryly.

Roger moved past her and knelt beside his wife and the baby. "Can I . . . sit with them for a while?"

"Goodness, you can do whatever you want, Roger. This is your wagon, and Dorothy is your wife." Angela left the rest of it unsaid, but Roger didn't seem to notice.

"Why don't you step outside and get some fresh air?" he said. "It might make you feel better."

Angela nodded. "Thank you. I'll do that." Roger was a considerate man, a good man. She had always liked him because of his devotion to his family, not just to his wife and son but to his brother and father and uncles too. He tried to do what was right and best for all of them. At least, he had until this fateful and ill-advised journey west.

She moved to the back of the wagon and climbed out. The sun almost blinded her. It seemed awfully bright to her after she'd been cooped up inside the wagon all day. And the air was even warm, a far cry from the icy temperatures of the past few days. Most of the snow had melted, and what was left was dripping.

She knew what Preacher would say if he were here: "Prob'ly be another one o' them blue northers in a day or two." Preacher seemed to know such things, no doubt because he had lived in the wild for so long and was somehow connected with nature to a greater extent than those who had spent all their lives in civilization.

Where *was* Preacher? And where were the children? The fact that Preacher had been gone for so long had to be a bad sign. The children hadn't just wandered off. Something had happened to them. Angela was sure of it.

Someone called her name, and she turned to see her

husband hurrying toward her. Peter had a rifle in his hand and a worried expression on his face.

"Aren't you supposed to be standing guard?" Angela asked him as he came up to her.

"My father is watching for trouble," Peter replied. "How are Dorothy and the baby?"

It would be so easy. She could look right at him and say, *Your mistress and your bastard son are sleeping.* At this moment, she would enjoy seeing the shock on his face if she said that to him.

And yet for some reason she held back. If she told Peter, she would have to tell Roger too, and she found that she didn't want to hurt him that way. There was enough trouble plaguing the family right now without all the added strain that such a revelation would bring. To be honest, she was so worried about the children that she simply couldn't summon up the strength to hate Peter right now.

"They're asleep," she said in reply to his question.

"The baby is all right?"

Angela nodded. "He seems to be fine."

"Well, that's good. I'm happy for Roger. But what about Dorothy?"

"I don't know. She came through the birth, and it was bad. But she could still take a turn for the worse."

"God, I hope not! That would be terrible. Terrible for Roger."

And for Dorothy's lover too.

Angela shoved that thought out of her head. "I hoped that Preacher would be back by now," she said, changing the subject, but not to a more pleasant one. She was more worried about her children than she was about the fact that Peter had cheated on her.

A grim look came over his face. "He should have let Roger and me go with him, instead of taking those two old men."

"Those two old men are your uncles," Angela reminded him. "They happen to love you, and the children, very much."

"I know that. But if it comes down to a fight with Indians or something like that, how much help will they really be?"

"Enough," Angela said softly. She had to hope so anyway, for the sake of Mary and Brad and Nate. For the sake of all of them really, because if Preacher got killed trying to bring the children back, there was a good chance that none of the immigrants would ever see civilization again.

The sun was lowering over the peaks to the west. Its rays cast dappled shadows under the aspens and cottonwoods that thickly lined the banks of the creek. Shadows through which Preacher glided like he was one of them, insubstantial, fleeting, there and then not there.

As he approached the spot where the Indians had stopped, apparently for the night, he hoped that Jonathan and Geoffrey were in position. He had carefully pointed out where they were to go, told them what to do, and then had given them time to get there, but that didn't mean the old-timers couldn't have been delayed somehow. If they weren't ready, Preacher was walking straight into big trouble.

He had considered waiting until night fell to make his move, but had decided that the warriors would actually be more on their guard then. They were less likely to be expecting trouble now, so now was when Preacher was going to try to snatch those young'uns away.

He bellied down and crawled, gliding noiselessly through the brush. He was close enough to hear the Indians talking among themselves. He also heard some miserable whimpering that came from one or more of the children. Probably the two younger ones, Preacher thought. He had seen enough of Nate to know that the younker had sand. Nate might feel like crying, but he would try to hold it back if he could.

Preacher had two pistols, both double-shotted, tucked behind his belt, and he carried his Hawken, sliding it carefully along the ground as he crawled. Dog followed, also on his belly. Jonathan and Geoffrey were armed with rifles and pistols. Preacher wished he'd had more time to work with the older men on their marksmanship during the first few days of this ill-fated journey. Once the ball started, every shot would have to be a true one.

Preacher came to a halt and parted some brush. He saw the Arikara warriors gathered on the bank of the creek. A couple of them were getting ready to build a small fire. The others were talking amongst themselves. Off to one side, Nate sat with his back against a rock. His younger cousins were on either side of him, and he had his arms around them as if to protect them. The rock had shielded the ground beside it from the sun during the day, so not all the snow had melted. There was still a thin layer of it where the youngsters sat. Had to be mighty cold on their behinds, not that any of their captors would give a damn about that.

Mart Hawley stood near the prisoners, close enough to be guarding them without really paying that much attention to them. He was busily engaged in digging a wad of chewing tobacco out of a pouch and packing it into his cheek. Preacher wouldn't have minded putting his first bullet into the son of a bitch, but the 'Rees were more of a threat. He had to deal with them first.

The sun was behind the mountains now. Dusk began to settle over the landscape with its usual swiftness. In the brush near the creek, Preacher came up into a crouch, then slowly straightened to his full height. Even though he was now in plain sight, the Indians didn't notice him until he stepped through the brush with a crackle of branches and said in a loud voice, "Howdy, boys!"

The Indians whirled toward him, grabbing for arrows.

Preacher knew which one of the Arikara warriors was the leader of this bunch: the tall, muscular, ugly one. He brought the Hawken to his shoulder and fired at the chief in one smooth movement, seeming not to aim at all. With a puff of flame and smoke from the muzzle, the rifle roared and kicked against his shoulder. At the last instant one of the other Arikara stepped in front of the chief. The heavy ball caught him in the middle of the forehead, caving his skull in on itself and blowing his brains out the back of his head in a grisly shower that splattered over the chief.

Preacher let go of the Hawken and had hauled out both pistols before the rifle hit the ground. The first man he had shot hadn't hit the ground yet either when Preacher's right-hand pistol blasted. Both balls struck one of the warriors, one of them thudding into his chest while the other just tore shallowly through the side of his neck. That slowed down the second ball and deflected it slightly, but it still had enough force behind it to carry it into the left eye of a third warrior, where it ripped into the optic nerve and then the brain.

Preacher had killed three members of the war party in a matter of a couple of heartbeats, but he knew that much luck probably wouldn't stay with him. In the next instant, however, two more rifle shots sounded. One of them came from a high rock off to the left, where Preacher had sent Geoffrey. The other originated on the far side of the creek. Preacher had had Jonathan cross the stream half a mile back and then work his way carefully along the creek until he was opposite the spot where the Indians had camped.

Both shots were well aimed and found their targets. Two more of the Arikara tumbled off their feet as lead smashed through them. That made five down. Preacher fired his left-hand pistol. One of the balls tore through a warrior's lungs and sent him to the ground spewing blood, but the other missed, traveling harmlessly over the shoulder of the chief. The ugly son of a bitch seemed to have a guardian angel. Preacher dropped the pistols and hauled out his knife, ready to go to carvin'.

An arrow whipped past his head as he lunged forward. The warrior who had fired it dropped his bow and grabbed for his tomahawk, but as his fingers closed around it, Preacher's steel drove deep into his body. Preacher twisted the blade and grunted with the effort as he ripped it to the side, opening the Arikara's belly and spilling his guts out on the ground. A hard shove sent the mortally wounded man sprawling into a couple of his companions as Preacher jerked his knife free.

He bent to scoop up the tomahawk that had been dropped by the man he'd just killed, and then in a blur of pantherish motion he was among the rest of them, swinging the 'hawk in brutal strokes and slashing with the knife. Drops of blood flew in the air and fell almost like rain. Dog was in the middle of the fighting too, pulling down one of the warriors and ripping his throat out.

More shots thundered as Geoffrey slid down from the rock and Jonathan splashed across the shallow stream. They fired their pistols at the Indians on the fringes of the melee, being careful not to aim toward Preacher. Some of the Arikara turned to meet this new threat, leaving Preacher with more manageable odds. He caved in a skull, slashed a throat, tripped another man, and then buried the head of the tomahawk in the back of the luckless warrior's head. It was slaughter, pure and simple. Even these hardened Arikara warriors were no match for the frenzy with which Preacher attacked.

Preacher swung toward the kids and saw Hawley trying to bring a pistol to bear on them. "Stay back, you bastard!" Hawley screamed. "Stay back or I'll kill these little—"

He didn't get any farther, because at that moment, Geoffrey bounded onto the rock beside which the young'uns huddled, and with a spryness that belied his years, he launched into a flying tackle that smashed Hawley to the ground. Hawley was bigger and younger and stronger, though, so he was able to throw Geoffrey off.

Preacher was about to go to the older man's aid when he had to dart aside to avoid a slashing blow from the war chief's tomahawk. The Indian swung the weapon again in a backhand that was almost too fast for the eye to follow. Preacher's eyes were not those of a normal man, however, and he was able to drop out of the way of the killing stroke. He rolled to the side and came up lithely onto his feet again.

He was in time to see Hawley drive a knife into Geoffrey's body. The renegade white man pulled the blade free and drew it back to strike again. Preacher threw the tomahawk that was still in his left hand. The throw was accurate. After turning over once in midair, the tomahawk smashed into the back of Hawley's left shoulder and lodged there. Hawley screamed as he fell forward, driven down by the impact of the tomahawk striking him.

That action had occurred in the blink of an eye. Preacher was already turning back to face the chief's challenge. The chief wasn't there anymore, though. Preacher couldn't spot him in the gathering gloom. He saw that all the other members of the war party were down. Jonathan rushed past him, shouting, "Geoffrey!"

Preacher turned and looked and saw that Hawley had staggered to his feet and was running away now, leaving Geoffrey sprawled on the ground behind him. Bending, Preacher snatched up a fallen bow and arrow and let the arrow fly after the renegade. The shaft whistled past Hawley as the man ducked into the brush.

Preacher didn't much like it, but he let Hawley go. The renegade vanished into the gloom of fast-approaching night. Preacher hurried toward Jonathan, Geoffrey, and the kids, anxious to see if the young'uns were all right.

21

On his way across the clearing where the Indians had planned to make their camp, Preacher picked up his pistols and quickly reloaded them. Dog was nosing around the sprawled bodies of the fallen warriors. Preacher knew if any of the Indians were still alive, Dog would let him know about it.

The kids were already clustered around their great-uncles. Jonathan propped Geoffrey up in a sitting position. "I tell you, I'm all right," Geoffrey insisted, but his voice held a thin edge of pain.

Preacher hunkered beside the two older men and said, "Let me have a look." He pulled Geoffrey's coat aside and saw the bloodstain on the man's shirt, just below his right shoulder. It looked like Hawley's knife thrust at him might have missed anything vital.

A quick further examination of the wound revealed that to be so. Preacher wadded up a piece of cloth and pressed it to the blood-leaking hole. "Hold that there," he told Jonathan, then turned to look at the kids. "Are all you young'uns all right?"

"I'm tired and hungry," Mary said. "And I was scared until you got here, Mr. Preacher."

"None of us are hurt," Nate assured Preacher. "Some of the Indians wanted to kill us when they first caught us, but the chief stopped them."

Preacher grunted. "Prob'ly figured to use you as hostages if'n he needed to. How'd Hawley come to throw in with them?"

Nate shook his head. "I don't know. He was with them when they found us." The youngster looked around. "Where did he go?"

"He got away," Preacher said in disgust. "So did the chief."

"Swift Arrow?"

Preacher nodded. "If that was his name. I wouldn't know."

"That was his name. He spoke a little English and talked to Hawley some." Nate pointed to one of the fallen warriors. "That one there was their medicine man. His name was Badger's Den."

That was the man whose throat had been torn out by Dog. His medicine hadn't been powerful enough to stop the big wolflike creature.

With Swift Arrow and Hawley still on the loose somewhere out there in the darkness, Preacher didn't think they could afford to lollygag around here all night. He said to Geoffrey, "You reckon you can travel?"

"Of course I can, if someone will just tie this bandage in place. . . ."

Preacher did that, and then Jonathan helped his brother onto his feet. Geoffrey was a mite shaky at first, but he steadied himself and nodded to Preacher. "Let's go."

The six of them—seven if you counted Dog—moved out quickly as soon as Preacher had gathered up all their weapons. He took some of the knives and tomahawks that the Arikara had dropped too. You never knew when something like that might come in handy.

Preacher kept up a fast pace, guiding them by the stars and by his own instincts. He wanted to put some distance between them and the scene of the fight with the 'Rees. The fact that Swift Arrow had survived the fracas was worrisome. Preacher didn't think the war chief would try to follow them and attack them by himself, but it was possible, even likely, that he would find the other groups that had split off from the war party earlier in the day and come after them.

Hawley still being alive didn't concern him as much. The renegade was wounded, and Preacher hoped that he would just crawl off in the brush somewhere and bleed to death. That would be just fine.

Preacher knew the kids must be worn out, but they bore up without much complaining. When he finally called a halt a couple of hours later, though, they flopped mighty gratefully on the ground. Jonathan and Geoffrey sat down on a log. Preacher asked Geoffrey, "How you holdin' up?"

"I'm all right," Geoffrey answered, but he spoke between teeth gritted against the pain. "I must admit, though, I'll be quite glad when we get back to the wagons."

"You saved us, Uncle Geoffrey," Nate said. "Hawley was gonna shoot us. I never saw you jump around and fight like that before."

In the moonlight, Preacher saw Geoffrey's rueful smile. "You may never see it again either. I'm, ah, not much of a brawler."

"You did fine," Preacher assured him. "In fact, both o' you fellas handled yourselves well back there. You'll do to ride the river with."

"Thank you, Preacher," Jonathan said, his voice thick with emotion. "Coming from a man like you, that's higher praise than I ever expected to hear."

Preacher said, "You two wait here with the kids while I scout around a mite on our back trail, just to make sure that Arikara chief ain't skulkin' around."

He faded off into the darkness with Dog padding quietly after him. When they came back a few minutes later, Preacher said, "No sign of Swift Arrow. If you're rested up enough, we'll get movin' again."

"Can't we rest a little while longer?" Mary asked.

"Come on," Nate told her in a tone that brooked no argument. "Don't you want to get back to your folks?"

"I do want to see Mama again," Mary admitted, and her little brother said, "I want Mama too."

"Let's go, then," Nate said as he prodded them to their feet.

Jonathan helped Geoffrey up, and the whole group set out again.

Preacher got them started down a long, narrow valley that they could follow in the moonlight, and then dropped back slightly to bring up the rear. If trouble was going to catch up to them, he wanted it to find him first, so that he could deal with it.

A moment later he saw Nate coming toward him. "Something wrong?" Preacher asked.

"No, I just wanted to come back here and walk with you."

Preacher started to send Nate back ahead with his cousins and uncles, but then he decided it would be all right to let the youngster accompany him for a little while. "All right, but if I tell you to get back with the others, you skedaddle, you hear?"

"Sure, Preacher." Nate hesitated. "Preacher, can I have a pistol?"

The question took him by surprise. "You know how to handle a gun?"

"I've shot one before. They're heavy, but if I hold it with both hands, I can manage."

Preacher chuckled. "You hit what you aim at?"

"Sometimes. And even when I don't, I don't miss by much."

Preacher figured he knew what was going on. Being captured and held prisoner by the Indians must have made Nate feel pretty helpless, and now he wanted a gun so he wouldn't have to feel that way again. Preacher could understand that. He drew one of the pistols from behind his belt and handed it to the boy.

"It ain't primed. You know how to do that?"

"Sure. I'll get some powder from Uncle Jonathan and put it in my pocket."

"Your ma might not like that."

"She won't like me carryin' a gun neither, but I'm goin' to do it," Nate said with a grin.

"Best you remember one thing . . . a gun comes in mighty handy, and it can sure enough save your life out here. But there's problems that it can't solve. You got to use your brain for that. A fella who can think fast and straight is gonna come out on top most of the time."

Nate nodded. "I'll remember." They walked along in silence for a spell, and then Nate said, "Preacher . . . that Indian Swift Arrow kept talkin' about how him and his people had vengeance coming, like we'd done something bad to them."

Preacher had felt all along like the Arikara must have some sort of blood debt they wanted to settle with the Galloway party. Otherwise they wouldn't have tracked the immigrants so far and so stubbornly.

"You got any idea what he was talkin' about?"

"No, not really. But he sure acted like *we* had done something bad to *them,* instead of the other way around."

"Maybe we can figure it out when we get back to the wagons and talk to your folks," Preacher suggested.

"It won't do any good for me to talk to them," Nate said. "I'm just a kid. They won't pay any attention to me."

Maybe not, but they would pay attention to *him,* Preacher thought. He was tired of not knowing what was going on and why the Arikara were so determined to kill them. When they got back to the wagons it would be time for a showdown, time for the Galloways to put their cards on the table.

Preacher intended to make sure of that.

As night fell, Angela sat inside the wagon and studied Dorothy's sleeping face by the light of the single candle that burned.

They had been friends, Angela thought, more like real sisters than sisters-in-law. Why had Dorothy betrayed her by sleeping with her husband?

Angela couldn't answer that question, but she knew what had to be done. She was waiting now for Dorothy to wake up.

John Edward squirmed in his little nest of blankets and pillows next to his mother. His lips made sucking noises. Soon he would be hungry enough to wake up, and when he did, he would demand to nurse and would raise a squalling ruckus if he didn't get the nipple. Angela hoped she would have things settled with Dorothy before then.

A few minutes later, as John Edward stirred even more, Dorothy's eyes flickered open. She was disoriented for a moment, her gaze darting around the room, but then her eyes focused on Angela's gravely solemn face and she whispered, "The baby . . . ?"

"He's right here," Angela assured her, "and he's fine. You'll probably have to nurse him in a few minutes."

Dorothy closed her eyes for a moment and nodded weakly.

"But before then," Angela went on, "we have to talk, Dorothy."

Dorothy looked up at her again and began, "I'm so sorry—"

"Don't. I don't want your apology." Angela saw the pain on Dorothy's face and went on. "I don't know what happened, but I forgive you for your part in it. What's important now is that things don't get any worse. Listen to me, Dorothy. . . . You haven't told Roger about you and Peter yet, have you?"

Dorothy's head moved from side to side, not much but enough to signify her answer. "I . . . I couldn't bring myself to . . . to tell him."

"Then don't." Angela's voice was firm with resolve. "No one needs to know about this but the two of us."

"But the baby . . . looks so much like . . ."

"Roger and Peter are brothers," Angela said. "Yes, the baby looks more like Peter, but that's not unheard of. Peter inherited his dark hair from one of their ancestors. John Edward could have gotten his from the same place."

"I . . . I suppose. But don't you think . . . Roger has a right to know?"

"Roger has a right to be proud of his new son. And since

you've been sick, Dorothy, you probably don't know everything else that's been going on. There's been some trouble . . . an Indian attack . . . and now we're headed back east, instead of trying to go on to Oregon."

She hoped that Dorothy was coherent enough to understand what she was being told. Angela didn't say anything about the children being missing. Dorothy was in no condition to do anything about that, and in her weakened, fragile state, the added worry over her son Nate might be enough to send her over the edge. She would have to be nursed along carefully. Anyway, Preacher would be back soon with the children, Angela told herself, and Dorothy wouldn't have to know about any of that until later, when she was stronger.

It was vital, though, for the sake of all of them, that the true identity of the baby's father remain a secret. They had to concentrate on getting safely to Garvey's Fort once Preacher returned with Nate, Mary, and Brad.

"Do you understand, Dorothy?" Angela pressed her. "You mustn't say anything to anyone about you and Peter."

Dorothy closed her eyes and nodded. "I understand," she replied in a hollow whisper. "But I'm so sorry, Angela."

"Don't worry about that," Angela said. She slipped her hands under John Edward just as he began to cry. "You've got something a lot more important to tend to right here."

22

Mart Hawley gritted his teeth against the blinding pain as he twisted his body and stretched his right arm in an attempt to reach the handle of the tomahawk. He felt blood trickling out around the edges of the wound. It would probably bleed even worse when he got the tomahawk loose, but that couldn't be helped. He couldn't leave the damn thing stuck in his back.

His fingers touched the branch from which the handle was made. He groaned and stretched a little farther.

He had crawled into this brush-choked gully after running until he collapsed. He expected Preacher to catch up to him at any second, and he knew he couldn't expect any mercy from the mountain man. Preacher was already legendary as a killer. He wouldn't waste any time. He'd just cut Hawley's throat and be done with it.

Hell, Hawley couldn't blame Preacher for that. He'd have done the same thing if the tables had been turned.

Preacher hadn't come after him, though, and the only reason Hawley could think of was that Preacher had probably wanted to get those kids back to safety as fast as he could. He'd been willing to let Hawley go in return for a quicker start.

Bastard was goin' to regret that, Hawley thought with a grimace as he finally got his fingers wrapped around the tomahawk. With a wrench, he pulled it free, crying out at the agony that flooded through him. He felt the warm flow down his back and knew he'd been right about the bleeding. It was worse now. He had to get something on the wound and slow it down, or he might bleed to death right here and now.

Moss was good for that, and he had already felt around in the dark and found some at the base of a tree. He reached out now and got a handful of the stuff. Grunting with the effort, he twisted around and tried to slap it on the wound. He didn't think he was going to make it. . . .

Strong hands plucked the moss from his hand and pressed it to the wound beside his shoulder blade. Hawley let out a yell of fear and surprise. Who the hell—!

"Quiet," Swift Arrow said. Hawley instantly recognized the war chief's harsh tones. "Be still. You not die from this."

"How . . . how did you find me?" Hawley gasped.

"You white man," Swift Arrow said with a grim chuckle. "And you not Preacher. Follow noise."

Hawley slumped in relief and let the Arikara tend his wound. Naturally, Swift Arrow had experience patching up tomahawk wounds. He packed it full of moss and then tied a pad of cloth torn from Hawley's shirt over the wound. The bleeding had already slowed considerably, and although Hawley still felt mighty weak, he didn't think he was going to pass out.

Still lying on his belly, he asked, "What are we gonna do?"

"Kill Preacher," Swift Arrow said. He didn't elaborate, didn't explain how he intended to go about that chore. It was just a simple statement of his intentions.

Hawley sighed. "Take me with you," he said. He was tired and his wounded shoulder hurt like blazes, but the fires of hatred deep inside him burned hotter than ever. Hatred for the mountain man . . .

"You keep up, you be there when I kill Preacher," Swift Arrow said.

"Wouldn't miss it for the world," Hawley said.

* * *

Preacher and the others traveled all night, stopping only now and then to rest. Even when he called a halt, Preacher didn't stay still for very long. While his companions caught their breath, he checked their back trail or scouted out ahead, Dog trotting along with him. By the time the moon set and the starlight waned, the terrain had become flatter and Preacher knew they were on the edge of the foothills. They ought to be getting back to the wagons any time now.

He spotted the humped white shapes of the canvas coverings in the gray light of dawn. By that time he was carrying Mary, who was sound asleep. Jonathan had Brad in his arms, with the boy's head resting on his shoulder, and Brad was asleep just like his sister. Nate had taken over the job of helping Geoffrey whenever the wounded man needed any assistance to keep going or to get over some obstacle.

The immigrant camp appeared to be completely asleep. No one moved around the wagons. There was no fire. Preacher had a bad moment during which he wondered if the other members of the Arikara war party had somehow found the wagons and wiped out everybody else. The two old men and the kids might be the only survivors of the group.

But then he saw Angela climb out the back of one of the wagons. She seemed to be all right and didn't act like anything was wrong. She got a bucket and filled it from one of the water barrels.

"Aunt Angela!" Nate cried, unable to restrain himself.

Angela turned sharply and in her surprise dropped the bucket. The water splashed out onto the ground, but no one paid any attention to that. She let out a sound that was half laugh, half sob and ran toward them.

Mary and Brad were stirring. Preacher set Mary on her feet and said, "There's your mama, gal. Go see her."

Mary knuckled the sleep from her eyes and then stiffened as she recognized Angela. "Mama!" she exclaimed as she hurried to meet Angela. A still half-asleep Brad stumbled after her.

Angela went to her knees and swept the children into her

arms, gathering them to her like long-lost sheep. She hugged them tightly and shuddered from the depth of the emotions coursing through her. All three of them were crying now.

Preacher, Nate, Jonathan, and Geoffrey stood there smiling as they watched the reunion. Over at the wagons Simon Galloway emerged, and Roger and Peter came hurrying from the trees, carrying the rifles that showed they had been standing guard until the commotion broke out at the camp. They hadn't been doing a very good job of it, Preacher thought briefly, but you couldn't expect much from city folks.

Of course, that wasn't quite fair, he reminded himself. Jonathan and Geoffrey still had a ways to go before they would be seasoned frontiersmen, but they had handled themselves pretty darned well during the rescue mission.

Preacher patted Nate on the shoulder and said, "Go see your pa." Nate looked up at him, and Preacher nodded. With a grin, Nate ran to meet Roger. Roger swung the youngster up into his arms and hugged him.

"Are you all right, Nate?" he asked.

"I'm fine. Not hurt a bit," Nate assured him.

Roger must have felt the gun Nate had tucked behind his belt, because he looked down and said, "What's that?"

"A pistol," Nate said, his tone indicating that that should have been obvious. "I reckon I'm gonna go armed from now on."

Roger looked surprised, but he didn't argue the matter. He was too glad to have his son back alive, safe and sound, when it must have seemed like a strong possibility that he would never see Nate again.

The two old-timers limped forward and were greeted by their brother Simon. Hands were shaken and backs slapped all around, and then Simon said to Geoffrey, "You're hurt!"

"It's nothing," Geoffrey replied. "Just a little knife wound."

"It needs some proper patchin' up," Preacher said as he ambled up. "Any trouble here while we were gone?"

Simon shook his head. "No, but there's a new member of the party. I have a new grandson. John Edward Galloway."

Nate twisted around in Roger's arms to look at his grandpa. "I got a new baby brother?"

"That's right, son," Roger told him.

"Can I see him?"

"Well, I don't know." Roger looked at his sister-in-law. "Angela?"

Angela raised her tear-streaked face. She was still smiling happily at being reunited with her children. "What?"

"Can Nate see his mama and his new baby brother?"

Preacher might have imagined it, but he thought he saw something odd flash in Angela's eyes at that moment. For a second he wondered if Dorothy Galloway had died giving birth. But then Angela said, "They're both asleep right now. Your mama really needs her rest, Nate, so it might be better to wait."

"Aww . . ." Nate said. "I guess it's all right, but I really wanted to see 'em."

"In a little while," Roger promised him.

Nate started to squirm and kick a little. "Put me down, Pa," he said. "I'm too big for you to be pickin' me up."

Roger looked like he might have argued that, but he lowered Nate to the ground.

The sun was almost up now, and the rosy glow in the sky matched the good mood in the camp. Not everything was rosy, though, Preacher reminded himself. There were still at least a couple of dozen vengeance-hungry Arikara out there somewhere, probably no more than a day behind them. Peter was still caught up in hugging and kissing his prodigal children, so Preacher motioned to Roger, Simon, Jonathan, and Geoffrey. They came over to him, with Nate drifting along behind Roger.

Quickly Preacher told Roger and Simon what had happened. He concluded by saying, "Swift Arrow, the war chief o' that bunch, got away, and so did Hawley."

"That bastard," Simon said. "I can't believe he allied himself with savages."

"Well, he did," Preacher said. "I ain't worried all that much about him. He might even be dead by now. But Swift Arrow wasn't hurt, as far as I know, and I reckon he'll be comin' after us as quick as he can. He'll likely try to round up the rest of his war party too. That'll slow him down some, but then he'll come on like a house afire. We got to start puttin' some miles behind us."

Angela heard that comment and came over to join the men. With an assertiveness unusual in women of her era, she said, "We can't go anywhere right now. Dorothy is too weak. I don't think she can stand traveling."

"We don't have much choice," Preacher said. "If we stay here very long, them 'Rees will catch up to us for sure, and then we'll be in for it."

Roger said, "Preacher, if my wife is too ill to go on, then we don't have any choice. We'll just have to hope that once she's a little stronger, we'll still have time to reach the fort—"

Preacher stopped him by swinging an arm toward the northern sky. "You ain't got that much time, and it ain't just 'cause of the Injuns neither. There's another snowstorm comin', and it'll be a lot worse than the last one."

"Oh, I say!" Simon exclaimed dubiously. "How can you know that?"

"Preacher knows things about this country that none of us do," Jonathan said, and Geoffrey nodded. "Take our word for it, Simon, you don't want to doubt what he says."

"But you're talking about my wife," Roger said miserably, his joy at the return of the children momentarily forgotten. "We can't take chances with her life."

"You stay here and you're takin' a chance with everybody's life," Preacher said grimly.

The others started talking all at once, trying to hash things out, and Preacher felt his frustration and impatience growing. He had told them how things stood, and while he hated to put Dorothy Galloway in any more danger, what he had said was absolutely right: They would all die if they squatted here for very long, and that included Dorothy.

"I'm goin'," he said curtly, cutting through their babble. "If you folks want to come along, best get ready to move as soon as everybody's eaten breakfast."

They all stared at him. Angela found her voice first. "You'd leave us?" she said. "You'd really abandon us?"

Whether he really would or not was a damned good question, Preacher thought, and he figured the answer was that he wouldn't. But they didn't need to know that, so he kept his bearded features stern and flintlike as he nodded and said, "If you-all are stubborn enough to throw your lives away, damned right I would."

"Then it seems we have no choice," Roger said with a sigh. "We can't get back without your help, so we have to go along. But I'm not going to forget this, Preacher. If my wife dies . . ."

"If you stay here, she will," Preacher said. "You can count on that."

He turned away and went to check on his dun, which he had left with the wagons when he went after the children. He could feel the others' eyes on him as they talked together in low voices, and he figured they were cussin' him up one way and down the other. That was all right, he told himself. He hadn't thrown in with this bunch of immigrants to make friends. His goal was to get them back safely to someplace where they could spend the winter.

He was going to accomplish that goal, and if it had to be in spite of the very people he was trying to help, then so be it.

23

Angela gave him the cold shoulder after that, which was probably a good thing, Preacher reflected. He knew that when he had first seen her that morning she had looked mighty damned good to him, and since she was married to somebody else, those weren't feelings he ought to be having.

He checked over all the horses and the mules while Angela was fixing breakfast. The animals were all right. They had probably benefited from having a couple of days to rest. They would need all the strength and stamina they possessed for the long, fast haul to Garvey's Fort.

Nate came over to him when the food was ready. "Preacher, come and eat," the youngster said.

"Much obliged. I'm glad to see you ain't mad at me, Nate."

The boy frowned. "Well, I'm worried about my ma, of course. I wish we could stay here and let her rest after havin' that doggone baby. But Aunt Angela and Uncle Peter and Pa . . . well, they didn't see Swift Arrow close up, nor spend time as his prisoner. Him and Hawley talked about killin' all of us, Preacher. We can't let them catch up to us, or my ma will die for sure."

Since Preacher had said practically the same thing himself earlier, now he just nodded. Nate had a practical streak to him that was a mite unusual in such a young fella. It would stand him in good stead out here on the frontier, Preacher thought.

He ate a plate of bacon and biscuits and washed it down with good strong coffee. When he was finished, he told the men, "Get those teams hitched up. We'll be pullin' out in a few minutes."

They followed orders without complaint, but he saw the resentful looks Roger and Peter gave him. He didn't give a damn how they felt. They would thank him when they got to Garvey's Fort and still had their hair.

Preacher saddled the dun and then swung up on the back of the rangy horse. He rode to the front of the first wagon and called, "Lead the way, Dog!"

Dog loped out in front of the wagons. Preacher pointed to him and told Jonathan, who had climbed to the seat of the lead wagon and taken the reins, "Follow him."

"We're being led by an animal?" Jonathan asked.

"He'll smell trouble 'bout as fast as I could see it, and he'll take the easiest path too. Fella can do worse in life than to follow a dog. A smart dog anyway." Preacher grinned. "They ain't all overly bright, but then neither are people."

Jonathan shrugged, flapped the reins, and got the wagon rolling.

Preacher reined the dun to the side and waved for the others to follow Jonathan. Roger's wagon came next, followed by Peter's and then the one usually driven by Geoffrey. He couldn't handle a team with his wounded shoulder, though, so Simon had been pressed into service.

When all the wagons were moving, Preacher turned and rode back the way they had come. His eyes roved constantly, searching for any signs of pursuit as he dropped back a couple of miles. He didn't see anything out of the ordinary, and finally he turned and headed east again. Less than an hour later, he caught up to the wagons and got waves of assurance from all the drivers as he passed, letting him know that they hadn't run into any trouble.

That morning, the breeze had still been out of the south. Before noon, the air went dead calm, which Preacher considered a bad sign. Sure enough, a little while later, it began to blow from the north, and it wasn't a breeze this time but rather a hard wind.

A *cold* wind.

Another storm was on the way, just as he had predicted. He had no way of knowing how bad it would be, but his instincts told him it would be worse than the one before. This might be the first of the season's real howlers.

By the time the pilgrims stopped for a late lunch, the temperature was plummeting. Roger looked at Preacher and said, "How in the world did you *know* it was going to do this?"

Preacher shrugged. "I can't explain it. You spend a few winters out here, though, and you get to where you can tell what's comin'. Somethin' about how the air smells maybe."

"Is it going to be worse than last time?"

"Reckon we'll find out," Preacher said. "Just hide an' watch. . . ."

Angela kept tucking extra blankets around Dorothy and John Edward as the temperature dropped during the afternoon. Unlike earlier in the trip when Dorothy had been running a fever, now her body temperature seemed to have gone down, just like the weather. Her lips took on a faint bluish tinge as she muttered incoherently. She was out of her head most of the time, and although Angela didn't want to admit it even to herself, she was losing hope. If Dorothy had been in a comfortable bed, in a nice snug house, being attended to by a physician, she might have stood a chance of pulling through. As it was, rocking along on a pallet in the back of a wagon with nobody to take care of her except a woman with no medical training whatsoever . . . Well, Dorothy's chances weren't nearly as good, Angela thought. She didn't know if Dorothy would make it. She just didn't know.

If Dorothy died, that would leave Roger without a wife and Nate and John Edward without a mother. Angela wouldn't wish that on anyone. Yes, she had been angry when she first discovered that Peter was really the baby's father. If Dorothy had been healthy and had told her that she had slept with Angela's husband, Angela would have cheerfully throttled her. Now, though, she didn't feel anything but sympathy for Dorothy.

The same could not be said about her feelings toward Peter. Speaking of cheerfully throttling someone . . .

But she couldn't do that either, couldn't do anything except keep what she knew to herself, at least until they got back to civilization. When that happened, there would have to be a confrontation. She would have to tell Peter that she knew what he had done. She couldn't keep it all bottled up inside.

"Peter . . ." Dorothy murmured. "Peter, don't, please don't . . ."

Angela leaned closer and frowned. That had sounded like Dorothy was trying to stop Peter from doing something. She was reliving the memory of something, unaware in her ill state of where she was or what was really going on. What could she be remembering except the obvious? Angela asked herself. Was it possible that Dorothy hadn't wanted Peter to do what he had done?

Had Peter raped his own brother's wife?

The thought made a chill go through Angela that had nothing to do with the weather. She had been married to Peter Galloway for almost ten years. She would have thought that she knew him about as well as one human being could know another. My God, she'd had two children with the man! To think that he might be capable of . . . of doing a thing like that . . . was almost beyond Angela's comprehension.

If it was true, she couldn't stay married to Peter. She didn't know what she would do, but she was certain of that much. Somehow, their marriage would have to come to an end.

Of course, between the weather and the Indians, they might all wind up dead, and then she wouldn't have to worry about it, Angela thought. She laughed softly, and even to her own ears, the sound had an edge of hysteria in it.

* * *

The wind blew in more than the cold. Clouds followed it, racing across the sky. As Preacher glanced at the tumbled gray masses, he thought about how much the weather had changed since that morning. It had been almost warm then, and now it was like there wasn't even a vestige of warmth left anywhere in the world.

The clouds overtook the sun and swallowed it whole. As Preacher rode past the wagons, he called encouragement to the drivers, who were huddled on their seats in thick coats and blankets, their hats pulled down tight and tied with scarves to keep them from blowing away. With the thick overcast, night would fall early, so Preacher rode on ahead and started looking for a good place to make camp. They were on the edge of the plains now, with the foothills having fallen behind during the day. The terrain rolled gently, which made for faster traveling but didn't provide much in the way of shelter. There would be no cliffs or caves where they could get in out of the wind. The best they could do would be to draw the wagons in a tight circle and crowd the livestock inside.

The wind was blowing so hard Preacher didn't even hear the shot. He *felt* the heavy ball go past his ear, though, only inches from his head. He reined in and twisted in the saddle, looking for whoever had just taken a potshot at him. He saw three riders come boiling over a nearby rise and gallop toward him. Feathered headdresses streamed out behind them as they rode.

Pawnee! Preacher thought. He never had gotten along well with the Pawnee, and now it looked like he had one more reason not to like them. The three attacking him carried rifles, and another one fired as they came closer. Preacher saw the spurt of flame and smoke from the muzzle.

The ball whined overhead, missing him by a good margin. Some Injuns were good shots, but most of 'em could barely hit anything, especially from the back of a running horse. Preacher lifted the Hawken he carried across the saddle in front of him and spoke quietly to the dun, calming him. Lifting the long-barreled rifle to his shoulder, Preacher drew a bead. The three Pawnee kept coming, riding stubbornly straight at him.

He fired.

One of the Indians went backward like a giant hand had snatched him from the back of his pony. He hit the ground, bounced a couple of times, and then lay still. Preacher knew he would never move again. Anybody who fell like that was dead. But the other two Pawnee were still alive and still after his hair.

Preacher spoke to the dun again as he swapped the empty Hawken for the one in the saddle sheath that was loaded. He cocked and primed the rifle, but by the time he went to lift it and nestle the smooth wood of the stock against his cheek, the Indians had split up and were coming at him from two different directions. So they weren't completely stupid.

He wished he knew which one of them had shot at him before. Whichever one it was hadn't had time to reload, so Preacher would have shot the other one first, figuring the Pawnee with the empty rifle was less of a threat. But he didn't know, so he just picked one and fired again, the Hawken roaring as it kicked against his shoulder.

As fire geysered from the muzzle of Preacher's rifle, the Indian he was shooting at ducked down, flattening himself along the neck of his mount. Only thing was, Preacher hadn't really aimed at the rider but at the horse instead. He hated like blazes to hurt a horse, but he had figured the Pawnee might do something like that. The heavy lead ball struck the horse in the neck. The animal's front legs folded up, and as the mortally wounded horse fell, the Pawnee on his back sailed through the air over its head. The Indian hit the ground hard, probably knocking the breath out of him and stunning him. A second later the dying horse rolled over him, and Preacher could practically hear the man's bones snapping, even from where he was.

That left only one of the Pawnee, and as he galloped toward Preacher, only twenty yards away now, he thrust out his rifle and fired it one-handed. At the sound of the blast,

Preacher knew he had chosen the wrong enemy to bring down first.

It was a lucky shot. The ball struck the barrel of the Hawken in Preacher's hands and tore the rifle loose from his grip. His hands tingled and throbbed from the impact. He kneed the dun and sent the horse lunging forward as the surviving Pawnee reversed his rifle and swung it at Preacher's head like a club.

The blow missed, but the Pawnee recovered with blinding speed and launched himself from the back of his horse just as Preacher was pulling one of his pistols from behind his belt. The collision jolted Preacher out of the saddle. He fell, smashing into the ground with the blood-crazed Pawnee on top of him. The Indian got the fingers of his left hand around Preacher's throat while his right groped for the handle of the knife at his waist. He pulled the blade from its sheath and lifted it high overhead.

Preacher slammed the pistol in his hand against the side of the Pawnee's noggin, sending him sprawling. Preacher rolled the other way, putting a little distance between them. As he came up on his knees, he saw the Pawnee drawing back the knife again, this time getting ready to throw it.

Not wanting to take any chances, Preacher palmed out the other pistol and thumbed back the hammers of both weapons as he lifted them. The pistols were primed and ready to fire, so he let loose with both of them as the Pawnee's arm flashed forward. The next instant he dove to the side so that the knife blade just clipped the top of his left shoulder, slicing his buckskins and nicking the flesh underneath.

The Pawnee wasn't so lucky. All four of the balls from the double-shotted pistols struck him, landing in such a tight pattern at this close range that they blew a fist-sized hole clean through him. He rocked back on his haunches and lived just long enough to gaze down in wonderment at the awful thing that had happened to him. Then he toppled over to the side and was dead when his face hit the ground.

Preacher heard growling and looked around to see Dog

standing over the Pawnee who had been thrown from his horse and then crushed by it. Preacher climbed to his feet and walked over to check on the man. He was still alive, but his arms and legs were broken, and from the looks of his body in the blood-stained buckskins, he was all busted up inside too. A swipe across the throat from Preacher's knife finished him off, and Preacher didn't feel bad about doing it either. If he had been hurt that bad, he would have looked on such an act as a kindness.

He straightened and looked around. Evidently the three Pawnee had been alone, because he didn't see any more of them. Probably out on a last hunting trip before the real snows came, and when they had seen a lone white man riding along, they had decided to have some fun with him.

Their sport had backfired on them. Preacher left the bodies where they had fallen, reloaded his pistols, found the Hawken that had been shot out of his hands, and then went back to looking for a place to camp. The storm wouldn't hold up just because he'd been forced to spend a few minutes killing those Injuns.

24

He kept a close eye out for more Indians, just in case those three Pawnee had split off from a larger group. He didn't see any, though. Except for him and the dun and Dog, Preacher thought, the vast plains might as well have been deserted.

A short time later he came upon a buffalo wallow and knew he wouldn't find a better place for the pilgrims to camp. The wide depression in the earth wouldn't offer much protection from the wind, but any was better than none. Preacher marked the spot in his mind and then wheeled the horse to ride back to the wagons.

As Preacher came up to the lead wagon, Jonathan reined the team to a halt and said excitedly, "We heard shots, and then we passed some dead Indians back there a ways. Did you see them, Preacher? Do you know anything about them?"

"Reckon I do," Preacher drawled. "They jumped me a mite earlier this afternoon."

Jonathan goggled at him. "You killed all three of them?"

"Seemed like the thing to do at the time, considerin' that they was shootin' at me and hell-bent on liftin' my hair."

"Yes, of course, I didn't mean to imply that you did anything wrong," Jonathan said quickly. "I was just surprised . . . although I don't know why I should be. I saw how you fought with those Indians when we took the children away from Swift Arrow. Three-to-one odds wouldn't mean anything to you."

"Don't be too sure of that," Preacher told him. "But sometimes a fella's just got to go ahead and do what has to be done, no matter what the odds."

Jonathan nodded. He had come to understand a lot more about life on the frontier than he had when he started this journey.

Following Preacher's orders, the men drove on to the buffalo wallow and bunched the wagons inside the depression, pulling the vehicles close to each other in a circle. The daylight began to fade with a swiftness that surprised even Preacher. The clouds had to be growing very thick overhead for them to shut out the sun that way. For a while, Preacher seemed to be everywhere at once, helping to unhitch the teams and bring them inside the circle of the wagons.

They would have to have a fire, and though there were still clumps of trees here and there, for the most part the landscape since leaving the foothills had become a treeless prairie. That meant firewood was in short supply . . . but not buffalo chips, and they would burn too.

Preacher put the young'uns to work. "See them buffalo chips on the ground?" he said. "I want y'all to pick up some of them and make a big pile of 'em."

"What are they?" Mary asked.

Nate leaned over and whispered in his cousin's ear. Mary made a disgusted face.

"Don't worry, they won't hurt you," Preacher assured her. "And the heat they'll give off when we make a fire out of 'em will feel mighty good tonight when the temperature gets down below freezin'."

"Do you think it's going to snow again?" Nate asked.

"It sure might."

The kids set to work. Preacher motioned for Geoffrey to come over, and when the older man had joined him, he said quietly, "I'd 'preciate it if you'd keep an eye on them young'uns. I know you got a bad arm, but you can handle a pistol a little with your left hand, can't you?"

"Certainly," Geoffrey replied, and from his enthusiasm

Preacher could tell that he was glad to have been given something to do. "I'll watch over the children and fire a shot if anything threatens them."

Preacher nodded. "That's the idea. Much obliged." He clapped a hand on Geoffrey's uninjured shoulder for a second, then went on about the task of seeing that the camp was set up properly and safely.

By the time full darkness had fallen, a small, almost smoke-less fire was burning next to one of the wagons. The mules and horses were on the other side of the circle, kept there by a rope strung from one wagon to another. That didn't leave the humans much room, but they would make do, Preacher thought. Right now, that livestock was just about as important as the people; that is, if any of them hoped to make it back alive.

Preacher went over to Roger Galloway and asked, "How's that new son of yours?" He hadn't seen Angela since that morning, so he hadn't had a chance to ask her about Dorothy.

Roger had a haunted look in his eyes as he nodded. "The baby seems to be fine. Angela says he has a good appetite and a healthy pair of lungs."

"But your wife ain't doin' so good, is she?"

Slowly, Roger shook his head. "Not at all. She's been either unconscious or out of her head all day." His voice shook from the strain he was under. "I don't know what to do, Preacher. I . . . I want to make things right, but I just don't know how."

"Ain't much you can do right now, stuck out here in the middle of the prairie like we are," Preacher said commiser-ating with the man. "Time for thinkin' about the right thing to do was before you ever took off for Oregon at the wrong time of year."

"I know that now. I guess we'll just keep trying to make it back to that fort you told us about."

"Pretty much all we can do," Preacher agreed.

Inside the wagon, Angela was thinking about how they would feed John Edward if Dorothy died. She felt terrible about even considering the possibility, but they had to face facts: If Dorothy sank much lower, she wasn't going to make it. If they'd had a milk cow, they might have been able to give that milk to the baby.

But the nearest cow was . . . Angela couldn't even make herself think about how far away. Too far to ever do them any good.

Dorothy broke into her reverie by murmuring, "Peter . . . Peter . . ."

Angela felt herself grow even more tense. She loved Dorothy like a sister, and she had meant it when she forgave her for whatever her part had been in the illicit affair with Peter. But Angela didn't need to be reminded all the time of her husband's adultery.

"Hush now," Angela said quietly as she leaned closer to Dorothy. "The baby's asleep, so you should rest too."

Dorothy's eyes blinked open, and she looked up at Angela with uncommon lucidity. "Angela . . ." she said. "How can you stand . . . to be around me?"

"Shhh. I'm here to take care of you. You have to get well, for the baby's sake."

"The baby . . ." Dorothy repeated weakly. "Your husband's baby, your own husband . . . You're so good, Angela. . . . I don't deserve . . ."

"Hush," Angela said again. Suddenly she felt the wagon shift slightly on its thoroughbraces as someone stepped up at the rear of it. More emphatically she said, "Be quiet now, Dorothy."

Dorothy ignored her plea, though, and her voice chose that moment to grow stronger as she went on. "But Peter is John Edward's father, Angela. You must hate us both."

"No, no, I don't, just . . . just please don't talk anymore—"

"No," Roger said flatly from behind Angela. "Let her speak if she wants to."

Angela jerked her head around to stare at her brother-in-law. Roger's face was bleak and dark with rage in the light from the single candle as he stepped on into the wagon and let the canvas flap fall closed behind him.

"If Dorothy has something to say," he went on, "let her say it."

Dorothy sighed, a long, fluttery sound that made Angela look around sharply. She saw that Dorothy's eyes were closed again. Her breathing was soft and shallow. She had slipped back into unconsciousness, exhausted from those brief moments of awareness.

Without turning to look at Roger, Angela said, "She can't say anything right now. She's resting."

"I heard her," Roger said. "She . . . she was crazy there for a minute, wasn't she? She didn't know what she was saying?"

Angela heard the desperation in his voice, the urgent need to cling to any hope, even the slimmest one. She knew she could lie to him, could agree that Dorothy had been out of her head, but she knew that in the end it wouldn't do any good. Roger had heard for himself the conviction in his wife's voice and knew that Dorothy had spoken the truth.

She turned her head at last to meet Roger's stricken gaze. "It's true," she said. "Dorothy admitted it to me after John Edward was born. Peter is . . . is the baby's father."

Roger stood there without saying anything for a long moment, his breath rasping in his throat as he visibly struggled to control his emotions. He stared past Angela at Dorothy, fixing his gaze on his wife's face. Slowly he moved his eyes down to the tiny, sleeping form nestled next to her. Angela held her breath, thinking that she might see hatred growing in Roger's eyes, but instead, to her great relief, his expression softened and nothing but love shone on his face.

"It's not his fault," he said quietly. "He had no part in this."

Angela shook her head. "No. No, he didn't."

"He's the only truly innocent one among us."

Angela nodded in agreement with that. Since Roger seemed a little calmer now, she ventured, "I think it would be a good idea if we didn't say anything to anyone about this. It won't help anything—"

She stopped as Roger's expression hardened again. "Oh,

there'll be something said about it," he told her. "You can count on that."

He turned toward the rear of the wagon.

Angela stood up and hurried to his side, catching hold of his coat sleeve. "Roger, wait! If you confront Peter now, it'll just cause trouble—"

He jerked away. "*He* caused the trouble already! He slept with my wife. The bastard!"

"We don't really know what happened—"

"We know enough." Roger thrust out a hand and pointed at the mother and child bundled up on their makeshift bed. "We know that that baby is no son of mine. I should have realized that! He looks so much like Peter. . . ."

Roger's voice trailed off, and then with a sudden cry he thrust the canvas aside and pushed his way out of the wagon. Angela caught at his coat again, but he pulled away from her with ease and leaped from the tailgate to the ground. As she hurriedly climbed out behind him, he strode toward the fire, where Peter stood along with Simon. Jonathan and Geoffrey were preparing supper, while the children stood nearby. The night seemed huge, with the small fire struggling to hold back the all-encompassing darkness.

"Peter!" Roger barked as he stalked toward his brother.

Peter turned to look at him. "What is it?" he said in alarm as he saw the look on Roger's face. "What's wrong?"

"Wrong?" Roger echoed. "I'll tell you what's wrong!" He jerked a pistol from behind his belt and leveled it at Peter's face, cocking the hammer as he cried, "My brother is a traitorous bastard, that's what's wrong! And I'm going to blow your damned brains out!"

25

Preacher was ranging outside the camp, Dog at his side, when he heard the commotion. Dog heard it too, and laid his ears back and growled.

"Yeah," Preacher agreed, "I reckon we better go see what sort o' trouble them greenhorns are gettin' up to now."

It was even worse than he thought it would be, he saw as he loped into the camp and stepped long-legged over one of the wagon tongues. Roger Galloway had a pistol in his hand and was pointing it right at his brother Peter.

Preacher didn't have any idea what had caused the falling out betwixt them, but he knew that with all the dangers still facing the group, they couldn't afford to go around killin' each other. He called out, "Hold it! Roger, put that damned gun down."

Roger didn't lower the pistol. He stood there with his arm straight out. His face was twisted with anger, and his hand shook a little. Peter stared into the muzzle of the gun. His face was drained of color. Clearly he realized that he was very close to death.

Off to the side, Simon, Jonathan, and Geoffrey watched the confrontation in shocked horror. Mary and Brad sobbed, knowing only that their father was being threatened by his own brother. Nate said urgently, "Pa, no! Don't do it, Pa!"

"Listen to the boy, Roger," Preacher advised. "I don't know

what you're so het up about, but it won't make it any better for you to shoot Peter."

"I don't know about that," Roger said tautly. "It might make me feel better to know that I killed the man who slept with my wife."

Carefully, so as not to spook his brother, Peter lifted his hands and held them palm-out toward Roger. "I don't know where you got that crazy idea, but I swear to you—"

"Save your swearing," Roger cut in. "I heard it from Dorothy herself. She was talking to Angela, and she said that you're the father of that baby in there."

Peter swallowed hard. Preacher could tell he didn't know whether to continue denying the charge or if it would be safer for him to admit it. Preacher didn't know either. Roger sure looked ready to pull the trigger on that pistol.

"Roger, please don't," Angela said from the back of the wagon where Dorothy was resting. "Put the gun down and think about what you're doing."

"Think about it?" Roger echoed. "All I've been able to do for the past few minutes is think about it! I can't get that picture out of my head. . . . I can't stop thinking about what he did!"

"Listen to me, Roger," Peter said. "I don't care what she told you, she wanted it as much as I did! I . . . I never forced her—"

"Shut up!" Roger roared.

Preacher wouldn't have thought that Peter could make the situation any worse, but danged if he hadn't just done so.

"You raped her?" Roger went on. "You attacked your own sister-in-law?"

"No, I'm telling you—"

"You've told me enough," Roger broke in coldly.

Simon made an attempt to reason with him. "Son, you can't do this. You can't shoot your own brother."

Roger took a deep breath, and for the first time the barrel of the pistol sagged a little. "You're right," he said in a hollow voice. "You're right, I can't shoot him."

He lowered the pistol the rest of the way and let down the

hammer. The gun slipped from his hand and fell with a thud to the ground. Preacher let out his breath when the impact didn't make the weapon go off.

"I can't shoot you, Peter," Roger said. His hands clenched into fists. "But I can beat you to death with my bare hands!"

With that he leaped forward, swinging a vicious punch at Peter's head.

Taken by surprise, Peter didn't have time to avoid the blow. Roger's fist smashed into his cheek and knocked him backward. Though Roger was smaller, he struck again with all the power that rage gave him, and the blow packed enough punch to lift Peter off his feet and drop him to the ground.

Roger went after him, even as those gathered around shouted for him to stop. Except for Preacher, who stood and watched calmly. Sometimes a situation got so bad there was nothing left to do except have it out. Given what he had heard about Peter and Dorothy, he reckoned this was one of those times.

Ignoring the shouts and pleas, Roger drew back his leg and aimed a kick at Peter's head. Peter shook off the effects of the punch just in time to roll out of the way. As he came over onto his back again, he reached up and grabbed his brother's leg. Since Roger was already off balance from the missed kick, it was easy for Peter to heave up on his leg and topple him. Roger fell, landing heavily on his back.

That gave Peter a momentary advantage, and he tried to seize it. He leaped on top of Roger and clawed at his throat, managing after a second to lock his fingers around Roger's neck. Peter planted a knee in Roger's belly to hold him down and began to squeeze.

Peter might have choked the life out of his brother, but Roger cupped his hands and slammed them against Peter's ears. Peter let out an anguished howl and jerked back, and that allowed Roger to break the grip on his throat. Roger bucked up off the ground, arching his back. The move threw Peter off to the side. Roger rolled away, gasping for breath.

"Both of you, stop it!" Angela screamed from the tailgate

of the wagon. Behind her the baby wailed, his sleep no doubt disturbed by all the uproar.

Roger and Peter climbed to their feet and faced each other again. A bruise was starting to purple Peter's face where Roger's first punch had landed. Before they could attack each other again, Simon and Jonathan rushed in to grab them and hold them apart.

"Stop it, you two idiots!" Simon commanded as he held on to Roger's arms from behind. "I'm your father! Do what I tell you!"

"You're . . . you're through giving orders to us, Pa!" Roger rasped. His throat was sore from being throttled by Peter. "Let go of me!"

With that he brought his heel down hard on his father's instep. Simon yelped in pain and let go. Roger leaped across the small open space. Peter tore away from Jonathan and lunged to meet him.

Nobody could have more of a knock-down-drag-out fight than a couple of brothers, Preacher thought, unless it was a father and son. For the next few minutes, Roger and Peter fought with all they had, standing toe-to-toe and slugging it out. The thick coats both men wore made it difficult for them to strike with much effect at each other's bodies, so they aimed their punches at each other's head instead. Blood began to fly as knuckles opened cuts, smashed lips, and pulped noses. It began to look like they might actually beat each other to death if the fight continued long enough. Preacher started to think about stepping in and ending it.

He didn't get the chance to. A gun roared, the loud noise echoing over the prairie. Startled by the shot, Roger and Peter both stopped swinging their fists. Everyone looked around to see Angela standing at the rear of the wagon, smoke curling from the barrel of the pistol in her left hand. In her right she held another pistol, and this one was pointed at the two combatants instead of into the air.

"I'll shoot the next man who strikes a blow," she declared. "That's a promise."

"Angela!" Peter cried. "Shoot him! Stop him!" When Angela didn't respond, he said raggedly, "For God's sake, I'm your husband!"

"You should have thought of that about nine months ago," Angela said, her voice flinty with anger.

"I don't care if you shoot me," Roger mumbled through swollen lips. "I'm still gonna kill him." He started to shuffle toward Peter.

Preacher got in his way. "You ain't gonna kill nobody, old son," he said in a flat voice that allowed for no arguments. He put a hand on Roger's chest. "Back off. Fight's over."

Roger's fists were still balled. For a second he looked like he was going to take a swing at Preacher, but the thin smile on the mountain man's bearded face must have warned him that that wouldn't be a good idea. Glaring, he stepped back, then turned and walked unsteadily toward the wagon where Angela stood. He went past her to lean against the vehicle, where he lifted a hand and dabbed the back of it against bleeding lips.

"Pa," Nate said as he came up to Roger. "Pa, can I help you?"

Roger summoned up a pained smile as he looked down at his son. "Thanks, Nate," he said thickly. "But I reckon it's too late for that."

Angela still had the pistol lined on Peter. He glowered at her and snapped, "For God's sake, put that gun down. It's liable to go off accidentally."

Preacher never had held a very high opinion of Peter Galloway's intelligence, and it went down another notch now. If Peter couldn't see that if that pistol went off it wouldn't be an accident, then he was damn near too stupid to live.

Still, they might need every warm body they could muster before this journey was over, so Preacher said, "Might be a good idea for you to lower that pistol, ma'am. We don't need any more shootin'."

His calm words got through to her. Slowly she lowered her arm until the pistol was pointed at the ground. Preacher took it from her and eased down the hammer. He set the weapon on the tailgate.

Angela turned away. Instead of going to her husband, she stepped over to Roger's side and put a hand on his arm. "Come inside the wagon," she said. "We'll put some salve and plaster on those cuts on your face, and your hand should probably be wrapped up too. You may have some broken knuckles."

Peter stared at her in disbelief. She ignored him as she helped Roger into the wagon. Nate climbed in after them.

Preacher tightened his jaw to hold in a chuckle as he looked at the expression on Peter's face. "You prob'ly made some big mistakes in your life, mister, but none bigger'n this'un."

"I don't need any advice from you," Peter said.

"Wasn't offerin' any, just commentin' on what a damned fool you are. A fella don't go messin' with his brother's wife." Preacher found himself growing a little angry. "And out here, a man who forces hisself on a woman usually winds up dead in a hurry—shot if he's lucky, kickin' his life out at the end of a hang-rope if he ain't."

"Are you threatening me?"

"Just tellin' it to you straight, so you'll know not to cross me."

Peter muttered a curse under his breath and turned away, clearly not wanting any further confrontations tonight. He pulled a rag from his pocket and started wiping at the blood on his face. His two young'uns just stared at him, unsure of what they were supposed to do. It had to be mighty unsettling for them, seeing their mama point a gun at their papa that way.

"Simon, grab a rifle and go stand guard," Preacher said. "Everybody else, go back to what you were doin'. Fight's over, and if we're lucky, there won't be any more trouble tonight."

Grudgingly the others went back to their chores, even Mary and Brad, who resumed piling up buffalo chips near the fire. Nate hadn't returned from the wagon where Angela was patching up Roger's injuries.

Preacher wasn't sure what to do with Peter. If the man really had raped his sister-in-law, he ought to be punished, but there was no law out here on the frontier to do it. The nearest law was back in St. Louis. Everywhere west of there, folks took care of their own problems.

And to complicate matters even more, there was still the threat of the Arikara war party lurking behind them. Peter might not be much of a man, but as long as he could point a gun and pull a trigger, he was valuable to the rest of them.

For the time being Roger was going to have to call a truce with his brother. They couldn't be tussling or threatening to shoot each other all the time. They had to find a way to get along. The safety of the whole bunch might depend on their cooperation.

Preacher hoped it never came down to that, though, because if things were that bad, then they were sure enough in trouble.

Roger climbed down out of the wagon, followed by Angela and Nate. He had bits of plaster stuck here and there on his bruised, battered face, covering up the worst of the cuts and scratches. He still looked very angry, but he was in control of himself again. Angela must have been talking to him as she worked on his injuries, Preacher thought. She must have argued some sense into his head.

"Peter," Roger said.

Peter had his back to his brother. He turned slowly and said, "What are you going to do now, take another punch at me?"

Roger shook his head. "No, I'm through fighting. You're not worth it. I can see that now. But you're no longer my brother."

"Oh, come on. Brothers fight. You know the old saying about blood being thicker—"

"No," Roger cut in. "I'll never forgive you, Peter. I see you now for what you are. You're nothing but a selfish coward, and you don't care about anyone except yourself. You've been causing trouble ever since this trip started." An even more bitter edge crept into Roger's voice as he added, "If it weren't for you, those damned Indians wouldn't even be after us."

Preacher's ears perked up. He had thought from the start that there was more to the story than he had been told.

Maybe he was about to find out what it was.

26

Preacher stepped forward even as Peter waved a hand and said disgustedly, "I don't know what you're talking about."

Preacher didn't believe him for a second, and judging by the stricken looks on the faces of Jonathan, Geoffrey, and Simon, they knew that Peter wasn't telling the truth either. Just as Preacher had suspected, something had happened back along the trail that had sent the Arikara war party after the immigrants. The men had hidden the secret among themselves, but it could stay hidden no longer. Preacher was about to drag it out into the light.

"All right," he said heavily. "Time you fellas put your cards on the table. Roger, what are you talkin' about?"

Roger hesitated now, as if he might regret what he had said. But then his resolve stiffened, and he ignored the warning looks from the others as he met Preacher's intent gaze and said, "Peter killed one of the Indians. A young man. It happened not long after we passed their village."

"That's a lie—" Peter began, but Preacher silenced him with a hard glance.

"Go on," Preacher told Roger. "I thought you said you hadn't never seen any 'Rees before."

"Well, we didn't stop at their village. We saw it before we got there, and we were afraid of them—they're savages, after all—so we went around. They didn't see us, didn't know we were there."

Preacher would have been willing to bet that the Arikara had known good and well the little wagon train was passing close by. They just hadn't bothered to do anything about it. The tribe had a habit of letting other people alone unless something happened to rile them, as it had in this instance.

"We moved on," Roger said, "and then the next day, while we were stopped at noon, Peter went out to do some hunting. We wanted some fresh meat."

Preacher looked at Peter and guessed. "Instead you ran into an Injun."

Peter looked like he wanted to deny it, but then he shrugged and shook his head as if to ask what was the use of that. "I didn't set out to hurt anybody," he said, a note of whining defensiveness in his voice.

"Just tell me what happened," Preacher said. "Don't leave anything out."

Sullenly Peter said, "I was walking through some trees along a creek, and then suddenly there he was. He looked, well, savage, like he wanted to kill me. He had bones in his hair, like those others, and he was carrying a bow. When he saw me, he said something—I didn't understand him, of course—and then he reached behind his back, like he was reaching for an arrow. You have to understand, I thought my life was in danger. I thought he was going to get an arrow and shoot me."

"So you shot him first," Preacher said, knowing where this story of misunderstanding and violence was going. It had been repeated many times across the frontier, ever since the white man had started pushing westward into the domain of the red man.

"I was defending myself," Peter insisted. "My rifle was ready, so I just lifted it and pointed it at him and pulled the trigger." He swallowed hard. "The ball hit him in the chest and knocked him back into the creek. I pulled him out, but it was too late. He was dead."

"What did he have behind his back?" Preacher asked, guessing that he still hadn't heard everything.

Peter looked down at the ground. "A couple of rabbit carcasses on a string. I . . . I think he was going to offer one of them to me."

Preacher's hands clenched tight in anger on the Hawken. "I expect you're right," he said. "As a rule, the Arikara are generous folks. The fella you shot was prob'ly out huntin' too, and he asked you if you wanted to share in the game he'd bagged." Preacher thought of something else. "Roger said the Injun was young. How young?"

"I don't know." Peter waved his hands helplessly. "Fifteen or sixteen years old, more than likely. But I thought he was a full-grown man when I first saw him. I . . . I never really took a good look at him until after I'd pulled him out of the creek."

"So you just blazed away and killed a fella who didn't mean you no harm." Preacher struggled to keep his temper reined in. "What did you do then?"

"There . . . There was a little gully close by. I put him in it and . . . put some brush and rocks on top of him."

"Hidin' what you'd done," Preacher snapped accusingly.

"I didn't want to take the time to bury him," Peter said. "I knew someone might have heard the shot."

"The other Injuns, you mean."

Peter shrugged again. "I just thought it would be best to put him where he couldn't be found easily. And it wasn't totally selfish on my part, you know. I . . . I was trying to lay him to rest the best I could."

Preacher knew such thoughts had never entered Peter's head; the man hadn't even considered anything except saving his own hide. But he didn't waste any breath arguing. He just said, "Then you went back to the wagons."

"That's right."

"And you told your brother and your pa and your uncles what had happened."

"Not right away, he didn't," Roger said. "I suppose he was too afraid of what he had done. But a day or two later, he told us. We all agreed that the best thing to do would be to go on and keep what had happened to ourselves. We didn't think it would matter once we got to Oregon."

"You didn't figure the rest of the Injuns would come after you?"

"We hoped they wouldn't find the body," Roger said.

And for a while they must not have found it, Preacher thought. Otherwise the wagons wouldn't have gotten such a big lead on the war party that had set out to avenge the young man's murder. It had taken time to find the body and then to locate the trail of the one responsible for the killing. The Arikara, in their quest for vengeance, wouldn't really care which of the immigrant party had pulled the trigger. They would wipe out all the whites in order to even the score.

Preacher wondered if the slain young man had been the son of the chief or the leader of one of the warrior societies. That would help explain a little more the determination of the Arikara to find and kill this bunch of pilgrims. It wasn't necessarily the case, though. They would have valued the life of any of their young men and considered his murder a debt that had to be paid in blood.

"Why didn't you tell me all this when I threw in with you?" Preacher demanded of the circle of men.

"We had agreed to keep it our secret," Simon said.

"And we didn't see how telling you would really change anything," Jonathan put in. "The Indians were already after us, and you seemed to be convinced those first ones who attacked us weren't just a small band of renegades, Preacher. How could you have done anything differently?"

Preacher dragged a thumbnail through the close-cropped beard on his jaw and frowned. "Maybe I would have staked out Peter and left him for the 'Rees. I reckon they would've figured out he was the one to blame for the killin' and might've been satisfied with torturin' and scalpin' him."

Peter stared at him, eyes wide with horror, and the others looked just about as appalled. "You can't mean that!" Simon exclaimed.

"Don't be so sure," Preacher grated. "Out here when a fella makes a mistake, he usually pays the price for it hisself, without draggin' a bunch of other folks down with him."

Geoffrey stepped over beside Peter and squared his shoulders, even the wounded one. "We never would have allowed such a thing," he said. "Peter made a mistake, all right, a bad one, but he's still family."

"That's right," Jonathan said, moving up alongside Geoffrey. Simon closed ranks on Peter's other side.

Preacher looked at Roger. "How about you? You was ready to kill him yourself a while ago."

Roger appeared to think it over for a moment, leading the others to glare at him for his hesitation, but then he said, "They're right. As much as I hate Peter right now, I wouldn't turn him over to the savages. I just couldn't do that."

"Suit yourself," Preacher said. "I don't reckon they'd take him now anyway. There's been too much fightin'. Too many of them have been killed. For them, it's all or nothin' now."

"You mean . . ."

"Either we die," Preacher said, "or all of them do."

Inside the wagon, Angela Galloway had listened to the men talking, and though she wouldn't have thought it possible, her loathing for the man she had called her husband grew even stronger. Peter had slept with his brother's wife, possibly even raped her, and now Angela discovered that he was a killer as well, the murderer of an innocent young man.

Of course, Peter had acted out of panic when he shot that Indian, Angela told herself. He probably really had feared for his life. But his impulsiveness was liable to cost them all dearly. The other Indians wouldn't turn back, wouldn't give up. She had heard Preacher say that the Arikara intended to kill all of them. She didn't doubt it for a moment.

The baby began to kick and fret. Angela turned and picked him up, holding him against her as she snuggled him tighter in the blankets around him. The wind was still blowing hard, and it was very cold inside the wagon. Drafts found their way in no matter how snugly she closed the canvas flaps over both entrances. Poor John Edward, she thought. He was cold and hungry, and his mother was dying and his father was a coward and a liar and an adulterer. How could any child stand a chance in the world with odds like those against him?

"I'll take care of you," she murmured, knowing that the baby couldn't understand her but feeling compelled to say the words anyway. "I know I'm not your mother, but I won't abandon you. Neither will Roger. He may not be your real father, but he loves you. That . . . That's more important. He loves you, and so do I."

John Edward settled down as she spoke quietly to him, and a moment later he was sound asleep again. He must not have been too hungry, Angela thought. She laid him down carefully and then brushed a hand over Dorothy's forehead. The poor woman was colder than ever, and when Angela checked her pulse, she found it weak and rapid. Despair gripped her, despair for Dorothy, for John Edward, for Nate and for her own children as well, because all of them were threatened by the weather and the Indians. If any of them survived, it would be a miracle.

But Preacher was still with them, Angela reminded herself, and if anyone on this wild frontier was equipped to work a miracle, it was the man called Preacher.

Simon Galloway had drifted back into camp when the argument over Peter's killing of the Injun youngster had started. Now Preacher sent him out again to stand guard, and he took Dog and the Hawken and went out himself, circling the buffalo wallow in the howling wind.

The night's revelations had been stunning ones, and yet Preacher wasn't all that surprised. He had known from the start that Peter was rash and reckless and inclined to get into trouble. He just hadn't known how bad that trouble was. It took a special breed of bastard to cuckold his own brother. As for shooting the Injun when it wasn't necessary, well, that was something that had happened before, all the way back to when Cap'n Lewis and Cap'n Clark had gone up the Missouri and set out for the Pacific. Lewis and Clark had been a good ways north of here, and it had been a Blackfoot Lewis had shot in a dispute over a gun, Preacher recalled, but still it was a hasty act that had had plenty of repercussions over the years. The Blackfeet never had been friendly toward the whites after that, and more than one scalped trapper could lay part of the blame for his grisly fate at the feet of ol' Meriwether Lewis.

Dog suddenly growled and bumped his muscular body against Preacher's leg. Preacher looked down at him and asked, "What is it, Dog? Somethin' wrong?"

A second later, he got the answer to that question as the blizzard hit him like a brick wall.

27

He had just *thought* the wind was blowing hard before. Now he staggered as it smashed at him with incredible force. Not only that, but he was blind, instantly surrounded by an ocean of white flakes driven with stinging force by that terrible wind. Preacher had been battered by heavy rainstorms before, but he had never known that *snow* could hurt.

He held his hat on and lowered his head so that the wide brim protected his face, at least to a certain extent. He went to a knee before he could be bowled over by the gale. "Dog!" he shouted, not knowing if the animal could hear him or not.

A moment later, the great furry body pressed against him and he felt Dog's warm breath against his ear. Preacher looped his right arm around Dog's neck and buried his hand in the thick fur.

"We got to get back to camp!" he shouted. "Come on!"

Relying on his inner sense of direction, he came up in a crouch and started moving toward the buffalo wallow. At least, he hoped that he was going the right way. If he wasn't, if he became completely disoriented by the storm, he might wander around out here for hours until he finally collapsed and froze to death. He kept his hand knotted in Dog's thick coat, knowing how keen the wolflike creature's senses were and knowing as well that Dog would head for the camp.

Preacher felt the ground under his feet change its pitch. He was moving down a fairly gentle slope now, and relief washed through him as he realized it was probably the buffalo wallow. He still couldn't see anything except the sea of white that had swallowed him, but a few moments later he ran into something big and unyielding. It took him only a second to get the feel of it and realize it was a wagon wheel.

He groped his way along the wagon until he came to the back of it. Stepping up on the tailgate, he pulled the canvas flap aside and tumbled inside. It wasn't much warmer, but at least he was out of the wind. For the most part anyway, since the canvas cover popped and billowed and let in some of the howling monster.

"Who's that?" someone exclaimed loudly as Preacher entered the wagon. "Who's there?"

Preacher recognized Jonathan Galloway's voice. "Take it easy, Jonathan," he assured the older man. "It's just me, Preacher."

"Thank God! We were afraid you were lost out there in the blizzard."

"I came damn close to it," Preacher told him. "But Dog helped me get back."

And speaking of Dog, Preacher thought, where was he?

As if in answer to the question, he heard claws scratching at the tailgate and turned to put his head and shoulders outside the flap. He reached down and caught hold of Dog under the animal's front legs. As big and heavy as Dog was, even Preacher had to grunt with effort as he helped him climb into the wagon.

"Hope you don't mind some more company," Preacher said as he settled back with Dog beside him. He pulled the flap closed and tied the thongs on it to keep it shut.

Geoffrey answered this time. "Not at all. Every bit of body heat we can get is more than welcome."

"Injuns sleep with dogs during the winter for warmth. The colder it is, the more dogs you need."

"Well, then, we could use a whole pack of them tonight," Jonathan said.

Preacher found himself warming up a mite now that he was

out of the worst of the wind. His teeth stopped chattering after a few minutes, and he said, "Is everybody else in the wagons? Everybody accounted for?"

"I think so," Jonathan replied. "The only one I'm not sure about is Simon. He was out standing guard, you know. But he wasn't very far away, and he must have come back when the storm hit."

Preacher frowned in the darkness. "You saw ever'body else? You know they're in the wagons?"

Geoffrey said, "That's right. Roger, Dorothy, and Angela are in Roger's wagon, and the children are with Peter in his wagon."

"But you don't know for sure about Simon?"

"Well . . . no. We just assumed. . . ."

"You don't think he's still out there, do you?" Jonathan asked.

"Only one way to find out, I reckon," Preacher said grimly.

"My God!" Geoffrey said. "You can't mean you're going back out there?"

"To the other wagons at least. Until I find Simon."

"Do you want us to come with you?" Jonathan asked. Preacher heard the reluctance in his voice, mixed with worry about Simon.

"No, we don't need any more lost sheep," Preacher said. "Stay here with Dog. I'll be back."

He ordered Dog to stay, then loosened the flap and climbed out of the wagon. The icy wind pounded at him and the snow stung him fiercely as he fastened the canvas behind him. He moved to the front of the wagon, keeping at least one hand on it all the time. When he came to the wagon tongue, he worked his way along it until he could reach out and touch the next wagon in the circle. He stuck his head in the back and asked who was there, but no one answered. That came as no surprise. According to what Jonathan and Geoffrey had told him, one of the wagons should have been empty, unless Simon had crawled into it, and obviously he hadn't.

With his head bowed against the wind, Preacher moved along the second wagon to the third one. This time when he climbed onto the tailgate and put his head through the flap, someone inside screamed. A childish voice yelled, "Indians!"

"No, it ain't Injuns," Preacher said. "Peter, you in here?"

In this catastrophic weather, the earlier conflicts had been forgotten. Preacher thought he heard relief in Peter Galloway's voice as the man answered, "I'm here. And all three children are with me. We're all right, Preacher."

"What about your pa?"

"What about him? He's in one of the other wagons, isn't he?"

"You ain't seen him since this blizzard started?"

Peter hesitated. "No. I don't think I have."

"You don't think so, or you're sure you ain't?"

"I'm sure," Peter said. "I got the children together and brought them in here when the storm hit, and we've been in here ever since."

The uneasy feeling inside Preacher began to grow stronger. He said, "All right. Stay here, and don't come out until the storm lets up. It'll last all night, and it might even last all day tomorrow."

"We have food," Peter told him. "We'll be all right."

Preacher nodded, even though they couldn't see him in the snow-choked darkness, and closed the flap. There was just one wagon to go, and if Simon Galloway wasn't in it, then the unavoidable conclusion was that he was out there somewhere in the storm, definitely lost and maybe already dead.

One more time, he felt his way along the wagon and came to the last one. As he paused at the tailgate, he saw a narrow strip of light coming from inside, through a gap in the canvas cover. The occupants of this wagon had managed to keep a candle going, even with the drafts that had to be blowing through there. He pulled the canvas aside, and the light flickered as the wind made the candle flame waver.

"Who—" Roger Galloway began excitedly.

"Preacher. Take it easy, folks. It's just me."

He climbed in and closed the flap behind him, and as the candle flame grew steady and bright again, he saw Roger and Angela sitting on either side of the thick pallet where Dorothy lay. Both of them were wrapped in blankets, and Angela had a bundle in her lap that had to be the baby. Preacher looked at the pale, haggard face of the woman lying on the pallet and realized he was seeing Dorothy Galloway for the first time. He had heard plenty about her during the time he had been with the wagons, of course, but until now he hadn't laid eyes on her.

There was no sign of Simon Galloway inside the wagon.

Preacher's spirits sank for a moment as he realized that. He hadn't particularly liked Simon—the man struck him as weak and lazy—but Preacher wouldn't wish freezing to death on him either. And he knew as well that he was going to have to go out in that blizzard and look for Simon. He had to at least make the attempt.

"It's good to see you, Preacher," Roger said. "We were worried about you. I thought, though, that if anyone could make it back here once that storm hit, it would be you."

"What about your pa?"

"What about him?" Roger asked with a frown. "He's with Peter, isn't he? Or Jonathan and Geoffrey?"

Preacher shook his head. "He ain't in any of the wagons."

Angela lifted a hand to her mouth. "Oh, Dear Lord. You mean . . ." She couldn't go on.

"He's out in . . . in that?" Roger finished for her, horror in his voice and on his face.

"I reckon he must be. There ain't no other place he could be."

Roger hurriedly started to get up. "We have to find him! It may not be too late!"

That was true. Simon was probably still alive, since he wouldn't have frozen in the time that had passed since the storm hit. But he wouldn't be able to last much longer.

Preacher put a hand on Roger's shoulder and held him down. "Stay here," he grated. "I'll find him."

"But how? We . . . We can't afford to lose you, Preacher."

"You got any rope? I need as much as you can muster."

Roger nodded. "We have several coils. If we tie them all together, they'll probably stretch six or seven hundred feet."

That ought to be long enough, Preacher thought. The

buffalo wallow was about a hundred yards across. Likely Simon wouldn't have gone any farther than that to stand guard. Unless, of course, he had tried to get back to the wagons when the storm hit, gotten turned around, and moved farther and farther away instead of coming closer. If that was the case, there was no telling where he could be by now.

"Stay put and tell me where the rope is." Preacher was ready to go. Waiting wouldn't make things any better.

Roger told him where to find the rope in one of the storage packs slung underneath the wagon. Preacher gave Roger and Angela a reassuring nod and then crawled out into the snow and wind once more. He found the ropes and began knotting them together. His fingers were stiff from the cold, and that, along with the gloves he wore, made the task difficult and awkward. Preacher took the necessary time, though, to make sure the ends of the ropes were knotted together securely. If they came apart while he was searching, he might be in big trouble.

Once he was satisfied, he moved around to the outside of the wagon, dragging the heavy coils of rope with him. He found an end and tied it around a wagon wheel, making sure that knot was secure too. Then he gathered the rope in his arms and started walking straight out from the wagon, paying out the makeshift lifeline as he went.

Of course, there were risks. As long as he had hold of the rope, he was confident that he could follow it back to the wagons. But if he lost it for any reason, he might not ever be able to find it again. Then too, there was no guarantee that he would find Simon Galloway by doing this. He might pass within five feet of the man and never see him. All he could do was work his way out to the end of the line, move over a little, and start back in. When he got to the wagons, he could move again and go back out. It would be a slow, tedious process . . . maybe too slow to do Simon any good.

But as far as Preacher could see, it was the only chance Simon had. He trudged ahead, buffeted by the wind, stung by the snow, hoping that once again luck would be with him.

28

It took Preacher a good ten minutes to walk to the end of the rope, leaning over into the wind the whole way. Keeping a firm grip on the lifeline, he faced back the way he had come, moved some ten feet to his right, and started back in, gathering up the rope as he went. The return trip went a little faster since the wind was now at his back. When he reached the wagon the rope was tied to, he turned around and started out at a different angle this time.

He was pretty sure he was checking the general vicinity where Simon had gone to stand guard. There was no way of knowing, though, how much Simon had moved around while he was out here. And Preacher's mind kept coming back to the possibility that Simon could have easily wandered off even farther after he was blinded by the blizzard.

The minutes seemed to race past, because Preacher knew that with each one that went by, the chances of him finding Simon alive were less. Out to the end of the rope, back to the wagons . . . Again and again, Preacher moved along the lifeline, back and forth, out of the buffalo wallow and then back in. He lost track of how many times he had made the trip and how long he had been out here. His fingers and toes were getting numb. He knew he couldn't stay out in the blizzard for much longer, or he would risk losing them.

A fella ought to be in somewhere snug and warm on a

night like this, he thought. In his own cabin maybe, with a fire roaring in the fireplace and a pretty gal with whom to share a buffalo robe in front of that fire. A girl like Jennie . . .

He saw it plain as day in his mind's eye, the two of them snuggled together while the storm raged outside, secure in the knowledge that they were together and would never be parted. With the kids asleep up in the loft and Dog at their feet . . . Jennie had loved Dog and he had loved her, had in fact nearly lost his life trying to protect her. It sure made a pretty picture, Preacher thought. Never would happen, of course, couldn't happen because Jennie was dead, but for a moment, as Preacher trudged through the snow, he felt almost warm as he thought of it. What might have been, Lord, what might have been if only things had worked out different. . . .

Maybe he was warm because he was freezing to death, a part of his brain warned him. He had heard that was what happened just before a fella drifted off to his final sleep, the one from which he never woke up.

A moment later, he tripped over something and went to his knees in the deepening snow.

The fall made the rope slip out of his left hand. It slid in his right too, so that only two fingers were around it. He clutched desperately at it, knowing that if he let go, the wind might whip the rope around so that he could never find it again. Should have tied it on to his belt, he thought wildly, but the idea hadn't occurred to him. Now that oversight might be the death of him.

His flailing left arm tangled in the rope. He grabbed on firmly with both hands and knelt there for a few seconds, letting his racing pulse slow down a little. When it had, he wrapped the rope completely around his waist and knotted it there. Then he reached out to feel around and locate whatever it was he had tripped over.

He knew what it was, of course, before he found it, or at least he was afraid he knew. And as his fingers touched something and explored it until he was sure it was a face, his guess was confirmed. He ran his hand over the man's head and felt the lack of hair on top. Simon Galloway had been mostly bald.

Preacher checked for a pulse, a heartbeat, a breath. Nothing. He even leaned down and pressed his cheek against Simon's. The flesh was cold and hard.

Preacher bit back a curse. He hadn't liked Simon Galloway, had considered the man pretty much useless most of the time. But his death still bothered Preacher, even though the mountain man knew it wasn't his fault. He had sensed that a storm was coming, but he'd had no way of knowing it would be as bad as it was. The frontier could be a harsh, unforgiving place, and Simon had been unlucky enough to bear the brunt of its fury on this night.

Simon was a good-sized man. Preacher couldn't pick him up and carry him. He had to settle for dragging the body back to the wagons. When he got there, he took it to the empty wagon, lowered the tailgate, lifted Simon enough to prop him against it, and slid the body inside. Then he untied the rope from his waist and went to tell the others.

He stopped first at the wagon where Jonathan and Geoffrey were. As he climbed in, Jonathan asked, "Preacher? Is that you?"

"It's me," Preacher said heavily. He recalled that these two didn't know he had been out searching for Simon. The last they had seen of him, he had been headed for the other wagons to check on everyone else.

He went on, "I've got bad news, fellas. Your brother wasn't in any of the other wagons."

"My God!" Geoffrey exclaimed. "You mean he's out in this storm somewhere?"

"We have to go look for him!" Jonathan said.

"I already did," Preacher said, "and . . . I found him."

The ominous tone in his voice told the two older men what they didn't want to know. Still, they had to ask. Geoffrey said, "Is . . . is he . . . ?"

"He's dead," Preacher confirmed. "I figure he tried to

make it back to the wagons when the storm hit, got turned around, and finally couldn't go any farther."

Jonathan muttered something, and after a second Preacher figured out it was a prayer for Simon's soul.

"I brought him back in," Preacher went on. "He's in that empty wagon."

"What can we do?" Geoffrey asked, his voice thick with grief.

"Nothin', at least not tonight. Come mornin', we'll see about diggin' a grave, if the ground's not frozen too hard already."

He left them talking quietly with each other, no doubt reliving some of the good memories of their brother's life. Bypassing the wagon where Peter was staying with the young'uns, Preacher went to Roger's wagon.

He pushed the flap back a little and called softly, "Roger, come out here."

A moment later, Roger climbed out of the wagon. He was followed, to Preacher's surprise, by Angela, who clutched a blanket tightly around her.

"Ain't no need for you to be out here, ma'am," Preacher told her. "You ought to be in there watchin' over the other lady and the little one."

"They're both asleep," Angela said. "They don't need me right now. And if you have news about Simon, I want to hear it. He's my father-in-law, you know."

"Yes, ma'am, I know. And I'm mighty sorry to have to tell you—both of you—that I found him out yonder a good ways. Looks like he froze to death, so I reckon he went pretty peaceful-like and prob'ly didn't really know what was goin' on."

Angela let out a sob, and Roger flinched almost like he had been struck. "Dear Lord, is there no end to the tragedy?" he said. He put his hands over his face for a moment, then found the strength to straighten slightly and ask, "Where is he now? Were . . . were you able to bring him back?"

Preacher nodded. "Yeah, I put him in that wagon with nobody in it. I already told your uncles, but I ain't said anything to Peter. Didn't want the young'uns overhearin' and gettin' upset any sooner than they have to."

"Thank you. I'll tell Peter." Roger took hold of Preacher's arm for a second, squeezing hard in his grief. "And thank you for . . . for finding him. I feel a little better knowing that he . . . he wasn't left out there in the storm all night."

Preacher didn't say anything. It didn't matter to Simon where he spent the rest of the night, but then, after a fella was dead, nothing mattered. All the gestures and rituals that went with death were for those who remained behind, not the one who had already crossed over the divide.

Angela said, "Come inside where it's at least a little warmer."

"I'm obliged, ma'am, but I reckon I'll go back and spend the rest of the night with Jonathan and Geoffrey. Quarters are already a mite cramped in there, and I don't want to disturb the baby."

"You're sure?"

"Yes, ma'am."

Preacher left them and felt his way back along the line of wagons. The storm hadn't eased any. The wind was blowing just as hard and the snow was just as thick as it had been earlier.

He climbed into the other wagon to find that Geoffrey and Jonathan had lit a candle too. They sat huddled over it, as if the tiny, flickering flame would ward off not only the darkness but the cold. It wasn't doing a very good job at either of those tasks.

Jonathan held out a jug as Preacher settled down beside them. "We're drinking to Simon's memory," he said. "We'd be honored if you'd join us, Preacher."

"Well, I ain't one to take a drink except ever' now and then . . . but I reckon this is a righteous time." Preacher took the jug and said, "To Simon Galloway," before lifting it to his mouth and taking a swallow of the fiery whiskey.

"To Simon," both of the older men said quietly.

It had already been a long night, Preacher thought, and it would be longer still until morning.

* * *

Jonathan and Geoffrey got roaring drunk. Preacher took a few more swigs from the jug, but for the most part he just passed it back and forth between the other two. When they weren't drinking, they were telling stories about the times when they and Simon had been kids and then young men. Preacher heard more yarns about the Galloway family than he ever wanted to hear.

They had been a pretty normal bunch, growing up in Philadelphia, the sons of a printer who had been friends with Ben Franklin, Tom Jefferson, and the other fellas who had led the colonies in their revolt against the English. Those must have been exciting times, Preacher thought. He had been born too late for the revolution, but he had taken part in the war that had finally finished it up, back in '14. Despite the fact that he had fought against them, he didn't bear any particular hatred or even dislike for the English. Like every other nationality, there were some good ones and some bad'uns.

"What did you fellas do when you grew up?" Preacher asked.

"Geoffrey and I took over the printing business," Jonathan replied. "Simon became a banker. He was the most successful one in the family. In fact, he paid for most of the wagons and supplies for this journey."

"Damn shame he didn't make it to see the end of it."

"Yes, it is," Geoffrey agreed.

"Any other brothers or sisters?" Preacher asked.

"Yes, but they're all back in Philadelphia." Jonathan laughed. "They all believe that we're insane for leaving the city and coming west. I'm afraid they don't have any adventure in their souls."

Preacher nodded. How well he understood that. He had left home at the age of twelve, determined to go out and see the world, to take care of himself and make his own way. He had been on his own ever since, his solitude broken only by occasional sojourns with friends, or with Jennie when she was still alive.

At times he suspected he would spend the rest of his life alone. That frightened him near as much as that grizz he had tangled with, back in the days when he hadn't been long in the mountains, but fate was called that for a reason. A fella chose his own path, his own way of getting there, but in the end he had a destiny to live out, and there wasn't much that could change it.

"What are you plannin' on doin' when you finally get to Oregon?"

"Well, we'll want to see Roger and Peter settled first, of course," Geoffrey replied. "They plan to have a farm . . . although, given the hard feelings between them now, they may have to have *two* farms. After that . . ."

"After that we're going to be mountain men and go exploring," Jonathan finished, eagerness in his voice.

Preacher grinned. "Mountain men, is it?"

"That's right." Jonathan frowned. "You think we can do it, don't you? I know we're rather old to be starting out on such a career, but . . ."

"If that's what you really want to do, you'll find a way to do it," Preacher assured them. "Don't forget, I've seen you fellas in action. You handle yourselves pretty good. Just keep your eyes and ears open, and learn as much as you can."

"Just being around you seems to be an education in itself, Preacher," Geoffrey said with a smile.

Preacher chuckled, glad that they had gotten their minds on something other than grieving for their lost brother. Sorrow was a good thing in many ways, but it had to be tempered with hope.

And he was a good one to be thinking that, he told himself, considering how he had felt since Jennie's death. Had he had any hope, truly, or was he just going through the motions? The Galloways still had time to mourn Simon. Maybe it was time for him to move on, though, Preacher thought.

"You know, if y'all are gonna be mountain men, you'll need some good nicknames," he pointed out.

"What's wrong with our real names?"

"Not a thing, but out here folks tend to be a mite less formal. You don't reckon I was born with the name Preacher, do you?"

"What is your real name?" Jonathan asked.

Preacher grinned at them. "Arthur." He didn't give them his last name; he had kept that to himself ever since the night he had sneaked out of his parents' house and gone out to see the world.

"Well, that's a fine name," Geoffrey said. "Like King Arthur and his knights."

"I ain't got no fellas in armor followin' me around, though, and I'd just as soon not. The Injuns had trouble sayin' the name when I first come out here, so they called me Artoor. That is, until they started callin' me Preacher like most ever'body else. Ever' now and then, though, I run across one of the old trappers who calls me Art."

"I think we'll stick with Preacher," Jonathan said. "What should our nicknames be?"

"Well, I'll have to think on that. It'll come to me, though, and when it does, we'll have a drink on it."

The older men nodded, and Geoffrey said, "That's a promise."

29

During his time in the Rockies and on the Great Plains, Mart Hawley had seen quite a few snowstorms and even raging blizzards. None like this one. This bastard was one for the ages.

He was glad that he and Swift Arrow had found the other two bunches of the Arikara war party and merged them back together into one group that would continue to pursue Preacher and the Galloways until vengeance was done. He was even more glad that they had come upon a small cave at the edge of the foothills before that blizzard hit. If they had been out in the open, with no shelter at all, they wouldn't have stood a chance.

Hawley's back still hurt like blazes where the tomahawk had lodged in it. Swift Arrow had given one of the members of the war party, a young brave called Corn Man, the job of caring for Hawley's wound. Corn Man didn't speak any English, or if he did, he was keeping it to himself. He was surly too, and Hawley could tell that he hated whites. Still, Corn Man's respect for—and fear of—Swift Arrow was enough to ensure that he followed orders. He had cleaned the wound and bound it up again when the blizzard forced them to halt, and now Hawley leaned against the wall of the cave with his right shoulder and felt drowsiness stealing over him. The Injuns had built a fire out of buffalo chips and a little wood, and enough of the heat it gave off was trapped in the cave to make the temperature bearable. It was still cold enough so that Hawley was grateful for the buffalo robe, though.

Swift Arrow came over to him and hunkered down to talk to him. "Where whites go?" he asked.

"Well, it's obvious that kid lied to us, or at least made us think he was lyin' on purpose," Hawley replied. "Tricky little bastard. The wagons didn't head south. They're still hittin' east, I reckon, makin' for Garvey's Fort. They won't be goin' anywhere in this blizzard, though."

Swift Arrow grunted. "Sahnish not travel in blizzard either. Whites freeze to death?"

"Hard to say," Hawley answered with a shrug. "They're bound to be a good ways out on the plains by now, and if they don't have any shelter 'cept those wagons, they might be in a bad fix. You got to be ready, Chief, for the possibility they might be dead already when we catch up to 'em."

"What good you be then?" Swift Arrow asked, and Hawley thought he saw cruel amusement glinting in the war chief's eyes.

"I been a friend to your people, ain't I? I done ever'thing I could to help you get your vengeance on that bunch. It ain't my fault things ain't worked out so far."

Swift Arrow didn't say anything, just regarded Hawley intently, as if trying to figure out what to do with him.

Hawley swallowed and went on. "Anyway, I didn't have nothin' to do with whatever it is that's got you folks so het up. You don't have any score to settle with me. 'Twouldn't be honorable to do me any harm."

Swift Arrow's hand shot out and gripped Hawley's injured shoulder. The war chief's lip curled in a snarl as he twisted Hawley's shoulder and brought a cry of pain from the trapper. The other Indians ignored the cry.

"Speak not of honor," Swift Arrow growled. "Your skin is white. You know nothing of honor."

"I . . . I didn't mean nothin' by it," Hawley gasped, blinking as tears began to roll down his cheeks into his beard. "I just meant that I'm your friend, and I want to stay your friend!"

Swift Arrow brought his face close to Hawley's. "You know why Sahnish kill whites?"

Hawley managed to shake his head mutely.

"Whites kill young Sahnish brave. Go hunting, never come back. Days go by. We look, find young warrior, killed by white man's rifle. Follow tracks that lead to wagons. Wagons that went by Sahnish village days before."

"I'm sorry," Hawley said, still struggling to control his pain. "Did they shoot him for no reason?"

"No reason to kill," Swift Arrow agreed. "Not painted for war."

"Reckon whoever killed him must not have known anything about that. Those greenhorns are pretty dumb, Chief. They really thought they could get across the mountains to Oregon at this time of year."

Swift Arrow shook his head at the sheer stupidity of that idea. Finally, he let go of Hawley's shoulder and allowed him to slump back against the rock wall of the cave. Hawley sighed in relief as the pain subsided a little.

"Who was the young fella who got shot?" he asked as an afterthought.

"Name Cloud Seeker." The war chief's face was as stony as the wall of the cave. "Was son of Swift Arrow."

When Preacher climbed out of the back of the wagon the next morning, he stepped down into more than two feet of snow. The stuff immediately worked its way into his high-topped moccasins and made his feet even colder.

The wind had died down some, but it was still blowing and snow still fell thickly from the leaden sky. It was impossible to tell for sure what the time was, but the sun was up; enough light made it through the snowstorm for Preacher to know that. He felt like the hour was pretty early.

Behind him in the wagon, both Jonathan and Geoffrey snored loudly. They had dozed off into a drunken slumber far into the night. Preacher had slept too, rolled in a couple of blankets. Eventually the cold and the racket had roused him.

He wasn't that worried about the Arikara war party right now, he thought as he took a look around the camp. Chances were, the Indians were holed up somewhere, probably back in the foothills. They didn't have even the meager shelter of covered wagons; if they had been out on the plains when the storm hit, they might be done for. That would certainly simplify matters, although Preacher wasn't sure he would wish such a fate even on his enemies.

The mules and the horses were all still alive, having huddled together for warmth during the long, cold night. They were pressed up against the wagon where Simon Galloway's body lay. Preacher moved outside the circle and headed on around to check on the people in the other wagons.

Peter Galloway climbed out in response to Preacher's soft-voiced call. The man's teeth chattered as he rubbed his hands wearily over his reddened face. "The children are all right," he said in reply to Preacher's question. "Cold, of course. Can we build a fire?"

Preacher nodded. "We'll clear off a space and build a shelter, and then we'll get a fire goin'. That'll make everybody feel a mite better." He paused for a moment, then said, "I reckon your brother told you . . . ?"

"About our father?" Peter nodded. "He did. Thank you for going out and finding him. Knowing that he's not lost out there is scant comfort, but it's better than nothing."

"You and Roger ain't gonna go to whalin' on each other again, are you?"

"I'm sure I deserve it," Peter said stonily, "but I think we've called a truce, at least for the moment. In a situation like this, we can't be trying to kill each other."

"That's the damned truth. Let me check on everybody else, and then I'll get started on that fire."

"Let me know if you need any help," Peter offered.

Preacher went on to the remaining wagon, pulled the canvas flap aside a little, and said quietly, "Roger? You awake?"

A moment later, Angela's face appeared at the opening as she answered the summons. "Roger's asleep," she whispered. "Do you need me to wake him?"

Preacher shook his head. "Nope. Just checkin' to see how everybody's doin' this mornin'."

Angela didn't say anything, but she pulled the flap back farther and slid out of the wagon. She stepped over the tailgate and held out a hand to Preacher. He instinctively took it and helped her leap lightly down into the snow. She wore a hooded coat and had a blanket wrapped around her in addition to that. A scarf muffled her throat and the lower part of her face.

"It snowed every winter in Philadelphia, of course," she said, "but it's been a long time since I've seen this much on the ground. And it's still coming down."

"May be four or five feet 'fore it's over," Preacher said.

"How can we travel in that?"

He shook his head. "We can't. We'd be stuck here until some of it melted or blew off. The wagons can manage about three feet, but that's all."

"Then if it snows the rest of the day and on into the night . . ."

"We likely won't be goin' anywhere for a week or more."

Angela frowned. "We have enough food. I suppose we could wait it out if we had to. But what about those Indians?"

"They'll be pinned down too, but they'll probably be able to move again quicker'n we will. So we better hope that we ain't stuck."

"There's no chance that they might just . . . give up? Go home because of the weather?"

Again Preacher shook his head. "It's hard to tell what a Injun will take a notion to do, but as stubborn as this bunch has been so far, I don't reckon they'll give up. They want blood too bad."

"Killing all of us won't bring back that young man, or any of the men they lost when they attacked us the first time."

"No, ma'am, it sure won't, and they know it. But that won't stop 'em from liftin' all our scalps if they get a chance to do it."

Angela shuddered. "I . . . I just don't understand how anyone can be so savage, so heartless." She glanced at the wagon where her husband was. "But then, there are a lot of things in life that I just don't understand," she added meaningfully.

"Yes'm, you and me both." To change the subject, Preacher asked, "How's the mama and the baby this mornin'?"

"John Edward is all right, though I don't think he's getting enough to eat. Dorothy is very low. I . . . I don't think she's going to last much longer."

"That's a terrible shame," Preacher said. "Things betwixt her and Roger, did they ever get worked out?"

With sadness on her face, Angela said, "Dorothy was lucid for a time during the night. She and Roger were able to talk for a while. I . . . I tried not to eavesdrop, but I couldn't help overhearing some of what they said. She begged for his forgiveness, and he gave it. He wanted to know if Peter attacked her, and while she wouldn't admit that, wouldn't blame him for what happened, I'm sure that none of it was Dorothy's idea, even if she did cooperate and he didn't have to rape her."

That was her husband she was talking about, Preacher reminded himself, and it was remarkable that she could stand there and say such things in such a calm, strong voice. The whole messy business had to be tearing her up inside too, but as long as the others needed her, she wasn't going to give in to what she was feeling, wasn't even going to show her pain.

In some ways, he supposed it had simplified things that the one woman he had ever loved was a prostitute. He had been young and inexperienced enough when he first met Jennie that he didn't fully understand what was going on in the back of that wagon owned by the man who had taken her in, but he had caught on quickly enough. It might have bothered some fellas to be in love with a whore, even a reluctant one, but for Preacher, that was just the way things had always been. Jealousy never really entered his mind.

"Well, it's good that they settled things," Preacher said now, referring to Roger and Dorothy. "Might make things easier . . . later on."

Angela nodded in solemn agreement.

"I'm gonna clear some ground, get a shelter up, and build a fire," he went on. "We can have some hot coffee and food in a while."

"That will be wonderful." Angela hesitated. "What about Simon?"

"It's cold enough the body'll keep," Preacher said. "I ain't tryin' to be callous about it, just practical. When the weather gets a mite better, we'll get a grave dug and say some words over him 'fore we move on. That's the best we can do."

"Yes, I suppose you're right. I just wish—"

Preacher never found out what she wished, because at that moment, a ragged cry came from inside the wagon. "Dorothy!" Roger Galloway wailed. "Oh, my God, no! Dorothy!"

And Preacher knew that before they left this place, they would have two graves to dig.

30

Dorothy's eyes were open but lifeless. Her face was so pale it seemed to have been completely drained of blood. Her lips were blue.

"She was still bleedin' inside somewhere most likely," Preacher told Jonathan. The older man had climbed into the wagon to help him with the body. Roger and Angela were back in the other wagon with Geoffrey. They had taken the baby with them, of course. Preacher wasn't sure how they were going to continue feeding the infant with Dorothy gone. Preacher was not optimistic about the poor baby's chances of survival.

"It never should have come to this," Jonathan said bitterly. "She was a good woman, and she shouldn't have died this way."

"Can't argue with that."

"If only Roger and Peter and Simon hadn't pushed so hard to leave Philadelphia. We could have waited until next spring, but no, they had to start. There couldn't be any delays. They were just too . . . too anxious to get to the Promised Land. But like Moses, Simon will never enter it. He won't even see it."

Preacher wouldn't have compared Simon Galloway to Moses, but he knew what Jonathan meant. "Best get on with the job at hand," he said. "Let's wrap this blanket around her nice and snug."

With Dorothy no longer needing all the blankets and quilts

that had been around her for warmth, the two men used only one blanket as her shroud. They wrapped the body securely, and Preacher tied the blanket in place with several lengths of cord. Then they picked up the body, Preacher at the head and Jonathan at the feet, and carried it out of the wagon.

It took them only a few minutes to place Dorothy in the other wagon with the body of her father-in-law. With that unpleasant task accomplished, Preacher got to work on the chore that he had hoped to have done by now, getting a shelter built and a fire burning.

Using a shovel from the farm tools stored in one of the wagons, Preacher cleared the snow as best he could from an eight-foot-wide circle and then angled some stakes in the ground, tying them together at the top. He used a couple of pieces of canvas to rig a makeshift tepee on the framework. It was crude but it would work. The canvas would protect the fire from the wind and snow, and the opening at the top would let the smoke out. If everyone crowded inside, it might even be halfway warm. Since it looked like they might be here for several days, they needed something like this in order to survive.

He dug buffalo chips out of the pile the young'uns had made, shook the snow off them, and carried them into the tepee. A few minutes of diligent work with flint, steel, and tinder got a tiny fire started. Preacher leaned over and blew on the flames until he was confident they wouldn't go out. He held his hands above the fire for a moment, enjoying even the little bit of warmth that the flames gave off.

Jonathan stuck his head in through the opening where the pieces of canvas came together. He said, "I've got the coffeepot and the frying pan and our supplies. If you'll move over, Preacher, I'll get to work on breakfast."

"Sounds mighty fine to me," Preacher said with a nod. "I'll go take a look around, just to make sure there ain't nobody tryin' to sneak up on us."

With Dog at his side, Preacher trudged up the slope and out of the buffalo wallow. Although visibility was much better than it had been the night before, the snow was still swirling and blowing enough so that Preacher couldn't see very far. He made a complete circle around the camp, knowing he had gotten back to the place where he had started because he could still see the path he had broken through the deep snow. The tracks might fill up if the snow continued coming down, but it would take quite a while. Not having seen anything threatening other than the weather itself, he went back down to the wagons and inside the circle. He caught a brief whiff of coffee brewing, and the aroma made his mouth water. He went to the tepee and bent over to step inside quickly, so as not to let out warm air and let in cold.

He found Jonathan, Geoffrey, and the two younger children sitting by the fire. Mary looked up at him and said, "Good morning, Mr. Preacher. This is just like an Indian's house, isn't it?"

Preacher hunkered on his heels next to her. "It sure is, little missy. They build 'em a mite better than I do, but I reckon we can get by with this'un."

The youngsters wore solemn expressions, and Preacher figured they had heard about their Aunt Dorothy's passing. He said quietly to Geoffrey, "Where's everybody else?"

"Roger and Angela and Nate and the baby are in our wagon," Geoffrey replied. "I'm not sure where Peter is."

Preacher felt a faint stirring of alarm. "He wouldn't wander off in this storm, would he?"

"I'm pretty sure he's in his wagon brooding. Don't worry about Peter; he's prone to doing foolish things, but not anything that will hurt him directly." Geoffrey spoke quietly, and the children didn't seem to be paying any attention to him. Preacher was glad of that, since Geoffrey was talking about their father. As sorry a human being as Peter Galloway was, Preacher didn't believe in talkin' down a man in front of his kids.

Jonathan had bacon frying and some left-over biscuits warming, and the coffee was ready. When the food was done, Preacher ate sparingly. These pilgrims might believe they had plenty of food, but Preacher knew first-hand how quickly supplies could disappear, especially when a trip took longer than anyone thought it would. He didn't want them to run out of rations before they got back to Garvey's Fort. He poured himself a full cup of coffee, though, and savored it.

The others had eaten by the time he swallowed the last of the strong, black brew. "Stay here," he told them. "I'll go let the others know breakfast is ready."

"Is there room in here for everyone?" Geoffrey asked.

"It'll be a mite cramped, but I reckon ever'body can squeeze in. Be warmer that way too." Preacher just hoped there wouldn't be any more ruckuses between Roger and Peter. Peter had promised that they would get along, but Preacher wasn't convinced of it yet.

He walked across the camp to the wagon where Roger, Angela, Nate, and the baby were and stepped up at the back of it to put his head through the flap. "Mornin', folks," he said, keeping his voice pleasant but not cheery. These people were bereaved, after all. Roger had lost a wife, Nate and John Edward a mother, and Angela a sister-in-law. "There's food and coffee, if anybody wants any. And I'd recommend that you eat. We all got to keep our strength up."

Angela sat on one of the bunks built into the side of the wagon, cradling the blanket-wrapped infant in her lap. Roger and Nate were on the other bunk. Roger had an arm around his son's shoulders. Preacher almost thought of Nate as Roger's older son, then reminded himself that Roger wasn't really John Edward's father.

It might be best all around if Roger *did* regard himself as the baby's pa. John Edward could be raised that way and might not ever have to know the difference. Preacher didn't pretend to be an expert on such things, though. He knew about huntin' and trappin' and trackin' and fightin', and everything else that went with staying alive on the frontier. He had explored places where no white man had ever set foot. But like most folks, the human heart was still largely uncharted territory to him.

"I don't think anyone is very hungry right now," Angela

said. She smiled sadly. "Except for this little fellow here." The baby squirmed a little in her lap and made tiny crying noises.

"Better eat anyway. Won't do nobody any good to starve, and it might even make y'all feel a mite better."

"My mama is dead, Preacher," Nate said dully. "How can I feel better?"

"Well, now . . . did you ever fall down when you was runnin' and scrape your knee or bust your shin against some-thin'?"

"Yeah. I guess I did."

"Whenever that happened, I'll just bet you your ma tried to make it not hurt quite as much, didn't she?"

Nate hesitated but finally said, "Yeah."

"Then I reckon she'd prob'ly like it if you didn't hurt quite so much now, wouldn't she? It'd make her happy if you weren't so sad?"

"Maybe," Nate said. "I never really thought about it like that."

"Well, you ponder it, and if you want some bacon and bis-cuits whilst you're ponderin', just come on over."

"Thank you, Preacher," Roger said in a voice choked with emotion. "I think we'll do that. Won't we, Nate?"

"Sure, Pa. If you say so."

Preacher looked at Angela. "Be warmer on you and the babe in the shelter I made too."

She nodded, and there was gratitude in her eyes for more than the offer of food and coffee. "Let's all go," she said to Roger. "Just let me wrap up the baby a little better. . . ."

A short time later, they had joined the group already inside the tepee. Dog was in there too, lying between Mary and Brad, enjoying the petting they were doing. There was a time when he'd been too touchy to let himself be loved on like that, Preacher thought. The big, wolflike creature was getting more tolerant as he got older.

That left Peter as the only one who wasn't in the tepee. Preacher figured he ought to go get him. That might make things a bit tenser, but they didn't need anybody else freezing to death right now.

Preacher tromped through the snow to Peter's wagon and thumped a fist on the tailgate. "Come get some breakfast!" he called. "Coffee and bacon—good for what ails ye!"

There was no response from inside the wagon.

"Galloway!" Preacher called. "You hear me?"

When there was still nothing but silence, Preacher frowned. Earlier, Jonathan and Geoffrey had said that Peter wouldn't wander off in the storm or do anything else to hurt himself, but Preacher wasn't so sure of that. If the man had even an ounce of humanity left in him, he had to be feeling pretty damned bad right now about everything that had happened. He hadn't put a pistol to his head—Preacher would have heard the shot—but there were other ways for a fella to end his own life if he was determined enough to do so.

Muttering under his breath, Preacher pulled himself up, stepped over the tailgate, and pushed into the wagon. It was very dim inside, and he couldn't see well. He could smell, though, and the reek of raw whiskey hit his nostrils. His foot bumped something lying on the floor of the wagon bed, and when he knelt and reached out, he put a hand on Peter's shoulder. The man groaned when Preacher shook him.

Dead drunk, Preacher thought. And if he stayed here like this, maybe just plain dead. The temperature was still below freezing, and Preacher had heard that cold weather was even harder on a fella when he was full of rotgut.

"Come on, damn it," Preacher said as he slipped an arm around Peter's shoulders and rolled him onto his back. "We better get you by the fire so's you can thaw out."

Peter was a big, muscular man. It took some effort for Preacher to get him onto his feet and wrestle him out of the wagon. Peter was only half-conscious, and he fell when Preacher tried to guide him over the tailgate. He plunged down into the thick snow, which cushioned his fall. He came up sputtering and pawing at the snow that covered his face.

The cold had shocked at least some of the drunkenness out of his system.

"What . . . what the hell—"

Preacher grabbed his arm and swung him toward the tepee. "We're gonna get some black coffee in you."

"Let go of me, damn you!" With that, Peter swung a wild, shaky punch at Preacher. The mountain man easily avoided the blow and gave Peter a shove that sent him stumbling several feet away. Preacher expected him to fall, but somehow Peter managed to remain on his feet.

"Listen to me," Preacher grated, and his voice was low and dangerous. "I know you been in there guzzlin' 'cause you feel sorry for yourself. But I reckon you're the only one who feels sorry for you. I sure as hell don't. And if you swing at me again, I'll bust you, sure as shootin'."

"I'm not . . . not afraid . . . of you," Peter said thickly.

"You damn well better be."

After a moment, Peter shook his head gingerly, mumbled a curse or two, and wiped the back of a gloved hand across his mouth. "You said something about . . . coffee?"

"Come on. And you best behave when you get in there. The mood ever'body's in, if you cause any trouble they're liable to line up to thump you." Preacher added grimly, "And I ain't gonna stop 'em neither."

31

It stopped snowing about the middle of the afternoon, but the sky remained thick with clouds. When Preacher stepped out of the tepee and regarded the heavens through squinted eyes, he couldn't tell if the snow was really finished or just holding up for a while. He hoped the storm was over. There were some three feet of snow on the ground. He thought the mule teams and the wagons could negotiate that much, if they avoided the deeper drifts. With any luck, they might be able to pull out early the next morning.

He took up the shovel he had used to clear the ground where the tepee now stood and said, "Come on, Dog." Together they walked up the slope to the edge of the buffalo wallow. Before he stepped out onto the prairie, he took a good look around. The thick white carpet of snow would make it easy to see anyone who was coming toward the camp. Preacher didn't spot any movement anywhere in the vast sweep of the plains.

He found a spot where the wind had scoured some of the snow off the ground, leaving only a thin covering. The shovel had a difficult time biting into the dirt when he began to dig, but the ground wasn't frozen so hard yet that it was impossible. He had been working at it a while, enough so that he was starting to feel a mite warm in his buckskins and heavy coat, when footsteps came crunching through the snow behind him.

"Let me help," Peter said. When Preacher turned to face him, he was holding out his hand for the shovel.

Preacher grunted and handed over the tool. Peter took it and began to dig. He went at it hard and fast, his breath fogging thickly in front of his face. After standing by and watching for a few minutes, Preacher said, "That ain't gonna change anything."

Peter paused and looked up at him, breathing heavily. "What?"

"No matter how hard you dig, it won't change what you did. And it won't bring back your sister-in-law or your pa."

Peter gave him a surly glare. "I'm just trying to help."

"And I appreciate the help. I'm just tellin' you not to think it means more than it really does . . . 'cause it don't."

Peter stared at him for a long moment, then finally said, "You're a hard man, aren't you, Preacher? Your heart's as cold as all this snow."

"I've stayed alive this long and aim to stay alive a while longer. And I don't really give a damn what you think of me."

Peter drove the shovel into the ground with a grating sound. "The feeling is mutual."

He went back to his digging. A few minutes later, Preacher saw another figure trudging up from the center of the buffalo wallow. As the man came closer, Preacher recognized him as Jonathan Galloway.

"I thought I'd come lend a hand," Jonathan said as he walked up to the other two men.

Peter stepped out of the shallow hole and handed the shovel to his uncle. "Don't work too hard at it," he advised, "or Preacher will insult you."

Jonathan frowned in confusion but didn't press the matter. He turned to Preacher and said, "Roger told me he thinks it would be all right to dig one grave for both Simon and Dorothy. They got along well enough in life, he said, that they can stand to be buried together."

Preacher nodded. That was the practical thing to do, of

course. He was glad Roger had suggested it, though, so *he* hadn't been forced to.

Jonathan worked on the grave for a while, but being older, he tired more easily. Preacher took the shovel back from him and went to town with it. The ground was softer the lower he dug, and the work went fairly quickly. By the time the light was beginning to dim, he had a big enough hole to do the job.

Peter had already gone back to the wagons, but Jonathan was still there, keeping Preacher company while the mountain man completed the grim task. As Preacher stepped up out of the grave, Jonathan said, "I'll go tell the others we're ready."

Preacher nodded. There was no point in putting it off. Now that the grave was dug, it would be better to go ahead and get it over with.

He followed Jonathan down to the camp and found Peter sitting alone in his wagon, rather than in the tepee with the others. "Come on," Preacher told him. "You and me'll take the bodies up there."

"Why me?" Peter asked, still surly from the earlier confrontation.

"Because you're the strongest of the bunch next to me. Besides, I'll be damned if I'm gonna make your brother carry his own wife's body."

"Don't you have any feelings?" Peter choked out. "I . . . I loved her too, you know."

"You keep your trap shut about that," Preacher warned. "Take your hat off when the words are bein' said over 'em and look sad all you want, but don't you say a damned word."

Peter glowered at him for a moment, then shrugged. "I'm not going to waste my breath arguing with you."

"Good."

They went to the wagon where the bodies lay and, one at a time, carried the blanket-shrouded figures up the slope to the grave. They took Simon Galloway first and then returned for Dorothy, and as they brought her to her final resting place, the others left the tepee and walked slowly and solemnly behind them. Angela held the hands of her children, while Roger carried the baby and Nate walked alongside him. Jonathan and Geoffrey brought up the rear of the gloomy procession, at least as far as the humans were concerned. Dog padded along through the snow behind them.

The grave was wide enough so that Simon and Dorothy could lie side by side. Simon was on the left, Dorothy on the right. The mourners gathered around the grave. Despite the cold, the men removed their hats.

"I'm now the oldest one in the family," Geoffrey began, "so I'll begin. We've come here to lay to rest these two fine people. Simon Bartholomew Galloway was brother, father, and grandfather to us, and we loved him very much. He was a kind man, a hard-working man."

Preacher thought Geoffrey was being a mite generous, based on what he had seen of Simon Galloway, but hell, the man was talking about his brother after all. It was understandable.

"And Dorothy Elizabeth Corrigan Galloway was a fine, loving woman, a dear wife to Roger, a devoted mother to Nathan and John Edward. So devoted to her children that she gave her own life to bring the newest member of the Galloway family into the world. She will be deeply missed." Geoffrey looked around. "If anyone else would care to say a few words . . ."

Preacher meant no disrespect, but his mind wandered some as Jonathan, Roger, and Angela all spoke glowing, emotional tributes to the two people who had passed on. He had buried quite a few friends over the years, and beyond a simple prayer, not much had been said at those services. The frontier taught those who dared to live there how to be practical and efficient in all things, including their ceremonies. Also, he was standing so that he could keep an eye on the country to the west, because that was where the pursuing Arikara war party would come from. He watched for any sign of movement now that the storm was over. It wouldn't surprise him a bit if the Injuns were already on the move again, coming after the wagon train they had tracked halfway across the plains, into the mountains, and back out again. He didn't see anything moving against the snow, however, except a distant animal that his keen eyes identified as an antelope. He found himself wishing the creature would come within rifle range. Some antelope steaks fried over the fire would be mighty good tonight.

He lowered his head and closed his eyes as he realized that Geoffrey was praying, commending the souls of the departed to the Lord, asking that He welcome them into heaven. If they were going to get there, Preacher thought, they were already there, having ascended the Starry Path to Man Above, as the Indians put it. Preacher knew he would take that Starry Path himself one of these days, even though he was still relatively young, and the prospect didn't worry him overmuch. He had already crossed the earthly divide several times; when he finally crossed the heavenly one, it would be just one more new country to explore.

"Amen," Geoffrey said, and everyone murmured, "Amen." Peter had done as Preacher told him and remained silent throughout the service. Now he remained behind with Preacher as the others turned and walked back down the slope to the camp. Out of consideration for them, Preacher waited until they had gone into the tepee before he picked up the shovel and went to work filling in the grave. Those folks didn't need to hear the thud of earth falling onto the blanket-wrapped forms.

"I'll help," Peter said after a few minutes. Just as he had earlier, he reached out for the shovel.

Preacher gave it to him and stepped back. As Peter tossed shovels of dirt into the hole, he went on. "You think I'm one sorry son of a bitch, don't you?"

Preacher's silence spoke volumes.

"Well, you don't understand," Peter grated as he pushed the shovel into the mound of earth beside the grave. "You can't understand what it's been like. You don't know everything that's happened."

"The Injuns have a sayin' about walkin' a while in the other fella's moccasins," Preacher said. "I reckon that's pretty hard to do, though. Why do you care whether or not I understand you, Galloway?"

"I don't," Peter snapped. "I'm just telling you not to be so damned high-and-mighty. If you were in the same position I was in, you'd probably do the same thing I did."

"I don't reckon."

"But you don't *know*. Nobody knows what they'll do until they're faced with a situation. You may believe you'd handle it a certain way, but you could be wrong."

"This conversation ain't gettin' us nowhere." Preacher stepped forward. "Gimme that shovel."

He took it and resumed filling in the grave. Peter moved back. A humorless laugh came from him.

"You know I'm right," he said. "You know it, Preacher. You just don't want to admit that you're fallible too. You try to act like you're not human, but you are. You make mistakes just like everyone else."

Preacher stopped his work and faced the other man. "Sure, I make mistakes," he admitted. "Make 'em all the time more'n likely. The difference 'tween you and me is that I don't try to excuse mine away or blame 'em on other folks. I own up to what I've done."

"Always?" Peter asked mockingly. "You didn't come to me and apologize after you looked at my wife with lust in your eyes."

Preacher's hands tightened on the shovel. "Miss Angela's a fine woman," he said. "I wouldn't never dishonor the friendship she's showed me."

"That didn't stop you from wanting her. Would you like to know what she's like in bed, Preacher? How it feels to have her under you—"

Preacher took a step toward him and drew back the shovel. "Shut your filthy mouth," he warned, "or by God I'll bash that head o' yours in!"

Peter laughed again. "Go ahead. Put me out of my misery. You'll just have to dig another grave."

Slowly, Preacher lowered the shovel. He glanced toward

the camp, hoping that none of the others had seen him threaten Peter. No one was in sight. He supposed they were all still inside the tepee. Even if someone had been out and about, it was getting dark, and they might not be able to see very well up here where the grave was.

"I'll finish this," he said. "You go on down."

"Suit yourself." Peter turned and stalked toward the wagons.

Preacher stood there for a moment, leaning on the shovel as he tried to get control of the anger roiling around inside him. When his pulse wasn't thudding quite so hard in his head, he went back to work and finished filling in the grave. He patted down the rest of the dirt and then stepped back.

Pausing before leaving, he took off his hat and said, "I didn't say nothin' before, I reckon because I never knew you hardly at all, ma'am . . . and Galloway, I knew you but didn't much like you. Still and all, none o' that really matters now. We walk our paths in life, and we walk our paths in death. Here's hopin' that y'all's have led you home."

He put his hat back on and started down the hill carrying the shovel, not looking back.

He was only about halfway to the camp when he heard the loud, angry voices and knew that the trouble wasn't over yet.

Somehow, that didn't surprise him at all.

32

When Preacher stepped over one of the wagon tongues into the circle, he saw that the argument had spilled out of the tepee into the open. Roger and Peter stood facing each other, fists clenched, faces red with anger.

"I won't allow it!" Roger declared. "I'll be damned first!"

"You don't have any say in the matter!" Peter shot back.

"The hell I don't! He's my son!"

Peter shook his head and said, "No, he's not, and you know it."

Angela came running from the tepee and got between the two men. "Stop it!" she cried. "Have you two no decency? Simon and poor Dorothy are barely in the grave, and you're ready to kill each other again!"

"No one is taking my son away from me," Roger said, his voice shaking with emotion. "Least of all *him*." Undisguised loathing dripped from the words.

"John Edward is my son, and you know it," Peter said. "You heard Dorothy admit it. Since I'm his father, I have a right to raise him as I see fit."

Angela swung toward him, her previous role as would-be peacemaker forgotten for the moment. "What about me?" she asked. "Don't I have any say in this?"

"No," Peter said flatly. "You don't."

"That baby will be raised believing that I am his father," Roger insisted. "It's only right and proper."

"It's neither of those things. You know you can't keep such a secret from him forever. Too many people know about this, Roger." Peter adopted a more reasonable tone. "Wouldn't it be better and easier for John Edward if he knew the truth all along?"

"Never!" Roger practically spat at him. "He'll never be your son!"

"Then go to hell!" Peter shouted as he shoved Angela aside and launched a punch at his brother's head.

Angela cried out as she stumbled, tripped, and fell into the snow. Roger ducked the blow and grappled with Peter. They swayed back and forth for a second, clawing at each other's throat, before Preacher reached them. He grabbed each of them by the coat collar and flung them in opposite directions, his great strength sending them flying through the air. They crashed to the ground and skidded in the deep snow.

Preacher reached to his waist and grasped both pistols. He brought them out and leveled them at Roger and Peter, earing back the hammers as he did so.

"No!" Angela screamed from the ground.

"Preacher, wait!" Jonathan called from the tepee, where he and Geoffrey had just pushed out through the gap in the canvas cover.

"Don't shoot them!" Geoffrey added.

Preacher stood there for a moment, then growled a curse and lowered the hammers on the pistols. "I wasn't goin' to shoot 'em," he said, "though I was shore tempted there for a spell." One at a time, he tucked the weapons back behind his belt. "You two get up," he snapped at the men on the ground. "What's all this about?"

Roger and Peter climbed to their feet and started brushing snow off their clothes. "He says he's going to take John Edward away from me," Roger said, nodding to Peter.

"Yeah, I reckon I got that." Preacher turned to Peter. "What ever gave you that idea?"

"He's my son," Peter insisted. "I have a right to raise him."

"His mama should have had a say in that."

"His mother is dead," Peter said flatly. "The decision is mine to make. Legally—"

"Now there's an idea you got to get out o' your head," Preacher cut in. "The nearest court is one hell of a long way from here, and the only judges who got any jurisdiction west o' the Mississippi are cold steel and hot lead. The only law is what's right, and you got to enforce it yourself."

"That's what I was trying to do."

Preacher turned back to Roger. "You want that boy, don't you?"

Roger wiped his mouth and said, "I . . . Yes, I do. He's part of Dorothy, and God help me, I love him, just like I loved her. I never stopped loving her."

Preacher looked at Jonathan and Geoffrey. Behind them, the three older children were peeking out of the tepee, curious about what was going on but at the same time scared to see all the grown-ups so upset. "What do you fellas think about this?" Preacher asked the two older men.

They looked uncomfortable at being caught in the middle of the dispute. Jonathan said reluctantly, "It seems to me that a child ought to have both a mother and a father. I know Roger means well by saying he'll raise the boy, but . . ."

"But if Peter and Angela raise him," Geoffrey said, "he'll have two parents—"

"Wait a minute," Angela interrupted. "You're assuming that Peter and I are going to stay married."

"What?" Peter exclaimed, thunderstruck by the implications of her statement.

She looked coolly at him. "I'm not sure I intend to remain married to you, Peter."

He gave a harsh laugh and said, "You can forget about that. You heard what Preacher said. There are no courts out here, which means there are no divorces. Such a thing is practically unheard of anyway. Why, it . . . it's unholy! A marriage is sacred and forever."

Angela crossed her arms over her chest and took a deep breath. "Yes," she said. "I can go in there and look at that poor baby, and see for myself just how sacred marriage is to you, Peter."

He didn't have anything to say to that.

Night had fallen while the argument was going on. Preacher said, "We ain't goin' to settle anything tonight, I don't reckon. And if it don't snow no more tonight, then first thing in the mornin' we'll be pullin' out, so there won't be time to fuss about it then. Seems to me that right now, we're all sort o' responsible for takin' care o' that baby, so let's just leave it at that."

"That's the best idea I've heard," Jonathan declared.

"I agree," Geoffrey put in. "We'll sort it all out later."

Preacher looked back and forth between Roger and Peter. "What do you say?"

"All right," Roger said grudgingly. "I'll never give up my son, though."

"We'll see," Peter said. "This isn't over yet."

Preacher was beginning to wonder if it ever would be.

Far into the night, the clouds began to thin, with stars peeking through the gaps. As the overcast sky broke even more, the moon appeared and showered silvery light that was reflected and made brighter by the snowfield. In fact, it was almost as light as the past couple of days had been.

That's what Mart Hawley thought as he trudged along in the wake of the Indians. Swift Arrow was in the lead, tirelessly breaking a trail through the snow for the others. The war chief drew strength from his hatred and his thirst for vengeance on the whites.

Swift Arrow had gotten them moving again when the clouds began to break. Hawley hadn't wanted to leave the warm, dry cave, but Swift Arrow had made it plain that his choices were: either going along with the war party or staying there with his throat cut. Hawley hadn't taken very long to make up his mind. He knew he was lucky that Swift Arrow had left him alive to start with. The Arikara didn't really need him, although it was possible they might be able to make use of him in a trap for the immigrants, if it came down to that.

The deep snow made it impossible to find any tracks left behind by the wagons, so Swift Arrow was steering his course by the stars and heading as much due east as possible. He thought they would be able to see the wagons against the snow if they passed anywhere within a couple of miles of them. Hawley figured that was pretty likely. And by starting out while it was still dark, they had a chance to cut down considerably on the lead that the pilgrims had. The snow hadn't stopped until mid-afternoon, and Hawley thought it was likely that wherever the Galloway party had waited out the storm, they wouldn't get moving again until morning. They might not leave even then; the snow could be too deep for the wagons.

The two dozen Arikara warriors strung out behind Swift Arrow, with Hawley bringing up the rear. His wounded shoulder ached, and he was cold, clean through. Walking in deep snow wore a man out about as quick as anything. It would have been better if they'd had snowshoes, but the war party hadn't expected to be away from their village this long and that was one thing they hadn't brought with them. They were running a little low on rations too. They wouldn't starve— they were Injuns after all, and able to live off the land where a normal man couldn't—but they were liable to be pretty thin and hungry by the time they got back home.

Hawley slowed down more and more and fell farther and farther behind the others. He began to wonder what would happen if he lagged far enough behind that the Indians forgot about him. Could he just stop and let them go on without him? Surely, sooner or later Swift Arrow would notice that he was gone. The question was whether or not the war chief would take the time to turn around and come back after him. The more Hawley thought about it, the more he doubted whether that would happen. Chances were, Swift Arrow would just keep going.

Hawley's mouth stretched in a thin smile under the muffler that was wrapped around his neck and the lower half of his face. He slowed down some more. The nearest Arikara warrior was now a good thirty yards in front of him. Hawley dawdled until that gap had increased to fifty yards.

The war party came to a gully where the snow had drifted even deeper. Swift Arrow paused on the lip of it for a moment, studying it. The gully ran north and south as far as the eye could see in both directions, and Swift Arrow didn't want to take the time to try to get around it. Besides, it might run for miles and miles, both ways. He slid down the bank, floundered through the drifts, and then climbed up the other side. The rest of the war party came after him. No words had been spoken; no words needed to be.

Hawley had hung back as much as he dared during that little delay. When he came to the gully, he climbed down into it as well. But instead of clambering up the far bank, he turned and began making his way along the bottom of the gully, heading south. The snow was above his waist, but he forced his way through it for several hundred yards until he came to an overhang. He rested there with his back against the bank and listened. The night was deathly quiet. He knew that angry voices would have carried well in the thin, cold air. Either the Injuns hadn't discovered that he was no longer with them, or they just flat didn't care.

Every minute that passed meant that he was safer, because it would take longer for Swift Arrow to come back and kill him. Swift Arrow knew that Hawley hadn't had anything to do with the death of his son. The war chief wouldn't waste the time to murder one white man just on general principles. Hawley clung to that hope.

Finally, when an hour or more had passed, he was convinced that the Injuns weren't coming back. He came out of his hidey-hole and climbed up the bank to the plains. Turning slowly, he looked all around and saw nothing in the silvery moonlight except the snow-covered prairie. He was alone, he thought exultantly. He had escaped.

And he was *alone,* he thought again, as the realization hit him that he was indeed by himself, wounded and without food, in the middle of a vast, snowy wilderness.

A sob of fear came from his throat as he asked himself what the hell he was going to do now.

33

The weather had improved by the next morning. Even before sunup, Preacher could tell that the sky was clear. Once again, a storm had come and gone.

Unfortunately, the atmosphere in the camp hadn't gotten better since the night before. That storm was still raging.

At least Roger and Peter didn't come to blows as everyone began to stir and get ready for the day. They made a point of avoiding each other as much as possible, although that was difficult given the close confines of the circled wagons.

Preacher had spent most of the night on guard, sleeping only for a short time early that morning. Peter had retreated alone to his wagon, while Roger, Angela, and all the children remained in the tepee. Jonathan had taken a short turn on watch while Preacher slept, and Geoffrey had gotten up before the rest of them to start on breakfast. His wounded arm was still sore, but it was healing and he was able to use it more now.

Preacher and Dog walked out onto the prairie to check the snow. It was deep, but not quite as deep as in the buffalo wallow. Preacher thought the wagons would be able to handle it, although the going would be slow. When he walked back down to the camp to report as much, he found Roger and Peter glaring at each other.

"Now what?" Preacher asked, not bothering to suppress the weariness and impatience in his voice.

"Now he's not only trying to steal my son, but my wife as well," Peter said accusingly.

"You're insane," Roger shot back. "If you make any more evil insinuations about Angela, I'll—"

Peter broke in by saying, "See? See the way he defends her? He's in love with her! And she spent the night with him in that tepee, like she was some sort of . . . Indian squaw! It's not proper, I tell you—"

He fell abruptly silent as Preacher stepped up to him and grated, "Shut your damned mouth. You ain't the one to be talkin' about what's proper and what ain't. Miss Angela spent plenty of nights in Roger's wagon whilst she was tryin' to save Miss Dorothy's life. Now she's lookin' after the kids. I reckon that's all."

Peter sneered at him. "You're just saying that because of the way you feel about—"

"Shut . . . up," Preacher whispered, "or I swear I'll take my knife and open you up from gizzard to gullet, you son of a bitch."

He ached with the desire to smash a fist into Peter's face and carve him up with the heavy hunting knife, just as he had threatened. Peter swallowed, paled slightly, and backed off a step. "I didn't mean to get everyone upset," he muttered.

"That's a damned lie," Roger snapped. "All you want to do anymore is upset everyone."

Peter turned his back, saying, "Go to hell." He headed for his wagon.

Preacher let him go. He wanted to get the wagons moving again as soon as possible, and wasting time on Peter Galloway just wasn't in his plans.

"Soon's we eat, we'll get the tepee taken down and them teams hitched up," he said, and Roger and Jonathan nodded in agreement.

The next half hour was a busy one. Everyone ate quickly, and then Preacher assigned each of them a job, even the young'uns, who helped Geoffrey take down the tepee. They rolled up the sections of canvas and stowed them away in one of the wagons, along with the stakes that had formed the structure's framework. If they needed to set up the tepee again, it would be faster and easier next time.

Roger and Jonathan hitched up some of the mules while Preacher and Peter tended to the others. Preacher didn't like working with the man, but he knew better than to tell Peter and Roger to work side by side. When the teams were all hitched and the supplies had been loaded, Preacher walked over to Geoffrey and asked, "Can you handle a team with that wounded arm?"

"I reckon I'll have to," Geoffrey replied, sounding more like a frontiersman than ever. "Angela can drive, but she'll have to take care of the baby and the other children."

"I can take a team if I need to."

Geoffrey shook his head. "We need you on horseback, Preacher, scouting ahead of us and watching our back trail."

"That's true, I reckon. We'll try to rest as much as we can along the way—"

"Not on my account," Geoffrey insisted. "Let's get moving, and put as much distance between us and those Injuns as we can."

Preacher grinned and said, "Sounds like a fine idea to me."

There was a solemn moment as the wagons rolled out of the buffalo wallow and then halted while everyone looked back at the lonely grave where Simon Galloway and his daughter-in-law Dorothy lay in eternal rest. Preacher sat his dun beside the lead wagon, where Jonathan was at the reins. The older man said, "It doesn't seem right to just leave them there like that, without even a marker." He looked at Preacher. "Could you find this place again come spring?"

"I reckon I could," Preacher said with a firm nod.

"Would you come back and put up a marker of some kind, so that if anyone else comes along and sees it, they'll know who's buried there? I . . . I hate to think about them being completely forgotten."

"Sure," Preacher said quietly. "I can do that."

"I'd be glad to pay you for your trouble—"

"No need. We've fought side by side. We're pards now, you and me, and Geoffrey too."

"You're sure?"

"You say anything else about payin' me, and I'm liable to get a mite insulted," Preacher told him.

"Well, all right then. I really appreciate it, Preacher."

Preacher shrugged to say that it was nothing. He didn't bother explaining to Jonathan that any marker he put up on the grave probably wouldn't last more than a year before the elements claimed it. After a few years had gone by, all signs of the grave would be gone for sure. It would be just another small stretch of prairie, just like the other hundreds of miles of prairie.

That didn't really matter, Preacher thought. The memories that folks kept in their hearts were the best and most lasting markers of all.

The wagons rolled steadily eastward all day, with only occasional stops to rest the teams or to clean out hard-packed snow that had piled up underneath the wagon beds and slowed them down. The snow had one other disadvantage besides making travel more difficult, Preacher thought: They were leaving a clear path behind them now, a trail that a blind man could follow. If those Arikara warriors stumbled on it, they wouldn't have any trouble knowing where their quarry had gone. And Preacher knew that once they had the trail, they would come on fast.

He rode back a mile or more, Dog bounding through the snow beside him. Stopping and scanning the plains for as far as he could see, Preacher didn't notice anything out of the ordinary. Then, suddenly, he did, his keen eyes picking out some small dark dots against the white sweep of snow.

"Damn it," he said under his breath. The Injuns were back there, and they were moving quickly. He wheeled the dun and put it into a trot, knowing it didn't matter if the Arikara had seen him or not. Chances were, they had, since he had spotted them and they probably had pretty good eyes too.

He rode hurriedly after the wagons. Peter was last in line, with Geoffrey handling the wagon in front of him, and then Roger, and finally Jonathan in the lead. Preacher didn't stop to talk to Peter, but he rode alongside the vehicle where Geoffrey was perched on the seat and said quietly, "I think I done spotted the Injuns back there a ways."

Geoffrey's breath hissed between his teeth. He looked at Preacher with a frown and asked, "Are they catching up? They can't catch up, can they? I mean, they're on foot and we have wagons and mule teams."

"Even with the snow, those warriors can run faster than them mules can pull the wagons," Preacher said. "If they keep on a-comin', they'll catch up. It's just a question of how long it'll take 'em."

"How long will it take us to reach Garvey's Fort from here?"

"With luck we might get there tomorrow, or more likely the next day."

"We're that close?" Geoffrey asked with despair in his voice. "We could make it in less than forty-eight hours?"

"I reckon."

"My God . . . What do we do now, Preacher?"

"Keep movin'," Preacher said. "When the Injuns get closer, maybe we can find someplace to fort up. If not, we'll just have to stop, circle the wagons, and fight 'em as best we can."

"We're only five men. There are still at least a couple of dozen of them."

"Nate can handle a rifle, I reckon, and maybe Angela too, unless we decide we want her to load for us. One way or another, we'll have some cover. The Injuns'll have to come at us over open ground. Don't give up, Catamount."

"I won't . . . What did you call me?"

"Catamount," Preacher said with a grin. "That's another name for a mountain lion. I figure you were fightin' about like one when we had that tussle with the Injuns back yonder in the foothills."

"Catamount," Geoffrey repeated. "I think I like it."

"It suits you," Preacher assured him. With a wave, he rode on ahead to break the news that they were being followed to Roger and Jonathan.

After Preacher had told him about the Arikara, Roger asked quietly, "Should I tell Angela and the children?"

Preacher thought about it, then shook his head. "No need to worry 'em just yet. They'll find out what's goin' on soon enough."

Roger nodded in agreement. "What should I do?"

"Just keep drivin'," Preacher told him. "Just keep drivin'."

Like his brother and his nephew, Jonathan took the news calmly. "I suppose this means a fight," he said.

"I reckon it does. Sooner or later. The Injuns won't turn back."

"Well, we have plenty of ammunition, and they don't outnumber us as much as they once did."

Preacher couldn't help but chuckle at the optimism in Jonathan's voice. "That's a good way to look at it, Silvertip."

Jonathan's face lit up in a grin. "Silvertip? Is that my mountain man name?"

"That's right. You got some silver in your hair, just like a silvertip grizzly bear. Built a mite like a bear too."

Jonathan threw his head back and laughed. "That's the greatest thing I've ever heard!" he exclaimed. "I'll carry the name with pride, Preacher. What about Geoffrey?"

"You mean Catamount?"

That brought another laugh from Jonathan. Then he grew more sober and said, "You've given us those names because we're running out of time. You think we may not survive the day."

"That's true of ever'body, every day they open their eyes

and go on livin'. I sure as hell ain't givin' up, if that's what you mean."

"No," Jonathan said, "I suppose you're not. And I don't intend to either. How do we proceed?"

Preacher leveled an arm and pointed east. "Keep goin'," he said. "I'll let you know when to stop."

Jonathan nodded, flapped the reins, and called out to the mules, urging them on. The wagon wheels continued turning, crunching their way through the snow.

The snow wasn't as deep here as it had been farther west, telling Preacher that the storm hadn't been quite as intense. A little less than a foot of the stuff was on the ground. The sky was a bright blue overhead, but the temperature was still below freezing. That was all right with Preacher. The wagons could move faster on snow-covered, frozen ground than they could through mud, and that was what they would have out here once all the snow melted.

By the time that happened, either the wagon train would have reached Garvey's Fort . . . or it would never get there.

34

A short time later, Preacher rode back to check on the pursuit. The Arikara were still back there, coming on at a steady pace that ate up the distance. He figured they were about two miles behind the wagons. When they had cut that lead to, say, half a mile, it would be time to stop and get ready for the inevitable attack.

Preacher glanced at the sky. The hour was well past noon, and that wasn't good. Darkness would be the ally of the Indians. It would be much easier to sneak up on the wagons after night fell. The immigrants would lose the slight advantage they had because of their rifles. Preacher had hoped to pick off some of the Arikara before the war party came within arrow range. The defenders couldn't hit what they couldn't see to aim at, though.

Preacher galloped back to the wagons, snow flying high as it was kicked up by the dun's hooves. Peter had found out somehow that the Indians were closing in on them, because he raised a hand and hailed Preacher. When the mountain man stopped, Peter said, "Is it true? Are they right back there?"

"A couple of miles," Preacher replied with a nod.

"Can we outrun them?"

"Nope. I don't think so."

"What if we keep moving all night?"

Preacher shook his head. "Then they'll sneak up on us and take the wagons one at a time. We'll have a better chance fortin' up and makin' a stand."

"Forting up where?" Peter waved a hand at the trackless expanse around them. "There's nothing out here!"

"It ain't quite as flat as it looks. If we can find a little rise, or somethin' like that . . ."

Preacher wasn't confident of finding such a place, but he wasn't going to give up hope either. He heeled his horse into a trot again and rode to the front of the wagon train, waving at Jonathan as he moved past.

About half a mile farther on, he felt his spirits begin to lift a little. The ground sloped down slightly into a broad, shallow valley that was at least a quarter of a mile wide. On the far side, the terrain sloped up to a small rise dotted with brush. The rise wouldn't provide much shelter, but Preacher knew it was the best he was likely to find in this mostly flat country.

Some people had started referring to the vast plains between the Mississippi River and the Rocky Mountains as the Great American Desert. Well, it wasn't a desert by any stretch of the imagination—Preacher knew the prairie teemed with life, both animal and plant—but it was a mite sparse when it came to geographical features. That little rise was the closest thing to a hill that this vicinity boasted, and Preacher was glad to have found it.

He reined in at the crest and waited. Before long, the wagons lumbered into view. He waved them on, and when Jonathan's wagon finally rolled up the slope and over the top of the rise, Preacher called to him, "This is where we'll make our stand!"

For the next few minutes, he was busy supervising the preparations for defending this high ground, such as it was. He had the drivers pull the wagons into a loose box shape, one on each side, with enough room left in the center for the livestock. By now Angela had figured out what was going on, and she came to Preacher to say, "I can fight. Just give me a rifle."

"Figured you'd say as much," he said with a smile. "Hold on a minute."

He called Nate over, and when the boy came running up, Preacher said, "Nate, you know how to load a rifle, don't you?"

"Sure, Preacher," the youngster replied.

"That'll be your job then."

Nate's face fell. "Aw, Preacher, I was figurin' that I'd get in on the fight too."

"You'll be in on it, never you worry about that," Preacher told him. "What you'll be doin' is just as important as anything we'll be doin'. Ever'body'll have two rifles, and it'll be your job to keep that second one loaded. Liable to be so much shootin', you can't keep up, but do your best."

Nate nodded. "I will, Preacher. I promise."

Preacher turned back to Angela. "I reckon that leaves you free to handle a gun, ma'am. The only thing is, can you shoot?"

"Well enough. We all practiced some with the rifles on the way out here."

"Shootin' at targets, you mean?"

"Well . . . yes. Does that make a difference?"

"A target don't shoot back at you," Preacher said. "It don't have a family neither. When you got one o' them Arikara in your sights, you got to be able to forget that he's just a fella who's probably got a squaw and a passel o' kids back in whatever village he comes from. You can't be thinkin' about how his old ma's gonna carry on when she hears he's dead." He made his voice deliberately harsh, so that he could be certain he was getting through to her. "All you can think about is how, if that warrior gets his way, him and his friends are gonna rape you until you're half-dead, and then he's gonna cut your throat and lift your hair."

Angela was pale and wide-eyed, but she kept herself under

control and nodded. "I can shoot a man, if that's what you're getting at," she assured him.

"Good . . . because it ain't just what he'll do to you that you got to remember. He'll kill your kids too if he gets the chance."

"Just give me a couple of rifles," Angela grated.

Preacher nodded. "You'll do."

He hated putting a woman on the front line of defense, but Angela was probably in better shape than Geoffrey, who, while stronger than before, would have trouble handling a rifle with that wounded arm. Preacher walked along the rise, glancing from time to time toward the west, where the war party was now visible. They were approaching the far side of the valley, moving out in the open and not bothering to hide. Everyone on both sides of this conflict knew exactly what was going on and what was going to happen. There was no need for secrecy.

The defenders would use the wagon parked just beyond the crest of the rise for cover. Preacher put Roger at the rear of the wagon and Peter at the front. Angela and Jonathan were stationed underneath the vehicle, where they could lie down side by side and fire over the crest. The kids, except for Nate, were all in the wagon that formed the back end of the box. Geoffrey would stand guard over them and was well armed with several pistols.

The Indians stopped on the far side of the valley. When they didn't come any closer, Preacher frowned. That war chief, Swift Arrow, was a cunning fella. He knew that the rifles wielded by the white men had a longer range than the Arikara bows. If he led his men in an attack on the wagons now, while the sun was still up, the defenders would have a chance to pick off quite a few of them before they ever got close enough to inflict any damage of their own.

"Damn," Preacher muttered as he stared across the quarter mile or so of open ground.

"What is it?" Roger asked. "What are they doing?"

"What I was afraid they'd do. They're waitin' for night. If

they came at us now, it'd be a turkey shoot for us. But if it's dark, we won't be able to see 'em comin', especially if they hit us before the moon comes up, and I reckon they will."

"What do we do?"

"Nothin' we can do but wait. At least they still have to come up a slope at us, and we ought to be able to see them a little against the snow, so that's somethin' else on our side too. But it'll still be mighty tricky shootin', and chances are they'll be amongst us before we can kill all of them."

"My God," Roger said softly. "They're going to overrun us, aren't they?"

"We'll give a good account of ourselves," Preacher said, his voice gruff.

"But we'll still die, no matter how many of them we kill. There are just too many. . . ."

"A fight ain't over until it's over," Preacher insisted. "And I ain't in the habit o' givin' up."

Roger looked toward the other end of the wagon and said bitterly, "None of this would be happening if it weren't for Peter. He doomed us all when he killed that Indian."

Preacher didn't say anything. What had doomed them was their decision to start west at the wrong time of year. Even if Peter hadn't shot that Arikara brave, the whole bunch would have died up in the mountains, probably when the first blizzard roared through. They were just too green to live.

But they still had a chance to fight their way out of this. They couldn't give up hope.

Suddenly, Peter stalked up behind Roger and grabbed his shoulder. As he jerked his brother around, Peter snapped, "I heard what you said! You're blaming me for everything, just like you always do!"

Roger knocked Peter's hand off his shoulder. "Get away from me. It's bad enough we have to fight on the same side. If I'm going to die, I don't want you anywhere near me."

"Damn it, we're brothers!"

"You should have thought of that before you . . . you . . ."

Roger couldn't bring himself to say it, but they all knew he was talking about Dorothy.

"This isn't my fault," Peter insisted stubbornly. "I only killed one Indian. Preacher killed a dozen of them! Jonathan and Geoffrey attacked them too."

Angela crawled out from under the wagon. "Peter, just stop it," she said with an infinite weariness in her voice. "It doesn't matter now. Go back where Preacher told you and do the best you can. That's all any of us can do now."

Peter turned to her and reached out. "Angela, at least you can say you forgive me," he pleaded. "We've meant so much to each other. You . . . You can't just turn away now. . . ."

"You turned away from me, Peter," she whispered. Her hands tightened on the rifle she held. "No matter what happens, it's over between us. I can't ever love you again."

"Angela . . ." Peter looked and sounded utterly wretched.

"I'm sorry, Peter. But we can't change what's happened."

He looked around. Confusion, anger, sorrow, resentment . . . All those emotions and more played across his face. Finally he said in a surly tone, "All right, if that's the way you want it, that's the way it'll be, I guess." He went back to the other end of the wagon and took up his position there, staring dully out across the open valley toward the Indians, who still waited there.

"Are they out of rifle range where they are now?" Jonathan asked from under the wagon when Angela had rejoined him there.

"No, but it'd be a heck of a shot if any of us hit one of 'em from here," Preacher said. "I could maybe do it, especially if I had a shot or two to sight in, but if we start shootin', they'll just pull back and then we'll have wasted some powder and lead."

"This waiting is hard," Jonathan mumbled.

"That it is, Silvertip, that it is."

The sun was low in the western sky by now, and its red glare reflecting off the snow made the defenders squint. Preacher wondered for a moment if Swift Arrow might try an attack just as the sun went down, in hopes that the white men on the rise would be blinded. He didn't think the war chief would risk that, preferring to wait until dark when sneaking up on the wagons would be even easier, but where Injuns were concerned, nothing could be ruled out. They usually did whatever they took a notion to, whether it made sense to a white man's way of thinkin' or not.

"Anybody wants anything to eat or drink, now's the time," Preacher said a short while later. "Or if you just want to stretch your legs."

Angela and Jonathan came out from under the wagon. Angela went to check on Geoffrey and the children while Jonathan got a dipper of water from one of the barrels. The water had ice crystals in it but hadn't frozen solid yet. He and Roger stood talking quietly while Preacher said to Nate, "How you doin', partner?"

Nate's head bobbed in a nod. "I'm all right. I'm scared, though, Preacher."

"So am I."

"Really?" Nate looked up at him as if he couldn't believe that. "I didn't think you ever got scared, Preacher."

"Sure. I been scared plumb half to death plenty o' times in my life. Like when I had to fight that grizzly bear. Only a fool wouldn't be scared goin' up against an ol' grizz like that. Or when we was at war with the British, and the outfit I was part of had to fight 'em at New Orleans. That was mighty scary too. I couldn't even begin to count the times I been scared."

"But you never quit. You never ran."

"Well . . ." Preacher rubbed his bearded jaw. "When the Good Lord was handin' out the things that fill up a man and make him what he is, He didn't see fit to put a whole lot of back up in me. It ain't somethin' I did a-purpose, you understand. It's just the way I am."

"I wish I could be as brave."

"You plan to keep them rifles loaded, like I asked you?"

"Yeah, sure," Nate said.

"If a fella does what's got to be did, no matter how scared he is, then he's just as brave as anybody else."

"As brave as you, you mean?"

Preacher squeezed the youngster's shoulder for a second. "I sure do."

Nate grinned. "Thanks, Preacher. I—"

Whatever he was going to add remained unsaid, because at that moment Angela let out a startled cry and said, "Oh, my God! Peter! What's he doing?"

Preacher wheeled around, feeling a flash of anger toward himself because he had let the conversation with Nate distract him. He hadn't been keeping an eye on the situation as well as he should have. He hadn't noticed when Peter Galloway left the wagons.

By now, Peter was a hundred yards away, striding out into the valley, heading straight toward that Arikara war party.

35

Preacher stared at Peter's retreating back, for a second unable to comprehend what the man thought he was doing. Then Preacher stepped out away from the wagons and bellowed, "Galloway! Damn it, get back here, Galloway!"

Peter ignored him and kept walking toward the Indians.

Angela clutched Preacher's arm. "Stop him!" she said. "For God's sake, he's going to get himself killed!"

Maybe that's just what he wants, Preacher thought. It sure as hell looked like that was what Peter was trying to do.

Preacher shook off Angela's hand and trotted forward, snapping a command over his shoulder. "Ever'body stay here. Take your positions and be ready to fire."

Then he hurried after Peter, who still didn't look back, even when Preacher shouted at him to stop.

Preacher kept an eye on the distances involved. Peter wasn't in range of the war party's bows, but if he kept up that fast walk for much longer, he would be. Preacher started to yell at him again, but before he could, Peter began to shout. The words were directed at the Arikara war chief.

"Swift Arrow! Swift Arrow, can you hear me?"

There was no response from the Indians, but Preacher knew they could hear Peter just fine.

"Swift Arrow, I'm the one you want! I killed your brave back there near your village! Take me, and let the others go!"

Preacher kept trotting after Peter, and finally Peter glanced back. He broke into a run, but he didn't stop yelling at the Indians.

"I surrender!" Peter shouted. "The others had nothing to do with it! Let them go, and you can have me!"

The damn fool didn't realize that the Injuns already had him. His surrendering now wouldn't change a blessed thing. The war party wanted vengeance, not only for the young man Peter had murdered, but also for the warriors they had lost when they set out to even the score. Peter thought he was making a noble gesture—maybe in an attempt to redeem himself at least partially in his wife's eyes, Preacher thought—but in reality all he was doing was throwing away his life and making the odds for everyone else even worse.

Preacher would have to catch the dumb son of a bitch, though, before he could explain all that. And there might not be time for that, because Peter was almost close enough for the Indians to risk a shot . . .

In fact, it was just a second later when an arrow came whistling through the air. It fell short, but Peter still didn't stop. "Kill me!" he shrieked. "Kill me and let the others go!"

"Galloway, stop now!" Preacher roared. His long legs had cut the gap between them until he was only about twenty yards behind Peter. "They're gonna—"

They did. The next arrow flew true and slammed into Peter's chest. He cried out in pain as the flint arrowhead tore into his body, burying itself deeply. He stumbled but stayed on his feet and kept running toward the Indians. "Take me!" he croaked. "Don't kill the oth—"

Two more arrows thudded into him, one in the chest, one in the belly. Preacher heard screams coming from the wagons far behind him as Angela saw her husband being pincushioned with arrows. Peter staggered and twisted around so that Preacher saw the shafts protruding from his body. Peter turned his head and looked back at Preacher, his eyes wide with pain and the realization that he was doomed. Preacher began to back away, knowing that he was dangerously close to being in range himself.

"I'm . . . sorry," Peter choked out, and then another arrow ripped into his side. He twisted the rest of the way around under the impact, so that he was facing toward Preacher and the wagons. He fell to his knees.

A final arrow hit him in the back of the neck and penetrated all the way through so that the bloody arrowhead emerged from his throat. Peter opened his mouth but couldn't scream or say anything else because of the flood of crimson that came from his mouth. He flopped forward, landing awkwardly because of all the arrows sticking out of his body.

Preacher wheeled around and lit a shuck for the wagons.

He heard the Arikara a-whoopin' and a-hollerin' behind him. An arrow zipped past him, and fluttering sounds behind him told him that more arrows were falling short. He risked a glance over his shoulder and saw that the war party was giving chase. One of their most hated enemies had come close to them, almost in their grasp, and they hadn't been able to resist the temptation to come after him.

A grim smile tugged at Preacher's mouth. This might work out after all. It would all depend on how fast he could run. . . .

It was a fantastic race with stakes of life and death there in the fading light. Preacher was a hundred yards ahead of the Indians, but he had to cover almost three hundred yards to reach the relative safety of the wagons. He was a fast runner, though. The snow slowed him down a little, but his pursuers had to contend with the same obstacle.

He remembered hearing about John Colter's epic race with hostile Blackfeet back in the fall of '08. This was nothing like that, of course; Colter had been stripped naked by his Indian captors and then had to run five miles to escape from them. Preacher had all his clothes and had to cover less than a quarter of a mile. But he still thought about Colter as he thudded across the open ground with the Arikara howling in pursuit.

Preacher slowed down. He could have run faster, but he didn't want to. If he drew away from them, they would realize they couldn't catch him and would turn back. He didn't want that. He wanted to pull them on, so he let them come closer and closer to him. Some of the Indians stopped, nocked arrows, and let fly at him again. The feathered missiles rained around him. Preacher kept going.

He was about a hundred yards away from the wagons when the defenders opened up. He heard the roar of exploding powder and saw puffs of smoke from around the wagon that was parked just beyond the rise. Behind him, one of the 'Rees yelled in pain, and when Preacher glanced back, he saw that two of them were down. The others came on, but they were slowing now that they realized Preacher had become the bait in a trap.

Jonathan, Roger, and Angela had had all the rifles loaded before they fired their first volley. That allowed them to fire again quickly, and they did so, the heavy lead balls whistling over the prairie to thud into the bodies of some of the onrushing Indians. Preacher stopped and whirled, throwing the Hawken to his shoulder. He cocked the rifle and drew a bead in the blink of an eye, then pressed the trigger. Flame spurted from the muzzle as the Hawken blasted. Another Arikara warrior spun off his feet as Preacher's lead tore through him.

Preacher pulled his right-hand pistol and fired, was rewarded by the sight of blood spraying in the air from a warrior's shattered shoulder. He didn't delay any longer. Turning toward the wagons, he broke into a run again, and this time he didn't hold back.

More shots came from the wagon, irregularly spaced now instead of together in a volley. With Nate's help, the defenders were reloading and firing as fast as they could. Preacher threw a look over his shoulder and saw that the Indians were retreating, leaving their dead and wounded behind for the moment, although he was sure they would come back for them later. He counted six bodies on the ground, and he thought one or two more of the fleeing warriors were limping and staggering from their wounds. Peter's crazy notion had allowed the others to strike a heavy blow at the enemy.

But they were still outnumbered by more than two to one, Preacher thought, and it would be dark soon. Swift Arrow wouldn't give up either. He would still rush the wagons as soon as night had fallen.

Preacher slowed to a trot as he went up the rise to the wagons. His heart slugged heavily in his chest. He was all whipcord, whang leather, and muscle, but that had been a hard run in cold, thin air. He would be glad for a chance to catch his breath.

Jonathan met him. "We got some of them!" the old-timer exulted. "I saw some of them go down!"

"You sure did," Preacher told him. "I figure we done for five or six of 'em, and there's a couple more wounded, maybe bad enough so they're out of the fight."

Jonathan's grin vanished, to be replaced by a solemn look. "Peter . . . ?"

Preacher shook his head. "He never had no chance."

Angela crawled out from underneath the wagon in time to hear that. A sob caught in her throat. Roger went to her and put an arm around her shoulder to comfort her. Both of them had lost a spouse in the past couple of days. Even though Angela had come to despise Peter and had declared their marriage over, there had still been enough of a bond remaining between them so that she felt his loss. It had to hurt, Preacher thought. Best to let her cry it out.

But only for a short time, because the sun was gone and its light was beginning to fade from the sky. In less than an hour, Preacher thought, Swift Arrow and the rest of the Arikara war party would be coming, and one way or another, this would be the end of the long chase.

While he had the chance, Preacher went to check on Geoffrey and the younger children. Mary and Brad were sniffling, still frightened by all the shooting that had gone on earlier. If they knew that their father was dead, Preacher couldn't tell it. He didn't say anything about what had happened to Peter, but he could tell from the bleak look in Geoffrey's eyes that the older man knew about it. "What now?" he asked.

"Same as before," Preacher said. "When the time comes, we fight as best we can."

Geoffrey nodded grimly. He sat on one of the bunks with four loaded pistols at his side. If it came down to it, Preacher was sure that Geoffrey would defend the young'uns to his last breath.

Preacher dropped down from the tailgate and saw Nate coming toward him in the dusk. "Preacher," the boy said, "did I do all right?"

"As far as I could tell, you done just fine. You ready to do some loadin'?"

"Yes, sir."

Preacher patted his shoulder. "Well, it shouldn't be too long now."

He went back to the first wagon and nodded to Roger, who stood there leaning on a rifle, the butt resting on the snowy ground. "That was terrible," Roger said quietly, keeping his voice low so that Angela, who was at the other end of the wagon with Jonathan, wouldn't overhear. "I didn't know Peter had that much courage. It was a grand gesture."

It was a stupid gesture, Preacher thought, and hadn't accomplished a damned thing except to cost them a defender. Still, Peter had been Roger's brother, and just as with Angela, there were still bonds there despite all the trouble. Roger had lost a father, a wife, and a brother in mighty short order.

Those deaths gnawed at Preacher's innards too. He had thrown in with these immigrants with the goal of getting them back to safety. *All* of them. He had known from the start how unlikely that was, of course, but still, losing any of them bothered him. He hadn't had anything to do with Dorothy Galloway's death, of course, and he had tried to get Peter to come back and not throw his life away. But there was a way of looking at Simon's death that made Preacher to blame for it. After all, Preacher had sent him out to stand guard before that storm hit and froze him to death.

Of course, somebody had to stand guard, and if it hadn't been Simon, it would have been somebody else. Jonathan or Geoffrey or Roger might be dead now instead of Simon. Preacher wasn't going to lose much sleep over what had happened—assuming he lived through the perilous night to come—but he wouldn't forget about it either. Tragedy had dogged this expedition even before he joined it, and he hadn't been able to prevent it completely since then.

"Got all the guns loaded?" he asked.

Roger nodded. "Loaded and primed. All we have to do is cock and fire. But once it's dark, how will we know the Indians are attacking?"

"We'll have to let them make the first move," Preacher said. "It's risky, but we don't have much choice."

"So they take the first shot and we hope they miss?"

"Yeah, pretty much," Preacher said with a grin.

"How many of them are left?"

"Twelve, fourteen, somewhere along in there."

"And there are five of us," Roger mused. "More than three to one odds."

"I've faced worse and come through all right."

Roger turned to look at him, but Preacher couldn't read his expression in the fading light. "Angela is quite fond of you. You'll take care of her, if you both live through this."

"This ain't the time to think about that."

"And the children," Roger said, ignoring Preacher's comment. "Someone will have to look after them."

"That'd be a good job for the two of you," Preacher pointed out.

"The two of . . . You mean Angela and me?"

"Y'all been through a lot together, and you both love them kids. I ain't sayin' or meanin' any more than that. I reckon right now you're thinkin' that you ain't got a lot to live for, Roger. I'm just sayin' that maybe you do."

For a moment, Roger didn't say anything. Then he said quietly, "You're an odd man, Preacher."

"So I been told," Preacher replied with a chuckle.

"You see hope where there shouldn't be any. You don't back down and you don't give up. Talking to you, I almost find myself thinking that maybe we will make it."

"Remember that," Preacher told him, "and keep on a-fightin' even it looks like there ain't no use. We'll pull through, one way or t'other."

Roger nodded and looked out across the open ground in front of the rise. "I'm ready," he declared.

That was good, Preacher thought, because the sky was black and the stars were out and in a matter of minutes the Arikara would be coming to wreak their vengeance on the hated whites.

That meant it was time for him to go.

36

He made sure everyone was back in position and ready for what was to come. Every gun in the darkened, makeshift stronghold was loaded. All the defenders were alert, their eyes turned in the direction the Indians would come from. When Preacher was sure he had done everything he could to prepare them for the battle, he drifted back into the shadows and said softly, "Dog." The big animal followed him soundlessly as he slipped away from the wagons.

It would be a few minutes before they noticed he was gone, he thought. They might not even tumble to that fact until after the Indians launched their attack. By that time it would be too late for the defenders to waste any time wondering about his disappearance. They would be too busy fighting for their lives.

He catfooted along in a low crouch just behind the rise, moving about seventy-five yards before he dropped to hands and knees and began crawling. Within minutes his hands and knees were soaked and cold from the snow, but he ignored the discomfort as best he could. Beside him, Dog bellied along, following Preacher's example. Neither of them could afford to be spotted, not until they were good and ready.

He stretched out flat as his senses warned him that someone was moving nearby. Several shapes ghosted past him about twenty yards away. The war party had spread out, and now the Indians were closing in. Preacher glanced toward the wagon at the top of the rise, barely able to make out its bulk in the thick darkness. The stars were bright, but what light they gave off seemed to be swallowed up by the heavens before it ever reached the earth. It was as dark as the bottom of a well, and as Preacher came up in a crouch again and began to move, he was guided by instinct as much as he was by sight.

Smell helped too. He caught a whiff of bear grease and knew he wasn't far now from the Injuns.

As he came up soundlessly behind them, he began to be able to pick them out better, indistinct shapes here and there, dark against the snow. He heard one of them take a deep breath and knew that was his signal to go into action. They were getting ready to charge.

Preacher stood up straight, about ten feet behind one of the skulking Indians, and leveled his Hawken. He snapped, "Dog!" and then pulled the trigger.

Dog leaped forward, choosing one of the other warriors as his prey. The rifle roared and bucked against Preacher's shoulder and the heavy ball that it launched exploded through the body of the Arikara brave, smashing him face-first to the ground. Dog hit his target an instant later, his ferocious charge landing him on the startled Indian's back. The man cried out as he went down, but the yell ended in a grotesque gurgle as Dog's teeth sank into his throat and ripped it out.

Preacher dropped the Hawken and yanked out the brace of pistols. They were double-shotted and loaded with heavy charges, and they boomed like pocket cannons as Preacher fired. Three more of the Arikara went down, knocked off their feet by the scything lead.

"Open fire!" Preacher yelled. "Open fire!" He knew the shout would reach the defenders at the top of the rise. He hoped that, once they realized he was right in there among the Indians they wouldn't hesitate for fear of hitting him. He had known what he was doing when he decided to hit the war party from behind, and he was willing to take his chances.

Welcome spurts of flame came from the rifles around and underneath the wagon as Preacher bounded forward. As a dark shape loomed in front of him, he struck with one of the pistols and felt the satisfying crunch of a skull being crushed by the blow. Preacher shoved the dying man out of the way and dropped the empty pistols. He reached behind his back and brought up two more, loaded and primed. His thumbs found the hammers and pulled them back as feet rushed at him from the side.

He pivoted smoothly, bringing up the right-hand gun. The flame that licked out from the muzzle as he fired briefly lit up the face of the warrior who took both balls almost point blank. Then most of his head disappeared in a bloody spray of brains and bone, blown right off his shoulders by the double charge.

Preacher heard fierce growling and screaming and knew that Dog was still in the middle of the fracas, pulling down his prey just as his wolf ancestors had done for untold centuries. A grunt of effort warned Preacher in time to prompt him to duck under the sweeping blow of a tomahawk. As the warrior who wielded the 'hawk stumbled against him, thrown off balance by the miss, Preacher slammed the barrel of the empty pistol across the bridge of his nose, shattering bone and sending deadly splinters up into the man's brain. Jerking as he died, the Indian toppled off his feet.

Preacher still had a loaded pistol in his left hand. The next instant, he needed it as two of the warriors rushed him. He fired, hoping to take both of them down with the double shot, but only one man was hit. That one died on his feet, his heart pulped by the ball, as he continued to stumble forward for a few steps before diving face-first into the snow. The other one crashed into Preacher and bore him over backward. The Indian landed on top of him and knocked all the air out of his lungs, and for a moment all Preacher could do was lie there stunned as the Arikara warrior drove the blade of a knife at his throat.

* * *

The defenders had been taken completely by surprise when Preacher started yelling and shooting from behind the Indians. None of them had realized he was gone. But the uproar about fifty yards in front of the wagons gave them something to aim at. Everyone who pressed the trigger of a rifle worried about hitting Preacher, but they fired anyway, knowing that the survival of the entire group depended on winning this fight.

The rifle in Roger's hands was empty when he saw one of the Indians closing in on him. The Arikara howled a war cry and fired an arrow that clipped the sleeve of Roger's coat as it went past. The warrior dropped his bow and grabbed his tomahawk instead, lunging at Roger with his arm upraised to strike a killing blow.

Roger reversed the rifle and leaned in, swinging it like a club. The stock shattered on the Indian's jaw and broke bone as well. The warrior went down. Roger struck again and again with the broken rifle, using the breech to batter in the enemy's skull. He knew he was fighting and cursing like a madman, but he didn't care. All the fear and grief and anger of the past few days came flooding out of him in an incoherent cry as he beat the Indian to death.

Under the wagon, Jonathan and Angela fired as fast as they could, taking the reloaded rifles that Nate slid up to them. But then several of the Indians were right there in front of them, and Jonathan shoved Angela back as he crawled forward to get in front of her and shield her with his own body. He rammed the barrel of an empty rifle into the belly of an on-rushing warrior, and as the Indian doubled over in pain, Jonathan reached up and got him by the neck. He came to his feet and slammed the man's head against the sideboard of the wagon.

Pain lanced into his side like fire. He gasped and reached down to grasp the shaft of an arrow. It hadn't lodged deeply, so he was able to rip it loose. As another Indian grappled with him, Jonathan jammed the arrowhead at the man's left eye. It went in cleanly. Jonathan heard the eyeball pop and felt the spray of liquid from it on his face. The Indian staggered back, shrieking and pawing at his destroyed eye.

Jonathan saw a couple of them run past him and tried to get in their way, but he was too late. They were heading straight toward the wagon where Geoffrey stood guard over the children, Jonathan saw. "Geoffrey!" he shouted in warning.

As one of the Indians leaped to the tailgate, a pistol roared inside the wagon and knocked him backward. The children began to scream. Inside the wagon, Geoffrey dropped the empty pistol and snatched up another one as he crouched beside the rear opening. He was too late. A buckskin-clad figure lunged through the opening and crashed into him. Geoffrey went down. He cried out as cold steel bit deep into his belly. The stench of bear grease filled his nostrils, mixed with a coppery smell that a detached part of his brain knew came from his own blood. Feeling himself about to pass out, he summoned up the last of his strength, jammed the barrel of the pistol under the Indian's chin, and pulled the trigger. The Arikara warrior had been grunting with effort as he ripped his knife back and forth in Geoffrey's midsection, but those sounds ended abruptly with the roar of the pistol.

Mary and Brad kept crying in terror, along with the thin wailing of the baby. The children's shrieks redoubled as another dark figure clambered into the wagon.

A fierce, furry shape barreled into the Indian just before the blade found Preacher's throat. Dog bowled over the warrior and went to work on him with slashing teeth. The Arikara tried to fight back and managed to land a long gash on Dog's shoulder before the powerful jaws crunched down on his throat, ending his life.

Preacher rolled over, came up on his knees, and dove to the side as he saw a tall, powerful figure lunging at him. Swift Arrow, he thought. Had to be. The war chief was the biggest of the Arikara.

Swift Arrow came at him, starlight glittering on the knife

in one hand and the tomahawk in the other. Preacher leaped to the side to avoid a flurry of slashing blows. He still had an empty pistol in his left hand. He used his right to pull his own hunting knife from its fringed sheath.

It was almost like a dance then, across the shadowed, blood-spattered snow, as Preacher and Swift Arrow darted and lunged and circled, each man attacking and parrying in turn, moving with blinding, deadly speed. Swift Arrow's knife slashed across Preacher's upper arm, leaving a bloody wound behind, fortunately not cutting deep enough to sever any nerves or muscles. An instant later, the barrel of Preacher's pistol thudded with numbing force on the top of Swift Arrow's left shoulder. The war chief stumbled but caught himself before Preacher could press the advantage.

Back and forth they struggled. Breath rasped in Preacher's throat. His foot suddenly caught on something concealed underneath the snow, and he staggered and went to one knee. Swift Arrow rushed in at him. Preacher went on down, letting the Indian's attack go over his head. He bowled forward, knocking Swift Arrow's legs out from under him. Both men rolled away to put some distance between them, then came up to face each other again.

Preacher had dropped his pistol, but the tomahawk had slipped out of Swift Arrow's fingers. They came together, knives flashing, and suddenly they were locked motionless, less than a foot apart, each man with the fingers of his free hand wrapped desperately around the wrist of his opponent's knife hand. They strained against each other's grip, putting all their incredible strength into the effort, but for long moments neither man could budge the other.

Then Swift Arrow's left arm buckled slightly, and the tip of Preacher's blade came nearer the war chief's chest. Though Preacher didn't know it, Swift Arrow's left shoulder was broken where Preacher had hit him with the pistol. Swift Arrow struggled on anyway, gritting his teeth against the terrible pain as shattered bones ground together.

Preacher had his own problems. The gash on his left arm

had bled quite a bit, and he felt himself weakening and growing light-headed. If he passed out, even for a second, the fight would be over. Swift Arrow's knife would be in his heart in the blink of an eye. Preacher reached inside himself, drawing on all the reserves he had left. He sensed that Swift Arrow was growing weaker too. If he could just hold out, hold out a little longer . . .

Swift Arrow's left arm buckled again, and this time there was no holding back the thrust that Preacher made. The knife penetrated the war chief's buckskins, slipped through skin and flesh and muscle. Preacher shoved hard and felt the steel grate on bone as the blade passed between ribs. Swift Arrow said softly, "Ahhh . . ." Preacher pushed harder, driving the knife through the tough fibers of the Arikara's heart. He twisted the blade.

Swift Arrow's knees buckled. His hand opened and he dropped his knife as he sagged. Preacher ripped his knife free and stepped back. Swift Arrow fell to his knees, looked up at Preacher, and died. He toppled to the side like a falling tree.

Then and only then did Preacher realize there was no more shooting going on. The battle was over, he told himself as Dog came up to him and nuzzled his hand. He looked around and saw dark shapes sprawled everywhere on the ground. Then he lifted his gaze toward the wagons and saw someone hurrying toward him. His fingers tightened on the handle of the knife. He didn't know if he could fight anymore, but damned if he was going to surrender.

"Preacher!" Jonathan Galloway shouted. "Preacher, is that you?"

"Damn . . . Silvertip . . ." Preacher husked as Jonathan came up to him and reached out toward him. "I'm mighty glad . . . that's you . . ."

Jonathan grabbed his arm and held him up long enough to get an arm around his waist. Then he began helping Preacher back toward the wagons.

"Anybody . . . hurt?" Preacher managed to ask.

"I've got a cut in my side from an arrow," Jonathan said, "but it's not too bad. Roger and Angela and the children are all right. None of them were hurt. It's a miracle."

"Not . . . a miracle. Just . . . hard fightin'." Preacher forced himself to concentrate on what Jonathan had just said. "Your brother . . . Geoffrey . . . ol' Catamount . . ."

"He . . . died . . . protecting the children. I found his body when I climbed into the wagon. The Indian who killed him was lying on top of him with his head blown off."

"Aw, hell," Preacher said, and meant it.

Tears sparkled on Jonathan's cheeks, sparkled in the light of the rising moon. "He died fighting, like a mountain man. That's another marker you'll have to put up, Preacher."

"I'll do it," Preacher promised.

"At least it's over now," Jonathan said. "All the Indians are dead. We're safe. All we have to do is make it to Garvey's Fort."

"That's right. Safe," Preacher repeated. They had suffered losses, heavy losses, but now the rest of them would make it. He was sure of it.

That same night, about twenty miles to the east, four men rode through the gate in a high wall made of sod and bricks. The wall ran around the compound of several buildings that made up Garvey's Fort, the trading post and lone bastion of civilization in this part of the country. The riders were lean, hard-faced men, and when they dismounted, they went into the trading post's barroom and asked if anyone knew the whereabouts of a family called Galloway. . . .

37

Again they dug a single grave in the morning, and laid Geoffrey and Peter to rest side by side in it. Preacher was getting mighty tired of lowering blanket-shrouded shapes into the ground. He figured Garvey's Fort was only about twenty miles away, though, and with the threat of the Arikara war party taken care of, he hoped they could make it the rest of the way without running into any more trouble.

One thing he noticed as he checked the bodies of the warriors was that Mart Hawley was no longer with them. He wondered what had happened to the renegade trapper. It could be that Swift Arrow had gotten tired of him and killed him, or maybe Hawley had sickened and died from the wound he'd suffered during the fight back in the foothills. Or maybe he had just frozen to death. Preacher hoped that whatever had happened, he had crossed paths with Hawley for the last time.

He didn't like leaving the bodies of the Arikara for the scavengers, but there was no handy gully or ravine where they could be placed, and he didn't want to take the time necessary to dig a grave big enough for a dozen corpses. Still, it bothered him, and when he said as much, Jonathan frowned at him and said, "Why? They were trying to kill us. I don't see why you'd worry about not burying them."

"You've learned a lot about frontier ways, Silvertip," Preacher told him, "but you still got some things to learn.

Them old boys were our enemies, sure enough, but they weren't without honor. They were tryin' to avenge a wrong that was done to their people."

"The murder of that young man," Jonathan said solemnly.

Preacher nodded. "That's right. The way they looked at it, they was just after justice. I can't say as I disagree with 'em."

"And yet you helped us. You probably killed more of the Arikara than the rest of us put together."

"And if they'd just gone after Peter, I might've stayed out of it. But it wasn't right for them to try to kill the rest of you either." Preacher shrugged. "Most of the time in life, there ain't no right or wrong answers, just shades of good and bad on both sides. You got to go with which side looks the best."

"Most of the time?"

"Yep. But there's such a thing as pure evil too, and now and then you run across it. When you do, you fight it. Simple as that."

Jonathan shook his head. "I don't think there's anything all that simple about you, Preacher."

"You just ain't known me long enough," the mountain man said with a grin.

There had been a heap of crying over Geoffrey and Peter, but everybody was dry-eyed again as the wagons rolled eastward later that morning. White clouds floated in the sky, pushed around by a breeze from the south that was still cold, but not as cold as it had been. Just as before, they would have a few days of better weather before another storm came roaring down out of Canada, Preacher thought as he rode out ahead of the wagons with Dog at his side. By the time that happened, they would be safe and sound at Garvey's Fort.

Angela and Nate had to each drive a wagon now. The young'un was nervous about handling a team, but his pa and his uncle had given him some pointers and Preacher was confident that Nate would do just fine. The boy had the right stuff in him.

Roger had come through the fight without a scratch, as had Angela. Jonathan had a shallow arrow wound in his side, but Angela had cleaned it and bound it up, and with any luck it would heal just fine. The injury was stiff and sore but not enough so to prevent Jonathan from driving one of the wagons.

The temperature remained cold enough to keep the snow from melting very fast, although the sun took care of some of it. The wagons made good time because Preacher kept them moving all day with only short, occasional stops. He wanted to cover enough ground today so that they could reach the fort the next day. By nightfall, he was fairly certain that they had. He thought he could have ridden ahead and reached Garvey's place that night, but that would have meant leaving the wagons and he didn't want to do that. He could wait until the next day and ride in with them.

That night they had a good fire and a hot supper, and although the mood was still solemn because of the losses the group had suffered, there was also talk about what would happen the next day when they reached the fort, and even a mention or two of going on to Oregon in the spring. Preacher sipped from a cup of coffee as he looked across the fire at Roger and Angela sitting together on a wagon tongue. They had been through a hell of a lot, and while the friendship they shared might or might not blossom into anything else, at least they would always have that friendship. Preacher hoped it stayed strong.

Far behind the wagons, Mart Hawley walked along, his feet scuffing in the thin coat of snow on the ground. He saw the faint, distant eye of the fire and knew the pilgrims were there. He wasn't trying to catch up. The shape he was in, he didn't want another showdown with Preacher. He had food now, and weapons, all scavenged from the bodies of the Arikara war party when he came on them earlier in the day. He would survive and grow stronger and recover from his wound, and maybe one of these days, when the time was right, his trail would cross Preacher's once again.

An ugly grin tugged at Hawley's mouth as he thought

about that. He wouldn't forget, and he sure as hell wouldn't forgive, all that Preacher had done. Sooner or later he would have his revenge.

One of these days . . .

The flat terrain meant that the walls of the fort were visible long before the wagons reached them. Preacher, ranging out ahead on the dun, saw them before anyone else and galloped back to tell the others. "Hallelujah!" Jonathan exclaimed. A short time later, when the wagons came in sight of the fort, the children began chattering excitedly. Preacher couldn't even begin to imagine what a grueling, terrifying journey this had been for them.

People inside the fort must have seen them coming, because the gates opened and several riders emerged. As they came closer, Preacher recognized one of them as a trapper he knew, Cephus Rattan. He lifted a hand in greeting and called, "Howdy, Cephus!"

Rattan reined his horse to a stop and stared at the wagons trailing behind Preacher. "Whoo-eee!" the lean, bearded trapper exclaimed. "What you got there, Preacher? Been pickin' up strays?"

"I reckon you could say that," Preacher replied with a grin. "I ran into a whole family of pilgrims who thought they could make it over the Rockies with winter comin' on."

Rattan shook his head at the sheer damned foolishness of that idea.

"I got 'em turned around and brought 'em back here," Preacher continued. "Figured they could try again next spring."

"That was smart of you," one of the other men said. He was tall, powerfully built, and sported a thick black mustache. "Fred Garvey," he said, introducing himself as he thrust out a hand. "This is my place."

Preacher shook hands with the trader, whom he had never crossed trails with before. "Pleased to meet you." He jerked a thumb at the wagons. "Those folks behind me are the Galloways."

"Galloway?" Rattan repeated, sounding surprised.

"From Philadelphia?" Garvey asked.

Preacher tensed. Something was wrong here. "Yeah, that's where they're from," he said. "How in blazes did you boys know that?"

Rattan, Garvey, and the other men, who looked like trappers but were unknown to Preacher, glanced at each other, and then Garvey said, "There are some men inside the fort looking for a family name of Galloway that came out here from Philadelphia. They rode in a couple of days ago."

"Hard-lookin' bunch too," Rattan said, leaning over in the saddle to spit on the ground.

"We told them we didn't know any Galloways," Garvey said, "and it was true at the time. They said they'd stock up on supplies and rest their horses for a day or two before they left."

"And they're still there?" Preacher asked sharply.

Garvey nodded. "Still there. They keep to themselves and don't say much, but like Cephus said, they look like hard cases."

"I'm obliged for the information," Preacher said with a nod of gratitude. "I'll try to find out what it's all about." He wheeled the dun and rode back to the wagons, about seventy-five yards behind him. Rattan, Garvey, and the other men trailed behind him.

Preacher held up a hand, signaling for Roger to stop. Roger was at the reins of the lead wagon now, with Jonathan bringing up the rear and Angela and Nate second and third in line, respectively.

"Why are we stopping?" Roger asked. "We're almost at the fort. I can see it right up there."

"There's somethin' we better talk about first," Preacher said, leaning forward to ease himself in the saddle. "Some men at the fort are lookin' for a family named Galloway. A family from Philadelphia. I don't reckon that's a coincidence, do you?"

Roger's face tightened. "What sort of men?"

"A bad sort, accordin' to what I been told. What's this all about, Roger? Who are those fellas?"

Roger sighed and said, "I was hoping . . . we all hoped . . . that no one would follow us."

The other wagons had stopped behind Roger's, and now Jonathan came forward, carrying a rifle. "What's the holdup?" he asked. "Why aren't we going on into the fort?"

Roger turned to look at his uncle. "There's trouble, Jonathan," he said. "Some men are there looking for us."

"For us? What in the world for?"

"Money, I suspect," Roger said heavily. "They've been paid to track us down."

"Spit it out," Preacher said, his voice like flint now. He had suspected all along that there was more to the story than he had been told, and he was tired of having the truth hidden from him.

Angela hopped down from the wagon she was driving and came forward too, in time to hear Roger say, "My father paid to outfit us for this trip, but what none of the rest of us knew except for Peter and myself was that most of the money was . . . well . . . stolen."

"Stolen!" Jonathan exclaimed. "Simon was a thief?"

"He took the money from his partner, but only because the man was a thief to start with! He had been cheating Pa for years." Roger's voice lost some of its certainty. "At least, that's what Pa said. . . ."

"So now this old partner of your pa's has a grudge against him and hired men to come out here and look for him," Preacher said, having no trouble connecting up the rest of the story. He added contemptuously, "Bounty hunters."

"That's what I suspect, yes," Roger said.

"Why didn't you tell the rest of us, or at least Geoffrey and me?" Jonathan wanted to know.

Roger shook his head. "I suppose Pa was ashamed. I . . . I

guess he really *was* a thief. But he asked Peter and me to keep it to ourselves, and we decided to honor his wishes."

"So that's why we had to leave so quickly," Angela said, "why there was such a hurry about getting out of Philadelphia. Simon wanted to get far away before his crime was discovered."

Roger nodded miserably. "That's right."

Well, things made a heap more sense now, Preacher thought, but there was still one very important question left unanswered: What were they going to do now?

"Those men who are looking for us . . ." Roger said. "When we tell them that Pa is dead, I suppose they'll go back where they came from and report that to the man who hired them?"

"Maybe," Preacher said. "It just depends on how much vengeance the fella wants. He may have given them orders to go after the whole bunch of you."

"But that's not right! Pa was the one who took the money. The rest of us had nothing to do with it."

"Yeah, and your brother was the one who shot that Arikara brave too, but that didn't stop the 'Rees from wantin' to lift the hair from all of you."

Roger paled. "My God! You mean they may try to . . . to murder the rest of us?"

"I wouldn't put it past 'em. I could be wrong, though. Only one way to find out."

"Yes, we'll go in and talk to them—" Roger began.

"Nope. *I'll* go in and talk to 'em, try to find out just how bad they want you folks."

"No, Preacher, that's not fair," Jonathan said. "You've done so much for us already, we can't ask you to risk your life for us again."

Preacher ignored him. "Keep the wagons right here," he told Roger. "Don't you come on in unless me or Cephus here rides out to tell you it's all right." He glanced at Rattan. "That all right with you, Cephus?"

The trapper nodded. "Sure, Preacher."

Fred Garvey spoke up, saying, "I can't take sides in this. I've got to do business here—"

"Sure," Preacher said. "I understand, Garvey. We'll settle this amongst ourselves, without gettin' anybody else mixed up in it."

"I'm obliged for that."

Preacher lifted the dun's reins, but Angela stepped forward and stopped him by laying a hand on the horse's shoulder. She looked up at him and said, "Why are you doing this for us? I'm not sure we deserve it."

Preacher wasn't sure they did either, and yet he had been around them enough to know that there was good in all of them, especially Angela and Nate and Jonathan. But he didn't know how to explain that, so he just said again, "Stay here. I'll be back."

Then he turned and rode toward the fort.

38

Rattan, Garvey, and the other men who had come out from the fort followed Preacher. The gates were still open. Preacher rode through them and turned to ask Garvey, "Where are those fellas now?"

"In the bar inside the trading post. That's where they've spent most of their time since they got here."

Preacher reined to a stop in front of the long, low building that housed the trading post. The building was constructed of blocks of sod carved out of the prairie, but instead of the usual thatched roof, it had a wooden one, made of thick planks that must have been carted out here by wagon from St. Louis. That had probably been expensive.

He swung down from the saddle and looped the reins around a hitchin' post next to the building's low porch. When he swung open the heavy door and stepped inside, it took his eyes a few seconds to adjust to the dimness. The trading post had no windows and was lit by candles and a few lanterns hung on pegs, so the air inside was close and stuffy, hazed by smoke, and smelled of the buffalo chips being burned in a potbellied stove in the corner. Even inside, Preacher's breath fogged a little from the cold. The stove didn't do much to ward off the chill.

Preacher's instincts helped him recognize the men he was looking for. There were four of them. They sat bunched around a rough-hewn table, a jug of whiskey and four cups in front of them. All of them wore thick coats and high boots. One sported a fur cap while the others all had floppy-brimmed felt hats much like the one Preacher wore. Their coats were open, and Preacher saw the butts of pistols sticking up behind their belts.

He walked toward them. They watched him warily as he approached. Coming to a stop a few feet from the table, he nodded to them and said, "I hear you fellas are lookin' for a family called Galloway."

"That's right." The words came from the man in the fur cap, who seemed to be the spokesman. "You know where we can find them?"

"How come you're lookin' for 'em?"

"That's our business," Fur Cap said. "Might make it worth your while, though, if you can put us on their trail."

Preacher shook his head. "You don't want to go messin' with the Galloways. They're pretty good folks. They've had a passel o' bad luck, and they need to be left alone."

That sharpened the interest of all four men. They leaned forward eagerly, and Fur Cap said, "It sure sounds like you know where they are, mister. You'd be well advised to tell us and then keep your nose outta our business."

"Never was too good at that," Preacher said, his voice deceptively mild. His tone hardened as he went on. "Simon Galloway is dead. He froze to death a few nights ago and is buried about thirty-five or forty miles west o' here. Go back to the man who hired you and tell him it's all over."

For a long moment, none of the men said anything as they studied Preacher. Then Fur Cap sneered and said, "You know the whole story, do you?"

"Enough of it."

Fur Cap shook his head. "No, you don't know enough. You don't know me, mister. Once I take on a job, I do it. I been paid to settle up with the Galloways, and that's what I intend to do. That's what we all intend to do."

The other hard cases nodded their agreement.

"What about the money?" Preacher asked harshly. "If you get some of it back, is that enough to satisfy you—and the man who hired you?" He didn't know how much of the stolen money, if any, the Galloways still had, but he thought it was worth a try.

Fur Cap shot down that hope by slowly shaking his head. "It ain't about the money anymore. Like I said, it's about settlin' the score."

"Well, then, you'll have to start with me," Preacher said quietly.

Fur Cap's eyes narrowed. "Who the hell are you anyway?"

Preacher would have answered, *A friend of the Galloways,* but he didn't get a chance to. Rattan and the others had followed him into the trading post, and now the lean trapper laughed and said, "Why, mister, that there is Preacher."

Fur Cap's breath hissed between his teeth. "Preacher!" His hand darted toward the gun at his waist as he kicked backward and came up out of the chair. "Get him!" The other three went into action an eyeblink later.

But that was an eyeblink too late, because Preacher's hands had already swept underneath his coat and closed around the butts of his pistols. He brought them out and up and flame spurted from the muzzles, throwing a garish red glare on the corner where the four hired killers had been sitting. One of the balls from the left-hand pistol thudded into the center of Fur Cap's forehead and blew a sizable chunk of his brains out the back of his head. The other ball missed, but it wasn't needed. Both lead missiles from the right-hand pistol struck one of the other men at the point where his arm met his shoulder and nearly tore the limb off. Blood fountained as the arm flopped loosely, held in place only by a couple of strands of gristle. The man fell back in the corner, screaming and gurgling as he bled to death.

Preacher threw himself forward as the other two men fired. The shots went over his head. The roar of exploding powder was deafening at such close range. Preacher slid across the table and barreled into both men, spreading his arms so he could take them down. They all crashed to the floor.

Swinging one of the pistols in a short, backhanded arc, Preacher broke one man's jaw. The man rolled away moaning, out of the fight for the moment. The other man grappled desperately with Preacher, forcing him to drop both pistols. The bounty hunter fumbled at the handle of a heavy-bladed knife sheathed at his waist. Preacher got a hand on the man's wrist just as the knife came free. He pinned the man's arm down and locked the fingers of his other hand around his opponent's throat. Preacher hung on tight as the man kicked and spasmed underneath him, face turning dark and tongue bulging. Finally the man went limp. Preacher didn't know if he was dead or had just passed out, and didn't particularly care which it was either.

The other man, the one with the broken jaw, hit him from the side then, mouthing incoherent curses as he knocked Preacher sprawling. He went for Preacher's throat, but Preacher was too fast for him. Preacher's arm looped around the man's neck and pressed down like a bar of iron, and as they rolled over and over on the hard-packed dirt floor, a sudden loud cracking sound signaled a broken neck. The last of the hired killers jerked violently and died.

Slowly, Preacher climbed to his feet. He wiped the back of his hand across his mouth, then bent to pick up his hat, which had fallen off when he tackled the two men. As he settled the hat on his head, he looked around at Garvey, Rattan, and the other men in the trading post and said, "I'm obliged to you for not mixin' in that, boys. It was my fight."

"Didn't figure you really needed the help," Rattan said with a grin. "Hell, there was only four of 'em. 'Tweren't really your fight, though, Preacher. You was just takin' up for them Galloways."

"Somebody's got to take up for folks what can't take up for theirselves." Preacher shook his head. "I hate to think what it'll be like in this world if people ever forget how to do that."

Then he walked out of the trading post, swung up onto the

dun, called Dog, and rode out to tell the Galloways it was safe to come in.

All four of the hired killers were dead. "The fella who hired 'em won't know for a long time, if ever, what happened to them," Preacher told Roger and Jonathan that night as they sat at a table in the trading post. "By the time he finds out, you folks ought to be in Oregon next year, makin' a new life for yourselves."

"You're sure you won't guide us there?" Roger asked.

Preacher shook his head. "No need. Cephus says he's got a hankerin' to see the Pacific Ocean, and he's a good man, damn near as good as me. He'll get you there just fine."

"And what will you do?" Jonathan wanted to know.

"Thought I might head south," Preacher said with a grin. "Find someplace warmer to spend the winter. There's a place called Texas I ain't never been to yet. It's part o' Mexico, but things like that don't mean much to me. Lines on a map only matter as long as a fella lets them."

"We'll miss you," Jonathan said. "We owe you more than we can ever repay. We've learned so much from you."

"Well, you're what they call the patriarch o' this family now, Silvertip. You'll do just fine. Take care o' each other, that's the main thing." Preacher looked at Roger. "You and Angela got kids to raise. Raise 'em up right."

"We will," Roger promised solemnly.

Preacher drained the last of the whiskey in the cup in front of him, then stood up. "Come next spring, I'll put those markers up," he promised.

"You're not leaving now?" Jonathan exclaimed, startled.

"No reason to stay. It's a clear night with a big moon. Dog an' me can put some miles behind us 'fore we settle down for the night."

"But . . . but you just got back to civilization!"

Preacher grinned. "For some of us, that's all the more reason to light a shuck."

He shook hands with both of them and left the trading post, walking out into the cold, clear night. He regretted a little bit not saying good-bye to Nate, but he figured the youngster would understand. Nate had some of the same restless nature in him that had always been a part of Preacher. He had already seen that in the boy.

"Preacher."

The soft word was spoken as he reached to untie the dun's reins. The horse had been fed and watered and rested and was up to traveling a ways yet tonight. First, though, Preacher turned and saw Angela come out of the shadows on the trading post's porch.

"You're leaving?"

He nodded. "I reckon it's time."

"I . . . I hoped you'd spend the winter here too."

"Oh, I don't reckon I could do that," he said. "Bein' around people all the time, sleepin' with a roof over my head . . . some of us just ain't made for that kind o' life. We need to be out in the wild, lonesome places."

"You . . . you never wanted to stay somewhere . . . to stay with someone?"

Preacher remembered Jennie, for a change seeing her face clear as day, seeing the smile of wistful farewell on her lips, and for the last time, he allowed himself to think about what might have been.

"Once maybe," he whispered in reply to Angela's question, "but that was a long time ago." Then he bent down, brushed a kiss across her forehead, and said, "Roger's got the makin's of a good man, but he needs a good woman, and all those kids need a mama."

Clearly embarrassed, she said, "Preacher, I . . . I don't know what to say. . . ."

"Don't say nothin,'" he told her. "Just think on it." Then he swung up into the saddle, said, "Come on, Dog," and galloped out through the open gate into the night.

Texas was waiting. Someplace he'd never been before.

LAW OF THE
MOUNTAIN MAN

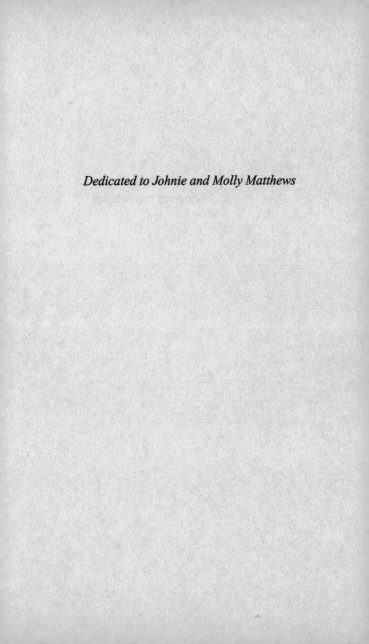

Dedicated to Johnie and Molly Matthews

I feel an army in my fist.
Friedrich von Schiller

1

He hoped this would be the last winter storm of the season. Probably wouldn't be, but there is that line about hope springing eternal.

He just wished it was spring. Period.

Smoke Jensen sat in a cave over a fire and boiled the last of his coffee. He knew he was in Idaho. He guessed somewhere south of Montpelier. All he knew for certain was that he was cold, and he was being hunted by a large group of men. He knew why he was cold; he didn't really have a clear idea why he was being hunted.

He poured a cup of scalding, strong coffee and fed a few more sticks to the fire, then leaned back against the stone wall of the cavern and once more went over events in his mind.

Sally's parents had come out from the East for a visit. Why they had chosen to come to northern Colorado in the middle of winter was still a mystery to Smoke. It was so cold during the winter that when someone died the body was placed in a cave until spring when the ground thawed and a hole could be dug.

It was even colder here in Idaho, Smoke mentally griped, his big hands soaking up the warmth from the tin cup. Dagger, Smoke's big mountain-bred horse, chomped on some grass Smoke had dug up for him.

Besides the cold in Colorado, the baby had taken sick—

some sort of lung ailment—and Sally's father had suggested they go to Arizona for the winter. Smoke had no desire to go to Arizona and there were a few things he needed to tend to around the spread.

With the house empty and matters tended to, Smoke had become restless. The pull of the High Lonesome had tugged at him, so he had saddled up and rode out one cold but sunshiny morning. He didn't have any particular place in mind. He just wanted to be one with the mountains again. Damn near got himself killed doing it. And he wasn't out of the fire yet.

He had headed northwest out of Colorado, staying on the west side of the Continental Divide, angling northwest. He was doing all right until he came to a little town on the Bear River, just about on the border, he reckoned. He had stopped at the general store to resupply and then to have a drink of whiskey. Not normally a drinking man, Smoke visited the saloons more for news than for booze, although in this sort of weather, a shot of whiskey did feel good going down.

Smoke was tall, broad-shouldered, lean-hipped, and ruggedly handsome with cold brown eyes. Smoke Jensen, called the last mountain man by some, was the hero of countless penny dreadfuls sold all over the country. He was also known as the fastest gun in the West. He wore two guns: on the left, a .44 worn high and butt-forward for a cross-draw; on the right, a .44 worn low and tied down.

When Smoke had been just a young boy, he was taken under the wing of a cantankerous old mountain man named Preacher. Preacher had taught the boy well, watching him practice with those deadly guns as they traveled all over the Northwest.

Outlaws had raped and killed Smoke's first wife and cold-bloodedly murdered their newborn son. Smoke had tracked them all down and killed them, had then rode into the outlaw town that had been their headquarters and had shot it out with the killers' friends. His reputation was then carved in granite.

Now Smoke poured another cup of cowboy coffee and let his mind drift back a few days.

"Whiskey," Smoke told the barkeep. "Out of the good bottle."

The saloon had quieted as Smoke walked in, something that did not escape his attention. He paid it little mind, though. A stranger appearing out of the dead of winter always drew attention.

Especially one who wore his guns like Smoke wore his.

"We don't serve no Box T riders in here, mister," the barkeep warned.

Smoke's eyes turned colder than the weather outside. "I don't ride for the Box T. I don't even know where it is or what it is. Now pour the drink." He laid money on the bar.

A man walked up behind Smoke, spurs jingling. "I say you're a liar. I say you're one of that old man and woman's hands. And I say you ain't gonna buy no drink in here. I say—"

Whatever the loudmouth was going to say, he didn't get the chance to finish it. Smoke spun and hit the man smack in the teeth with one big, work-hardened fist. The cowboy's eyes were rolling back in his head and he was out cold before he hit the floor.

Smoke shifted positions, moving to the end of the bar closest to the door so he could keep an eye on the rest of the riders in the room.

"Pour the damn drink!" Smoke told the barkeep. "And make it out of a new bottle. Let me see you pry the cork and pour!"

"Yes, sir!" the barkeep barked. "Right now. Then will you please get the hell out of here?"

"I'll think about it." Smoke held the glass in his left hand. His right hand was hidden by the bar. His right hand was close to the butt of his .44. Out of habit, he always slipped the hammer-thong from his .44 as soon as his boots left the stirrups and touched the ground.

Preacher's lessons had stayed with him.

"Mister," the voice came from a table near the back of the room. "That there is Jud Vale on the floor. He's gonna kill you when he gets up."

"If he doesn't handle his guns any better than he flaps his mouth he's going to be in for another surprise."

"You won't say that to his face!"

Smoke laughed at the man.

"You can't take all of us," another voice added.

"Bastard looks like Perkins, don't he?" yet another said.

Perkins? Smoke thought. Who is Perkins? "Maybe not. But I can kill the first six or eight. Anybody want to start?"

Apparently, no one did. No more voices were heard.

Smoke sipped his drink as Jud Vale moaned and stirred on the floor. "Isn't anyone going to help this stumble-bum up?"

Several men stood up and warily approached the groaning Jud Vale, all of them keeping an eye on Smoke, who was standing by the bar smiling at their antics. Whoever this Perkins person was, he was respected, for sure.

"You a dead man, Perkins, or whoever you are," one of the men said, helping Jud to his feet. "You got one boot in the grave now."

Jud Vale, his bloody mouth puffy, glared at Smoke. "I'm gonna let you ride, you punk!" he snarled. "Take this message back to Burden: I'm gonna kill him and then run that old broad off the land. You tell him I said that."

Smoke started to tell the man that his name wasn't Perkins and he didn't know anybody named Burden. Then he thought better of it. He'd play along for a time. The idea of somebody like this loudmouth Jud Vale bothering some old couple rankled him.

Smoke nodded, finished his whiskey and then backed away from the bar, finding the doorknob with his left hand. He stepped out into the cold-blowing winds and closed the door behind him.

* * *

He stopped at a farmhouse a few miles from town, spotting a man carrying a slop bucket out to his hogs.

"Mister, where can I find the Box T spread?"

"South of here. It's right around Bear Lake. You got any sense, you'll stay away from there."

"Why?"

"'Cause Jud Vale wants it, that's why. And whatever Jud Vale wants, he gits. Now you git!"

Smoke got.

Jud Vale's men came after him hard. So far, not a killing shot had been fired from either side, but Jud's men kept Smoke in a box, warning him back with well-placed rifle shots and causing Smoke to wonder what in the hell was going on.

He was south of Montpelier, a town settled by the Mormons back in '63, first known as Clover Creek and later as Belmont; Brigham Young gave it its present name. He was not too far from the Oregon Trail. Smoke was close to Bear Lake and the Box T spread, but could not figure out a way to get to the place without killing some of Jud Vale's men, and that was something he did not want to do. Not just yet, anyway.

How do I get myself in these messes? he wondered, drinking the last of his coffee. All I wanted to do was see some country, not fight a war.

He walked to the front of the cave and looked out. It was getting light, and soon the hunt would continue. Smoke sighed and did his best to keep his patience. He didn't want to get riled up. When Smoke Jensen got angry, somebody was sure to get hurt.

Dagger snorted and scraped a steel-shod hoof on the floor of the cave. The big horse was getting restless, and was letting Smoke know it.

"All right, Dag," Smoke said, turning to walk back into the wider area of the cave. "I'm getting tired of it myself."

Smoke packed and saddled up, then checked his guns. He

led the big horse outside and swung into the saddle, riding with his Winchester across the saddle horn.

"We're headin' for the Box. T, Dag. And come Hell or high water or Jud Vale, we're going to make it."

The big horse shook his head as if in agreement.

He had not gone a mile before he saw smoke from a fire. Dagger's ears perked up as he caught the scent of other horses. Smoke smiled grimly. "You wanna go visit that camp, boy? All right. Let's just do that."

When he got close, Smoke dismounted and slipped nearer—on foot. A half-dozen of Vale's men were huddled around a fire, drinking coffee and eating bacon. Smoke recognized several of them from the saloon.

He lifted his rifle and plugged the coffeepot, then dented the frying pan with another round. He put several more rounds directly into the fire, scattering hot coals all around the clearing and sending gunhands scrambling for what cover they could find.

He emptied his rifle into a tree where the horses were picketed, and several of them panicked, reared up, and broke loose, taking off into the timber.

Chuckling, Smoke ran back to Dagger, swung into the saddle, and skirted the camp, heading for the Box T range on the Bear.

He had sure ruined breakfast for those ol' boys.

As he rode, he saw smoke from several more fires, but decided not to press his luck.

Twice he heard the sounds of horses and men and both times he slipped back into the timber and waited it out as the men rode past him. And they came close enough for him to see that Jud Vale really meant business. He recognized Don Draper, the Utah gunslick, and Davy Street, the outlaw from down New Mexico way. As the second bunch rode by him, Smoke picked out Cisco Webster, the Texas gunny; Barstow, a no-good from Colorado; Glen Regan, a punk kid who fancied himself a gunfighter; and Highpockets, a long, lean drink of water who was as dangerous as a grizzly and as quick as a striking rattler.

What the hell was going on in this part of southeastern Idaho?

Smoke rode on as the day started to warm some.

He began to see cattle wearing the Box T brand, really no sure sign that he was on Box T land, for cattle wandered miles to grass, but Smoke figured he was getting close.

Then he found out why the cattle were so scattered—miles of cut fences. Somebody, probably Jud Vale and his men, had really caused some damage.

He topped a ridge and could see, far in the distance, a house and barn, and off to the south, a winding road leading to the house. He cut toward the road, riding slowly and cautiously, for if those in the house were under siege, he would probably be considered hostile.

He stopped several times as he drew nearer, taking off his hat and waving it in the air.

Nothing from the house.

He came to a closed gate and stopped, dismounting. He wasn't about to open that gate unless invited to do so.

But no invite came.

The snow was just about gone from the grounds but the wind was still whistling around him.

"Hello, the house!" Smoke yelled.

He was just about to call again when the response came "What do you want?"

A female voice. And not an old voice.

"Some food and coffee would be nice," Smoke called.

"Have this instead," the voice said, sending him a bullet that had Smoke diving for the ground.

2

Several more slugs cut the air above his head. Smoke noticed that none of the slugs came close to Dagger. The big horse trotted away a few yards and looked back at Smoke, his expression saying, "What have you got us into now?"

"I'm friendly!" Smoke called, crawling to his knees. "I mean you no harm!"

"You ride for the Bar V?" This time it was a man's voice.

"Hell, no! They've been chasing me all over the country for the last week."

"Why?"

"Because they think I'm somebody named Perkins!"

A full minute ticked by. "All right, mister." This time it was the female voice. "Get into the saddle and come on in. But you put a hand on a gun and you're dead. And close the gate behind you."

It suddenly came to Smoke. Perkins! Clint Perkins. The outlaw that some called the Robin Hood of the West. He was always helping farmers, nesters, and the down-and-outers. He would rustle cattle from big land barons, butcher the carcasses, and distribute the meat to the needy. He'd been known to give the money to the poor, after holding up rich folks.

But what connection did Clint Perkins have with the Box T?

Well, he might find out . . . providing he didn't get shot first.

He swung into the saddle, leaned down and opened the gate, and rode on in, carefully closing the gate behind him. He walked Dagger toward the house. Smoke stopped at the hitchrail and sat his saddle. Damned if he was going to get down until he was invited.

"What's your name?" the voice came from inside the house, speaking from behind the open but curtained window.

"Mamma," a child's voice said excitedly. "I seen him on the cover of a book. That's Smoke Jensen!"

After a lot of apologies and much embarrassment on the part of those in the house, Smoke was invited to sit down and eat. A small boy took Dagger to the barn. Children could handle the big mean-eyed stallion, but Dagger would kill a grown man who tried to mess with him.

Smoke tried to put some family resemblance between the young woman and the old couple. He could not see any. And he didn't ask—none of his business.

Smoke put away a respectable bit of food and started working on his third cup of coffee.

"I like to see a man eat well," Alice Burden said. "Our boy used to eat like that."

Walt gave his wife a warning look that closed her mouth.

Smoke picked up on the glance but said nothing.

"Just passin' through?" Walt asked, lighting his pipe.

"Something like that." Smoke sugared his coffee. "'Til I had a run-in with a loudmouth name of Jud Vale. I busted him in the mouth and put him on a barroom floor."

"I'd sure like to have seen that," Walt said with a sigh. "That man has sure caused us some problems."

"Why?"

The old man shrugged his shoulders. "He wants our land. Jud Vale wants everything he sees. Including her." He cut his eyes to Doreen, a slim but very shapely woman who looked to be in her mid-twenties.

Got to be more to it than that, Smoke thought. "What has Clint Perkins got to do with all this?"

Walt looked at his coffee cup. His wife busied herself at the sink, washing dishes. Doreen met Smoke's eyes. "He's my husband. Sort of."

Odd reply, Smoke thought. "Father of the boy?"

"Clint is from this area, right?"

"Not too far from here," she replied. "It's a long story, but I'll make it short. When Clint was just a boy he saw his father and mother killed by greedy cattlemen who wanted their land and didn't like farmers. The boy took to the high country and raised himself. He hates rich people to the point of being a fanatic about it. But he has a few good points. More than a few. I married him, but it just didn't work. He refuses to stop his outlawing. I just couldn't live like that."

"So you took the boy and left?"

Smoke didn't believe her. She was lying through her teeth, but damned if he knew why.

"This is a big spread, Mr. Burden. Where are your hands?"

"Don't have none no more. Jud's men run them off; killed a couple. They're buried on that crest to the east."

Smoke had seen the graveyard. More than two crosses there. "And Jud's men cut your fence?"

"Yep."

"Tell me about this Clint Perkins."

"What is there to say?" Walt said. "Nobody 'ceptin' Doreen has seen his face in fifteen years."

"You two look alike," Doreen said. "I can see where someone might think you were him."

What to do? Smoke thought. All three of these people were lying to him. But why? What were they hiding? Walt and Alice Burden were too old for Clint Perkins to be their son. So that was out. So where was the connection? There had to be one.

"How'd you get here?" he asked Doreen.

"Runnin' from Jud Vale," she answered simply. "Walt and Alice took me and Micky in and let us stay."

Why? Had they known Doreen that well? Had they been neighbors? What? Too many unanswered questions. It made Smoke uneasy. Very uneasy.

"You have any idea how many head of cattle you have?" Smoke asked the old man.

"Not no more. Jud and his gunhands been runnin' 'em off for a year or more. The one herd they can't get to without a lot of fuss is west of here, next to the Bear River."

"How are you getting your food?"

The question seemed to make all three of them nervous. Walt finally said, "Friends slip food to us."

Smoke nodded, not satisfied with the reply but sensing he wasn't going to get much more out of the trio. Micky was outside, playing. Smoke figured the boy to be about eight years old.

"There is no point in my trying to restring the wire," Smoke said. "Without hands to ride fence, Jud's people would just cut it again come night."

"True."

"Do you have the money to pay hands, providing I could find some who'd work for you?"

"Oh, sure. I got money up in Montpelier. That's a Mormon town. Jud ain't gonna mess with them folks."

Smoke knew that for an ironclad fact. Mormons tended to stick together, and folks who thought they wouldn't fight because they were so religious soon learned how wrong they were—providing they lived through it.

Walt was saying, ". . . You ain't gonna find no one to work for me, anyways, Mr. Smoke. Jud's got the folks around here buffaloed."

"You let me think on that for a few hours. You just might be wrong." He smiled. "However, the hands I get might not be the type you're used to seeing."

Smoke stowed his gear in the bunkhouse and fired up the old potbelly stove in the center of the room. Dagger was warm and content and chomping away on corn in a hay-filled stall in the big barn.

Smoke had noticed that at one time—not too long ago—the Box T had been a money-making spread. So why the sudden downfall? Was it just because Jud Vale wanted the land? Smoke didn't believe that for a minute. There was more to it than that—a lot more.

Smoke hated bullies. If it were just a simple matter of Jud Vale's greed, the problem could be easily solved—with a gun. Smoke wanted the whole story, though, before it came to that, if it came to that. And he sincerely hoped it would not. He, however, had a hunch that it would. Usually all loud-mouthed, pushy, bullying types could be handled without being killed, for bullies are cowards at heart. Give them a good beating and you've got their attention. But Smoke felt that Jud wouldn't go down that easily. If Jensen stayed around, he would have to drag iron against Jud Vale.

He felt pretty sure he was going to stick around. Nothing like a good mystery to pique one's interest.

Over supper, Smoke asked, "Lots of small farmers in this area, huh?"

"Oh, yeah," the old rancher said. "Most of them just barely hanging on. That's another thing that got me in trouble. I never minded farmers like a lot of ranchers seem to. Never had any trouble with them. I used to help a lot of them time to time. A little money, food, clothing, what have you. Used to hire some of the kids during the summer to work on the spread."

"Does Montpelier have a newspaper?"

"Sure."

Smoke nodded. "I'm going to be gone for several days." He noted the alarm that quickly sprang into the eyes of those around the table. "But I'll be back," he assured them. "And that's a promise."

"Jud Vale is a no-good," the farmer said bluntly. "And I'll say it to his face."

"Chester . . ." his wife warned.

"No, Mother." The man in the patched overalls shook his head. "Time for backing down is over. Mr. Burden is a good man who's hit on some hard times. We can't just turn our backsides to him and forget all the times he's helped us. 'Sides, we need hard cash desperate."

"Ralph is only twelve years old," she reminded him.

"And been doin' a man's work since he was nine. You seen how excited he is about Mr. Smoke's offer. And you heard Mr. Smoke say he ain't gonna put the plan into action unless the newspaper agrees to print the story and send it out to other papers."

"Well . . ." She shook her head. "I just don't know, Chester."

"Aw, Mom!" the boy finally spoke. "I can handle a gun good as the next feller!"

"No guns!" Smoke said it quickly and firmly. "If it comes to gunplay, I'll handle that. Any boy who shows up with a gun doesn't work."

"Yes, sir!" Ralph said. "You're the boss, Mr. Smoke, for sure."

"You pass the word around to your friends and neighbors. And keep it inside the circle. We want this to be a total surprise to Jud Vale when we spring it."

The farmer grinned and stuck out his hand. Smoke shook it. "You got it, Mr. Smoke."

The editor of the newspaper chuckled and rocked back in his swivel chair. "I like it, Mr. Jensen. I really like it. Jud Vale doesn't throw that big a loop around this town, but he's made life pretty miserable for those in his area. I've been curious about just why he hates Walt Burden so. Of course I'll print the story, and I'll send it out to newspapers all over the state. We want to be sure those young boys are safe. And there is nothing like the power of the press to insure that. Hire your . . . cowboys,

Mr. Jensen, and put them to work. I'll ride down and do a follow-up on the story in a few weeks, to keep interest alive."

"Damnedest bunch of cowboys I ever seen in all my born days," Walt said, looking at the new hands.

"Looks like we better get to cooking, Doreen," Alice said. "Some of those boys look like they haven't had a decent meal in weeks."

The youngest was ten and the oldest was fourteen. Of the boys, that is. In Montpelier, Smoke had rounded up three slightly older punchers. Dolittle, Harrison, and Cheyenne were in their sixties . . . they claimed. Smoke suspected they might be a tad older than that. He didn't know much about Dolittle and Harrison, except that they could sit a saddle and knew cows, but Cheyenne was quite another story. Smoke remembered Preacher spinning yarns about a mountain man he knew by the name of Cheyenne O'Malley from back in the '40s. Cheyenne was one of those born with the bark on; he didn't have to grow into it—mean from the git-go.

Cheyenne was about seventy, Smoke reckoned, and looked so skinny he might have to drink a glass of beer to keep his britches up. But he still wore his Colt low and tied down and Smoke knew the old mountain man could and would use it.

"All right, Cheyenne," Smoke told him. "You're the range boss on this job." Cheyenne nodded. "You boys know what that means. Cheyenne tells you to make like a frog, you just jump as high as you can. You don't have to ask if it was high enough. If it wasn't, he'll let you know. Dolittle and Harrison will be carrying orders from Cheyenne to you boys, and you boys will be spotted all around this spread.

"Now then, the first thing we're gonna do is round up some horses and top them off; settle them down for you." Smoke glanced at the animals the boys had used to get over to the Box T. Mules and plow horses. "Then you boys can turn your own animals out to pasture and let them rest." He looked at Walt. "All right, Boss, what's the first order of the day?"

The old rancher smiled. "The wife says the first thing we do is feed these boys."

All the boys cheered at that.

Jud Vale balled the newspaper up and hurled it into the fireplace. "That no good—" He proceeded to cut loose with a stream of cuss words that almost turned the air blue.

When he had calmed down enough to try to catch his breath, his foreman said, "Boss, this is bad. If one of them kids gets hurt by a bullet, the governor will send the law in on us—that is, if some vigilantes from around here don't hang us to the nearest tree first."

"I know, Jason. I know. That damn Smoke Jensen! Jesus God, why didn't I recognize him right off and let him alone?"

"Didn't none of us recognize him, Boss. But we should have, I reckon." He wore a sheepish look. "Damn bunkhouse is full of them penny dreadfuls writ about him."

"I better not see any of them around!"

"I'll pass the word."

"Do that. Damn!" Jud yelled. "Pass the word, Jason: stay off of Box T range and don't bother the boys. Don't even go near them. Jensen can't stay up here forever and them damn kids got to go back to school come fall. We can wait."

"Them high-priced gunhands is about next to worthless when it comes to workin' cattle, Boss. Most of 'em is just salivating to get a chance to brace Smoke Jensen."

"I'll give a thousand dollars to the man who kills Jensen. You pass that word along, Jason."

"That ought to get something stirred up, for sure!"

While in Montpelier, Smoke had arranged for a wire to be sent to Sally, advising her where he was, and for a courier to bring any reply to the ranch.

One was forthcoming quickly.

Darling Smoke. STOP *Doctors say baby must remain in a*

warm dry climate for at least two years. STOP *Mother and Father arranged to stay with me.* STOP *Father bought a bank here in Prescott.* STOP *We are fine.* STOP *Miss you terribly.* STOP *Come when you are finished.* STOP *Love Sally.* STOP.

"Bad news?" Doreen broke into his thoughts. He had not heard her come up.

The girl moved like a ghost.

"Yes and no. Our baby has to stay down in Arizona for quite a long time. Lung problems."

"Then you'll be leaving . . . ?" She let that trail off with a catch in her voice.

"No. Sally knows I don't go off and leave a job half-finished. I'll see this through. If it hasn't ended by midsummer, then I'll finish it."

She didn't have to ask how he would do that. She knew. "That is very kind of you, Smoke."

She moved closer. Doreen was a mighty comely lass. Smoke could smell the lilac water on her. Mayhaps, he thought, her middle name was Eve.

He moved back just a tad. "That is, I'll make up my mind about staying when and if you people ever get around to telling me the truth."

Her eyes turned frosty as an early morning chill. She spun around and stalked away, her rear end swaying like women's rear ends have a tendency to do.

Mighty shapely lassie. And Smoke didn't trust her any further than he could pick up his horse and toss him.

3

On the first full day of work, Smoke didn't know whether to laugh or cry.

The boys were sure willing enough. but the trouble was that none of them knew diddly-squat about ranch work. They were farm boys, used to gathering eggs and slopping hogs and plowing and such as that.

Little Chuckie fell off his mount, and landed in a fresh horse pile. The only other britches he had were hanging on the line to dry. He had to work the rest of that morning dressed, from the waist down, in his longhandles. With a safety pin holding up one side of the flap.

Of the boys, Jamie was the oldest and the strongest. He was built like the trunk of a large tree. And he could ride and was a fair hand with a rope.

Matthew was a frail young man who wore glasses and was in dire need of boots.

Smoke was making a list of what the boys needed; and he was going to see to it that they got it. One way or the other.

Ed meant well and tried hard, but it was plain that he would never be a cowboy. Smoke put him to running errands and taking messages back and forth.

Leroy would do. He never complained, even after being tossed a half-dozen times. He just got back up, dusted himself off, and climbed right back in the saddle and stayed there until he showed the bronc who was running this show.

Eli was the son of a carpenter and, like Ed, was no horseman. Smoke put him to work fixing up the place, and there was a lot of fixing up to do. A ranch starts to run down mighty quick, and this spread had been neglected for a long time.

Jimmy and Clark and Buster would do fine, Smoke concluded.

Cecil was fourteen, like Jamie, and solid and mature for his age. A fair horseman.

Alan was a grown-up thirteen, from a hardscrabble farm family. A good solid kid.

Rolly, Pat and Oscar were all twelve and showed promise.

All in all, Smoke thought, a pretty good bunch of kids. But, he had to keep this in mind: they were kids. He could not chew on them like he would adults. He didn't want them screwing up their faces and bawling like lost calves.

"All right, Cheyenne!" Smoke called, with Dagger under him. "Take the men to work!"

Smoke rode over to a three-building town located on Mud Lake, leading a pack animal. He would buy the boys as much clothing as possible here. Maybe all of it if he were lucky. And he could pick up any talk about how Jud Vale was taking this new twist.

As soon as he walked in, he could tell by the barkeep's reaction that the name Smoke Jensen was known. Somebody had been talking about him, and fairly recently.

The barroom was separated from the general store by a partition, so the men could talk and cuss without bothering any ladies who might be shopping in the store. The only door connecting the store and saloon was closed.

Smoke ordered a beer and leaned against the bar, observing the very nervous barkeep draw the suds. Three men were sitting at a table in the back of the room. It was gloomy in the small saloon, and the men were shrouded in shadows, but Smoke could see well enough to recognize the men as part of one of the groups who had chased him all over half of the southeastern part of Idaho days back.

And one of them was Sam Teller, a gunfighter from over Oregon way. Sam wasn't known for his easy disposition and loving nature.

A local man, a farmer by the look of him, opened the door and stepped inside, closing the door behind him. He stopped cold when he saw the tall man at the bar. His eyes cut to the three gunslicks sitting at the table. He swallowed hard, then walked on to the bar and ordered a beer.

"All of a sudden it smells like a hogpen in here," one of the gunhawks commented.

The farmer's face hardened but he was smart enough to keep his mouth shut.

"What'll it be, neighbor?" the barkeep asked.

"Beer." The farmer took a position at the end of the bar, near the curve of the planks, so if matters deteriorated into gunplay, he could hit the floor and be out of the line of fire.

Smoke was a cattleman, so he could understand, at least to some degree, why ranchers disliked farmers. But Smoke Jensen was living proof that rancher and farmer could live side by side and be friends. And he knew that not all of the blame for the hard feelings could be laid at the doorstep of the ranchers. Some farmers flatly refused to work with the ranchers, fencing off the best water; homesteading in line shacks that the ranchers had built and maintained; and sometimes rustling cattle, not always for food to feed hungry families. Sometimes just to aggravate the rancher.

The bartender had moved to the end of the bar, just as far away from Smoke Jensen as he could get.

Smoke sipped his beer and waited for the gunplay that he knew was just around the corner, lurking in those invisible shadows that drifted around and clung to those who lived by the gun.

"There ain't much to that pig slop, Burt," Sam Teller said. "Hell, he ain't even packin' no gun."

Burt. Smoke searched his memory. Could be Burt Rolly. Smoke had heard of him. A gunfighter of very limited ability, so he'd been told. Usually a back-shooter.

"You're a long ways from home, Jensen," Sam said. "I figured you was still in Colorado, hidin' under your wife's dresstail."

"You figured wrong on a lot of counts, Sam," Smoke told him. "But then, the way I hear it, you never were very bright."

"Huh?"

"I said you were stupid, Sam. Dumb. Ignorant. Slow. Mentally deficient. Am I making myself clear now?"

The farmer moved further away from Smoke and if the barkeep pressed any harder against the rear wall, he was going to collapse the entire end of the store.

"I don't think I like you very much, Jensen," Sam said, finally realizing he was being insulted.

"I don't like you at all, Sam. And I'm not real thrilled with those half-wits with you."

Burt pushed back his chair and stood up, his hands at his sides. "You take that back, Jensen! I ain't no half-wit."

Smoke smiled at him. "You're right, Burt. You're not a half-wit."

Burt relaxed.

"You're all the way a fool," Smoke finished. "The best thing you boys could do is pay for your drinks and ride out of this area of Idaho. Forget about Jud Vale and Walt Burden. And for damn sure, forget about trying to brace me."

The third man at the table slowly stood up and walked to another table. He sat down and placed both hands on the table.

Smoke recognized him. "Smart move, Jackson."

"The timin' ain't right, Smoke," the gunhand said. "Man, you're walkin' around with your tail up in the air, huntin' trouble. That ain't like you. What's got you on the prod?"

"I don't like Jud Vale." Smoke spoke to the man without taking his eyes off of Sam and Burt.

"Hell, I don't like him either! But he's payin' top wages for fightin' men."

Smoke laughed. "To fight an old man and an old woman? To fight a young woman and her eight-year-old kid? For that, Jud Vale hires two dozen gunnies? He must be a mighty skittish man."

"They's a lot more to this than that, Smoke."

"I figure so myself. One of these days somebody's going to tell me the whole story."

"I'm tired of all this jibber-jabber!" Burt shouted, just about scaring the pee out of the barkeep. "I'm a-gonna kill you, Jensen!"

Smoke stood tall and straight, facing the two men standing by the table. "No, you're not, Burt. All you're going to do is get buried. Think about it, man. I've faced more than a hundred gunhands. most of them better than you. They're all dead, Burt. Every last one of them. Pike and Shorty. Haywood and Ackerman and Kid Austin. Canning and Poker and Grisson. Clark and Evans. Felter and Lefty and Nevada Sam. Big Jack and Phillips and Carson. Russell and Joiner and Jeff Siddons. Jerry and Skinny Davis and Cross. You want more names, Burt? All right. Simpson and Martin and Reese. Turkel and Brown and Williams and Rogers. Fenerty and Stratton and Potter and Richards. And half a hundred more whose names I can't recall or never even knew. They're all dead and rotting in the ground. But I'm still here."

"Listen to him, boys." Jackson spoke the words softly. "I'm tellin' you, the timin' ain't right just yet. Back off."

"You could buy in!" Sam said hoarsely.

"Not just yet."

"Then you jist yellow!"

"No. But I'll be alive," Jackson told him.

The farmer was on the floor, belly down. The barkeep had slipped down to his knees and was peering around a keg of beer.

"Make your play, damn you, Jensen!" Sam yelled.

"Your deal," Smoke replied. "Bet or fold."

Sam and Burt grabbed for iron. Smoke's guns roared and belched fire and death. Sam stumbled back against the wall, his gun still in leather. Burt was plugged twice in the belly. He fell down on the floor and began squalling as the intense pain reached him. Sam cursed Smoke and managed to clear leather and level the pistol. Smoke shot him in the head. Burt tried to lift his pistol. He managed to cock it and fire, shooting himself in the foot, the slug tearing off his big toe. He dropped his gun to the floor and started yelling in pain.

Smoke glanced at Jackson. The man's hands were still on the tabletop, palms down.

"Holy Hell!" the barkeep hollered.

The farmer was praying to the Almighty.

"Can't say I didn't warn 'em." Jackson broke the silence.

"For a fact," Smoke replied, punching out empty brass and reloading. "Is there a bounty on my head, Jackson?"

"Thousand dollars."

"I don't have to ask who put it there."

"I 'spect you know."

"I imagine the bounty is going to go up on me after this."

"It wouldn't surprise me none."

"What about them?" Smoke jerked his head at the dead and dying gunslicks.

"Don't ask me, Smoke. Hell, I didn't take 'em to raise!"

"I'll bury 'em iffen I can have what's in they pockets!" the barkeep said.

"Suits me," Smoke told him. He picked up his beer mug and drained it, wiping his mouth with the back of his hand. He set the mug back on the plank. "Fill it up, barkeep."

"Git it yourself! It's on the house. I ain't movin' 'til I know all the lead's through flyin'!"

Smoke walked around the bar just as the farmer was getting up off the floor. He looked at him. "You want another beer?"

"Hell, no!" The farmer hit the air and didn't look back.

"I'm gonna stand up now, Smoke," Jackson said.

"Go right ahead."

"Then I'm gonna walk out the door and get my horse and go."

"See you around, Jackson."

"Maybe. I ain't made up my mind about this job. You showin' up sorta tipped the balance some."

"Whatever pops your corn, Jackson."

The gunfighter nodded, turned, and left the smoky barroom. Within ten seconds, the sounds of his horse's hooves echoed down the short, silent street.

Burt started hollering something awful.

"Ain't he gonna die?" the barkeep asked. "I'd lak to have them boots of his."

"Sooner or later. Is there any hard candy for sale in the store?"

"Hard candy!"

"Yeah. I got some kids working for me. They all probably have a sweet tooth."

"Hell, I don't know!"

Smoke shrugged and walked into the store area of the building. He was thinking that he'd better buy a couple boxes of .44's. Way things were going, he'd probably need them.

The news of the gunfight had reached the ranch before Smoke returned. Walt and Cheyenne met him in the barn.

"Did you run into some trouble, boy?" the old rancher asked.

"Couple of two-bit gunhands who thought they were better than they really were." Smoke stripped the saddle off Dagger, hung up the reins, rubbed him down, and began forking hay into his stall.

Cheyenne and Walt were silent for a time. Walt broke it. "Swenson came by here, all flusterated. Said you cut them boys down faster than the blink of an eye."

"Like I said, they weren't as good as they thought they were."

Cheyenne grunted and spat a brown stream onto the barn floor. "I knowed Burt Rolly's dad. He wasn't no good neither. Utes kilt him years ago. Died bad. They never sung no songs about him. What was that other hombre's name?"

"Sam Teller."

The old mountain man and gunfighter shook his head. "Must not have been much to him. I never heared of him."

Cheyenne limped off. He still carried a Sioux arrowhead in his hip. Slowed him down when the weather changed.

"Doreen finally got around to telling me that you two had a little run-in, Smoke."

"Not much of one. I would just like to know why everyone is lying to me."

The rancher was silent for a time. "You want to explain that remark, Smoke? 'Cause if you don't, old man or not, I'm goin' in the house for my six-gun and call you out!"

Smoke chuckled. "Yeah . . . you probably would, too, Walt. But I'm going to let my statement stand. None of you have leveled with me. I've seen the quick looks passed between you whenever I touch on certain subjects. What's going on, Walt?"

"Doreen is a good girl, Smoke."

"I never said she wasn't."

"She isn't married to Clint Perkins."

"I didn't think she was. The boy is a wood's colt, huh?"

"How'd you guess?"

"Just that, a guess. Is the boy's father Clint Perkins?"

"Yes. They went together for a time—on the sly. Then he got her all puffed up and ran out on her. He kept tellin' Doreen how they was gonna move to California and he was gonna change and . . . lies and lies, that's all they was. He'd climb a telegraph pole for a lie and leave the truth layin' on the ground."

"So Doreen figured that a make-believe outlaw husband was better than no husband at all?"

"That's about it. Clint is a no-good, Smoke. He started out doin' good, I'll give him that much; he really did do good. Then he turned bad. The young man is not right in the head."

"All that about him seeing his parents killed and running off into the timber . . . ?"

"Lies. You got to understand something, Smoke. I was the first white man to settle in this part of Idaho. Back in '38. The first one. I built me a cabin and got settled in and then went back for Alice. When we got here, the Injuns had burned the cabin down. We built again and fought off Injuns until they got to where they'd leave us alone. I prospered. Found some color and panned it. Found some more color and mined that out. I got money, Smoke. Plenty of it. I got money in a half-dozen banks. Hell, I don't need this ranch or the cattle. I kept on to it for my boy."

The old man paused to light his pipe and Smoke waited.

"But he married into trash. Pure trash. That woman—damn her black heart wherever she is—wasn't nothin' but a whore. That's all she was. Anyways, they had a son. Clint. His name ain't Perkins, it's Burden. But she run off with him and changed it."

"Wait a minute, wait a minute! This is getting confusing. Back up. Where is your son?"

"Dead. Ten years back. He turned into a drunk after that woman run off and left him. Staggered around here drunk and crazy in the head and heart for years. He never hurt nobody. He was just a fool there at the end. Jud Vale killed him. Shot him for sport one night over at the tradin' post where you was this day. Made it last a long time. Shot his legs out from under him, then busted his hands and arms with .44's. It was a awful thing for one human to do to another. Jud and that no-good foreman of his, Jason, just left my boy there in the mud to bleed to death. He ain't never hired nothing but trash over there at the Bar V. Most of them runnin' from the law somewheres."

"Where does Clint fit into all this?"

The old man laughed bitterly. "That's funny, son. Really funny. You see, I hired some fancy detectives to hunt that witch-woman down and bring my grandson back to me. They found her and brung him back. Bad seed, Smoke. He's just bad. But the more I got to lookin' at him, the more I began to suspect he wasn't none of my blood. The day he run off for the last time, he told me. My boy Clint didn't father him. Jud Vale did."

4

Smoke walked outside the barn with Walt and paused to roll a cigarette. "Does Jud Vale know about Clint being his son?"

"Oh, yeah. That's why he wants Clint dead and Doreen so bad. He suspects, and rightly so, that I changed my will, leaving everything to Doreen. He don't want no woods colt hanging around, messin' everything up. And with Doreen his woman, willing or not, he could produce a false weddin' license and claim it all. At worse, he could tie it up in court for years."

"Jud sounds like a real nice fellow."

"A regular Prince Charming," the old man said sourly.

"I'm glad you told me this, Walt."

"Me and the old woman talked about it last night. We agreed that it wasn't right for you to come in here and lay your life on the line for us, and us not to level with you. I'd have gotten around to tellin' you, son."

"You say you found gold around here?"

"A small pocket of it. I panned it plumb out. There was enough for me to invest in one thing or the other and become a well set up man. That's another thing, Smoke. Jud Vale knows about me panning the gold. But I never could convince the hard-headed no-good that there ain't no more gold. The gold I panned washed in here from God knows where, and the small pocket I mined is gone. Nature is a funny critter, Smoke. She'll sometimes put precious minerals in a place where they just ain't supposed to be. And when it's gone, it's gone forever. There just ain't no more."

"But Jud Vale doesn't believe that." It was not a question.

Walt sighed. "No. The man's a fool when it comes to money. Greediest man I ever saw in all my life. Got hisself a regular palace on his spread. And Doreen believes the man is in love with her; 'obsessed,' is the way she put it. He's finally found something that he can't have; he can't buy it or steal it, and he's furious about it."

"He might try to take her by force."

"That thought has come to me from time to time."

"You going to tell her that you leveled with me?"

"Yes. Oughta ease the tensions around here."

"For a fact. Let's go all the way with it and then we'll speak no more of it. How were you getting your food in here?"

"Shoshone friends of mine. But rations was gettin' kinda sparse since Jud found the trail they was usin' and posted guards on it."

"Toward the end of this week, once the boys have settled in, we'll take a ride to the trading post and stock up. I imagine Alice and Doreen would like a little outing."

"I reckon so. Ain't none of us been off this spread in months. And them boys you brung eat like starvin' animals!"

The boys settled right in and soon needed very little supervison. They began stringing wire and doing a good job of it. Smoke took Cheyenne and several of the older boys and went looking for Box T cattle. He felt he knew where most of the cattle would be, and his hunch paid off.

"We been on Bar V range for a time," Cheyenne pointed out.

"And seeing more and more of Walt's cattle. Jamie, you boys start hazing them out and bunching them."

"Yes, sir, Mr. Smoke."

They hadn't gone another half-mile before Jud Vale and half a dozen of his hardcases came galloping up, punishing their horses needlessly. That was another way you could judge a man's character—by the way he treated his horse. Smoke's dislike for Jud Vale deepened as he looked at the lathered-up gelding he was riding.

"What the hell are you doing on my range, Jensen?" Jud demanded.

"Looking for Box T cattle, Vale. And finding them. You got any objections?"

Cheyenne had shifted positions so the muzzle of his Winchester was aimed right at a Bar V rider's belly, and the Bar V man didn't look a bit happy about it.

Smoke had pulled his Winchester out of the boot and had his thumb on the hammer. Jud didn't seem to be too terribly thrilled about that either, since the muzzle was pointed in his general direction.

"Yeah," Vale finally replied. "I got objections. I can't help it if that old coot's cattle wandered onto my range, eatin' up all my grass."

"Well, then, you should be glad to see us, Vale. We're going to take them back to home range and then you won't have to spend your nights worrying about them. Now we can either do that, or I can wire the territorial governor and ask for range detectives to be sent in here. How do you want it, Vale?"

The man puffed up like a 'possum and gave Smoke some dark looks. "Well . . . git your damn cattle and git the hell off my land then. I'm tired of lookin' at your damn ugly face, Jensen."

"Unless you want us over here every day for a couple of weeks, Vale, why don't you have your boys assist us? It would move a lot faster."

Cheyenne's leathery old face struggled to hide his grin. Smoke was pushing the big blowhard into a corner, and the man couldn't find a way out.

Vale blustered and hissed like a spreadin' adder and shifted around in the saddle. "I ain't helpin' you do nothin', Jensen.

I don't give a damn how often you come over here. You just make sure all the beeves you push across the crick are wearin' Box T brands, or by God, you'll answer to me."

"We can do that now, Vale," Smoke told him. He booted the Winchester and dropped his right hand to his thigh, close to the butt of that deadly .44.

Jud didn't like that idea at all. It was seven against two, for a fact. But it was also a fact that this was a no-win situation. Cheyenne was an old he-coon from way back. Jud's men might take him, but the old man was sure to empty two, maybe three saddles before he went down; and even down the old goat was as dangerous as a cornered grizzly. Even dying, if you got too close to the old bastard, he'd sure likely come up with a knife and cut you from brisket to backbone.

Smoke Jensen was quite another matter. Everybody knew he'd been raised by Preacher, and Preacher was a legend. Jensen had killed more than a hundred men—and that wasn't counting Injuns. Jud Vale knew the first thing to happen should he grab for iron, was that Smoke was going to blow him right out of the saddle.

And there just wasn't no percentage in dying.

"Round up your damn cattle and get off my range," Jud finally backed down. He savagely jerked his horse around and galloped off, his men following him.

"I hate a man treats a horse like that," Cheyenne said. "A horse or a dog. You show me a man who's unkind to animals and I'll show you a man that just ain't no damn good."

"I'm going to have to kill that man someday, Cheyenne. I can see it coming."

"I 'spect, Smoke, they's a long line of folks ahead of you thinkin' the same thing."

Saturday, they went to the trading post on Mud Lake.

Walt drove the wagon with Alice by his side, and Doreen, all prettied up, and Micky sitting on boxes in the back of the wagon.

Doreen was a looker, no doubt about that, and a flirty thing, too. Smoke did his best to avoid her sliding glances. The heat coming out of her eyes could fry an egg. Although Smoke didn't think kitchen cooking was what she had on her mind.

Cheyenne, Winchester across his saddle horn, rode on one side of the wagon, Smoke on the other.

As they rode and rattled up to the big store, Cheyenne pointed out the two fresh graves in back of the building.

Doreen and Alice and Micky went into the store part of the building to shop, and Smoke, Walt, and Cheyenne went into the bar to have a beer.

"Not you agin!" the barkeep moaned, as Smoke stepped inside.

"I'm peaceful." Smoke grinned at him.

"Haw! You won't be when some of them no-count hard-cases from the Bar V show up. Just don't wreck my damn place," he warned.

"Why don't you just shut up and get us a bottle," Cheyenne told him. "You prattle on like a scared old woman."

The bartender looked at the skinny old mountain man with the wicked look in his eyes and shut his mouth. He placed a bottle on the bar and several shot glasses. Smoke pushed the shot glass away and ordered a beer.

Cheyenne downed one quick belt and poured another, taking the shot glass and moving to the far end of the bar where he could watch the door. He had left his Winchester in the saddle boot. If anything happened in the barroom, he would rely on the old Colt with the worn handles hanging low on his right side. Or on the Bowie knife sheathed on his left side. Or on the .44 derringer in his boot. Or anything else he could get his hands on. If it just had to be, the old mountain man would pick up a porcupine to use as a weapon and damn the needles.

Micky had a bottle of sarsaparilla and was sitting on a bench in front of the store. Coming to town was quite an outing for the boy.

Alice and Doreen were oohhing and aahhing over some new dress material in the store.

Two farmers were sitting at a table, nursing mugs of beer, talking quietly. They finished their drinks and left. A fat man, a drummer from the looks of him, was sitting alone at a table next to a window. He kept shifting his eyes to Smoke, stealing fast sly glances.

"Say!" he finally spoke. "Aren't you Smoke Jensen, the gunfighter?"

Smoke cut his eyes. "I'm Smoke Jensen."

"Well, I'll just be hornswoggled! I just read a big article on you in the *Gazette*. The writer said you've killed more'un five hundred men."

"Not quite that many," Smoke corrected.

"Kilt two right in here a few days back," the barkeep said with a grin. "This is my place. I'm Bendel." He pointed. "Kilt 'em right over yonder. They's buried out back."

"You don't say!" The drummer bobbed his head up and down. "I'm from St. Louis myself. I got the finest line of women's underthings and unmentionables on the market today, I do."

"How kin you sell 'um if you cain't mention 'um?" Cheyenne asked him.

The drummer looked startled for a moment, then burst out laughing. "Oh, that's a good one. I'll have to remember that." He stared at the old mountain man. "Are you somebody famous?"

"I have been a time or two," Cheyenne grumbled.

"That's Cheyenne O'Malley," Smoke informed the drummer.

"No kidding! You once fought off a hundred hostile savages."

"More like fifteen," Cheyenne told him. "And they wasn't savages or hostile. They was just mad at me 'cause I bedded down with the chief's oldest daughter. She was due to marry the war chief who led the band who come after me. Never could make no sense out of that. I enjoyed it and so did she. I went back about ten years later and looked her up. Sorry I did that. She was about the size of a tipi. Hit me upside the head with a rock and called me all sorts of vile names. Damned if I didn't have to fight the same bunch all over again. But this time that war chief was mad 'cause I hadn't toted her off ten years back. I don't think they got along too well."

"That's incredible!" the drummer said.

Cheyenne belched. "Damn squaw follered me from the Sun River all the way over to the Bitterroot. Hollerin' and cussin' and raisin' hell. I finally lost her around Lob Pass. Things like that tend to take some of the joy out of messin' with wimmin."

"What stories I'll have to tell when I get back to St. Louis!" He looked out the window. "Bunch of riders coming."

Smoke walked to the batwings and looked out. "Gun-hands," he said.

"Is there going to be a Wild West shoot-out?" the drummer questioned

"I hope not."

"Oh, that would be so exhilarating!"

"Not for them that gits shot," Cheyenne said, slipping the hammer thong from his pistol. "All they git is plugged."

Half a dozen Bar V hands began crowding into the barroom. They pulled up short and fell silent when they saw Smoke.

Smoke knew two of them. Blackjack Morgan and Gus Fall. The others might well be hell on wheels with a short gun, but they just hadn't made a name for themselves as yet. And if they decided to brace Smoke Jensen and Cheyenne O'Malley, the only name they were going to get would be carved on their gravestones.

"Jensen," Blackjack said, walking past him, his spurs jingling.

Smoke nodded his head.

Gus stopped by the bar and stared at Smoke. He shifted his chew around in his mouth and spat toward a spittoon near Smoke's boot. He missed the cuspidor, the tobacco juice striking Smoke's boot.

Gus grinned at him. "You can get the boy out front to come lick it off."

His grin was wiped off his face in a bloody smear as Smoke swung the beer mug, hitting Gus's jaw and knocking a couple of teeth out of his mouth. Gus was propelled backward, his boots slipping on the freshly mopped floor. He slammed through the batwings, tearing one off, and fell into the dusty street, on his back, out cold.

Micky sat on the bench and stared, mouth open, eyes wide.

Smoke tossed the handle of the mug onto the plank. "Another beer, please."

"There wasn't no call to do that," one of the young so-called gunslicks told Smoke. "'Sides, Gus is my friend. I feel obliged to take up for him."

Cheyenne laid the barrel of his Colt against the young man's head and he dropped to the floor like a rock.

One of the young man's buddies thought it was a dandy time to grab for iron. He changed his mind as Cheyenne eared back the hammer on his Colt and put those cold old eyes on the kid.

"Boy," Cheyenne warned him, "I'll blow a hole in your gawddamn belly a horse could ride through."

"That's Cheyenne O'Malley!" the drummer blurted out as a warning.

The young man's face turned gray and shiny with sweat. He let his eyes slide away from the eyes of death searing at him from the face of the mountain man. Slowly, very slowly, he let his hands drop to his sides, as far away from the butts of his guns as humanly possible. He would have grabbed the boards on the floor if his reach had been long enough.

Cheyenne eased the hammer down and holstered the Colt. He turned his attentions back to his shot glass.

"See about Gus," Blackjack told one of the men. He cut his eyes to Smoke. "You're right touchy today, Smoke. Who twisted your tail?"

"Two-bit gunhands have a tendency to annoy me." Smoke lifted his fresh mug of beer with his left hand and took a sip.

"When Gus gets up from the dirt, he's gonna kill you, Smoke."

"He'll try." Smoke turned his back to the gunfighter and sipped his beer.

Blackjack moved to a table and sat down, ordering a bottle.

The drummer was scribbling frantically in a notebook; he wanted to be sure to get all this down. He might write a book about this.

Gus was helped back into the barroom, his mouth bloody and his eyes wild with hate and fury. Smoke turned to watch him, his right hand by his side.

Gus shook himself away from the men on each side of him and faced Smoke. He was so mad he was trembling.

"Gus," Blackjack warned. "Back off, son. This is not the time."

"Go to hell!" Gus said, without taking his eyes off of Smoke.

"You better do what he says, boy," Cheyenne told him. "You're just about to step off into where the waters is deep and dark."

"You go to hell, too, old man!"

Cheyenne shrugged his shoulders. "Nobody can ever say I didn't try to warn you about the currents."

"You ready, Jensen?" Gus asked.

"I'm not finished with my beer, Gus. I would suggest you get you a cool one and calm down some."

"You, by God, don't tell me what to do, Smoke."

"I'm just trying to save your life, Gus."

Gus cussed him. "Here or in the street, Jensen?"

"It doesn't make a damn bit of difference to me, Gus." Smoke set his beer mug down on the plank.

Gus reached for his guns.

5

Smoke's left-hand Colt roared and bucked as his cross-draw flashed.

The slugs hit Gus in the chest and belly, doubling him over. He stumbled back and grabbed onto a table's edge for support. He finally managed to drag iron just as Smoke fired again, the .44 slug slamming into his chest. The light began to fade around him as the men in the barroom took on a ghostly appearance, drifting into double images as the sounds of the pale rider grew louder in his ears.

Gus looked down at his hands. What had happened to his guns? His hands were empty. But he had drawn them. He was sure of that.

Gus sat down heavily in a chair and the legs broke under the sudden weight, spilling him to the floor. The last thing he would hear was the sounds of the pale rider's horse galloping closer. And finally, the feel of that cold and bony hand reaching down to touch his shoulder.

"Did anybody even see Jensen draw?" the drummer asked, his voice filled with awe. "Jesus God, I didn't."

The young man whom Cheyenne had bopped on the noggin with the barrel of his Colt finally sat up and moaned, both hands to his head. "What happened?" he asked.

"Gus finally saw the critter," Blackjack told him.

The young man looked up into the cold eyes of Smoke

Jensen. Right then, and unfortunately for him, only for a very brief moment, did the old homeplace farm back in Minnesota pull at him slightly.

The young man who had just recently taken to calling himself the Pecos Kid pushed those thoughts out of his head and began to think about how he could kill Smoke Jensen. Yeah . . . the man who killed Smoke Jensen would be famous all over the world. He'd have fame and money and all the women anybody could ever want. So he very wrongly thought.

Smoke stared down at him from the bar. His words momentarily chilled the Pecos Kid. "Put it out of your head, kid. Don't even think about it."

Smoke turned and Walt and Cheyenne followed him out of the bar and into the general store.

When Smoke was well out of earshot, Pecos said, "I bet I could take him."

Blackjack just shook his head in disgust.

It appeared that the bitterly cold and long winter had finally given way to spring as the warming winds began to blow. The syringa began to bloom, as did the balsam and lupine, and the marsh marigold and blue columbine lent their hues and fragrances to the cacophony of color. Harrison had ridden to the store by the lake and came back with bad news.

"That Clint Perkins done struck agin, Mr. Walt. This time he killed a man over on the Little Malad. Some big landowner over thataway."

Walt kicked at a rock and cussed.

"And that ain't all. Jud Vale—had to be him—done upped the ante on Smoke's head. Five thousand dollars to the man who kills him."

Smoke had walked up, listening. The news came as no surprise to him.

Walt looked at him. "Jud knows that with you out of the picture this whole operation would fold. Me and Cheyenne and Dolittle and Harrison could hold on for a time, but not for long. Maybe it's time for me to sell out and move on; take Doreen and Mickey with me and the old woman and just get gone."

"Is that what you want to do, Walt?"

"Hell, no!" There was considerable heat in the man's voice.

"Then don't. But here's what we can do: round up the rest of your herds and sell off the older stuff. That would take some strain off the range. We could use the boys to drive them to the railhead at Preston. Me and Cheyenne would stay here on the place with you to make sure Jud's men don't burn the house down."

Walt thought for a moment, then nodded his head. "All right, let's do 'er."

Leaving Cheyenne in charge of the roundup, Smoke saddled up and headed for the nearest telegraph office to find a buyer for the cattle. He did not take the normally traveled roads or trails, but instead cut across country, blazing his own trail.

Smoke wasn't worried about the men Jud Vale had hired. Most of them were stand-up, look-you-in-the-eye gunfighters. They had a reputation to defend or to build, and back-shooters they were not. It was the bounty hunters that Smoke knew would be coming in who worried him.

That scum had no scruples or morals or anything that even remotely resembled those attributes.

And they would be coming in once that five thousand dollar ante on his head was spread about the country; that would not take long to accomplish.

He made the ride to the wire office with no trouble, and sent wires out until he found a buyer who knew him and was interested in the cattle. He made arrangements over the wires to meet the shipment at the railhead with a bank draft.

He walked over to the hotel and checked in, then got himself a bath and a shave and changed clothes while his range clothing was being washed, dried, and ironed. Then he headed for a cafe for a meal.

Smoke was a handsome, striking-looking man, tall and muscular, and he turned many a female head as he strode up the boardwalk, spurs jingling. And he caused many a man to step back as he passed, for even though Smoke did not know it, and would have scoffed at it if someone had told him so, there was clear and present danger in those cold brown eyes. And by the way he wore his guns, there was no denying that he was very comfortable with those Colts, and knew how to use them. And more importantly, would use them.

He had changed into dark pinstripe trousers over his polished boots, a white shirt with a black string tie, and a leather vest.

He decided to have a beer before he ate his lunch and pushed open the batwings of the saloon, stepping inside.

The bounty hunters and the gunfighter locked eyes.

John Wills, Dave Bennett, Shorty Watson, and Lefty Cassett were sharing a bottle and playing poker.

Smoke told the barkeep he wanted a beer and walked over to their table, pulling out a chair and sitting down. "Deal me in, boys."

"You got a lot of brass on your butt, Jensen," Lefty told him. "Who the hell invited you?"

"You're hurting my feelings, Lefty. Makes me think I smell bad. And to think I just spent good money to have a bath and a shave."

"Very funny, Smoke," Wills said. "Notice how we're all laughing."

"I can see that. You boys gonna deal me in or not?"

"Closed game, Jensen," Shorty told him. "Just like you're gonna be soon. Closed. Like in a box."

They thought that was funny. Hysterically so. Smoke smiled with their laughter. They stopped laughing when they heard the almost inaudible click of a hammer being eared back.

"Is the joke over so soon?" Smoke asked, an innocent

expression on his face. "Keep your hands where I can see them, boys."

"You can't shoot us like this, Jensen," Wills said, a very hopeful note in his voice. "That'd be murder!"

"And you law-abiding boys certainly don't hold with murder, now, do you?" Smoke's voice was low-pitched and deadly.

Lefty softly cursed Smoke.

"Boys," Smoke told them, as he tapped the barrel of his Colt off Shorty's knee, that action bringing a sheen of sweat on the man's face. "I'm going to have myself a nice quiet drink and then I'm going to the cafe for something to eat. While I'm having my drink, you boys finish yours. While I'm in the cafe, I'd better see you scum ride out of town, and don't come back while I'm here."

"And if we don't?" Dave Bennett challenged.

"I'll come out of the cafe with both hands full of Colts and one thing on my mind: killing all four of you."

Wills swallowed hard and said, "This ain't like you, Smoke. You've usually had to be pushed into a gunfight."

"I came out here for a vacation. Soon as I crossed over into Idaho Territory, folks started pushing me. Now I'm pushing back. Keep another thought in mind, boys: if you ride out of here heading east, I'll know what side you're on."

"And . . . ?" Shorty asked.

"I will officially declare open season on bounty hunters."

Smoke holstered his Colt, much to the relief of all the men around the table. He stood up, turned his back to the men, and walked to the bar, ordering a drink.

Lefty exhaled slowly. "We got some talkin' to do, boys. We cross the Bear headin' east. This here job ain't gonna be no cakewalk."

"I say we take him as a group," Wills said. "Winner take it all."

"Here and now?" Shorty asked, doubt in his voice. "Standin' up and lookin' at him?"

"Hell, no! We'll ambush him. But we're gonna wait. The ante

is sure to go up as Jensen puts more and more punk gunslingers into the ground. We'll just lay back and let them reputation-huntin' gunhands get kilt. Then we'll make our move."

Smoke sat at a table by a window, eating his meal, and watched the bounty hunters ride out of town, heading west. The move was not unexpected and didn't fool him one bit. He'd bet a sack of gold nuggets that Wills and his bunch would get a couple of miles out of town and then swing around and double back, try to get ahead of him and maybe set up an ambush. For sure they were going to head east where the trouble was, and the blood money was waiting for the man or men who killed Smoke Jensen.

Right then and there, over his apple pie and third cup of coffee—for Smoke was a coffee-drinking man—he made up his mind that he was in this fracas to stay, come Hell, Jud Vale, or that hot-eyed Doreen.

Smoke Jensen just did not like to be pushed.

Smoke left before dawn the following morning. He rode straight south out of town and did not turn east until he came to a canyon very close to the Utah line. He built a hat-sized fire and cooked his supper, then mounted up and rode until dusk before finding a place to bed down for the night. The bounty hunters might find him, but Smoke was going to make it as difficult as possible for them.

He was back in the saddle again before dawn, and did not stop to boil coffee until the sun had bubbled its way up into the sky and he'd found a place that was easily defended.

He crossed the Wasatch Range and pointed Dagger's nose north, keeping on the west side of Bear Lake. He was on home range by late afternoon.

"Any trouble?" Cheyenne asked in the barn.

"None. But I did run into four bounty hunters."

"More than that drifted in the last couple of days. And Jud Vale is hirin' more guns. I think the no-count is gonna hit the herd and to hell with whether the boys gits hurt."

Smoke smiled. At the wire office he had sent and received more than one telegraph. He handed a copy to Cheyenne. The man read it and his leathery face crinkled in a smile.

Received your wire. STOP *Would be delighted to accompany the boys on a cattle drive.* STOP *Expect me at the ranch in three days.* STOP.

It was signed by the editor of the Montpelier paper.

"Tomorrow morning, I'll ride over to the trading post and tack this to the wall," Smoke said. "Jud will have it in his hands within hours. Then we'll see how he reacts to this news."

"Son of a bitch!" Jud shouted. Then he tore the wire to small bits, flinging the paper to the floor and kicking at the shreds. "Damn that Smoke Jensen to Hell!"

"This shore changes the plan," Jason said.

With a long sigh, Jud nodded his head. "Tell the boys to relax. We can't hit the herd with a damn newspaperman along. Public opinion would crucify me. The territorial governor would have this place swarming with U.S. Marshals if just one of those damn kids got hurt and it was reported."

"But they might not have a ranch to come back to," Jason said with a wicked smile.

"Yeah," Jud said softly. "You damn right!"

"You boys take 'er easy," Walt told the gathering in dawn's first light. "Ten miles a day is fine with me."

The editor of the newspaper had brought three men with him, a cub reporter from back East and two tough-looking men from his church. The men were heavily armed and ready for trouble.

Smoke knew there would be no trouble against the herd on this run. Jud was arrogant and perhaps crazy in the head, but he wasn't stupid. Smoke expected the drive to make it through with only the normal mishaps that took place on any cattle drive.

But he was equally certain the ranch would be attacked.

They stood and watched as the men and boys began moving the cattle out, the cattle setting their own pace.

After the dust had settled, Smoke began his preparations for the attack he was sure was forthcoming.

Cheyenne would stay in and defend the bunkhouse. The old mountain man and gunfighter had loaded up several rifles and half a dozen pistols. He had plenty of food prepared by the ladies and a couple of barrels of water to use against fire, should it come to that.

Before the drive began, Smoke had fortified the horses' stalls with extra boards. The stalls were as safe from bullets as they could make them.

Both Alice and Doreen could handle a rifle or pistol as well as, or better than, the average man. They would stay in the house with Walt and Micky.

Smoke would station himself in the loft of the barn. He had placed loaded rifles and shotguns at both ends of the building, and he had plenty of food and water to last out any siege.

Now all they had to do was wait, and sometimes that was harder than the actual battle.

The next move was up to Jud Vale and his men.

Probably forty or more men were to wage war against an old rancher, his wife, a young woman, her eight-year-old son, three old men, a group of boys whose average age was twelve, and one gunfighter.

Smoke had to laugh and question the bravery of those who rode with Jud Vale.

Just before dark, Smoke did a once-around of the buildings, looking in first on those in the house.

"We're set, Smoke," the rancher told him. "We've got Micky in the basement, guardin' the potatoes and the canned goods."

Smoke grinned and nodded. "No bullet can reach him down there, for sure." He noticed that both Alice and Doreen had changed into men's britches, so they could get around faster. Doreen did things to those jeans that the manufacturer never dreamed of.

She noticed the direction his eyes were taking and smiled at him.

"I got to go," Smoke muttered, and left the house.

In the bunkhouse, Cheyenne waved him toward the coffeepot. "I went over to the house about an hour ago," the old mountain man said. "Both them wimmin was prancin' around in men's britches. I never seen the like. This goes on, wimmin'll be votin' 'fore long and that'll be the ruination of the country." He was reflective for a moment. "Not that I ever voted that much myself. Quit altogether about a year after I cast my vote for Millard Fillmore. But, hell, anybody can make a mistake. I was gonna vote for that Abe Lincoln. But by the time I made up my mind and got to where I could vote, somebody had done up and shot him. Plumb-disheartenin'. Damn shore ruined Abe's night out, too. You much on votin', Smoke?"

"I wasn't until I married Sally. Kind of hard to find a ballot box at Brown's Hole."

"For a fact. Fort Misery, we used to call it. But I 'spect Preacher told you that."

"Yes, he did."

"Ol' warhoss is still kickin'. He's got to be eighty-five if he's a day. But them Injuns is takin' right good care of him. And I understand they's some old gunslingers and mountain men got together and in the process of building a retirement home for us old coots."

"That's my understanding."

"Won't that be grand! I'll have to go check that out—if I ever live to be old, that is."

Smoke laughed at him and walked back to the barn.

It was full dark when he crawled into the loft and made himself comfortable at the east end of the barn. He figured that was the direction from which the attack would most likely come.

Before taking his position, he watched the lamps go out in both the house and the bunkhouse as the defenders made ready for war.

Smoke settled down and waited.

6

Arrogant! Smoke thought, as he heard the sounds of hooves drumming on the road. Jud is so sure of himself that he just rides right up the road to the gate.

He heard the gates being torn down and then the wild screams of the hired guns as they galloped up the road toward the house.

Smoke quickly shifted positions and sighted a man under the hunter's moon that illuminated the night sky. He took up slack on the trigger and the butt-plate slammed his shoulder. A saddle emptied just as gunfire from the house and bunkhouse roared, shattering the night and emptying half a dozen more saddles.

He heard Jud's voice, hollering for his men to fall back to the ridges.

Smoke fired again, and saw a man jerk in the saddle. He managed to stay on his horse, but one arm was hanging uselessly and flopping by his side.

The attackers had been able to fire no more than half a dozen shots before they were beaten back.

One man struggled to his boots in the road and began staggering and lurching toward the gates. The defenders held their fire and let him go. Just before he reached the gates, he collapsed facedown in the hard-packed dirt and did not move.

That sight must have done it for the riders. Someone shouted, "Hell with this! The luck ain't with us this night."

The attackers rode off, heading back for the friendlier range of the Bar V. They left their dead and wounded behind them.

Smoke and the others waited a reasonable length of time, to see if it was a trick, and then slowly and cautiously gathered in the yard.

Smoke and Cheyenne roamed about, checking on the men sprawled on the ground.

They found several alive. "What do we do with those still alive?" Cheyenne questioned.

"Patch them up and get word to Jud to come and get them," Smoke told him. "Maybe pile them in a wagon and send them back to Jud. We'll see." He was kneeling down beside a man who was alive, but not for long. He had been shot in the center of the chest.

"He'll never quit, Jensen," the dying man gasped. "Vale's a crazy man."

"Why is he doing it?"

The man ignored that. "As long as he's got a dime in his jeans he'll hire fighting men."

"Why?" Smoke persisted.

"King. To be king. Wants to control everything from the state line to Preston. Everything and everybody."

"Shut up, Slim!" another wounded man growled, mercenary and loyal to the gun right to the end.

"You go to hell, Lassiter!" Slim told him. He cut his eyes to Smoke. The light was slowly fading from them. "Vale's got gunhands comin' in on the train. This is shapin' up to be the biggest range war in . . . the state. He'll overpower you just by . . . numbers, Jensen. And he's just about reached . . . the point where he don't give a damn if the kids git hurt."

Slim groaned and closed his eyes. He did not open them again.

Smoke rose to his boots and took the blanket that Doreen handed him, spreading it over the dead gunfighter. Cheyenne had taken all the guns and ammo from the dead and wounded men. They would be added to the arsenal of the Box T. Smoke felt sure they would be needed before all this was over.

He knelt down beside Lassiter. The man had a bullet-burn on the side of his head and a slight shoulder wound. Painful but not serious. "I ought to call the U.S. Marshals in here and file charges against all of you, Lassiter . . ."

The gunfighter sneered at him.

". . . But that would take weeks and we'd have to keep you prisoner and look at your ugly face every day. It just isn't worth it."

"You better kill me, Jensen," Lassiter warned. "Davidson was a friend of mine."

"You should choose your friends more carefully, Lassiter. No, I'm not going to kill you. Not like this, anyway. Not at this time."

"Then you're a damn fool, Jensen!"

"Maybe. But I can sleep at night, and I don't make war against kids and women and old people."

"Who gives a damn what happens to a bunch of snot-nose brats!"

Smoke was a hard man in a harsh time and environment, and he had killed many, many men. But he had to shake his head at the cold-blooded callousness of Lassiter.

"Back away and let me finish him," Cheyenne said, walking up. "We got it to do sooner or later."

Doreen stood looking at it all through wide and scared eyes.

Smoke had no doubts about the old mountain man's ability to do just what he suggested. And he knew the old man was right: they would have it to do sooner or later. But he just couldn't kill the wounded man that way.

He shook his head. "Get him patched up, Doreen. We'll put him in a wagon."

He walked over to where a young man lay, gut shot. The young gunfighter, no more than a couple of years out of boyhood, lay with both hands clutching his belly. The blood seeped darkly through his fingers, glistening wetly under the light of the hunter's moon.

"You got a mamma you want me to write, boy?"

He shook his head, wincing with the painful movement. "They throwed me out of the house a long time ago. I wasn't about to spend the rest of my life . . . sloppin' hogs and milkin' cows."

"Beats what you got now," Smoke coldly and bluntly informed him.

The young man cussed him. Smoke watched as his right hand slipped toward his large belt buckle. Smoke reached down and pulled a derringer from behind the buckle before the gunhand could reach it. The young gunfighter cursed him even more.

"How much was Jud Vale paying you, boy?"

"A hundred a month and found!" He moaned the words as the pain reached higher levels in his bullet-shattered belly.

"Maybe you can buy something in Hell."

"They'll kill you, Jensen! This is one fight you ain't gonna win. Your reputation . . . ain't gonna hep you none this time around. Jud Vale's better than you. His real name is . . . is . . ."

"Shet your mouth, you bastard!" Lassiter shouted at the young man.

But the admonition fell on dead ears. The young gunny's eyes rolled back in his head as his soul went winging to a fiery, smoky eternity. His boot heels and spurs drummed and jangled against the ground and then he was still.

Smoke walked over to Walt. "How long has Jud been in this area, Walt?"

"'Bout twenty-five years. He just appeared one day with that damn Jason fellow."

"He doesn't look that old to me."

"He's older than he looks. But he's one hell of a man still. Don't sell him short none. I'd peg him in his late forties. He might be fifty even. Hard to tell with a man like that."

"No idea where he came from?" Smoke got the strong impression that Walt was lying. But why?

"Not a clue."

Cheyenne walked up, hearing the last of the conversation. "He come up here by way of Texas," the old mountain man told them "But I doubt he was Texas born. I 'member when he got here. Like all them hands of his, I think he's runnin' from the law somewheres."

"And you would guess . . . ?"

Cheyenne shrugged. "Back East. But that's just a guess. It'd be hard to read his backtrail after all these years."

"What's the count on those still alive, Cheyenne?"

"Four dead and three wounded. None of them hurt too bad."

"Can one of them drive a wagon?"

"Oh, yeah."

"Let's hitch up a team and get them on their way. We'll pile the dead in with them."

"Beats the hell outta diggin' a hole," Cheyenne said with a wicked grin.

Walt, Smoke, and Cheyenne took turns standing guard that night, but as it turned out, they could have all slept soundly, for Jud Vale and his so-called fighting men had had quite enough of the Box T for this go-around.

"Four dead," Walt said, holding a cup of coffee in his hands, warming them against the early morning chill.

"They'll be more," Smoke told him. "This battle is just getting started. Now I'm afraid that some of the kids are going to be hurt."

"I don't think that even Jud Vale would do that. Not deliberately. One of those kids gets hurt, the whole area would turn agin him, and he knows it. But they might catch a bullet that was meant for one of us."

"The kids desperately need the money for their families," Smoke concluded. "I think what I'll do is ride around the area and speak to the mothers and fathers about it. Lay it on the line. Whatever they say, that's it."

Walt spoke around the stem of his pipe, "With most of the herd gone, we could do without the younger ones. Whatever the parents say, Smoke."

Smoke began seeking out and questioning the parents early the next morning, riding first to Little Chuckie's house—if that's what the shack could be called. It wasn't that his parents were rawhiders, they were just having a tough time getting the farm operation going—with Jud Vale and his men no small part of that struggle.

"It would really be a blow to Chuckie's pride iffen you was to send him home, Mr. Smoke," the father said. His wife nodded her head in agreement. "The boy is right proud of being able to bring in some money this summer. We'll leave it up to him."

Smoke rode over to the parents of Matthew, the frail little boy with the thick glasses. He got the same message as before. The parents were not unconcerned about their children; it was simply that this was still the raw frontier, and one grew up and pulled his or her weight from the git-go. It was called survival.

Smoke spent that day and most of another day talking with the parents of the boys. The message he got, though worded differently, came out to mean the same thing: it was up to the boys whether to stay or leave.

Smoke drifted on over to the railhead, arriving there about the same time as the herd. He watched through hard, chilly eyes, as the passenger car spewed forth a dozen or more booted, spurred, and two-gunned men. Smoke did not need a telegraph wire to tell him that these were the men the kid had told him about before he died in the front yard of the Box T spread.

Jud Vale was going for the brass ring this time, for Smoke recognized many of the newly arrived hired guns.

He watched as Gimpy Bonner limped off the train and made his way back to the horse cars. Gimpy was deadly quick and had no backup on him. He had a horse shot out from under him years back and the horse rolled on his leg, breaking it in several places, leaving him with a permanent limp.

Shorty DePaul, all five feet five inches of him followed Gimpy. Short he may be, but those guns of his, and his ability to use them, made him as tall as the next man.

The editor of the Montpelier newspaper had walked over to stand by Smoke's side and watch the gunfighters leave the train. "Who is that one?" he asked.

"Scott Johnson. From down Arizona way. That stocky fellow with him is called Yates. Right behind them is De Grazia and Jake Hube. They work as a team; they'll shoot you front or back. Doesn't make any difference to them."

"Looks like Jud Vale is pulling out all the stops, doesn't it?"

"For a fact," Smoke said, as he watched two gunfighters named Becket and Pike step out of the car.

Jaeger, the German immigrant turned gunfighter, stepped down right behind them. Molino was right behind him.

Smoke ticked the names off to the editor.

Chato Di Peso, the much feared and very dangerous New Mexico bounty hunter, stepped down, hitching at his gun belt as he walked.

There were several young punks, with fancy guns and silver-adorned gun belts, tagging with the better-known gunnies. Smoke counted them out as two-bit never-would-be's with no sand in them.

"I think," the editor said, "that I shall inform the governor of this gathering of trash."

"Go ahead. But it won't do any good."

"Why?" the man asked indignantly.

"There isn't a man over there who is wanted for anything that I know of. And there is no law against hiring tough men to work for you."

"There is going to be a bloodbath around the Bear, Mr. Jensen."

"Yes. And the only way I know to avoid it is for Walt and Alice Burden to turn tail and run; just give up their holdings to a madman and leave the country. Would you want to see them do that, Mr. Argood?"

"No," the editor replied quickly. "I would not. Is there a joker in this deck, Smoke?"

Smoke smiled. "Yes. And his name is Clint Perkins. He's an unknown. Have you ever seen him?"

"No. Few people have over the years. Or at least, if they have, they aren't talking. But I can tell you that many still look upon him as some sort of Robin Hood."

"But you don't."

Argood snorted in disgust. "He's no better than a common outlaw. And personally, from what I know about him, I think he's insane."

"Is he headquartered in this area?"

"No one knows. He's a mystery man. And a master of disguises." He looked at the most famous gunfighter in the West. "You think he'll show up here?"

"I think so. This is just too good for him to miss." He didn't know how much the editor knew, so he chose his words carefully. "I think there is a lot of hate in the man; all bottled up and ready to explode. When it does, it's going to get very interesting.

"That, young man," Argood said drily, "is one way of putting it."

7

Smoke took the bank draft from the cattle buyer and tucked it safely away in a money belt around his waist. He had a letter from Walt giving him the authority to endorse the draft and deposit it in the bank over in Malad City, a wild, rip-roaring town with a history of murder, lynchings, and stage holdups. But the Overland Stage Company—whose run stopped at Malad City—had a good record of foiling holdups, so Walt's money would be reasonably safe after being deposited.

Smoke told Dolittle and Harrison to keep the boys close until he got back.

He crossed the Bear and headed for the wide-open town of Malad City. The town was named by French trappers, who, after becoming sick from gorging on beaver meat, named the town Malade, thinking the area unhealthy.

Smoke had a hunch that with the news of Jud Vale's hiring of gunhands now so widespread, Malad City would be crawling with guns for hire stopping for liquid refreshments—and a fling with the hurdy-gurdy girls—as they made their way to the Bar V. And he also wondered if the ante on his head had been upped past the five thousand dollar mark.

It wouldn't surprise him a bit.

As he rode, Smoke tried to put some more reason behind what Jud Vale was doing. Or was what Walt had told him the sum total of it all? Smoke concluded that Walt was probably right in his assessment of the situation. If Vale could get his hands on the Box T, he would then have the largest spread in the state, and would certainly be a powerful man, a man to reckon with.

On this trip, Smoke stayed with the main road leading to Malad City, and a sorry road it was.

He met several groups of men, riding in twos and threes, all looking like hardcases, and all heading east. They either did not recognize him, or did not want to brace him with such short backup.

Since he had been late getting away from the railhead, Smoke made camp just to the south of Oxford Peak, the snow-capped mountain thrusting up more than a mile and a half into the air. He was boiling his coffee and frying his bacon when he heard the faint sounds of hooves approaching his camp from out of the fast falling dusk, the rider coming from the north.

"Hello, the fire! I'm friendly."

"Then come on in and light and sit. Coffee's almost fit to drink."

Smoke saw the young man's hair sticking out from under his hat before he saw anything else. Flame red. He'd bet the young rider was called Rusty. The man's outfit was old, but well-cared for, and Smoke liked the way the young rider saw to his horse's needs before he took care of his own. He carefully rubbed the animal down with handfuls of grass and saw that it was watered and picketed on good graze. Smoke also noticed that the redhead's gun was tied down—which might not mean anything, or everything.

As he approached the fire, tin cup and plate in his left hand, his grin was genuine and his handshake firm and quick.

"Sure am glad to see a friendly face. Most of the hombres I been seein' the past couple of days all looked like they could eat a porcupine and not feel the quills!"

Smoke filled his coffee cup without comment.

"My folks dubbed me Clarence, but nobody calls me that. Just Rusty."

"I guessed right at first glance." Smoke speared some bacon out of the pan and handed a hunk of bread to Rusty.

"Much obliged." He let his eyes drift over Smoke's rig, noting the two guns, one butt-forward.

"You ridin' east like all them others?" Smoke asked.

"West for a day, then I'll do a turnaround back to the Bear. Any work over yonder?"

"I'm lookin' for hands."

"You shore found one. My poke's as flat as a sit-on pancake."

"Might be dangerous signin' on with me."

Rusty's eyes narrowed. "What kind of work you got in mind, mister-whatever-your-name-is?"

"Punching cows. Fixing fence. Cleaning out waterholes. Cowboy work. You up to it?"

"Shore! That's what I been doin' since I was big enough to sit a saddle. What's the danger you talkin' about?"

Smoke sipped his coffee before replying. "Big rancher who is about half nuts is trying to run the old man and woman who own the spread off their land. They hit us the other night. We emptied seven saddles."

"How many is us?"

"You talking about hands?"

"Yep."

"Three old men who are about seventy and a handful of kids, average age twelve."

Rusty looked dead at him. "Are you serious?"

"As a crutch."

"What're you payin'?"

"A hundred a month and found."

"A hundred a month! Shoot, man! You just hired yourself a hand."

"Those are fighting wages, Rusty."

"I kinda figured they was. But I got to tell you, I ain't never hired out my gun."

"Can you use it?"

"Oh, yeah. I reckon I'm as good as the next man. I've drug iron a time or two."

"Any family?"

"Ma and Pa died years back. I got some cousins somewhere that I ain't never seen."

"Just curious. I want to know who to notify if you catch one."

"Just plant me where I fall, I reckon. And make sure my horse is taken care of. He's a good one."

"I'm heading over to Malad City. Then we'll head back to the Box T."

"Sounds good to me. You got a name?"

"Doesn't everyone?"

"You are a most exasperatin' feller! You 'shamed of your handle?"

"No."

Rusty cussed and then ate his bacon, mopping the grease out of his tin plate with bread. He poured another cup of coffee, rolled a cigarette, and leaned back. "You a gunfighter?"

"Some say I am."

"You look familiar to me. I seen you somewheres before. On a wanted poster, maybe?"

"No. I'm not wanted. I own a ranch down Colorado way. The Sugarloaf. I'm just helping out an old couple. I don't like to see folks shoved around."

"Right nice of you. I kinda get riled up some myself when somebody tries to roll over other folks. You gonna tell me your name?"

Smoke smiled faintly. "I tell you my name, you might not come to work."

"For a hundred a month and found? You could tell me your name was Satan and I wouldn't back away."

"All right," Smoke replied. "Come to think of it, you just might be riding into a corner of Hell after all." He left it at that.

* * *

Smoke and Rusty reached Malad City at mid-morning, just as the town was catching its breath after a wild and raucous night. Things had been reasonably quiet the previous night, with only one killing.

"Don't never ask nobody for directions in this place," Rusty told him. "When they laid out these streets, they just tossed a handful of sticks on the ground for a blueprint . . . and then followed it."

They stabled their horses and Smoke pointed out a cafe, telling Rusty he'd meet him there in a few minutes. He took care of Walt's bank draft and walked the boardwalk to the cafe. He saw several gunslicks he knew by name and a dozen more who had the hardcase brand stamped all over them. And a half-dozen punks who were looking for a reputation, but more than likely would find a grave to hold their swagger long before they found a reputation.

Smoke Jensen had been elusive for over a decade, surfacing outside of his ranch in Colorado only briefly. Many people knew his name but could not put a face to it, unless they had memorized the covers of the many penny dreadfuls, most of which were rarely accurate.

He received many a furtive glance as he walked toward the cafe, for danger clung to him; it was an aura that made many strong and brave men step aside until he had passed.

Smoke was scarcely into his thirties, just now approaching the prime years of his life, but he was already a living legend, and not just west of the Mississippi. Had he elected to cut notches into the handles of his Colts after each kill, he would have gone through half a dozen sets and still not have any handles left. But only tinhorns did that.

He opened the door to the cafe and stepped in, the good smells of cooking making him realize how hungry he was. Rusty was already working on his first plate of bacon and eggs and fried potatoes—and the first of several pots of coffee.

The redhead pushed out a chair with his boot and Smoke sat down.

"Been several folks wonderin' who you are," the newly hired puncher said. "Most I heard come to the conclusion that you was a lawman of some sort."

"I've worn a badge a time or two," Smoke admitted, then called out his order to the counterman. He picked up his cup and allowed the waitress to fill it.

She met his eyes. "I seen you two or three years back." She spoke the words softly. "You be careful in this town. It's filled up with hired guns, all of them just burnin' to kill you."

"I appreciate that."

She nodded and walked back into the kitchen.

Rusty's freckled face screwed up with disgust. "Seems like ever'body knows who you are but me!"

Smoke sugared his coffee and stirred. "The name is Jensen."

The redhead's fork froze midway to his mouth. *"Smoke* Jensen?" he finally managed to say.

"That's it. Now close your mouth before a bug decides to fly in there."

Rusty filled his mouth with food and then closed it. "Boy, I sure know how to pick 'em," he muttered. "I'm beginnin' to wonder if a hundred a month is enough."

"And found," Smoke reminded him.

"Food ain't too tasty with a bellyful of lead," the puncher said mournfully. But there was a definite twinkle in his eyes.

"You didn't sign a contract," Smoke reminded him. "Feel free to ride."

"Naw! Hell, I'll stick around. I ain't never ridden with such highfalutin' company before. Might be interestin'."

"I'm not looking for trouble, Rusty. After we eat our meal, I plan on saddling up and riding out."

"That must be why you walk around with them hammer thongs off your guns."

Smoke grinned. "I just believe in being a very cautious man, that's all."

"Right. With your name, you damn well better be."

The two men cleaned their plates, Rusty eating two plates of food without apology, then finishing off another pot of coffee. Not as strong as they liked it, but it would do. Then they leaned back, rolled cigarettes, and lit up. The cafe was gradually filling with the lunch crowd, all of the diners giving the two men short and cautious looks as they took their seats.

Then the door opened and four hardcases stepped inside.

Bob Garner and Montana Slim were the only two that Smoke recognized. The other two were unknown to him. But Garner and Montana Slim were quite enough to face on a full stomach.

Or an empty belly for that matter.

Slim's eyes widened as they settled on Smoke and recognition set in. Then he grinned, his hands close to the butts of his guns.

But the humor—if that's what it was—did not reach his killer eyes.

"We done got the hotshot all bottled up, boys," Slim announced, in a too-loud voice. "And some funny lookin' pup with him."

"This dog's got teeth, partner," Rusty told him. "An' I ain't been a pup in a long time."

"Little puppy dog done got up on his hind legs, boys," Garner said with a nasty grin. "I just might have to find me a stick and whup his tail back between his legs. What'd you boys think about that?"

"I wouldn't try it," the redhead warned. His quietly spoken words had steel behind them. "You just might find that stick stickin' out of a part of you that you didn't figure on."

Several of the men in the cafe laughed at that.

Several more men in the cafe softly pushed back their chairs and took their leave before the lead they knew was coming started flying.

And a stray bullet doesn't give a damn who it hits.

"You got a fat mouth, red on the head," Slim told Rusty.

"You wearin' a gun, ugly face?" Rusty popped right back at him.

Slim's face turned as red as Rusty's hair. "In here or outside?" He challenged the soft-voiced but hard-talking puncher.

"It don't make a damn to me."

The counterman came up with a sawed-off shotgun, pointed right at Slim's belly. "You hardcases ain't gonna shoot up this place," he informed them, earing back both hammers. "So this is my way of tellin' you to take your guns and your big mouths and your quarrel out into the street. And I mean lak raht now!"

Slim nodded, then looked at Smoke and Rusty. "We'll meet you boys at the south edge of town. That is, if you've got the belly for it."

"We'll be there," Smoke told him, finishing his cigarette and stubbing it out. "Watching our backs all the way."

Bob Garner spun around, red from the neck up and his ugly face turning even uglier. "What the hell does that mean, Jensen?"

"It means, Garner, that I think you're all a bunch of back-shooting cowards!"

"Git outta here!" the counterman hollered. "Afore I turn loose both of these barrels!"

The four hired guns and bounty hunters stomped out of the cafe. Smoke poured another cup of coffee and Rusty did the same. They sugared and stirred and sipped.

"How do we handle this?" Rusty asked, his voice low so that only Smoke could hear. "And what's this about them bein' back-shooters?"

"They're not back-shooters. I just said that to make sure they wouldn't try it. It's a matter of pride for them now. Some of their own kind would shoot them if they tried to set up an ambush."

They both looked up as the waitress set two thick slices of apple pie on the table before them.

"On the house, boys," the counterman said. "I ain't never

had nobody as famous as Smoke Jensen come in my place afore."

The men nodded their thanks and fell to eating the pie, chasing it down with gulps of coffee. Around them, men were beginning to place wagers on the outcome of the impending gunfight. Most of the bets went to Smoke and the red-headed cowboy with him.

Their pie and coffee finished, Smoke and Rusty pushed back their chairs, settled their hats on their heads, and stood up, hitching at their gun belts.

"Good luck, boys!" the waitress called, as they were stepping out the door and onto the boardwalk.

The street that had been bustling with people when Smoke entered the cafe was now barren of human life as the two men began their lonely walk toward the edge of town. The word had been quickly passed among the townspeople that lead was about to fly.

A dog looked up from its midday doze and wagged its tail, its eyes seeming to say: you leave me alone and I'll do the same for you.

They walked past the animal, their spurs softly jingling. They stayed in the shadows of the buildings until coming to the very edge of town.

"I got a hunch that Slim and Bob will stay together," Smoke said. "So we play it like that. I'll take Montana Slim and Bob Garner. You handle the other two. I don't know them; they might be fast as lightning."

"I ain't all that fast," Rusty conceded. "But I don't hardly ever miss."

"That's the main thing. Many so-called fast guns usually put the first bullet into the dirt. There they are, Rusty. I got a hunch they'll want to jaw a little first; work up some courage. We'll let them. You ready?"

"As I'll ever be."

The men stepped off into the dirt of the street and began the short walk toward destiny.

8

The hired guns and bounty hunters had positioned themselves by a falling-down old barn, obviously one of the first structures to be built in the town. And it was just as obvious that the men had done so with a plan in mind. Smart, Smoke thought.

"After the first rounds are fired," Smoke told Rusty. "Any left standing are going to dive for the protection of that old barn. You hit the ground behind that log pile and I'll take the back of the building." His words were spoken low, so only Rusty could hear.

But the hired guns could see his lips moving. "What the hell are you two whisperin' about?" Montana called. "You workin' up some sort of sneaky play?"

"Neither one of us need sneaky plays to deal with scum like you," Smoke called, his voice easily carrying the distance.

Montana Slim cursed them both, loud and long.

All four of the men Smoke and Rusty faced were wearing two six guns, low and tied down.

"Most men can't use but one gun at a time. And some of them can't use that one very well," Smoke pointed out as the gunfighter and the cowboy continued their shortening of the distance to death.

"And you . . . ?"

"I'm the exception," Smoke said without a single note of bragging. He was simply telling the truth.

There was about fifty feet between them when Smoke halted the parade.

"All right, Montana," Smoke called. "You made your brags back at the cafe. Now let's see if you've got the sand to back it up."

"Ten thousand on your head, Jensen!" Bob Garner called out. "We'll live nice on that money."

"You have to collect it first, Garner." Smoke tossed that reminder out to him.

Garner's laugh was full of confidence.

Ten thousand, Smoke mused. Surely it can't go much higher than that.

But then, after a second's thought, he changed his mind, realizing that perhaps there was no limit to Jud Vale's obsessions with being king.

"Ten thousand!" Rusty muttered. "Man, I am choppin' in some high cotton, Smoke. Somebody is shore scared of you."

Smoke did not reply, nor did his eyes leave Montana Slim. It was as he had thought: Slim and Garner were partners and were staying together. Rusty would have to deal with the two bounty hunters—if that's what they were.

Smoke could hear faint rustlings on the boardwalks behind them. He knew that the crowds were gathering to watch the show. It was a dangerous sport for spectators, and many an onlooker had caught a stray bullet. But entertainment was scarce in western towns; many folks packed picnic lunches and would drive a wagon for a hundred miles, bringing the entire family to make an all-day event out of a public hanging.

"I'm tired of all this jawing, Slim," Smoke told him. "And I really don't want a killing. Why don't you boys just get on your horses and ride out of here?"

There was something unnerving about Smoke, something that shook even a hardened gunfighter like Montana Slim. He was just so damned sure of himself. Maybe he ought to be,

Montana admitted silently. *He's put more than a hundred men in the ground and there he stands, lookin' at me.*

But Montana Slim knew he had backed himself into a corner with only two ways out: either walk away victorious, or be propped up in front of the undertaking parlor on a board for all the folks to see.

"And I'm just damn tarred of your mouth, Jensen," Montana yelled. "Grab iron!" His hands flashed to his guns.

Montana thought he heard Smoke say, "All right, Slim." Then he felt twin hammer-blows slam into his chest as his knees began to buckle. Out of the corner of his eyes, the light fading fast, he saw Bob Garner run into the old barn. Montana Slim, the veteran and victor of half a hundred gunfights, lifted his hands and looked at them.

They were empty! Jensen had been so fast, he hadn't even grabbed iron. But that was . . . impossible! That thought was Montana's last as he pitched forward into the dust, dead.

Rusty had taken his time and placed his shots well. One bounty hunter was down on his belly, his blood staining the dirt from two bullet holes in his belly, and the other so-called gunfighter was holding up his one good arm in surrender; his other arm, his shooting arm, was broken at the elbow and hanging at a very queer angle.

Smoke was off and running between the old barn and another building that looked to be in just as bad a shape as the barn. He quickly reloaded as he ran.

A bullet whammed into a corral post and Smoke dropped to his belly, scooting behind an old watering trough. He caught a glimpse of a red and white checkered shirt and snapped off a shot. He didn't think he hit Garner, but the slug came close enough to bring a yelp of surprise from the man.

Smoke triggered off five more rounds, then holstered that Colt, drawing his left-hand pistol just as Garner ran briefly into view.

Smoke dusted him from side to side, spinning the man around and holding him there long enough for Smoke to take careful aim and put another slug into the man's chest. Bob Garner went down slowly and didn't get up.

It was over.

For this go-around anyway.

Smoke reloaded both guns and walked over to where he'd seen Garner fall. The gunny was lying on his back, very close to death.

It was not a pretty sight. Of course, Garner hadn't been very pretty to start with.

Smoke squatted down beside the man. There was not much life left in him.

And much of what life remained was spent in cussing Smoke.

Smoke waited until the dying man coughed up blood and tried to catch his breath. "Anybody you want me to write, Bob?"

A funny look came into the gunfighter's eyes. He shook his head. "Best . . . if the wife . . . just don't never see me agin. I ain't . . . been much of a husband or . . . father."

"Any money you got you want me to send them?"

"Spent it last . . . night on the . . . whoors."

Rusty walked up and stood listening.

"I'll swap your guns for a buryin', Bob," Smoke assured him.

"Right kind . . . of you. See you . . . boys in Hell!" Bob Garner closed his eyes and died.

Rusty was quiet as they rode out of Malad City that afternoon. The dead gunman had, for the moment, taken the fight out of those remaining in the town. They stood on the boardwalk and watched Smoke and Rusty clear town. Most would continue on toward the Bar V. But there were some, mostly older and wiser, who would elect to seek another trouble spot where they could ply their deadly trade. It was not that they were cowards, far from it. They simply knew Smoke Jensen's reputation and their own capabilities and limitations.

"Mean right up to the end," Rusty finally broke his silence.

"What are you talking about?"

"Garner. What makes a man like that, Smoke?"

"Some folks back East and in the cities are claiming it comes from bad rearing."

"Huh!" Rusty summed up his opinion of that. "I ain't disputin' your word, Smoke, but I just don't believe in that at all. I been on my own for years. And my pa was a mighty mean man. He liked to whup up us boys and girls. Didn't make no difference to him. My older sister run off when I was just a little shaver. I heard she was doin' good out in California. My other brother died from a beatin' Pa give him. Hell, Pa knocked me unconscious with his fists or with a chunk of stovewood more'un once. And I ain't never stole nothin' in my life, or rode the hootowl trail or done nothin' much that was ag'in the law. And nobody could have had a worser home life than me. So them folks that think what you just said don't know a pot of beans from a pile of cow droppin's."

Smoke grinned. "I had to be a man grown just after my thirteenth birthday, working a hardscrabble farm back in Missouri and looking after my sick mother. Wasn't ever enough food; just enough to keep body and soul together. So I know what you mean, Rusty. And no, I don't believe those so-called experts either.

"What makes men like Montana Slim and Bob Garner and all the rest be what they are?" He shook his head. "I think they were born to it, Rusty. They could have had all the advantages in the world and they would have turned out bad. A different kind of bad, maybe, but bad just the same."

"What do you mean, a different kind of bad?"

"Oh, they might have been bankers cheating old ladies or grocers cheating people and being mean-spirited folks. That type of thing."

Rusty thought about that for a mile or so. "You know, Smoke. You're right. There sure are a lot of mean-minded and mean-spirited people in this world. Why, I know a few people who was born into money, and come from nice parents. Kind parents. But their kids would steal the pennies off'n a dead man's eyes."

"That's what I mean, Rusty. Born to it. I call it the bad seed theory."

Rusty settled into the bunkhouse with the old men and the kids. Smoke had taken to sleeping in a room out in the barn.

And Doreen stopped batting her eyes at Smoke and seemed to be quite taken with Rusty—much to the relief of Smoke. She got to getting all gussied up and swishing around him until it was embarrassing for all the others around them. Rusty, he just grinned like an egg-suckin' dog and stood around in sort of a daze.

There had been no trouble from Jud Vale or his men during the time Smoke had been gone.

But gunfighters kept drifting into the area, in groups of twos and threes. Pretty soon, Smoke thought, Jud Vale was going to have his own private army. And he was going to have to make his move pretty quick, for he was paying out a lot of money for all his hired guns to sit around and do nothing. While many of the bounty hunters and hired guns could work cattle, Smoke had a hunch that damn few were going to. Most of them were just downright lazy.

On a bright, sunshiny morning, Smoke lined the boys up and laid it on the line to them, telling them what their parents had said, and leaving the final decision up to the young cow-punchers.

The boys huddled together for a time, and then Jamie stepped out of the group and faced Smoke.

"I allow as to how we'll stay, Mr. Smoke," the boy said. "We got to have the money to help out at home. And it ain't as if we never faced outlaws and the likes of Jud Vale before, 'cause we all have. I figure it like this, and you tell me if it don't meet with your approval and we'll work something else out."

Smoke waited, as did the other adults.

Jamie took a deep breath. "You see, sir, me and Alan and Cecil and two or three of the others, well, we know more about Jud Vale than you do, we think. We know it won't make no difference to him whether it's a grown man or a boy—not when it comes to standing in his way when he's a-goin' after something he wants. Like this ranch and Miss Doreen. So we went ag'in your orders and each of us stuck a pistol in our saddlebags."

Smoke sighed. He couldn't really blame the boys. He would have done the same thing had he been in their position. Smoke had been toting a pistol since he was thirteen. A Navy .36 caliber that had been given him back in '63 by the as yet unknown Confederate guerrilla fighter named Jesse James.

"Way we all figure it, Mr. Smoke, it's gonna be comin' down to the nut-cuttin' right shortly. And it ain't fair for no one to ask us to ride unarmed when we might catch a bullet at any moment. I reckon that's all I got to say, Mr. Smoke."

Smoke towered over the boy, staring down at him. Finally, and with a sigh, Smoke nodded his head. "All right, Jamie. I fear for your lives, but I can't ask you to disarm yourselves. I been packing a pistol since I was just a boy. But I have to ask you all to show me that you know how to use those guns."

"That's fair, sir," Jamie agreed. "When do you want us to do that?"

"Nothing like right now."

Cheyenne took one group of boys, Rusty took another, and Smoke took the third.

But damned if Smoke was going to have ten-year-olds packing pistols. Any boy under the age of twelve would stay close to the house and work in the yard or in the barn or corral. The boys packing iron would be Jamie, Matthew, Ralph, Leroy, Cecil, Alan, Rolly, Pat, and Oscar.

The frail Matthew, thick glasses and all, surprised Smoke. The boy was a born gunhand, the pistol seeming to be a natural extension of his arm. And his aim was deadly true. Even

Jamie took a backseat to Matthew. Smoke had held the very strong suspicion that Matt had been secretly practicing his draw and firing for some time. He asked him about it.

"Yes, sir," the boy said, blushing. "Whenever I could scrape up a few pennies to buy ammo, I been ridin' out far from the house and workin' at my draw."

"It's a natural talent you have, Matt. But it's not one your ma and pa will look upon with favor. You know that, don't you?"

"Yes, sir. I reckon that's right. But if a feller's got a knack for something, he ought to polish on it, shouldn't he?"

Should he? Smoke silently pondered, staring down at the frail boy packing the short-barreled sheriff's model Peacemaker. Should he? *What would I be doing now if I had not discovered and polished my talent for weapons?* Smoke thought.

How many graves have I filled because of my quickness with a gun? And did this boy have enough sand in him to live with a gun by his side and not use it recklessly?

But can I stop him? Should I stop him? This was still the frontier, and it was filled with hard, tough, and often cruel men. Men like Jud Vale and his hired guns.

"Yes, Matt," Smoke said slowly. "Yes. Conditions being what they are, I guess you should polish it. As long as there are men like Jud Vale around, and with us being miles from the nearest law, I guess you should. But use that gun wisely, boy. If the law can handle it, let them. If you're pushed into a corner, then it's all up to you. I reckon that's the way it's always been and I suppose that's the way it's always going to be."

"I ain't smart like no grownup," Matt said. "But that's the way I think, too."

Matt turned, drew, cocked, and fired. All in one smooth, quiet motion, the bullet striking true. Smoke experienced a hard push of memory, winging him back in years. Back to when he was a boy, traveling with Preacher. Back to his first real gunfight with white men.

* * *

Preacher and the boy, Smoke, had stopped in a rip-roaring mining camp just west of the Needle Mountains. It would soon be named Rico.

They had bought their supplies and were just about to leave when two rough-looking and unshaven men stepped into the combination trading post and barroom.

"Who owns that horse out yonder?" one demanded, trouble plain in his voice. "The one with the SJ brand?"

The boy Smoke laid his purchases on the counter and slowly turned. "I do."

"Which way'd you ride in from, boy?"

Preacher had slipped to his right, his left hand covering the hammer of his Henry rifle, concealing the click as he thumbed the hammer back.

Smoke's hands were at his sides, his left hand just inches from his left hand gun. "Who wants to know—and why?"

No one in the room said a word.

"Don't sass me, boy!" the bigger and uglier of the two said. "My name's Pike, and I say you come through my camp yesterday and stole my dust!"

Smoke smiled grimly. "You're a damn liar!"

Pike grinned, an ugly peeling back of the lips, exposing blackened rotting stumps of teeth. His right hand was hovering close to the butt of his pistol. "Why you smart-mouthed little punk. I think I'll just shoot your damned ears off."

"Why don't you try. I'm sure tired of hearing you shoot off your mouth," Smoke told him, no fear in his voice.

Pike looked confused for a moment. This kid didn't seem to be at all afraid of him. Odd. Pike was as big and strong as he was ugly. And he had been a loud-mouth bully all his life. People just didn't talk to him like this kid was doing. "I think I'll just kill you for that, kid."

Smoke laughed at him.

Pike and his partner reached for their guns.

Four shots thundered in the low-ceilinged room. Four shots so closely spaced, they seemed as one thunderous roaring. Dust and bird's nest droppings fell from the ceiling. Pike and friend were slammed out through the open doorway. One fell off the rough porch, dying in the dirt street. Pike, with two holes in his chest, died with his back against a support post, his eyes wide staring in disbelief that the kid, any kid, could be so fast. Neither man had managed to clear leather before the death blows hammered them into the hot, yawning, smoking gates of Hell.

All eyes in the black, powder-filled and dusty barroom moved to the young man standing by the bar, a Colt in each hand.

"Good God!" a man whispered the words in awe. "I never even seen the draw!"

Preacher had moved the muzzle of his Henry to cover the men at the tables. The bartender put his hands slowly on the bar, indicating that he wanted no trouble.

"We'll be leaving now," Smoke said, holstering his Colts and picking up his purchases from the counter. He walked out the door without looking back.

Outside, Smoke stepped over the sprawled, dead legs of Pike and walked past his dead friend.

"What are we 'posed to do with the bodies?" a man asked Preacher.

"Bury 'em."

"What's that kid's name?" another called.

"Smoke Jensen."

Smoke brought himself back to the present, standing and watching Matt shoot. The boy turned with a smile on his lips, waiting for approval from the most famous gunfighter in all the West.

"You'll do to ride the river with, Matt," Smoke told him.

9

Smoke walked back to his room in the barn, his thoughts still lingering back over the years—long and bloody years. He tried to recall the year he'd killed that trash over at Rico—1868, he thought it was.

He'd have to watch Matt, and watch him carefully.

He looked up as Cheyenne entered the room, his wise old eyes still startled at the speed of the young boy.

"Cheyenne, take the boy under your wing, just like Preacher did me. Teach him what Preacher taught me. He's going to need all the help he can get, I'm thinking."

Cheyenne nodded. "First time one of them so-called gun-slicks of Jud Vale tries to draw down on that boy and gets plugged in the brisket, the boy is gonna be legend. Like another young man I do seem to recall from some years back."

Smoke nodded. "Yeah, I've been recalling it myself. Matthew's sure got the speed and the eye, Cheyenne. But I don't think it's God-given. I think it's passed up from Hell!"

"Mayhaps you be right. I have thought the same thing myself more'un a time or two. Now then, Jamie ain't real fast, but he's shore enuff a good shot. And Leroy is a fine rifle shot but ain't worth a puma's poot with a short gun. Damn near shot hisself in the foot a while ago."

"How about the others?"

Rusty walked in, hearing the last. "They'll do, Smoke. They

ain't no burnin' firebrands with short guns, but they generally hit what they aim at. I been teachin' them to take their time and aim, even though the lead might be flyin' around them."

"Good advice. Sometimes hard to follow, though." He said the last with a grin.

"I heard that." Rusty returned the grin. "Been there myself a time or two."

Cheyenne poured a cup of coffee from the ever-present battered old pot and squatted down on the rough board floor. "I been doin' some head-figurin' whilst you was gone, Smoke. Jud's got hisself a regular army now. I figure he's got nearabouts thirty gunslicks recent hired on the payroll. That ain't countin' his regular hands, which is about fifteen on any given day. That comes to about fifty men ag'in us. And that ain't countin' the bounty hunters snoopin' and a-salivatin' around the countryside, lookin' for a shot at you."

"Yeah, we were lucky the other night. Jud won't be fool enough to try that move again. But it bothers me about the boys carrying guns."

"They've had 'em in they saddlebags all along. And you can bet that whilst they was out of our sight, they was haulin' 'em out and showin' 'em around. Bet, too, that Jud Vale's had snoopers out lookin' us over through spyglasses and seen them boys with the guns."

"I hadn't thought of that, Cheyenne. You're right." He glanced at Rusty. "Think you can do a day's work without your mind on Doreen?"

Rusty grinned. "That woman can walk into a room and raise the temperature fifteen degrees."

"Do we have to tell you what to do to cool it off?" Cheyenne grinned at him.

The flush on Rusty's face was a pretty fair match with his hair. He mumbled something about having to see his horse and left the room while Cheyenne and Smoke had a good laugh at his expense.

* * *

The days began to drift together, each one bringing with it the promise of full summer. And still Jud Vale made no more moves against the ranch. Smoke couldn't figure out what he was waiting on. Then an idea came to him.

"Is Mr. Argood Mormon?" he asked Walt.

"Big time Mormon. Big worker in the church. It's just about time for him to take his annual trip down into Utah. Church meeting of some sort."

"That's what I figured," Smoke said.

"Figured what?" Cheyenne asked.

"That's what he's waiting on. For the editor of the paper to be gone. No news would be reported if Argood was not around to cover it. And you can bet that Vale will create some incident around Montpelier to keep that young reporter busy while he's striking at the ranch."

"You may be right," Walt said, touching a match to the tobacco in his pipe. "He's sorry, but smart."

"It's time for another run into the village for supplies. I'll take two of the boys with me. I want to leave as many defenders behind as possible. We'll pull out in the morning."

Leroy drove the wagon; Smoke and Matthew rode beside the wagon as it bumped and bounced along the narrow, rutted road toward the trading post. Smoke knew he was taking a chance bringing Matt along, but the boy needed some personal things for himself and wanted to buy his ma a present with money he'd earned himself. Smoke had not asked Matthew to stow his pistol in the saddlebags. The gun had become a natural part of the boy—a feeling that Smoke knew only too well.

But Smoke had talked hard to the boy just before leaving. "Matt, I want you to realize that out here, once you strap a gun on, there are those who won't give a damn how young you are. The only thing they're going to see is that hogleg on your hip. If any of Jud Vale's hired guns are at the post, they're going to taunt you, try to pull you into a fight. And because the West is what it is, I won't interfere unless they gang up on you."

"I understand, Mr. Smoke," the boy replied solemnly.

"You won't reconsider and stay at the ranch?"

"I reckon not, sir."

"Very well."

Smoke breathed a sigh of relief as they approached the post. Only a couple of horses were tied at the hitch rail, and he recognized them as belonging to some area cattlemen, men whose holdings were so far to the west of Jud Vale's spread that they really had little to fear from the man and his obsessions—so far.

Smoke felt that they might be able to pick up the supplies and get away safely. At least he hoped so. But he wasn't going to put any money on it. Once again, doubts assailed him. He could have ordered Matt to stay behind at the ranch. But the boy had earned his money and had a right to spend it. Matt was not a slave to the Box T; he could come and go as he pleased.

Smoke swung down from the saddle and looped the reins around the hitch rail, Matt doing the same. Out of the corner of his eye, Smoke watched the boy slip the hammer thong from his pistol. Cheyenne had drilled that into the boy's head. With a sigh, Smoke stepped up onto the porch. He handed Leroy the supply list and told Matt to stay with his friend. Smoke turned away and stepped into the saloon for a cool beer.

The barkeep eyeballed him dubiously as he pushed open the batwings.

"You agin! My stars and garters. I was in the hopes you'd left the country!"

Smoke grinned at the man. "It's me in the flesh. Pull me a cool one."

Drawing the brew, the barkeep said, "Did my eyes deceive me or did I really see that four-eyed kid wearing a gun?"

"You saw it."

The barkeep snorted in disgust. "Some of Jud Vale's men is liable to take that thing off'n him and spank his butt with it!"

"I'd hate to be the one who tried it," Smoke told the man.

"They might decide to do it in a bunch."

"Then if that happens I reckon I'll just have to step in."

"Naturally," the barkeep said mournfully. "And I just had new tables and benches built"

Smoke sipped his beer and kept his eyes on the outside, as best he could through the dirty, dusty, and fly-specked window.

One of the two cattlemen broke the short silence. "Why don't you just ride on outta here, Jensen? Jud Vale will settle down if you was to leave."

"You really believe that?" Smoke had turned, his back to the plank that served as a bar.

"That's what he told us," the other cattleman said. He had noticed that the hammer thongs had been slipped from Smoke's Colts.

Matt was sitting quietly on a bench in front of the store, minding his own business and sipping a bottle of sarsaparilla. Leroy was still inside the store, picking out the supplies from the list Alice and Doreen had given him. Smoke wished that Matt had stayed inside the store. He reflected sourly that people in Hell wished for ice water, for all the good it did them.

"Jud Vale is a good, decent man," the cattleman said. "He's gonna bring changes to this area. Good changes. Progress and all that."

Smoke smiled grimly. He wondered if these men really believed that, or had Jud bought them off with more than just words?

"Yeah," the other rancher said. "And if that little snip Doreen had any sense, she'd grab ahold of the offer Jud's handed her. She could live like a queen in that big mansion of hisn."

"She doesn't love him."

"Love!" the other said contemptuously. "Hell's fire, man! What's that got to do with anything?"

"Yeah," his drinking buddy agreed. "Love ain't got nothin' to do with livin' well. All a woman's got to do is perform her wifely duties when the lantern is turned off and keep her mouth shut 'cept when she's told to talk. And I'll tell you something else, gunfighter: you best get shut of them snot-nosed squatters' brats you hired to work on the BoxT."

His buddy gave him a dark look and the cattleman shut his mouth.

"Is that a threat or a warning?" Smoke asked.

"Tain't no threat, gunfighter," the man said, his mind quickly working through the murk the alcohol had caused, as he realized just who he was talking to. "Jist a fact, is all. Jist lak 'at four-eyed little turd rode in with you with a man's iron strapped on. I've a good notion to go out there and take it away from him. But you'd stick up for him, wouldn't you?"

"No," Smoke surprised them both by stating. "Not as long as it stayed one on one. But I'd leave that boy alone if I was you."

The cattleman muttered something that Smoke could not make out. His buddy said, "He ain't gonna bother that boy, Jensen. That's just whiskey talk."

"Why did he say to get rid of the boys?"

"I don't know," the man said, then fell silent.

Smoke sipped his beer and ignored the drunk and near drunk cattlemen. He had thought all along that the age of the boys would make no difference to Jud Vale—when the man decided to make his move. In a way, he was glad the boys had taken to carrying guns.

He walked to the door that opened into the store, looking in. Leroy was still buying supplies. The boy caught his eye.

"It's gonna be a few more minutes, Mr. Smoke. Miss Alice and Miss Doreen really gave me a long list"

"Take your time, Leroy. I'll have another beer."

"Yes, sir."

Smoke walked back to the bar and ordered a refill. "And pull it from a new barrel," he told the barkeep. "That last one was flat."

The barkeep grinned. "Cain't blame a man for tryin' to

drain the barrel, now, can you?" He pulled a fresh brew. "This one's on the house, Mr. Jensen."

Smoke nodded his thanks and leaned against the plank. He had a bad feeling about this day. One he just could not shake. At the sounds of hard-ridden horses, he knew his premonition was about to turn into reality.

Four Bar V riders came to a halt in an unnecessary cloud of dust, fogging everybody and everything in a brief dust storm. Smoke silently cursed as he recognized one of the riders as a man called Smith. Smith had a shallow-made reputation as a gunslinger but Smoke knew there wasn't much to the man. He was a bully who picked his fights, fists, and guns very carefully.

"Lookie here!" Smith hollered, spotting Matt sitting on the bench, a disgusted look on his young face as he brushed the dust from his clothing. "Would you boys just take a look at that little piss-ant with the big iron strapped on!"

Smoke forced himself to stay put. He had warned Matt. Warned him several times. Smoke would not interfere unless the Bar V riders tried something in a bunch. As long as it was one on one, with both parties armed, it was an unwritten code that the fight was fair. It was not always a fair code, but that was the way it was.

Leroy heard the commotion and went out the back door to the wagon, getting his Winchester and jacking a round in the chamber of the carbine, easing down the hammer. He re-entered the store and moved to the open doorway, staying concealed from the Bar V riders.

He had been getting something extra for Miss Alice. Some candles. She was going to surprise Matthew with a birthday cake. Tomorrow was his birthday. His fourteenth.

If he lives through this, Leroy added that to his thoughts.

Then his thoughts turned grim as he gripped the Winchester. Matthew would live through it. One way or the other. It was time for everybody in this section of the state to stand up to Mr. Jud Vale. And if it had to begin right here and now? . . . Well, let it come.

The Winchester he carried was a hand-me-down from some-body. His dad never said where he'd got it. It was a .44-40 that some owner had sawed the barrel off to make into a saddle gun. It was several inches shorter than the short .44 carbine. It kicked something fierce, but when that bullet hit, it packed a wallop, especially at short range.

Leroy had never shot a man before—and didn't especially want to now, but if his friend Matt got into it with that trash from the Bar V . . . well, there was a first time for everything. He wished he could have had his first time with a girl before having to kill a man. But if wishes were horses, then nobody would have to walk, would they? He inched closer to the door and settled down, waiting.

"Yes, siree!" Smith said. "I think we ought to get us a bottle of whiskey and hold the little craphead down and pour it in him. Since he's totin' a man's gun, he ought to have hisself a man's drink."

Matt wisely ignored the bully's comments. He had finished brushing himself off and then calmly wiped the neck of his soda pop bottle on his shirtsleeve and proceeded to take a big swig.

"Hey, piss-ant!" Smith hollered. "I'm talkin' to you, pig farmer's boy!"

"I'm not deaf," Matthew said softly. "Do you eat bacon, mister?"

"Haw?"

"I said do you eat bacon?"

"Why . . . hell, yes, I eat bacon. Don't ever'body?"

"Where do you think it comes from—grown on trees?"

"Are you gettin' sassy with me, punk?"

"No, sir," Matthew replied respectfully. "I was just curious. If you enjoy eating bacon, why do you make fun of those people who raise the hogs?"

Smith—no mental giant, any way one wanted to view it—wore a look of bewilderment on his face. "I don't think I lak you very much, four-eyes. As a matter of fact, I *know* I don't lak you."

"That's a shame. I have nothing against you, mister."

"Let's take his pants down and make him ride back home buck-assed nekkid!" another Bar V hand suggested.

The four men all agreed that would be a great idea. They made some crude remarks about what they might find when they shucked Matt's jeans. And what they might do if one of them could find a corncob.

"No way," Smoke muttered, as he stepped away from the bar.

The two cattlemen suddenly looked very sorry, sober, and sick.

The barkeep shook his head in disgust at the Bar V hand's suggestion.

Leroy eared back the hammer on the .44-.40.

Matt set his soda pop bottle on the bench and stood up, his right hand hanging by his side.

"Well, now!" Smith said, surprise in his voice. "The little piggy's done gone and thought hisself to be all growed up."

"I'll get the corncob, Smith," a Bar V hand said.

"You'll get a bullet," Matt told him, his quiet words stopping the man and turning him around.

"You threatenin' me, pig-boy?" the hand challenged.

"Aren't you threatening me?" Matt countered.

Leroy stepped to a dusty window and pulled the Winchester to his shoulder, sighting in one of the Bar V hands.

Smoke moved closer to the batwings.

"Why, you little turd-faced punk!" the Bar V hand hissed at the boy. "I think I'll just kill you!"

"You have it to do," Matt said softly.

The Bar V riders spread out, all of them grinning, seconds away from a killing.

10

Smoke pushed open the batwings and stepped out onto the porch. "I'll take these two so-called gunslicks on the right, Matthew."

"And I've got that ugly, skinny, bowlegged one on the far left in rifle sights!" Leroy called from inside the store.

"I guess that leaves you and me, doesn't it?" Matt told Smith.

The Bar V riders looked sick at the appearance of Smoke Jensen. This was not something they had counted on.

"You got no call to interfere in this, Jensen!" Smith hollered. "This ain't none of your concern."

"It is when four of you gang up on one boy, you sorry piece of buffalo droppings." Smoke then proceeded to hang a cussing on the Bar V riders, and having been jerked up, so to speak, by the old mountain man, Preacher, Smoke could let the cuss words fly when he had a mind to. And today was one of those days.

The riders took it for a time, and then pride got the best of them.

"I've had it, Jensen!" one yelled at him. "You don't cuss me like some saddle bum!"

"Then make your play, damn you!" Smoke lost his temper and started to push.

The puncher held his hands away from his side. "No way,

Jensen. I ain't no match for you with guns. But I'll tear your damned head off with my fists if you've got the belly for it."

"I'll take you up on that, partner. Whatever your name is."

"Larry Noonan."

"Oh, yeah!" Smoke said, his voice filled with scorn. "I know enough about you to know you're a yellow little two-bit punk. You killed an unarmed sheepherder. Shot him in the back—so I recall reading on the dodger."

Noonan flushed but did not deny the damning charges.

"I still got something to settle with this loud-mouthed, sassy pig-farmer's kid!" Smith said. "You gonna interfere with that, Jensen?"

"No. I'm as aware as you concerning a fair shoot out between two armed men. In this case a man and a boy. But I'll kill any of your buddies who try to step in."

"You ready, punk?" Smith sneered at the boy.

Matt had stepped to the edge of the porch. Smoke glanced at him. There was no fear to be seen about the boy. His face was impassive and his hands were steady. He stared at Smith through his thick spectacles.

"Too bad, boy." Smith tried to rattle Matt. "You got about ten seconds left to live."

"I have a whole lifetime ahead of me, Mr. Smith. Let's just say this is payback time for you."

"Huh?"

"Don't you remember that time you and those other hooligans rode your horses over my mother's garden? Ruined it. We didn't eat very good that winter, Mr. Smith. It was too late to replant. I remember it very well."

"You gonna bawl about it, kid?" Smith sneered at him.

"No, sir. But I am going to kill you."

Smith stared at the boy while something crawled slowly across his face. He wanted to brush away the invisible sensation, for he knew what it was. Fear.

"My baby sister died that winter, Mr. Smith. I won't say it was all because of what you done, even though you did kill our milk cow. She needed milk bad. You had a hand in her dying."

Smith said nothing. There wasn't very much left to say.

"Goddamn nesters should have stayed out this area," Smoke heard one of the cattlemen in the bar say.

Smoke ignored him for the time being. The man had his own conscience to live with. Providing he had one at all.

"Are you ready, Mr. Smith?" Matthew asked, very politely.

"Smith," one of the Bar V hands said softly. "Back away. I don't like this. The kid's too damn sure of hisself."

"I ain't backin' up for no damn snot-nose pig farmer's whelp!" He stared at Matt. "All right, boy. You've made your brags. Now do something 'sides talk!"

"After you, Mr. Smith."

Smith hesitated. Something was terribly, awfully wrong here. He'd seen any number of two-bit, show-off, would-be gunhands in his time. At the last minute, they always backed down. And even before they backed down, they were nervous, their voices shrill, faces shiny with the sweat of fear. But not this kid. Kid, hell! He was just a *boy*—barely in his teens.

"My little sister suffered, Mr. Smith. I don't think I'll ever forget that."

"Shut your mouth, damn you!" Smith screamed. "Draw, you punk!"

Matt waited, waited in his worn-out, low-heeled farmer's boots. In his faded and patched old jeans and carefully mother-mended shirt. His eyes were calm behind his thick glasses.

Smith jerked iron. He just managed to clear leather as Matt's pistol belched and roared smoke and sparks. The first slug hit Smith in the belly, spinning him around in the dirt. The second slug struck him in the side and knocked him down to one knee. The expression on his face was one of utter disbelief that this could be happening to him. The third slug hit him in the face, entering between nose and upper lip and making one God-awful mess. Smith trembled once and died.

The three remaining Bar V hands stood in open-mouthed

shock, all of them knowing they were not nearly as fast as this fresh-faced, as-yet-to-shave farmer's kid standing on the porch of the store, and all of them so very, very glad they had not tried to brace him.

Leroy stepped out of the store, his short-barreled .44-.40, hammer back, in his hands. The barrel of the carbine was pointed straight and rock-steady at the belly of a Bar V hand.

"I'm out of this, kid!" the hand said quickly.

"You interfere in the fight between Mr. Smoke and Noonan and you'll be out of it forever," Leroy told him, his young voice holding hard steel.

Matt had quickly reloaded and holstered the Peacemaker. His calm eyes, magnified behind the thick glasses, looked at the other Bar V hand.

"That goes for me, too, kid!" the hand said.

"Mr. Smoke?" Matt said.

"Matt?"

"If you'll excuse me for a minute, I got to go behind the building and throw up!"

"Go on, Matt."

The boy ran from the porch.

"I done the same thing my first man," a Bar V rider admitted. "It ain't nothin' to be 'shamed of." He didn't know what else to do with his hands—only wanting to keep them as far away from his pistol as possible—so he stuck them into the back pockets of his jeans.

Noonan looked at the bulk of Smoke Jensen and swallowed hard. "Come on, boys!" he urged, panic in his voice. "They's three of us. We can take them two."

The Bar V rider with his hands in his back pockets told Noonan what he could do with his suggestion, together with the same corncob they had originally had in mind for Matthew.

"That goes double for me," the remaining Bar V rider added. "You wanted to fight Jensen, you just go right ahead, Noonan." He removed his gun belt and hung it on his saddle horn.

The other hand thought that was a dandy idea, and did the

same. Leroy shifted the muzzle of the .44-.40 to Noonan's belly and the man let his gunbelt fall.

The shopkeeper, his wife, the barkeep, and the two cattlemen had walked out on the porch, to stand and stare. The body of Smith was, for the moment, being ignored. Matt walked around from behind the building, wiping his mouth with his shirtsleeve.

Smoke took off his guns and laid them on the bench. He stepped off the porch, walked up to Noonan, and knocked the puncher down in the dirt with one very quick and unexpected hard left hook.

Noonan rolled and came to his boots, the side of his jaw beginning to bruise from the blow. He shook his head, clearing it of stars and chirping birdies, and backed up, lifting his fists.

He swung at Smoke. Smoke ducked the punch and busted the cowboy in the belly with a hard right. Noonan whoofed out air just as Smoke came around with another left that connected on the man's ear, spinning him around and seriously impairing his hearing for a few moments.

Just as Noonan regained his balance, Smoke stepped in and blasted him in the mouth with another straight right punch. Noonan's boots left the dirt and he sat down hard on his butt, his mouth bloody.

Smoke backed up. He wasn't even breathing hard; hadn't even worked up a sweat yet.

Noonan wisely sat on the ground. He took another good long look at the gunfighter who stood above him, his fists balled, hanging at his sides, waiting. Smoke looked awesome. A big man, six feet or more, with a massive barrel chest and shoulders and arms that were packed with hard muscle.

Noonan came off the ground in a rush, a long-bladed knife in his right hand.

Smoke slipped the first swing of the knife, bending down as he parried the thrust, his left hand scooping up dust from the road. When Noonan closed in on him, Smoke tossed the dirt into the man's eyes, momentarily blinding the man.

Smoke kicked the man on the knee, bringing a howl of pain. Smoke hit the man twice in the face, a left and a right. The knife dropped from his hand just as Smoke's right hand clamped down on the man's fingers. Smoke bore down, using all his strength. Noonan began screaming as the bones in his fingers were crushed, the crunching sounds causing all the spectators to wince.

Still holding on to Noonan's now ruined hand, Smoke began battering the man's face with short, hard, chopping blows from his left fist. Within a minute, the man's face had been turned into a bloody, misshapen mask. His nose was flattened, his lips smashed into bloody pulp, several teeth knocked out of his mouth. Both eyes were beaten closed.

Smoke let him drop to the dirt. Noonan was unconscious.

Smoke walked to the horse trough and washed his face and hands and buckled his gun belt around his lean waist. He looked up at Leroy.

"All the supplies loaded, Leroy?"

"Just about, sir."

"I'll get right on that, Mr. Jensen!" the store owner said. He and his wife rushed back into the store.

Smoke looked at the now completely sober cattlemen. They were standing on the porch, faces pale under the tan, staring at the crippled Noonan.

Smoke pointed first at Smith, then to Noonan. "When you men decide to take a stand in this issue," Smoke told them, "I would suggest that both of you keep this sight fresh in your minds."

Smoke turned and swung into the saddle.

The news of the gunfight between the seasoned Smith and the nester's kid, and of the short but brutally crippling fight between Smoke and Noonan, spread like unchecked wildfire throughout the southeastern corner of Idaho. Noonan would never regain the use of his right hand. The so-called badman drifted out of the country, sucking on a bottle of laudanum to ease the pain. He would drift far away, change his name, and work the remainder of his life as a cowboy with a crippled hand, his true identity hidden forever, even to the grave.

Jud Vale had been oddly silent after the shooting and the beating at the trading post. Smoke had a hunch all that would abruptly change as soon as Editor Argood left on his journey to Utah. And that was just about a week away.

At Smoke's suggestion, the ranch house and the bunkhouse had been fortified against both an attack and a siege—Smoke suspected the latter would be tried, with Jud Vale's marksmen in carefully placed positions attempting to pick off the defenders one by one.

The remaining Box T herd had been moved to safer pastures—a huge valley with good grass and water, difficult for rustlers to get the cattle clear without being seen.

On a warm, bright late spring morning, Smoke walked around the compound, inspecting the work that had been done. He could not think of anything else they could do.

And Smoke was growing restless. "Edgy" might be a better word for it. Calm it might be—for now—but he knew their position was lousy, and if Jud would just do a little thinking and planning, logically instead of emotionally, and then turn his rabid dogs loose, there was no way that Smoke and the defenders could hold back a well-planned and well-executed attack against them.

So what to do?

Cutting down the odds would certainly help. Perhaps a little night work? Like headhunting?

Smoke smiled a warrior's smile, thinking: Why not?

He remembered Preacher's words: "You'll always be a fighter, boy—a warrior. You'll take the quiet home life for a time; then the itch will git to where you cain't jist sit at home and scratch it. And then you'll head for the high lonesome, lookin' for trouble. And knowin' you, boy, you'll find it."

Smoke rounded up Cheyenne and Rusty and took them to one side. "I'll be gone for a couple of days, maybe longer. I don't like the odds, so I think I'll do something about them."

"You crave some company?" Cheyenne asked.

Smoke shook his head. "No. This is something that's best left to one man. I'll be pulling out at dusk."

"You going to tell Walt and the wimmin what you're up to?" the old gunfighter asked.

"I'll tell Walt. If he wants to let the women in on it, that's up to him."

"If anybody can pull it off, you can, son. You had the best teacher in the world in Preacher."

Smoke certainly agreed with that last sentence. There had been no finer night fighter in the world than Preacher. "I'll start getting my gear together. Rusty, fix me up with a packet of food enough to last two days."

The cowboy nodded and walked away. Smoke turned back to Cheyenne. "My horse is too well known. Put a rope on that steeldust for me, will you? He's mean as hell but he's mountain bred and quick as lightning and can go all day and still have his bottom left."

"He's a good one. I'll dob him for you."

Smoke filled up all the loops in his gunbelt and filled up a bandoleer, slinging that around his shoulder. He slipped another box of .44's into his saddlebags and made sure his moccasins were tucked into the leather. He would soon slip out of his boots and into the moccasins when it was time for the night stalking to begin. He sat down on his bunk and began putting a finer edge on his bowie knife. That done, he walked to a stone building behind the barn and opened the locked door with a key he had found in a cabinet in the storeroom. He had a hunch what he would find, and his hunch was correct

He filled a small sack with sticks of dynamite and caps and fuses. He might not be able to cut the head off the snake, but he was sure intending to tweak its tail.

11

Smoke talked to Jamie and Matthew before he pulled out into the night.

"Tell the boys to ride carefully and keep a sharp eye out. I'm going into the lion's den, and there is no telling what Jud Vale will have his men do in retaliation after I'm through."

"There used to be a lot more farmers in this area than there is now, Mr. Smoke," Jamie said. "Women and girls has been tooken and misused by Vale and his riders. Men has been tarred and feathered and horsewhipped and killed. Killed outright if they was lucky. A deputy sheriff come in here once. He just disappeared. There ain't been no more lawmen come around the Bear. Jud Vale is pure trash, Mr. Smoke. Trash livin' in a big fancy house, with servants and such as that. When he can get them to stay, that is. He fancies young women all around, to wait on him. And he abuses them in ways we heard that would make you sick to your stomach, so they leave as soon as they can get a way out. You cain't tell us nothin' about Jud Vale and what he might decide to do."

"The more I hear about this man, the more I think the best thing to do would be to just go in and chop his head off, so to speak," Smoke said.

"Ain't gonna be that easy, Mr. Smoke. Not even for you. Jud ain't never alone. He's got half a dozen bodyguards with him all the time. Men that have been with him for years, my pa says."

"We'll see, boys. We'll see. I might not be able to do much more than rattle the bars on his cage this time around. But, by God, he will know that his territory has been violated."

Walt came out to the barn just moments before Smoke was to pull out. "Clint Perkins is in the area, Smoke. Don't ask me how I know—I can't explain the feelings I get when he's close. I just know. You be careful."

"Whose side is he on, Walt?"

"His own," the old rancher said bluntly. "He's like a goose; wakes up in a new world every day. I always knew he was about half nuts. Now I think he's gone slap dab crazy."

Smoke led the steeldust out of the barn and swung into the saddle. "I'll see you in two or three days, Walt."

"Be careful, boy."

Smoke rode slowly away from the ranch and into the night. He stayed shy of the roads and well-traveled trails as he worked his way toward the range of the Bar V. Editor Argood had told him that there was not one single person on the Bar V payroll that was worth the gunpowder it would take to blow his brains out. To a man, Argood said, they were bullies and trash and petty criminals and all wanted by the law somewhere. The people in the area put up with them because Jud Vale kept them all on a tight leash. Jud had forbidden them to enter Montpelier, restricting their carousing to a few small towns and trading posts in the area around the Bar V range.

All in all, Smoke concluded as he rode through the night, a snake pit could best describe the Bar V . . . and that included the owner.

With a tight smile on his face, Smoke thought that the next couple of days and nights should prove to be quite interesting.

Before leaving the Box T, Smoke had taken tape and silenced anything that might jingle. Only the clop of the steel-dust's hooves and the occasional creak of saddle leather could be heard. By midnight, he was on the Bar V range. He would ride for a while, then dismount and stand listening for several moments. He began passing bunched and sleeping cattle and slipped his rope free, knowing he would soon make contact with a night herder. If his luck held, the night herder would think him one of the Bar V riders—at least long enough for Smoke to dab a loop over the man and cause a little mischief.

He rode parallel to a series of ridges for a few moments, before finding a pass that would, hopefully, take them to the flats on the other side. He let the steeldust set his own pace and pick his way through the night. On the flats, reined up in the opening of the draw, Smoke spotted the night herder as the man worked his way around the herd, riding slowly so as not to spook the cattle, which was an easily done job. The cattle had, as usual, risen about midnight, grazed for a few moments, and then settled back down.

As the night herder passed Smoke's position, the gunfighter let the loop fly and jerked the rider out of the saddle. The man hit the ground hard, knocking the wind out of him. Smoke was off and running as the loop settled and he further silenced the herder by a hard right fist to the side of the man's jaw. He then tied him up, using cut-off sections from the Bar V rider's own rope. He gagged the man with a dirty bandana taken from the man's equally dirty neck and then squatted down beside him, waiting for him to regain consciousness.

The man's eyes opened and widened as he recognized who he was looking at.

"You want to live?" Smoke asked softly.

The man nodded his head up and down vigorously.

"You know who I am?"

The rider nodded.

Smoke took out his long-bladed knife and laid the cold sharp steel against the man's throat. "I've a good notion to cut your throat and just have done with it."

The Bar V man made desperate choking sounds behind the gag, being careful not to move his head, for fear the sharp blade would slice him.

"On second thought," Smoke told him, "I think I'll just strip you and tie you between two steers and then stampede the herd."

More frantic choking sounds.

"Unless you agree to ride out and never show your face in this part of the state again."

The muffled sounds from behind the gag were definitely in agreement with Smoke's last remarks.

Smoke very slowly moved the knife point, just scraping the man's unshaven jaw, and the Bar V night herder looked like he was developing the first stages of a heart attack. With one flick of his wrist, Smoke cut the gag from the man's mouth.

"Oh, Jesus!" the rider softly moaned.

Smoke grabbed him by the hair and jerked his head back, exposing the softness of his throat. He laid the blade against the man's skin and the sharp odor of urine filled the night.

"If I see you again, I'll kill you," Smoke told him.

"Mr. Jensen, if you was to cut me a-loose, I'll be two counties away come the dawn."

Smoke cut his bonds and stood up. "Ride. Ride like you've never ridden before. Forget your warbag back at the bunkhouse. Just get clear of this area."

"I'm gone, mister!"

The cowboy staggered to his boots and ran to his horse and swung into the saddle, wet drawers and all, and was gone into the night, heading west. Smoke had not disarmed the cowboy, but the man made no moves toward his six-gun. The night became quiet as the rider got the hell gone from Smoke Jensen.

Smoke removed his spurs and stashed them in a saddlebag. Back in the saddle, he guided the steeldust out to the edge of the herd and began making the night herder's rounds, working in a slow, rough circle. He soon spotted another night rider.

Smoke rode up to the man, and just as the rider realized he was not looking at a Bar V hand, Smoke leaned over and knocked him clear out of the saddle. He was on the ground and standing over the man as the cowboy came up fighting mad and cussing to beat sixty. He reached for his gun and Smoke knocked it out of his hand, then proceeded to beat the man to an unconscious bloody pulp. Smoke tossed him belly-down across the man's saddle, tied him securely, and slapped the horse on the rump, knowing the animal would head straight for the corral.

Smiling, Smoke swung back into the saddle and went in search of more night herders.

Long before first light, he had cleared the Bar V range of nighthawks. He had sent three packing, riding hell-bent for leather toward a more hospitable climate; and had either whipped with his fists or clubbed over the head four more, tying them across their saddles and sending the horses racing back to the corral and jumping and bucking under the strange load.

Smoke headed for the high country and some food and sleep. He was still smiling as he plopped his hat over his eyes and leaned back on his saddle as a pillow. The sun was just coming up. He was less than a mile from Jud Vale's mansion.

Jud Vale threw his hat on the ground and stomped around, cussing and hollering. "Get him!" he finally screamed, his face beet-red, spittle spraying over his lips. "Put a rope on him and drag that bastard back here! Ten thousand dollars to the man who brings him in, dead or alive! *Ride,* dammit!"

Forty riders hit their saddles and left the ranch complex in a cloud of dust, which was exactly what Smoke planned on them doing. He knew they would not expect him to be within ten miles of Jud Vale's mansion, much less standing on a brush-covered ridge overlooking the estate.

Smoke had carefully picketed the steeldust over good graze and a small pool of collected water—water enough for a couple of days. If Smoke did not return, the steeldust could break free with little trouble and head back to Box T's range.

Smoke took his time studying the ranch layout through

field glasses, including ways to reach it and ways to get out, once there. Jud had chosen his building site carefully, including a little creek that ran some three hundred yards behind the out of place mansion.

Smoke removed his boots and slipped on moccasins. He carefully checked his guns, wiping them free of any dust they might have collected. He removed his Winchester from the boot and checked it, making sure it was loaded full up. He patted the steeldust on the neck and spoke to it for a moment; then he started to move out.

Movement on the other side of the creek halted him. He squatted down and watched. He was sure he had seen movement. Or had he? He waited. There! He'd been right. Somebody, or something, was sure enough down there. He went back to his saddlebags and got his field glasses.

He moved several hundred yards closer to the mansion, adjusted the glasses for range and once more settled down to wait. Then he picked out the shape of a man. It startled him as the face of the man came into view. It was almost like looking into a mirror. There was some difference, of course, but the facial features of the man were startlingly similar to Smoke's own.

Clint Perkins. It had to be. But what the devil was he up to?

He watched as the man left the creek and ran to one of several privies behind the house. The privies surprised Smoke. He thought Jud would have installed some of those newfangled indoor water closets he'd seen back East.

Clint began working his way closer to the mansion, finally ducking into a shed not far from the back porch. The call of a meadowlark drifted to Smoke, and Smoke could tell the call was not real. Within a moment, a young woman stepped out onto the porch, shaking out a small rug.

Someone must have said something from inside the house, for the girl turned her head. Smoke could see her lips move in reply. She had an angry expression on her face. Her reply must have satisfied the questioner since she moved off the porch and walked toward an outhouse.

She angled toward the privy just behind the shed; that move would effectively block the view of anyone watching from the house, but not from the ridge and Smoke's magnified eyes.

The girl did not go into the outhouse. But she did disappear from view. So the shed either had a back door or a couple of loosened boards. Clint Perkins, the so-called Robin Hood of the West, either had him a girlfriend, or was planning to rescue the lady from the sweaty evil clutches of Jud Vale. Probably a combination of both, Smoke thought. This Clint Perkins, as it was turning out, was quite the ladies' man.

Smoke wondered just how many starry-eyed women Clint had loved and left and how many woods colts this dubious Robin Hood had in his backtrail?

After only a few moments, a man wearing two guns belted around his waist stepped onto the porch and, judging from the expression on his face, started yelling. The girl appeared, seeming to come from out of the privy. And from the expression on her face, she seemed to be yelling at the man. When she reached the porch, the man slapped her, staggering her, only the railing preventing her from falling off the porch. He grabbed her by the arm and hurried her into the house, slamming the door behind them.

Interesting, Smoke thought. Then he wondered how many more young ladies Jud Vale was keeping against their will in the huge mansion.

Smoke settled back in a more comfortable position, his back to a tree, his hat on the ground beside him, and waited and watched. This might prove to be a very interesting morning.

And Smoke might not have to do anything for a change.

Except enjoy the show.

12

Smoke shifted his attention to the front of the mansion as Jud Vale stepped out onto the porch with a cup of coffee in his hand and took a chair. Smoke envied him that cup of coffee, for a fact. His had been a cold camp the night before, and he sorely missed his usual full pot of hot, strong, black cowboy coffee upon waking up.

He contented himself by chewing on a biscuit sandwich made with fried salt pork, and chasing it down with sips of water from his canteen.

The girl Smoke had seen meeting with Clint Perkins came out onto the porch and began talking to Jud, gesturing with her hands.

Jud shook his head a couple of times and then, with an angry expression on his face, pointed toward the door. The girl, her shoulders slumped in defeat, walked back inside the house.

Jud stood up and hollered something; Smoke could see his lips move but could not make out the words. Three men stepped out of a bunkhouse and walked toward the house. Three more men, with the girl in tow—quite unwillingly, Smoke noted, by the way one held onto her arm—came out of the mansion to stand by Jud on the porch.

The man holding onto the girl nodded his head and the three went back into the mansion. Shifting his glasses, Smoke watched as Clint ran the short distance from shed to back porch and then disappeared into the mansion.

Going to get interesting very soon, Smoke thought.

Jud's horse was saddled and led to the porch, and Jud and three of his bodyguards rode off. Smoke finished his biscuit and salt meat and waited for something to start popping.

It wasn't long in coming.

One man was suddenly hurled through a side window, the side of his head bloody. Gunfire shattered the early morning quiet and one of Jud's bodyguards came staggering out onto the back porch. He fell over the railing and lay still.

More gunfire came from within the house and the third bodyguard fell out of the front door, on his back, on the porch. The front of his shirt was bloody.

Wisps of smoke began leaking out of an open window in the rear of the house as Clint and the girl ran out the back door and toward the creek. Several moments later, Smoke watched as two horses pounded away, the girl riding astride. They topped a hill and were gone.

"Robin Hood strikes again," Smoke muttered, as he took out another biscuit and settled back, just as Jud Vale and his bodyguards came galloping back to the ranch.

The fire had been confined to the kitchen and had been extinguished in a few minutes. Jud was talking to the man who had been bashed on the noggin and tossed out the side window.

"So it wasn't Jensen all along," Jud said, standing up, his face tight with anger. "It was that damn Clint Perkins!"

"They look enough alike to be brothers," Jason reminded his boss. "Be easy to mistake them in the dark."

"Maybe they're brothers?" a hand suggested. "And Smoke Jensen come in here to help him out?"

But Jud Vale rejected that on the spot. He'd been in the West for some years when the stories about Smoke Jensen first began surfacing. Jud knew that Jensen's father had died and that the mountain man, Preacher, took care of the boy's raising after that. Smoke had always been a loner, with no family to speak of, certainly no brother.

He shook his head. "No. He doesn't have a brother. Not anymore. His brother was killed in the war. Tortured and killed by a group headed by three men who later moved into Idaho. Jensen killed them all and destroyed the town."

"Then what's he doin' here, Boss?" Jason asked.

"Exactly what he said he was doing," Jud replied, bitterness in his voice. "He was just seeing the country when we braced him. That got his back up, and he stayed." Jud shrugged. "We brought it on ourselves."

"And we do what about it?" a gunslinger asked.

"Kill him."

A Bar V hand had gotten close to Smoke's hiding place while taking a shortcut to a search area. He now found himself flat on the ground looking up into the cold eyes of Smoke Jensen, with a knife blade across his throat. There were any number of questions he wanted to ask, but he wisely kept his mouth shut, figuring if Jensen wanted him to talk, he'd tell him so.

"Who is in the house besides Jud Vale and his men?" Smoke asked.

"Nobody! I swear it!"

"The girl who got away—who is she?"

"Susie somebody-or-another. Nester's kid from over Wyoming Territory."

"She was the only servant?" Smoke moved the razor-sharp knife blade and the man cringed in fear.

"If that's what you want to call what she done. Yeah. She cain't cook and don't clean house. It's like a boar's nest in that house. There was two more girls. One run off—never seen her agin—and Jud kilt the other. But it was an accident, Jud said. He broke her neck whilst they were messin' around. You know."

"Sounds like a nice gentle fellow, this Jud Vale does."

The hand didn't know how to respond to that, so he kept his mouth closed.

"What's Clint Perkins's beef with Jud?"

"Lord, man, I don't know! 'Ceptin' that Perkins is crazy, I reckon. He hates rich folks, I do know that."

Smoke stared hard at the man. The Bar V hand was scared and sweating, even though the day was cloudy and cool, threatening rain. "Where are you wanted?"

The hand hesitated. Smoke moved the big blade. That loosened his mouth. "Kansas!" he blurted out.

"What for?"

"I robbed a store. I was down on my luck and needed some cash."

Smoke grabbed him by the hair and jerked his head back, exposing his throat even more. "Tell it all!"

"Nebraska! I robbed a bank, kilt a teller! You gonna turn me in?"

"Not if you level with me."

"Anything you want. Jist anything at all, Mr. Jensen. You want me to git down and howl lak a dog, you jist say so."

"Is there any puncher on Vale's payroll who isn't wanted by the law?"

"Lord, no! Jud laks to hire people on the hoot-owl trail. He's got more control over 'em. They's more outlaws down yonder than at Robbers' Roost."

"And Jud Vale wants to be king of this part of the state?"

"Mister Jensen, he *is* king!"

"Uneasy lies the head that wears a crown."

"Huh?"

"Shakespeare wrote that."

"I ain't never heard of him. What outfit does he ride for?"

"Forget it." Smoke stuffed a gag into the man's mouth and tied him to a tree. He picked up his rifle and began making his way toward the creek that ran behind the mansion of Jud Vale. He wasn't worried about being spotted by any ranch hands; there weren't any hands left on the ranch, except those gunslingers and bodyguards in the house with Jud. Every hand, including the cook, was out looking for Clint Perkins and the girl. According to the tied-up and gagged Bar V hand, no one believed Smoke was within thirty miles of the mansion. And by this time, there wouldn't be a puncher, bounty hunter, or hired gun within ten miles of the ranch.

The day had turned cloudy along with the coolness, and any gunfire would be muffled by the humidity, not carrying nearly as far as on a fair, sunshiny day.

Smoke followed the creek to the rear of the house and then made his way to a pile of wood stacked behind the great two-story mansion. He poked his rifle through a good-sized crack in the stack and let a few shots bang.

The first shot tore through the kitchen wall and ricocheted upward, shattering a chandelier in the fancy dining room and sending bits of glass and coal oil spraying from the expensive lamps. Jud Vale and his men hit the floor, yelling and cussing. The second .44 round whined off the polished wood of the dining room table and stopped in the china hutch, destroying several plates and cups. The third round bounced off a kettle in the kitchen and whined wickedly around the stove before rolling across the floor and coming to rest about three inches from Jud Vale's nose.

The men began crawling across the floor, toward the rear of the house. Smoke anticipated that move, and lowered the muzzle of the Winchester, letting it bang.

"Somebody get around to the side of the house!" Jud yelled. "Try to get him in a crossfire."

But Smoke was off and running, coming to rest behind the gazebo in the side yard. He saw the bodyguard come chugging around the corner and knocked a leg out from under him. Dragging his limb, the man crawled back around to the front of the mansion.

Jud and his men moved to the side of the house, but by this time, Smoke had again changed locations, back to the rear of the house. He decided he'd pressed his luck enough for this day, and took a stick of dynamite out of his pocket, capping and fusing the thunder stick. He lit it and let it fly and was heading for the creek before the sputtering stick landed.

The charge landed on the ground and rolled under the porch. When it blew, it tore the whole porch off the rear of the house and busted most of the windows in the back of the mansion.

Smoke stopped at the creek bank long enough to empty his rifle into the back of the house and then ran toward the ridge and his horse.

Inside the mansion, their hearing momentarily impaired from the booming of the giant stick, Jud and his men hugged the floor until the rifle fire stopped. Their ears ringing, the men crawled to their knees.

"That wasn't Clint Perkins," Jud said, his voice seeming to come out of a well. "That was Smoke Jensen. Bet on it!"

Chuckling, Smoke cut the Bar V hand loose, laid the barrel of his pistol on the back of the man's head, ensuring that he would be out for some time to come, and mounted up, riding off.

He had a full day of headhunting to do.

The hand Smoke had busted on the noggin finally found his horse and rode back to the mansion, a lump on his noggin the size of a hen's egg.

"Jensen," he told Jud.

"Which way did he ride out?"

"Don't know. He busted me on the head. I just now come to my senses. I don't know how long I've been out."

Jud cussed and stomped and paced up and down behind the mansion and the ruined porch. He fought to keep his anger under control and managed it.

"Get the boys in," he told Jason. "Jensen was raised by Preacher. Probably the best Injun fighter the West ever seen. He's gone headhunting, bet on it. If the boys stay out, he'll do us some more damage. Get them back here, pronto."

Jason looked confused. "Jesus, Boss. How? They're scattered all forty miles."

Jud Vale sat down on a stump and cussed. Smoke Jensen planned all this, he concluded. He didn't know how, or even the why of it, but it was all Smoke Jensen's fault. He convinced himself of that. Damn Smoke Jensen to the pits of Hellfire!

Jud again calmed himself and did a little mental figuring. As of last evening, he had 18 hands on the payroll. He had hired 25 men at fighting wages—God knows they hadn't earned a penny of it—and he was giving another 15 or 20 men—he forgot the exact number—money just to hang around. Three riders had deserted him last night, thanks to that damn Clint Perkins; or had it been Perkins? And two more had been so badly beaten they were out of it for several days. Maybe a week. So savagely mauled that they hadn't even been able to leave the bunkhouse when Perkins and then Jensen attacked the house. He had lost two of his most trusted men to the guns of Perkins. Jensen had busted the leg of another. And a third had his head busted open.

"Damn!" he muttered. He looked up at Jason. "You boys stick close to home. I reckon them forty-odd men out in the field can deal with Smoke Jensen."

A gunslick whose Christian name was Wilber Hammersmith—his friends called him Hammer—thought a damn puma had done jumped onto his back, knocking him from the saddle. Then he looked up into the eyes of Smoke Jensen, sitting on top of him, and suddenly he felt an urgent need to relieve his bladder.

He cut his eyes as Jensen balled his right hand into a huge fist. "Aw, hell, man!" he managed to say before his whole head exploded in pain.

And speaking of his head . . . when he finally awakened, he had a whale of a headache, his whole world was upside down, and his head was unnaturally cold.

Hammer figured out why his world was upside down. It wasn't the world—it was him! Jensen had taken Hammer's rope and strung him upside down from a tall limb. After stripping him down to his longhandles and taking his boots and socks and guns.

But how come his head was so cold? He had always been right proud of his blond hair. He finally managed to get his hands free and to his head.

He screamed as if he'd been mortally wounded, the sound echoing around the hills and ridges.

That damn Smoke Jensen had taken his knife and shaved his head!

"Halp!" Hammersmith started hollering as he swayed in the breeze at the end of the rope. His own rope. "I'm a-gonna kill you, Jensen!" Hammersmith squalled. "Damn your eyes, you heathen! This ain't right. Halp!"

Buck Wall thought he heard someone hollering. He pulled up and listened. Yep. Someone was sure hollering all right. Coming from over that next ridge, he thought. He eased over that way and found the source of all the noise.

"Boy," he said to Hammer. "How come you got yourself all tied up like that there?"

"Cut me down, damnit!" Hammer squalled.

"All right, all right." Buck was in the process of dismounting when the loop settled over his shoulders and he felt himself jerked from the stirrups. He landed heavily on the rocky ground.

Then Smoke Jensen was all over him, fists flying. The last thing Buck recalled, for a few moments, was that getting the living hell beat out of him was not a very pleasant experience.

When he woke up, his world was also upside down. And his clothes were gone, right down to his socks and boots and guns. And there was not a horse to be seen anywhere.

"Hammer," he managed to speak through battered lips. "The next time you get in trouble, I wish you would please keep your mouth shet!"

"Halp!" Hammer hollered.

"Will you stop that! You're makin' my head hurt!"

"Halp!"

"Who said that?" Hammer asked.

"Well, it damn shore wasn't me!"

By twisting around, they could just see a newly hired gunny name of Ben Lewis. Someone—Jensen for sure—had peeled him buck naked and tied him backwards in the saddle. And from the looks of him, he'd been sitting in that saddle for some time. Looked worn to a frazzle.

"I'm a-gonna kill that crummy Smoke Jensen!" Ben hollered.

"Yeah," Buck said drily. "Right. Shore you are. Me, too. But furst I'd like to get shut of this damn tree limb!"

13

The hired guns and bounty hunters and would-be toughs began drifting back to the ranch one by one, and they were a sorry sight to behold. Jud Vale sat on the front porch sipping whiskey and viewing the unfolding scene with disgust in his eyes.

Glen Regan, the punk who fancied himself fast with a gun, was the first back. Hoofing it. Naked, except for his fancy silver conchoed gun belt, all the shells shucked out of the loops. He wore his empty holsters in strategic locations.

"Plumb pitiful," Jud said mournfully.

"What do you want done with him, Boss?" Jason asked.

"Get him out of my sight. And, Jason? Get ready for a lot more of the same. Jensen's playing games."

Barstow, the no-good from Colorado way, was the next to come limping in. Barefoot and clad only in a bush he had up-rooted. Jensen hadn't even left him his guns. Jud just pointed to the bunkhouse and poured another drink.

Three of Jud's own regular hands came staggering in about fifteen minutes later. They were drawerless and had been tied together in such a way that they had to move in a circle to get anywhere. They were so dizzy they fell down in a heap in the front yard.

Jud looked at the pile of struggling flesh in his front yard. "Jason?"

"Boss?"

"Get me a headache powder, will you?"

"I believe I'll join you," the foreman said. "But it cain't get much worse than this."

"Don't bet on it."

Jaeger, the German gunhand, came in riding his own horse and wearing clothes. But he had a bloody bandage tied around his big head and a very grim expression on his broad face. "Jensen shoot ear off," he said, and rode on toward the bunkhouse.

"Least he left you your britches," Jud told him.

"I vould ratter have mein ear!" the German called.

The bounty hunter, John Wills, came riding in without his clothes, his hands tied to the saddle horn. But Smoke had neatly wrapped him up, from neck to waist and both his legs, in poison ivy. He was already breaking out and swelling.

Jud pointed to the bunkhouse. "Ointment in the cabinet over yonder," he said with a sigh.

Hammersmith and Buck had found their horses and came riding in with Ben Lewis, the last two in their birthday suits. No guns or rifles. Jensen was going to have quite a collection before this was over.

Of course, Jud knew what Jensen was doing: arming the kids to the teeth.

"I don't want to hear it," Jud told the three, and pointed to the bunkhouse.

It just got worse. But the numbers were fewer. Hazelhurst came in draped over his saddle. His partner explained, "He wanted to make a fight of it. Stupid thing to do with Jensen. I figured my life was worth more than my britches and guns. Jensen said the shirts and jeans was gonna have to be altered some—and shore washed—but the kids would have work clothes a-plenty."

"Get a shovel and some boys and plant Hazelhurst," Jud told him, a weary note to his voice.

Vale got up and walked into the house, closing the door behind him. He just did not want to see any more of this.

* * *

Smoke stampeded the Bar V horses that night. He jerked down the corral bars and tossed a stick of dynamite outside the corral so no horses would be hurt—just scared half to death.

It was a move that no one expected. After the damage he had done all that day, all thought he would head back to the Box T.

Smoke put an end to those thoughts by emptying his six guns into the bunkhouse, then grabbing two more hung on the saddle horn and blasting away at the mansion, sending Jud Vale jumping out of bed, skinning his knee, banging his big toe on the chiffonier, and ultimately falling down his own fancily curving stairs. In his longhandles.

"You son of a bitch!" Jud hollered, holding his aching head where he'd banged it on his way down the stairs, head over butt. "I'll get you, Jensen. I swear by my mother's grave—I'll kill you for this!"

But Smoke was smiling as he crossed over the series of ridges that would lead him out of Bar V's range, leading a Bar V packhorse carrying clothes and guns.

"Don't you look like the cat who licked the cream," Cheyenne told him when Smoke rolled out of bed and walked outside to wash and shave.

When Smoke had finished telling him what he'd done, the old mountain man and gunfighter was cackling and slapping his knee.

"By God, I'll just bet that was some sight to see! I'd have give a month's wages to seen 'er."

"Well, it was fun," Smoke admitted with a smile. "Most of it. But there is no telling what Jud will do in retaliation."

"And Clint Perkins come up and stole the girl away, huh?"

"Yes." Walt and Rusty had walked up, to stand and listen.

"He's a tough one. Don't ever sell him short on courage. He's got his share and more of that."

Smoke had collected thirty pistols and fifteen rifles and more than five hundred rounds of .44 and .45 caliber ammunition. He distributed the weapons and ammo and gave Alice and Doreen the clothes to wash and alter for the boys. He had tossed the boots in a pile in the barn for the boys to prowl through.

"Argood has gone to Utah," Walt told him. "Be gone for a month or more."

"Then Jud will throw everything he's got at us," Smoke said. "It'll be open warfare from this point on." He smiled. "And after what I did to the Bar V, I sure can't blame them."

With little else to do, Chuckie, Ed, Eli, Jimmy, Clark, and Buster busied themselves at the creek, picking up and carefully selecting rocks for the weapons they had been working on. The rocks they picked up were just the perfect size, round and smooth, flawless. They would fit well in the pockets of their slingshots. Maybe they couldn't carry guns around, but they could sure use those slingshots with deadly accuracy.

And the youngsters had just as carefully picked out the spots from which they would launch their small war when Jud Vale's men attacked the ranch. And it was there they stashed their carefully chosen hoard of rocks and spare slingshots, telling no one else about it.

But Cheyenne, wise and watchful old man that he was, had seen the boys scurrying about and he became curious as to what they were up to. When he had satisfied his curiosity, he sat down and chuckled.

"Brave little lads," he muttered. And he knew just how deadly a slingshot could be in the hands of a boy with a steady eye. They might not kill anybody with those propelled little rocks, but they could spook some horses and cause some fearful bumps and dents in the head and some painful bruises in the flesh of any attacker.

"I do believe it's gonna get right interestin' around here," he quietly said to himself.

Matthew had been practicing daily with his Peacemaker. One hour a day, faithfully, every day, he practiced his draw. And with lots of ammo available, he could also practice his marksmanship.

The boy was a natural. Better than good, he was awesome in his ability with a short gun.

"I hate to see it," Smoke said to Cheyenne, after watching Matt practice.

"He'd a-done it with or without us, Smoke," the old gun-fighter said. "I allow as to how it was best that we was here to hep him along."

"Maybe you're right. But the West is slowly changing, Cheyenne. Perhaps not all for the better, but law and order is coming and fast guns will be a thing of the past before we know it."

"I'll never live to see it," the old man said flatly. "And for all the lawyers and judges with their fancy words, and hand-sewn duds, it's gonna be years afore all the West is tamed— maybe never. Matthew will be a growed-up man afore he'll be able to hang up his guns. And who knows, Smoke? Maybe he'll go on to become a fine lawman. There ain't a bad bone in the lad."

"I'm going to encourage him to do just that."

"I already been doin' that," Cheyenne said. "He seems interested in it, for a fact."

Smoke's eyes came open out of sleep. Something, or some-body, was in the barn. He looked out the open window with-out moving from his bunk. About three o'clock, he guessed.

He lay still, his right hand around the butt of a Colt. When the sound came again, Smoke eared back the hammer.

A soft chuckle came out of the darkness, just outside the open door to his room. "I didn't think I'd be able to get this far without you hearing me," the voice said.

"Perkins?" Smoke returned the whisper.

"Oh, my, yes. I've come to lend whatever assistance I can to this little war."

"I watched you the other day. From the ridges."

"Careless on my part, not seeing you. You're very, very good. As good as your reputation makes you out to be, I must admit."

Smoke felt that Perkins was not alone. All his senses were working overtime. "The girl with you?"

"Good guess, *compañero.*"

With that correct usage, Smoke knew the man had spent some time below the border. "Going to leave her here?"

"I really have no choice in the matter. She'll be much safer with Walt and Alice."

"Why do you hate them so? They seem like good people to me."

"Oh, I don't hate them. Not at all. I know they think that, but it isn't true. There is a medical term for my mental condition, but I shan't bore you with ten-dollar words when a single word can sum it all up rather well. I'm crazy."

"You have good days and you have bad days."

"Umm. Gunfighter you may be, but you are not overcome with ignorance. Yes. That is correct."

"Have you sought help?"

"Oh, my, yes. But unfortunately, the field of psychiatry is still in its infancy, and the methods they use are really quite primitive. And they don't work." He added the last with a note of bitterness.

"There ought to be some coffee left in the pot. Help yourself."

"Thank you, but I'm afraid I must decline your kind offer. How is Micky?"

"He's a fine boy."

"Ah, good. Doreen thinks I deserted her out of pure callousness. That was not the case. When these twilight moods strike me, I can kill anybody who stands in my way, who speaks to me in a cross manner, or simply because of a wrong word. I would be sorry for it immediately afterward, but apologizing to a corpse is a rather futile gesture, don't you agree, Mr. Jensen?"

"I would think so, yes."

"Should our paths cross again, Mr. Jensen, and I have a rather obvious wild-eyed look about me, leave me alone. Depart the area immediately. It's for your own good, I assure you."

"I'll remember that."

Silence.

"Clint?"

But he was speaking to shadows. Clint Perkins had vanished as softly and silently as he had arrived.

"Susie?"

"I'm right here, Mr. Jensen."

Smoke rose from his bunk and dressed. Then he lit the lamp. Susie was perhaps eighteen—no more than that. A very pretty girl, she had a wide-eyed, scared look on her pale face.

"You don't have to be afraid of me, Susie," Smoke told her. "Come on. Let's go wake up the house and get you settled in."

Over coffee and bear signs, the story Susie told was one of horror, clearly indicating that Jud Vale was as nutty as a tree full of squirrels. She told of beatings, of being forced into Jud's bed—and into the bed of Jason when Jud was feeling magnanimous. And of being forced to do things, things about which no decent person should know. Walt looked sick and Alice and Doreen almost had an attack of the swooning vapors, both of them fanning themselves vigorously.

Cheyenne wore a very uncomfortable look on his leathery face. Rusty's face was red as a beet. Smoke had heard the boys gather around the windows, outside the house, but said nothing about it. They were getting an earful, no doubt about that. Dolittle and Harrison had not been awakened.

"Have you seen Jud kill other . . . slaves?" Smoke asked her.

"One. But half a dozen have just disappeared. I know where they're buried, though."

"Your parents?"

"Dead. I was on my way to California to stay with my uncle and aunt when outlaws robbed the train. They took me and sold me to Jud. If he finds out I'm here, he'll attack this ranch."

"He's going to do that anyway, girl," Walt told her. "Just relax. You'll be safe here with us. When this is over, we'll get you to California."

"How did Clint find out you were at the Bar V?" Smoke asked.

"How does he find out anything?" she countered. "He's like a ghost." She looked at Doreen. "And no, there was never anything between us. He's just been a good friend."

The look Doreen gave her silently stated that she believed that about as much as she believed elephants wore pink tights and danced the can-can.

Susie met Doreen's eyes and accurately read the other woman's expression. She shrugged indifferently.

"Micky can sleep in with his mother," Alice said, stepping between the hot looks. "Susie, you take the boy's bedroom until we can fix up the other bedroom. Go on, dear. Walt's put fresh water in the basin and the towels are on the rack and the bedpan's clean. You get some sleep. We'll talk more in the morning."

"Good idea," Walt said, knocking the ashes from the bowl of his pipe and standing up. His wife joined him and they left the kitchen, Doreen and Susie following.

Smoke, Cheyenne, and Rusty sat around the table for a few more minutes, with Rusty and Cheyenne eating up every doughnut they could find.

"Near four-thirty," Smoke said, refilling his coffee cup. He was almost forced to break Rusty's hand as he reached for the last bear sign. "No point in going back to bed."

Rusty looked frantically around for another platter of doughnuts.

He found a fresh chocolate cake and his smile almost added new light to the room as he whacked off a hunk that would choke a bull.

"Growin' boy still," Cheyenne said with a grin. "Cut me a piece of that, too, Rusty."

"Smoke?"

"I'll pass, Rusty, thanks. I'm fixing to rustle me up some bacon and eggs before long."

"Fix some for me, too," the young puncher said around a mouthful of cake.

"Yeah. Me, too," Cheyenne said.

Smoke grinned and shook his head at the two characters. Then he sobered when he thought of what Jud Vale might do in retaliation. And another matter had been nagging at him off and on for a week or so.

"What you ruminatin' about?" Cheyenne asked.

"Jud Vale, for one thing."

"Just ride over and call him out and kill him. Me and Rusty and Walt will go with you."

"The odd thing is, Cheyenne, I don't want to kill him. He's not right in the head, and therefore he isn't responsible for what he's doing. It might come to a killing, but I hope it isn't me who has to do it."

Cheyenne thought about that for a moment. "And the other thing?"

Smoke sighed and finished his coffee. He nodded his head toward the outside. Rusty cut the lamps low and followed them. They walked over to the corral and Smoke pulled out the makings and built himself a cigarette.

"Walt has confided in me that he is a wealthy man," Smoke said. "Why doesn't he hire guns and let them bang it out with Jud's men?"

"I've pondered over that my very own self," Cheyenne admitted. "I can't come up with no firm answer."

Rusty looked startled for a moment. Then he shook his head in disbelief. He threw down his own cigarette and stomped it out, his spurs jingling with the movement. "I can't believe you two guys!" he finally blurted.

"What do you mean, you red-headed pup?" Cheyenne looked at him.

Rusty just laughed at him.

"I'll bust you upside your punkin head," Cheyenne told him, balling a hand into a fist and drawing it back.

"Whoa!" Rusty stepped back.

"You better explain yourself, Rusty. If you know something we need to know, spit it out."

"I didn't mean to laugh at neither of you. I just figured that you both knew."

"Knew what, you knothead?" Cheyenne growled at him.

Rusty looked at Smoke. "Soon as you told me I was workin' for the Box T, I figured the fire had done reached the grease. But it never dawned on me that Mr. Walt hadn't leveled with you. Hell . . ." He paused. "Well, maybe the old bunch has died out and the new bunch of folks in this area don't know. Jud Vale is Walt's kid brother!"

14

After recovering from his shock, Cheyenne said, "I been in and out of here for the last fifty years, Rusty. I ain't never heard that story."

"Rancher up in Montana told me some five or six years ago. Sorry, boys, I just figured you knew."

"So Clint is really Walt's nephew." Smoke spoke the words softly. "I wonder what surprises Doreen has in store for us."

Rusty blushed.

"Not those surprises, Rusty! I wonder if she's kin to Walt and Alice."

"Beats me. I done told you all I know."

"You shore this rancher wasn't just pullin' your leg?" Cheyenne questioned.

"I don't think so. We was sittin' around the fire one night during roundup, passin' a bottle around. Lemme see if I can remember all, or most, of what was said." He rolled another cigarette, deep in thought while he was shaping and licking and lighting the tube. "Mr. Randolph—that was the rancher I was workin' for at the time—he said that Walt come out to this part of Idaho 'way back. The first white man to settle in this part of the territory."

"That much jibes with what Walt told me," Smoke confirmed.

"Mr. Randolph said that Walt had left a baby brother

behind. I believe he said Ill-o-noise or O-hi-o or some of them faraway places like that. Said that Walt never really knew the kid all that good. He was in diapers when Walt left. The kid started gettin' into trouble right off the mark. Then as the kid got older, the trouble got worser. He's supposed to have raped and kilt a woman when he was 'bout fourteen or fifteen and had to flee, two steps ahead of the law."

"And Walt didn't know what was going on back home?"

"No way he could have. A thousand miles away like he was. Sure wasn't no letters bein' posted to this part of the territory. Mr. Randolph said that the kid turned to a life of crime—bad stuff. Robbin' and murderin' folks and abusin' women. He robbed a U.S. gold shipment, hundreds of thousands of dollars, and him and his gang come out this-aways. Jason's been with him from the git-go, way Mr. Randolph told it. That gold was what set him up in the ranchin' business.

"Walt went to see the rancher one day, and was shook right down to his boots when Jud Vale—that's the name he took—started talkin' about where he was from. Walt started writin' letters to folks he figured was still alive back to home. He started puttin' two and two together and soon realized that Jud Vale was his baby brother.

"But he never let on to Jud. Not until about ten years ago, I reckon, maybe more than that. Mr. Randolph never did say; or if he did, I forgot. Way Mr. Randolph told it, Jud went into a screaming rage for some reason, and told Walt he would destroy him and take all the gold that Walt had found. Walt tried to tell his brother that there wasn't no more gold on the Box T, that the strike had been a fluke and had been played out. But Jud wasn't havin' none of that."

"I wonder why Editor Argood didn't tell me all this?" Smoke questioned, his voice soft in the night.

"Well, he probably figured you knew already. Just like I done."

"And now you know it all." Walt's voice came from behind them.

The trio turned around to face the rancher.

"I wish you had told me," Smoke said.

"Shame. It was shame that prevented me from telling you."

Smoke swore an ugly streak. "You're lying, Walt. You've lied to me right from the start and I'm telling you now: clear the damned air and level with us!"

Walt came to the corral and hung his arms over the railing. He lit his pipe and sighed. "There isn't much else to clear. He's my brother, boys. Our blood is the same. I had him in rifle sights once and couldn't pull the trigger. I just couldn't kill him. Even knowing what trash he is—what he had turned into. I just couldn't do it. That's why, until recently, at least, I was just letting him run all over me. Then I got mad. I sent out word that I was hiring gunfighters." He laughed sourly. "But if I paid a hundred a month, Jud would pay two hundred. And so on. I had half a dozen. They left me and went to work for Jud. I hired some straight punchers. Jud and his men drove them off or killed them. I finally reached the point where I just didn't know what to do. I was confused, alone with the wife and Doreen and Micky. Scared for them and for myself. I'm not a young man. There is more than twenty years' difference between me and Jud Vale. His real name is Paul Burden. Then, Smoke, you showed up."

For the first time since arriving at the Box T, Smoke believed the man. "Doreen is no kin to you? No blood kin?"

"No."

"Walt, I've told Cheyenne that I don't want to kill Jud. He needs killing, I'll be the first to admit that. He's a vile, loathsome person, for a fact. But I don't want to be the one to pull the trigger on him. And I won't unless he pushes me to it or gets caught up in gunfire while attacking this ranch. The man is insane. He needs to be confined in an asylum. For the rest of his life."

Walt's laugh was bitter. "You think I haven't tried to do that? I personally called on the territorial governor and informed him of Jud—without telling him that Jud was my brother. He sent people in to talk with Jud. Jud charmed them. He has that ability. Just like his son, Clint. And just like Clint, he can go off the beam into a raging, killing darkness at the smallest slight or word. Smoke, I don't know what else I can do. I have reached my wit's end in this matter."

Smoke felt an intense sorrow for the man. A grandson that wasn't his, and a blood brother who was a raging lunatic and invariably would have to be destroyed like a rabid dog, were enough to fell all but the strongest of men.

"We'll work it out, Walt," Smoke assured him.

After Walt had returned to the house, Cheyenne asked, "Just how do you figure we're gonna work it out, Smoke?"

"I don't have any idea," Smoke admitted.

Susie slept late, it being almost noon when she walked out into the front yard. When the weather was good, the boys took their meals at a long setup table in the yard. When the weather was bad, they had to take shifts eating in the house.

Susie was amazed at the youth of the hands, and equally amazed at the ages of the old men. No one asked her to lend a hand with the cleaning up; she just fell to it as one by one the boys finished their nooning and got up, going back to work.

"Rider comin'," Cheyenne said, squinting his eyes.

"Who is it?" Rusty asked.

"Blackjack Morgan," Smoke told them. "You never know about Blackjack. Or Jackson, for that matter. They operate under a strange code."

Matthew had moved over from the table, to stand by the rosebushes planted in front of the house. The hammer thong was off his Peacemaker.

"You just steady down, boy," Smoke said. "Blackjack's not looking for trouble."

Blackjack reined up at the hitchrail and waited for an invite to dismount.

"Coffee's hot, Blackjack," Smoke told him. "You're welcome to a cup and something to eat if you're hungry."

Blackjack swung out of the saddle. "Neighborly of you, Smoke. Coffee sounds good." His eyes widened and he smiled. "Is them bear sign I spy?"

"Yes. Help yourself, Mr. . . . ah, Blackjack," Alice said.

"Thank you kindly, ma'am." He poured coffee and got a couple of doughnuts. He looked at Smoke. "But I got to say that this ain't what you'd call a social visit. At least not right off, it ain't."

"I didn't figure it was." Smoke moved to the table and sat down.

Blackjack munched on a doughnut and sipped his coffee. "That editor feller is gone to Utah. Won't be back for a month or more. And that youngster he hired to cover the news has recently got hisself a bad case of jitters. Didn't take much; just a little talkin' to, is all. He won't be comin' around here no more."

"We expected that."

Blackjack's eyes held a visible light of amusement as he looked around at the boys and the old men. "Damnedest outfit I ever did see. Pardon my language, ladies. These boys doin' a man's work. Drove that herd all the way to the railhead without a bobble. You boys is all right in my book. I brung a message from the Bar V," he said abruptly.

Smoke took a bite from a doughnut and waited.

"Jud Vale has done de-clared war on anybody ridin' for the Box T. Man, woman, or child. That don't set too well for a few of us. Me and Jackson, most especially. I don't believe in mistreatin' women or hurtin' no kid or dog. So, I ain't a-gonna do it. Neither is Jackson."

He finished his bear sign and wiped his mouth with the back of his hand. He drained his coffee cup and thanked Susie as she refilled it.

"But that's just two out of about forty-five . . . with more comin' in shortly. The odds is too high, Smoke. You can't win this one."

"These folks have noplace else to go, Blackjack. So we have to win it."

"Figured you'd say that. You bein' who you is and all that."

Blackjack sipped his coffee. "Now I ain't got nothin' personal ag'in you, Smoke. But that ten thousand dollars that Jud's done hung on your scalp is just too good for me to walk away from. That money would get me a right nice spread down in Texas and I can hang these guns up."

"You ain't never gonna hang them guns up, Blackjack," Cheyenne told him. "You been around too long. You're one of the old breed. There's always gonna be some punk kid who wants to make hisself a rep."

"Not me, Cheyenne. I'm a-gonna change my name and bury myself down near the Barrillas. Me and Lassiter. We done talked it over. So me and Lassiter will be waitin' for you over at Preston, Smoke. That's the way it's got to be, and you know it."

Smoke nodded.

Blackjack cut his eyes to Matthew. "Git shut of that gun, boy. It ain't nothing but grief. You already got the stamp on you, but it ain't too late to shake it off. As young as you is, you kill another man, you're gonna be marked."

"I plan on becoming a lawman," Matt told him.

"Huh! That's even worse. Puttin' up with drunks and whoors and tinhorns and gamblers. It ain't no life." He smiled sadly. "O' course, my life ain't been all that great, neither." He stood up and smiled at the women. "Much obliged for the coffee and bear sign, ladies." Turning, he looked at Smoke. "Lassiter's just over the ridge. We're headin' for Pres-ton. I 'spect we'll see you there, Smoke."

Blackjack Morgan walked to his horse and swung into the saddle. He rode off without looking back.

"Now that is interesting!" Walt said.

"Not really." Smoke began rolling a cigarette. "They're setting me up, that's all."

"You can bet on that!" Cheyenne agreed. "Blackjack and

Lassiter will prob'ly have four or five men with them. Their plan is being the only ones standin' after the battle."

"That's the way I read it at first. Now I'm not so sure."

"What do you mean, son?" Walt asked.

"Jud wants me away from the ranch, probably figuring I'll take someone with me."

"And he'll hit the ranch when you're gone," Alice stated, a sick expression on her face.

"That's the way I see it."

"And if you don't go into Preston, Blackjack and them others will spread the word that Smoke Jensen has turned yeller," Cheyenne added that.

Smoke shrugged that off. "That kind of talk never bothered me, Cheyenne."

"Son, you can't face seven or eight men alone," Walt told him.

Smoke smiled. "I faced eighteen alone one time. I did take some lead. But I put them all down. Don't worry, Walt. I have no intention of riding into a setup. If I just stay put, that will probably make Blackjack and the others so mad they'll do something rash."

"Like what?" Rusty asked.

"Oh . . . like moving their ambush a lot closer than Preston. Like over to the trading post."

"And you'd ride over there to face them?" Susie asked. "One man against seven or eight gunslingers?"

"I'd give it some serious thought," Smoke told her, pouring another cup of coffee.

"That man said that more gunfighters would be coming in shortly," Doreen said.

"I'm fresh out of ideas, Doreen. What do you want me to do, girl?"

"You could put the ranch up for sale. Advertise it in the paper, in papers all over the state. That would draw a lot of attention to our situation and maybe make Jud Vale back off."

"She's got a point, Walt," Smoke told him.

But the old rancher shook his head. "I been out here goin'

on fifty years. Me and Alice fought Indians and outlaws, blizzards and droughts. We come close to packin' it in several times. This ain't one of them times. If you all was to leave—and I wouldn't blame you none if you was to pull out—I'm stayin'."

His wife moved to his side. *"We're* staying, Walt."

He put his arm around her waist and pulled her close.

The younger of the boys looked at each other, all thinking they had best head back to the creek as quickly as possible and gather up some more stones for their slingshots.

Matthew hitched up his gun belt.

"This here is a right good job of work," Dolittle said. "So me and Harrison is stayin' put. If I'm gonna die, I'd druther it be with food in my belly and some coins to jingle in my jeans."

"I'm stayin'," Cheyenne said.

"So are we!" the boys shouted as a unit.

Rusty shrugged his shoulders. "Count me in, too."

"That's settled," Smoke said. "Let's get back to work."

15

The sheriff rode out to the ranch two days after Blackjack Morgan had tossed down the challenge. He had three tough-looking deputies with him.

He told Walt to get his crew together. His adult crew.

Only Smoke, Cheyenne, and the women were close to the house. They sat at the long table in the front yard and talked.

"Lines bein' what they are," the sheriff said, "I ain't rightly sure this place is even in my jurisdiction. But I know damn well that Preston is. Excuse my language, ladies. And I ain't a-gonna have no gunfights in my town." He looked at Smoke. "I thank you for not ridin' in."

"I'm waiting for them to move it closer to the ranch."

The sheriff nodded his head. He waved his hand at the three deputies. "This is it, folks. You're lookin' at the law enforcement in this county . . . providing, that is, the Box T is even in my county. New lines was drawn up last year and it's still all confused. But that ain't the point. The point is that Jud Vale's done hired himself about sixty men, all drawin' fightin' wages, and there ain't a damn thing I can do about it. Oh, I could ride over to the Bar V and try to throw my badge around. But you all know how much good that would do. Jud's a charmer. He'd just tell me be was gettin' ready for roundup and hired all them men to punch cows."

He sighed. "Walt, there may still be warrants out on Jud

back East. I know the story. And I've sent telegrams to them folks back yonder. The parents of the girl that Jud was supposed to have killed is dead. The lawmen who were in charge when it happened are gone. So that's a dead end. No help there."

"What you're trying to say, Sheriff," Smoke said, "is that we're on our own here."

"That's blunt put, Jensen. But yeah, that's just about it. You say that Jud attacked your ranch. Can you prove it in a court of law?"

"I doubt it," Walt admitted.

"There still ain't no laws about two growed-up men fightin' each other over gun barrels. There will be someday, but that time ain't here yet. I talked to a man from the governor's office. The governor ain't got the manpower to step in and settle every dispute between ranchers. Territory is just too big. I've said what I come to say, Walt. I wanted to tell it to you face to face."

"I appreciate that."

"You've told us, Sheriff," Smoke said. "Now let me tell you."

The sheriff cut his eyes to the gunfighter.

"Just stay out of it," Smoke said flatly. "I roughed up a few and killed one the last time out. The next time I go headhunting, I'm going to leave bodies all over the range."

The sheriff flushed, but wisely kept his mouth shut.

"And that goes for me, too," Cheyenne said. "In spades. I'm gettin' tarred of all this dilly-dallyin' around. I'm an old man; I ain't got many years left me. So it don't make a damn to me if I check out now, just so long as I take a few, or a bunch, with me. And I plan on doing just that."

The sheriff stood up and his deputies followed suit. "I wish you luck." The lawmen walked to their horses and rode away.

"He's a good man, the sheriff is," Walt said. "I ain't takin' what he said nearabout as hard as you boys. Maybe I just understand the feelin's around here better than you."

Smoke stared at the man. "What do you mean, Walt?"

"I've tried to tell you time and again, boy: folks around here is scared of Jud Vale. He's had them buffaloed for years, and it ain't got much better—if any better—since you come along. Man told me last time we went to the post that most of the bettin' money was with Jud and against you."

"You should have told him he was a fool."

"I did. Problem was, I don't know how convincing I sounded."

Walt and Alice, with Doreen and Susie right behind them, went back into the house. Smoke and Cheyenne walked to the corral and stood in silence for a few minutes.

"You changed your mind any 'bout just ridin' up to Jud and pluggin' him?" Cheyenne asked.

"No."

"Didn't figure so. Still think that would be the smart thing to do."

"You're probably right, Cheyenne. But it just isn't my style."

"You want me to do it? He ain't nothin' but a rattlesnake."

"No." Smoke looked off into the distance. "But it worries me about him declaring war on the women and the boys."

"It don't surprise me none," the old gunfighter said with a snort. "A rattlesnake don't give a damn who he strikes. Sometimes they'll just lay there on the trail still as death and watch you go past without even a short rattle. Next time you come by, they'll hit you. Jud Vale ain't got no more sense than a rattler. And is just about as useless. Come to think of it, a rattler might be worth more. Least they kill rats and mice."

The old rounder limped off, toward the bunkhouse and a cup of coffee.

Smoke stood for a time by the corral, deep in thought. Maybe Cheyenne was right. Maybe he should just ride over to the Bar V, line up Jud Vale in rifle sights, and end it.

But Smoke knew he wouldn't do that. At least not yet.

But if one of the boys got hurt . . . ?

He shook his head. He didn't even like to think about that.

With his back to the corral rails, he watched the boys ride out, heading back to work—a gutsy bunch of kids.

Smoke wondered where Clint Perkins had gotten off to. The so-called Robin Hood of the West had not been heard from since he had rescued Susie from the Bar V. But Smoke had no doubts about his being near, waiting for that invisible trigger in his brain—always on half-cock—to fire his unstable mind into action.

Smoke went into the house, told Doreen to fix him a bait of food, and with the food packet in his hand, went to the barn, saddling Dagger. Rusty had ridden in and was seeing to his horse.

"You headin' out?"

"Yes. Is the herd bunched?"

"And boxed."

"I want you and the others to stick close to the ranch. I don't know how long I'm going to be gone. Three days; maybe a week. However long it takes me to cut the odds down some."

"You goin' to face Blackjack and them others?"

"Probably. But it will be on my terms, not on theirs. Nobody has to leave the ranch. We're well-stocked with food; God knows we have enough guns and ammo to stand off a dozen attacks. Keep an eye on the boys, Rusty." He swung into the saddle.

"I'll do it. You watch your back trail, Smoke."

"I've been doing that since I was fifteen years old," Smoke said with a smile.

He rode for the Bar V range, keeping to the timber and the brush, riding slow and stopping often to sit his saddle and listen. He marveled at the size of Jud's herds. The man was worth a fortune in beef alone; there wasn't a rancher anywhere who wouldn't be satisfied with these herds. Only Jud Vale wanted more. But then, Smoke concluded, Jud wanted everything.

Especially Doreen.

Smoke had warned her to stick very close to the ranch, and to stop wandering out into the meadows to pick wildflowers. Jud had made his brags that he would have Doreen, one way or the other. But whether Smoke's warnings had gotten through to the girl was something only time would prove out.

Smoke steered clear of Jud's mansion. What he wanted to see was whether anyone was working Jud's cattle, and after spending most of the afternoon carefully watching from the hills and ridges, he concluded that the cattle had been pretty much left on their own.

So Jud had pulled in all his hands. For what? An attack on the ranch? Maybe. But somehow he doubted that.

He had tried that once, with disastrous results. So if not an attack against the Box T . . . then what?

Smoke could come up with no reason for leaving the herd unguarded. Of course, Jud probably felt—and rightly so— that no one would have the nerve to rustle cattle from him, so his herds were safe.

So what was going on? And why had he not run into any of the Bar V hands this day? Odd. Very odd.

With about three hours of good light left and guessing that he was a good ten miles—maybe more—from Jud's mansion, Smoke rode to near the top of a high ridge. Keeping in the timber, Smoke dismounted and took his field glasses, making his way to the top of the hill. There, on his belly and under cover, he began carefully sweeping the area.

Far in the distance, he picked up the small figures of men, some on foot, some on horseback. They were making a meticulous sweep of the area. Looking for what? Smoke silently questioned. Or for whom? Certainly not him. Jud knew he was at the Box T . . . or had been for days.

Had to be looking for Clint. That was all that Smoke could come up with. Had Clint pulled something over the past few days that Smoke did not know about? It was certainly possible.

Smoke studied the tiny figures of searching men through

his field glasses. At least twenty-five or thirty. And that brought yet another thought to Smoke's mind: where were Jud's other hands and hired guns? That question made him uncomfortable.

He decided to get the hell gone from there.

He mounted up and rode toward the deep timber that lay to the east of the mansion, but still well on the Bar V range. As he rode, he began seeing signs that this area had been searched and searched thoroughly. He reined up suddenly, knowing then where the other Bar V men were.

All around him, waiting to see if Clint—if that's who they were searching for—would double back.

Smoke found a place which offered deep cover and a good two days' graze and water for Dagger, picketed him, and slipped into moccasins. He filled any empty loops with .44's and, taking his rifle, began Injuning his way through the brush and timber.

Smoke was under no illusions: these were dangerous men he was surrounded by, and after Smoke's initial attack against the ranch, and his making fools of the men, they would be doubly alert, with more than one of them mad as hell and looking for blood.

Smoke's blood.

Making about as much noise as a drifting ghost, Smoke wormed his way under a pile of blown down brush and dead limbs—hoping that a rattlesnake had not made this spot his home—and settled in for a time.

As he waited, Smoke ran some questions through his mind: why the systematic search for Clint? Had the man staged another raid, or had Jud just decided to take out his enemies one at a time? Then Smoke rejected both ideas as another thought came to him.

Clint Perkins was a wanted man, a fugitive from justice. So what better way for Jud to show the people that he was a straight-up, honest, and law-abiding citizen than by killing or capturing the most wanted man in southern Idaho. That would certainly swing public opinion in his favor.

And there was something else, too; after Clint was taken—and Smoke felt the man would not be taken alive; Jud simply could not risk that—Vale could, and probably would, charge that Walt and Alice and Doreen had been hiding the outlaw. That would further erode Walt's credibility with his neighbors.

Slick! Smoke thought, as his eyes continued to sweep the terrain from his hiding place. Jud Vale was beginning to think in a more rational way.

And that, Smoke reflected bitterly, was something he had not even considered Jud doing. He had been counting on the man to continue behaving in his usual emotional and irrational manner.

A stick popped not far from Smoke's hiding place. Smoke cut his eyes, not moving his head. That was no animal, for animals seldom stepped on sticks unless they were running in fear. And Smoke heard no follow-up sounds of any animal in panic.

He waited, motionless, his breathing very shallow and through his mouth to cut down even the slightest sound.

He saw the man move; a fatal mistake on the man's part, for movement attracts attention much faster than sound in any deadly game of hide or be killed.

The man was dressed in earth tones, blending in well with his surroundings. Smoke concluded that the man was a skilled woodsman, and the stick was the only mistake he had made.

It just took one mistake in this game, and the man had made his.

The manhunter moved closer, moving stealthily through the timber. As he drew closer, Smoke could make out his features. It was one of those he had seen stepping off the train some days before. A bounty hunter.

The man carried a Winchester in his hand, a bandolier of cartridges slung over one shoulder. The manhunter stopped, tensed, and suddenly dropped to the ground.

Smoke watched through a small space in the pile of brush

and dead limbs. What had the man seen? Or had his hunter's sixth sense alerted him of the unseen danger?

Probably the latter.

Now it was a game of wait and see.

Smoke waited. Several minutes passed. He could detect no other men, so the bounty hunter was probably working alone. But Smoke couldn't be certain of that, although he believed it to be true.

A bird flew into the timber, started to settle on a branch, then abruptly took once more to the air, its wings flapping furiously.

Smoke's smile was a grim one. Thank you, bird, he thought. Have a long and happy life.

He had yet to move his head. Only his cold hunter's eyes had shifted. Now they remained fixed on the dangerous brush where the bounty hunter lay.

The top of the brush moved ever so slightly, the movement indicating the man was coming toward Smoke's location, making his way very cautiously.

Had he been spotted? Smoke didn't think so.

Smoke waited for several minutes, watching the slow movement of the man. He wanted him much closer; close enough to use his knife. He did not want to risk a shot, not knowing how many others were within earshot of his location.

Then the bounty hunter rose, all in one fluid motion. He was so close that Smoke could see the hard cruelty in his eyes.

The bounty hunter moved closer, pausing a few feet from the brush pile where Smoke lay.

Smoke exploded out of the brush, his knife in his hand.

16

The bounty hunter wheeled around, his eyes wide with panic, the rifle in his hands coming up. But Smoke's forward charge knocked the man sprawling, loosening his grip on the Winchester. The man opened his mouth to yell a warning. With one hard swing of the long-bladed knife, Smoke ended the life of the hunter.

He took the man's rifle, pistol, and ammo, and then dragged the body into the pile of brush. Smoke made his way back to Dagger, using a different route, stashed the weapons, patted the big stallion on the neck, and once more headed out into the woods.

This time out, he was going to show Jud Vale what he thought of a man who would declare war on women and young boys.

And he would write the message in blood.

Smoke stayed near the top of a ridge, working his way along, keeping to the brush and timber, not skylining himself. At the highest point of the ridge, Smoke bellied down and made his way to the crest.

A Bar V hand chose that time to stick his head up and look Smoke right in the eyes. Smoke recovered from his shock before the puncher and clobbered the cowboy right between the eyes with the butt of his Winchester, sending the man sprawling backward, his forehead bleeding.

Smoke was over the crest and on top of the hand before the man could recover. Smoke busted the man on the side of the jaw with the butt of the rifle and the hand's eyes rolled back in his head. He was out for a long time, with a broken jaw.

Smoke tossed the man's pistol into the brush and smashed the man's rifle useless against a tree trunk. He moved down the ridge, mad and on the warpath. A Bar V gunny spotted him and raised his rifle to fire. Smoke leveled his Winchester and shot the man in the belly, doubling him over and bringing a scream of pain.

Now the fire had reached the hot grease and the war was on.

The landscape seemed to erupt with ugly and very hostile gunhands as Smoke dived for cover just as unfriendly fire began zinging and popping and ricocheting all around him.

Jumping behind a fallen log, Smoke wriggled his way to the other end and rolled into a small depression in the earth. Below him, the Bar V gunnies were shouting and cussing.

Smoke leveled his Winchester and put an abrupt and permanent halt to one gunfighter's swearing. The .44 slug caught the man in the chest. The hand's rifle went flying as blood stained the front of his shirt.

Smoke lunged out of the depression and made the timber before the others could get him in gun sights; shooting uphill was just as tricky as shooting downhill.

On the crest of the ridge, in deep timber, Smoke settled in for the siege. He dusted one Bar V gunny's position, making the man hug the earth and lose his hat. Just for spite, knowing what value western men put on their hats, Smoke lifted his rifle and knocked the hat spinning, ventilating the Stetson.

The gunny cussed Smoke, loud and long.

Smoke ducked down as the lead began whining wickedly all around him, bringing the thought to his mind that now would be just a dandy time to haul his ashes out of that particular location.

During a break in the firing, Smoke eased back, clearing the crest of the ridge, and began making his way west, working in a slow, careful semicircle until coming to a better, if temporary, area in which to work.

He lifted his Winchester, sighted in a foot sticking out from behind a large rock, and squeezed the trigger. The yowl of pain that followed told him he had taken another gunny out of the fight. The man was screaming in pain from his bullet-shattered ankle.

Another gunny, with more guts than sense, left his safe position to move to what he felt was a better one.

Smoke shot him, the bullet going in his left side and tearing out the right side, spinning the man like an out-of-balance top and dropping him to the hard, rocky ground. He did not move.

Smoke punched more .44's into his Winchester and made life miserable for a gunhand who was crouched behind a tree. The man decided to seek better cover and made a run for it. Smoke knocked a leg out from under him and the man rolled down the hill, hollering and cussing. He finally managed to break his downhill rolling by grabbing onto a small tree and painfully working his way behind it. Smoke let him be, and concentrated on the others.

But the fight was gone from this bunch. Smoke watched without firing as they began working their way down the hill, staying in cover, carrying and helping the wounded back out of range of Smoke's deadly rifle fire.

He left his position and worked his way back into deep timber, paralleling the gunnies' retreat, sensing from their urgency and the direction of their travel that they were heading for their horses. He was waiting for them when they reached the picket line.

Smoke shot one badman in the belly and dusted another gunhand before they all left in a confusing and disorderly retreat, some of them losing their weapons as they stumbled and ran away.

Smoke ran into the camp, grabbed up the fallen weapons, and stuck them in empty saddle boots. He grasped as many reins as he could, swung into a saddle, and led the horses back to where he had left Dagger. There, he tied and grouped the horses and headed back for the Box T range.

All in all, it had been quite a profitable day.

It was late night before Smoke reached the ranch house. He put the horses into the corral, told the boys to strip the gear from them and clean and store the weapons. He switched horses and then filled a sack with dynamite and caps and fuses, and was back in the saddle, heading once more for the Bar V range.

He made a cold camp, slept for a few hours, and was up about three in the morning. He checked his guns and then saddled up. With a grim smile on his lips, Smoke went head-hunting under the stars.

About two miles from the main house, and not running into a single Bar V hand, Smoke moved several hundred head of cattle toward the direction of Jud's mansion and then tossed two sputtering sticks of dynamite near the bunched-up herd of Bar V cattle. The explosions sent them into a snorting, wild-eyed stampede heading straight for the mansion.

Smoke tagged along to see what other mischief he could get into this fine night.

The hard-running cattle hit the mansion grounds at full speed, demolishing several outhouses and destroying one corral. Smoke drove half a dozen of the frightened cattle into the mansion and then circled, tossing a stick of dynamite into a bunkhouse.

The charge of giant powder blew out one entire end of the bunkhouse and sent gunhands—in various stages of undress—rolling and running and crawling in all directions.

The dust kicked up from the wildly stampeding herd only added to the confusion, limiting visibility to only a few yards in any direction. Smoke's horse ran into one long handle-clad gunhand, knocking the man to the ground. The gunhand screamed as the horse's steel-shod hooves ripped flesh and cracked bone.

Jud Vale appeared on the balcony of the second floor of the mansion, clad only in his underwear. He was jumping up and down and screaming almost incoherently. "Somebody come up here and get this goddamn cow out of my bedroom!" he finally managed to squall.

With his six gun, Smoke put several slugs around Jud's bare feet. The man did a frantic little dance and, hollering to beat sixty, leaped back into the bedroom, obviously preferring the company of a smelly wild-eyed cow to the lead that was sending splinters into his tootsies.

A puncher grabbed onto Smoke's leg, trying to pull him out of the saddle. Smoke laid the barrel of his Colt against the man's head, splitting it wide open and dropping the man to the ground.

Hot lead came awfully close to Smoke's cheek and that convinced him that it was time to move. Bending low over his horse's neck, Smoke galloped around to the back of the house. Jud had just rebuilt the back porch and replaced all the windows at the rear of the house.

Smoke lit another fuse with the small can of burning punk and tossed the stick under the back porch.

Jud's wild cussing could just be heard over the confusion.

Smoke had cleared the creek and was heading into the starry darkness as the porch blew up. The giant powder demolished the newly rebuilt porch and once more broke all the windows from the rear of the mighty mansion.

"Goddamn you, Jensen!" Jud's voice rang out over the dusty night. "I'll get you for this. I swear I'll get you! I'll stake you out over an anthill and let them eat your eyes. I'll . . ."

Laughing as Jud's voice faded, Smoke headed for the deep timber.

Dawn found him cutting fence wire and scattering Jud's cattle all to hell and gone. An hour later he had blown two dams and torn down several line shacks.

He looked up at the sounds of pounding hooves and cut his horse toward a long-deserted cabin and barn about half a mile away. The story was that the cabin and barn had belonged to a rancher and his wife. Jud had moved in and moved them out, after killing the rancher's son and badly wounding the rancher.

Smoke chanced a glance over his shoulder. There were ten or twelve riders coming hard at him, but still too far away for accurate shooting on their part.

As he rode toward the cabin, Smoke made his plans as he bent over the horse's neck, keeping a very low target. The cabin was built into a hill. The sod roof had long since become a living thing as the grass from the hill caught life and flourished.

Smoke dismounted at a run and threw open the door, leading the horse inside. He knelt in the open doorway and leveled his Winchester, clearing one saddle of a hired gun. The horse trotted on toward the cabin as the other gunhands veered off, left and right, seeking some sort of cover. They all knew how deadly Smoke was with any type of weapon.

Smoke grabbed the reins of the spooked pony, pulled the rifle from its boot, tore loose the canteen—that would give him three full canteens—and jerked off the saddlebags. He slapped the pony on the rump, sending it on its way.

Smoke slammed the door and dropped the old bar across it just as rifle shots began slugging into the logs of the cabin. He led the horse into the rear part of the house, as far out of harm's way as possible, gave it a hatful of water, and returned to the front of the cabin. If worse came to worst, he could pull grass from off the roof and feed the animal.

He smiled when he saw the kitchen. Luck was with him. Some of the Bar V hands had used the cabin as a line shack, and used it recently. Staying low, Smoke closed the still sturdy inside shutters—put there long ago against Indian attack—and tried the pump in the kitchen. Cold clear water gushed forth. He opened the cabinet. Cans of beans and peaches looked back at him. He selected a can of peaches and opened it with his knife, then ate the peaches and drank the juice.

"All the comforts of home," he muttered, then checked the Winchester he'd jerked from the boot of the riderless horse. It was full up.

He looked into the saddlebags of the hired gun who now rested face down on the ground. Several biscuits with salt meat, three boxes of .44's and a spare pistol and holster under one flap. Dirty underwear under the other flap. He kept the biscuits, the pistol, and the .44's.

Smoke moved to a gun port and looked out. He could see a man slowly working his way toward the house, but still too far off for a shot. Smoke let him come on.

He moved to the other side of the house just in time to see a man run from tree to tree. This one was well within range. Smoke eared the hammer back on his Winchester and waited. The gunhand broke cover and made a run for the corral. Smoke stopped him at midpoint, the .44 slug turning him around as it hit his side. Smoke didn't finish the man, choosing instead to let him lie on the ground and scream in pain. That would work on his buddies much more than a death shot.

Smoke sat down on the floor, his back to an overturned table as the lead really began to fly in his direction. He ate one of the salt meat biscuits and sipped water from his canteen and let the attackers expel all the ammunition they wanted to.

After a time, the hostile fire slacked off and then died. Smoke smiled in a grim curving of the lips and moved to the window. He let out a long groan. He waited, and then groaned again.

"We got him!" a man shouted. "We really got the bassard this time!"

"Oh, yeah?" came the sarcasm-filled question. "And who wants to be the one to walk up and look inside the cabin to be sure?"

No one replied.

"That's what I figured," the man said.

Smoke removed the bar from the door and moved back to the overturned table, laying his rifle on the floor, pulling his Colts and easing back the hammers. He waited. When they opened that door—and he figured they would come all bunched up for moral support—more than a few of them were going to be in for a very nasty surprise.

Once more, the outside air was filled with lead. Smoke waited.

"Hell, he's had it," a man called. "I'm goin' in."

"I'll go with you," another called, and several more added their agreement to that.

Smoke waited.

He heard the jingle of spurs as the hired guns and bounty hunters approached the cabin. Smoke had removed his boots and arranged them behind the table, placing them so it appeared he was lying dead, his body concealed behind the table. He slipped on moccasins and then stepped back into the shadows of another room.

The front door was pushed open with the barrel of a rifle.

"See anything?" a man asked.

"Hell, are you crazy? I ain't stickin' my head in yonder!"

"I see his boots," another said, looking through a gun slit. "He's all sprawled out and stone cold dead behind a table."

The room crowded with men.

Smoke opened fire, the Colts belching sparks and flames and death. He pulled the pistol he'd taken from the saddlebags and ended the lopsided gunfight. One lone gunhand tried to rise up and shoot him. Smoke shot him between the eyes. "Your mamma should have told you there'd be days like this," Smoke said.

He then counted the bodies. Six. He figured maybe three were left on the outside still alive, and that included the badly wounded man by the corral.

He reloaded and moved toward the open door, staying close to the log wall. "Come on, boys!" he shouted. "Come join the party."

"Hell with you, Jensen!" a man shouted. "They's always another day. We're gone!"

"Then ride, scumbag!"

The man cursed him. A moment later, the sounds of horses galloping away reached Smoke.

Smoke gathered up all the weapons and tied the rifles together. He found a bounty hunter's horse and stuffed the saddlebags full of pistols and gun belts, looping some over the saddle horn. He secured the rifles to the saddle and led the horse to the cabin. Shoving the dead out of the doorway, Smoke led his own horse outside and mounted up. He walked his horse over to the corral and looked down at the man lying on the ground. The man was dead. He left him there and rode out into the plain. The first man he'd shot out of the saddle was lying on the ground, on his back, his eyes open and staring at Smoke. His shirt front was covered with blood.

"You're a devil!" the man gasped.

"I've been called worse," Smoke acknowledged from the saddle.

"I ain't gonna make it, am I?"

"Not likely."

The man cussed him but made no attempt to reach for the pistol still in leather.

Smoke waited until the man stopped cussing and tried to catch his breath. "Anything you want me to do for you?"

"Fall out of the saddle dead!"

Jud Vale had hired hardcases, for sure. No give in them. "Would you really have shot one of those little boys over at the Box T?"

"Just as fast as I'd shoot you, Jensen."

"Then I don't think I'll turn my back to you."

"It wouldn't be a smart thing to do, for a fact."

Smoke sat his saddle for a few minutes. The gunny began to cough up blood. Twice he tried to pull his pistol. But the thong covered the hammer and he could not clear leather. The gunny died with a curse on his lips.

Smoke turned his horse and slowly rode toward the Box T range.

17

Jud Vale pulled in his horns, so to speak. Even with his monumental ego and glaring arrogance, he was shocked to the bone at the havoc and carnage that Smoke Jensen had wreaked upon his possessions and hired guns. He had not believed it possible that one man could do so much.

A half dozen of his older and wiser hardcases bided their time and drifted out of southeastern Idaho, wanting no more of Smoke Jensen. Had most of those who left known Jensen was involved in this matter, they would not have signed on in the first place.

Jud spent a lot of time on his front porch—while his back porch was being rebuilt, again—drinking coffee and wallowing in his festering anger. He had sent out the word that he was still hiring men at fighting wages, and men were drifting in. But even Jud Vale could see that most of them were trash and scum. That made no difference; he hired them anyway.

And then the gunfighter Barry Almond and his four brothers came riding up to the mansion. They were dressed in long dusters and were unshaven, with cruel eyes their hat brims could not conceal.

Jud sat on the porch staring at the men while Barry sat his saddle and met the man's eyes.

"I'm Barry Almond." The gunslick finally broke the silence.

"I know who you are."

"That ten thousand dollars still on Smoke Jensen's head?"

"It's still there."

"Me and my brothers come to claim it."

"I've heard that from fifty other men over the weeks," Jud snorted.

"This is the first time you've heard it from me, though."

Jud nodded his head in agreement with that. "All right, you're all on the payroll."

"I ain't punchin' no gawddamn cows," Barry bluntly told him.

The rancher laughed, but the short bark was void of humor. "Nobody else is either," Jud replied, the bitterness thick on his tongue. Ranch was going to hell in a bucket. "So what else is new?"

"We'll just drift around some."

"You do that." Jud poured another cup of coffee and watched the gunfighter brothers head for the long new bunkhouse which Jud had been forced to build because of the overflow of hired guns and because Jensen had destroyed one end of the other bunkhouse.

Jud silently cursed Smoke Jensen. It made him feel better. But not much.

On the day that Smoke accompanied the supply wagon to the trading post, Blackjack Morgan, Lassiter, and four bounty hunters headed for the post for a drink of whiskey. The men were in a bad mood and ready for a killing. Especially if it meant Smoke Jensen or some of those snot-nosed brats on the Box T payroll. . . .

Clint Perkins lay on his ground sheet in his hidden camp and tried with all his might to fight the madness that once more began to slowly muddle his brain. He lost the battle. Clint stood up, pulled on his boots, and buckled his gun belt around his waist. With a strange smile on his lips and an odd look in his eyes, he saddled up and went looking for trouble. . . .

Matthew and Cheyenne were moving some strays toward the huge box canyon that was the home for what was left of Walt's herds. The old gunfighter and the young boy had become good friends in a short time. . . .

Doreen slipped out the back door of the ranch house to go walking toward a meadow about a mile back of the house. She had seen some lovely wildflowers there and felt that a bunch of them would look very nice on the kitchen table. She didn't think Jud would be foolish enough to try anything in the daylight. . . .

Jud Vale and Jason and Jud's bodyguards chose that time to make a daylight foray into Box T country. They were heavily armed and one of Jud's men had a gunnysack filled with dynamite and caps and fuses. If they could get close enough to Walt's place, they intended to return in kind what Smoke had given them. Twice. And if some of those snot-nosed nester brats got killed . . . ? Big deal. It would serve them right and send a message to the rest of the nesters in what Jud considered to be his territory. . . .

Don Draper and Davy Street and half a dozen other Bar V hired guns had left the bunkhouse to see if they could cause some trouble for the nester brats working the Box T herd. They headed straight for the area where Matthew and Cheyenne were working. . . .

Rusty was about a mile from the box canyon, working alone. . . .

It was ten o'clock in the morning when all the ingredients that were needed to bring to a full boil what would turn out to be the bloodiest range war in all of Idaho Territory's history were dropped into the cauldron.

Smoke stepped down from the saddle in front of the trading post/barroom, and slipped the leather thongs from the hammers of his guns. Walt went into the store to give the shopkeeper his order for supplies.

Doreen sat amid a wild profusion of flowers and began carefully picking out the most lovely ones and putting them into her basket.

Susie stepped out of the ranch house at Alice's request to go looking for Doreen. She waved Alan over and asked him if he'd seen her. The boy pointed to the meadow rising among wild and beautiful colors above the ranch, a good mile and a half away, he figured.

"She hadn't oughta get that far from the ranch alone," he added. "You want me to go fetch her, Miss Susie?"

"We'll both go, Alan." She looked at the gun belted around the boy's waist. "You really know how to use that thing?"

"Yes, ma'am. I sure do."

Susie hesitated for a moment. "Get a rifle, Alan. Just in case."

"Yes, ma'am. I'll be back in a couple of minutes."

Susie looked toward the meadow. She suddenly had a very bad feeling about this lovely day.

"Riders comin'," Cheyenne said, twisting in the saddle.

Matt turned and spotted the riders. He slipped the leather from the hammer of his six gun.

The movement did not escape the eyes of Cheyenne. "You just stay out of this, boy."

Rusty had seen Cheyenne and the boy working the strays. Then he saw a bunch of strays moving toward a coulee and went after them. Cheyenne and Matt were quickly lost from his sight as he followed the strays down into the deep coolness of the ravine.

"Boss!" one of Jud's bodyguards said, pulling up and pointing to the tiny figure sitting amid the wildflowers in the meadow.

Jud squinted his eyes and an evil smile turned his mouth. His lips were suddenly dry and he licked them as all sorts of wild, lustful and immoral thoughts, all involving Doreen and himself, raced feverishly around in his brain.

"Get her!" Jud ordered. "I'll have that woman. She'll come around. She'll learn to love me. I'll make her my queen!"

The bodyguards spurred their horses.

Doreen looked up at the sounds of pounding hooves, fear in her eyes. She jumped to her feet, her heart racing. She dropped the basket of wildflowers and began running just as Susie and Alan were beginning the long walk to the meadow.

Alan took stock of the situation quickly. He jerked Susie to the ground, knowing that he could not shoot—the distance was far too great. And there was no point in their being spotted and taken prisoner—or worse. At least for Susie.

All they could do was lie amid the flowers and watch.

Doreen ran for her life, screaming as she ran. Strong and hard hands jerked her off the ground and swung her across a saddle. She felt the horse turn and gallop back across the meadow. The horse slowed, then stopped, and she was dumped to the ground. She looked up into the hard eyes of Jud Vale.

"My queen," the rancher said. "You'll be my queen; you'll reign by my side. Together we'll rule this whole country."

"You're crazy!" Doreen hissed at him. "You're plumb loco!"

Jud laughed at her as his eyes roamed over her young body. "Hoist her up here, boys. I want me a handful of that woman."

Doreen began screaming.

Cheyenne had wheeled his horse to face the Bar V gunhands. The old gunfighter's face was hard, his eyes narrowed to obsidian slits. He looked straight at Don Draper. "What the hell are you and this bag of crap ridin' with you doin' on Box T range, Draper?"

"For a skinny old man, Cheyenne, you got a big fat mouth, you know that?"

"And for a punk, Draper, you're way over your head and outclassed facin' me, you know that?"

Draper flushed. "Anytime you're ready, Cheyenne. Then me and the boys will take that kid and have some fun with him."

"You'll visit the privy ever' day if you eat regular," Cheyenne popped back. "And you ought to, 'cause you shore full of it."

Draper's face darkened further at that remark. But still he hesitated, as did Davy Street. Cheyenne was known throughout the West as an old he-coon who had never backed down from anybody or anything at anytime. If the truth be known. Cheyenne had killed as many men, or more, as Smoke Jensen or John Wesley or Rowdy Joe or Tom Horn—and maybe as many as all of them combined.

Old he might be, but Cheyenne was still a man not to be taken lightly.

It was an old man and a young lad that faced the eight Bar V gunhands that hot morning, but the smell of fear was coming from the so-called gun slicks, not from Cheyenne or Matthew.

"You're a fool, Cheyenne!" Draper spoke, stalling for time.

"Naw," the old gunfighter said, amused at the man's reluctance to drag iron, but at the same time worried about Matthew. "I'm just an old man who's lived a long, long time, that's all. Now I'm ready to see the varmint and rest for a time."

"We gonna kill you and this snot-nosed brat!" a gunhand sneered at him, cutting his shifty eyes to the bespectacled Matthew.

The boy waited, his right hand close to his six gun.

"You might," Cheyenne admitted. "But they's gonna be a fearful toll taken on you boys whilst doin' it."

"You say!" the gun slick said.

"I say," Cheyenne replied calmly. He had faced this a hundred or more times, and he knew the time was now. This was the entire world. No one else existed. This little pocket was all there was. Time had stopped. Eternity was looking them all in the eyes.

"Now!" Davy yelled, grabbing for his gun.

Cheyenne drew, cocked, and fired, all in one smooth and practiced motion, blowing Davy out of the saddle, the slug taking the man in the center of the chest and knocking him backward.

Don jerked iron and fired, the slug striking Cheyenne in the side. Cheyenne leveled his long-barreled pistol and fired just as Matthew's Peacemaker barked. One slug struck Don in the belly, the other one took him in the chest, the bullet nicking his heart. He stayed in the saddle, one dead hand still holding onto the reins.

A Bar V gun blasted the smoky air, the bullet passing through Cheyenne's lungs. Cheyenne grinned a bloody smile and put a slug between the man's eyes as he was sliding from the saddle. The old gunfighter fell to the ground, on his knees just as Matthew put hot lead into the Bar V hand's stomach.

Cheyenne managed to lift his six gun and drill another hired gun before that pale rider came galloping up to touch him on the shoulder.

The old mountain man and gunfighter died on his knees, still wearing his hat and boots and holding on to his six gun.

Matthew was knocked out of the saddle by a slug that hit his left shoulder and tore out his back. But he held on to his Peacemaker and even though he had lost his glasses he could still see well enough to shoot. The boy leveled the Colt and shot the gun slick in the throat just as Rusty came galloping up, the reins in his teeth and both hands filled with guns.

When Rusty had emptied his Colts, only one Bar V man was left in the saddle and he was hard hit and fogging it back to the more friendly range, just barely managing to stay in the saddle.

Rusty took one look at Cheyenne and cursed at the loss of a friend and another man who had helped in the uneasy settling of the West. Rusty hoisted Matthew back into the saddle, found his glasses for him, and tied Cheyenne across his saddle.

"All hell is gonna break loose now, boy," the redhead told the boy. He had inspected the boy's wound and found it to be very painful but not too serious. The bleeding was slow, indicating that no major artery or vein had been hit. Rusty plugged the holes with a torn handkerchief and stabilized the arm in a sling.

"Feels like to me it has broke loose," Matthew said, his voice grim and old for his age. He looked at Cheyenne. "He was my friend."

"He was my friend, too, boy. Let's ride."

Both Alan and Susie had raced back to the ranch compound, yelling as they ran. Alice started crying and Micky joined her.

The boys wanted to ride after the kidnappers and shoot it out and rescue Miss Doreen. Jamie yelled them into silence and literally had to slap some sense into a couple of them. They would wait for Mr. Smoke and that was that. There wasn't no point in going off half-cocked and getting killed.

"Oh, hell!" the barkeep moaned, as Smoke stepped into the saloon. "Not you agin!"

"If this keeps up I'm going to get the feeling that you don't like me," Smoke said with a grin. "But of course," he added, "you would be at the end of a very long list, I reckon."

Bendel shook his head. "That don't seem to worry you much." He returned the smile. "One thing about it, Mr. Jensen—with you around I don't never have to worry about bein' bored." He drew Smoke a mug of beer and set it down on the bar.

"I had hoped this place would not be filled up with Bar V riders."

"Stick around," the barkeep said mournfully. "It will be."

"We won't be here long. Just long enough to get supplies."

"I'm glad you didn't bring that four-eyed kid with you. That youngster is so calm he spooks me."

"He'll do to ride the river with, for sure." Smoke sipped his beer while he waited for Walt to finish with his supply ordering. They were making a trip a week to resupply, for with fifteen growing boys to feed, the food went fast. And Rusty was no slouch when it came to grub. He could eat up a whole apple pie all by himself if the girls didn't keep a good eye on him.

Smoke heard the sounds of horses coming up to the post and inwardly he tensed.

The barkeep cursed.

"What's the matter, Bendel?"

"Some of Jud Vale's hired guns ridin' up. A whole passel of 'em."

Smoke sighed. "One of these days I'm going to get to finish a beer in peace."

18

Doreen had been dumped into an upstairs bedroom. It wasn't long before Jud opened the door, his arms filled with boxes and a big grin on his broad face. He dumped the boxes on the bed.

"Them's the finest gowns and underthings all the way from Paris, France," he boasted. "Silks and satins and the like. And in that little box, they's a diamond and ruby thing you wear in your hair. I forget what it's called."

"Tiara?" she asked.

"Yeah! That's it, all right. I bought it all just for you, Doreen."

"But I don't want any of these things!"

Jud ignored that. Waved it away. Then he began to pout. "But I bought them just for you," he said, a sulky tone in his voice.

Doreen looked at the bulk of the man, lifting her eyes to his. She could plainly see the madness in his eyes, the same kind of madness she had refused—at first—to see in Clint's eyes. Clint Perkins, Jud Vale's own flesh and blood. And in that instant, she realized something else: that if she was going to survive, she had best humor Jud.

But that thought, or warning, flew right out the window as Jud opened more boxes. Grinning at her, he laid the gold and jewel-encrusted headpiece on the bed and shook out the garment. "See what I bought for myself, Queen Doreen. My, oh, my, won't we both look fine!"

Doreen couldn't help it. She burst out laughing and laughed until the tears were running down her cheeks.

"You stop that this minute!" Jud screamed like a petulant child.

But Doreen could not stop laughing. And her laughter became uncontrollable when Jud stamped his boot on the floor and began to jump up and down, behaving very much like a naughty boy caught with his hand in the cookie jar.

Her laughter almost put her on the floor. Where it failed, Jud's fist succeeded. "You're really not going to wear that on your head, are you?" she questioned, just as Jud swung a big fist.

Doreen got her reply as her head exploded in pain and she lost consciousness.

When Rusty brought Matthew in, the hysteria of the women vanished and they took over the doctoring of the boy while Rusty solemnly cut the body of Cheyenne loose and told Jamie and Leroy to get shovels and start digging. They'd wait and have the funeral in the morning. The body would keep that long.

What to do about Doreen?

Rusty didn't know. He looked at Alan. "Boy, could you positive say in a court of law that Jud took her?"

The boy looked at Susie. Both of them shook their heads. "No, sir," the boy replied. "We was too far off to say positive it was him."

"What are you getting at, Rusty?" Alice asked.

"He'll hide her if anybody gets within ten miles of that ranch. You can bet he'll have lookouts posted ever'where. He may be crazy, but he ain't stupid."

"So we wait for Smoke to come back?" Susie asked.

"That's all I know to do." Rusty would have liked to go charging into the mansion, both hands filled with Colts. But he was forced to put his anger and his feelings for Doreen aside and do his best to think logically, knowing that even if he should manage to reach the mansion without catching a slug, he would never breach the big house—not alive, and he would certainly be no good to Doreen dead. Or anybody else for that matter.

He would wait for Smoke to return.

Bendel looked out the dusty window. "Six of them, Mr. Jensen. I know two of them by name."

"Who are they?"

"Blackjack Morgan and Lassiter. But them others look just as tough."

Smoke signaled for another beer with his right hand as his left hand touched the butt of his left-hand Colt. Of late, he had been loading the Colts up full. You never knew when that extra round might save your life.

Boots and jingling spurs sounded on the porch of the trading post. The batwings squeaked open. Smoke did not turn around.

Blackjack paused at the bar and spoke to Smoke's back. "Well, well, boys. Look what we done come up on here. The famous gunfighter, Smoke Jensen. You reckon we ought to bow down or something like that?"

His friends laughed. Smoke did not acknowledge the presence of any of them. He sipped at his beer and spoke to Bendel. "I thought I just heard a jackass bray, Bendel. You certainly do have a very strange clientele."

Bendel got a sudden case of the jumps and moved to the end of the bar, carrying a couple of bottles of whiskey with him. He knew the drinking habits of Blackjack and Lassiter and could guess at the tastes of those with them. A tray of shot glasses were bottoms up on a towel near the end of the bar.

"You callin' me a jackass?" Blackjack demanded in a loud voice.

Smoke slowly turned to face the man. "Why . . . it isn't a

jackass, after all. It's Blackjack. Excuse me, Morgan. I must have been mistaken."

"That's the damnedest apology I ever heard," Lassiter said.

"Who said I was apologizing." Smoke cut his eyes to the gunfighter.

"What'll it be, boys?" Bendel hollered.

"We ain't deef," one of the bounty hunters said sourly. "Whiskey."

Blackjack still stood by the bar, facing Smoke. Smoke had noted that all the men wore their guns loose in leather, free of hammer thongs. And Blackjack wanted to try Smoke something awful; Smoke could read the challenge in the man's dark eyes.

"Don't do it, Blackjack." Smoke spoke the words softly, so softly that only Morgan could hear them. "It isn't worth it, friend."

"Don't give me orders, Jensen." Blackjack's returning words were equally soft, less than a whisper; a scant moving of the lips. "I want you before the Almond Brothers find you."

Smoke had heard of the Almond Brothers. A trashy bunch of no-goods that had drifted out of the Midwest some years back. A pack of back-shooting scum who would steal the pennies off a dead man's eyes. Jud was certainly scraping the bottom of the barrel by hiring that bunch.

"If they take me, Blackjack, it won't be facing me."

"They'll still have the ten thousand and you'll still be just as dead."

Smoke smiled and turned his back to the man.

"Don't you turn your backside to me!" Blackjack snarled, putting out his hand and dropping it to Smoke's shoulder, spinning the man around.

Smoke hit him with a left to the belly and followed that with a beer mug to the side of Blackjack's head, knocking the man to the floor.

Blackjack was up like a rubber ball, blood streaming down his cheek from the gash on his head. He swung a fist and

Smoke ducked under it, again popping the man in the gut and bringing a grunt of pain.

Blackjack connected with a left to Smoke's head that backed him up. Blackjack was no stranger to brawls and he could punch.

Smoke faked him with a left and Blackjack took the bait, grinning and dropping his guard. Smoke punched through the hole and erased the grin, as he connected with a right to the mouth that smashed Blackjack's lips and loosened some teeth. Blackjack shook his head and came in swinging.

Smoke sidestepped and stuck out a boot, sending the man to the floor, clubbing him on the back of the neck as he went down.

With a curse, Blackjack got to his boots just in time to receive a left and right combination to both sides of his jaw that staggered and stunned the man. He fell back against the bar planking.

Smoke pinned him there and went to work, smashing at the man with big work-hardened fists. Smoke flattened Blackjack's nose and ruined his mouth. One of the man's ears was swollen and pulpy and the gunfighter's eyes were glazing over.

Smoke stepped back and let Blackjack fall to the floor. The man did not move.

Lassiter chose that time to stand up. "By God, Jensen, you'll not do that to another good man," and Lassiter went for his piece.

Smoke shot him.

He drew, cocked, and fired in less than a heartbeat, his slug striking Lassiter in the belly and knocking him back against a table, splitting the wood right down the middle. Lassiter was drawing iron as he was falling, and managed to get off one shot, which dead-centered the painting of a nude female that was hanging on the wall behind the bar.

"Why, you sorry son!" Bendel hollered. "I paid good money for that." He came up with a shotgun just as one of the bounty hunters was dragging iron.

Lassiter lifted his six gun as blood was leaking from his mouth.

Smoke shot him between the eyes just as Bendel's shotgun roared, the buckshot creating a terrible mess at close range. The torn-apart bounty hunter was literally lifted off his boots and flung across the room. He bounced off a wall and fell to the floor, lying still in a bloody mess. Two of his buddies cursed and then tossed good sense and caution to the gods of fate as they grabbed for their six guns.

Bendel gave one the other barrel just as Smoke shifted the muzzle of his Colt and let the .44 bang, the slug taking the second man in the chest and dropping him to his knees.

The lone bounty hunter left alive lifted his hands out from his body and held them wide apart to show that he was out of this affair.

Walt stuck his gray head into the gunsmoke-filled barroom. He held a six gun in his hand, the hammer eared back.

"It's over," Smoke told him, just as Blackjack moaned on the floor and tried to sit up.

Smoke jerked the man to his boots and spun him around, so he could see the carnage in the saloon.

Blackjack's eyes were swollen from the beating he'd just received, but he could see well enough to know that the best thing he could do would be to keep his mouth closed.

"Get on your horse and ride, Blackjack," Smoke told him. "And if you have any sense at all you'll keep going and not look back until you've cleared a couple of counties."

Blackjack broke his silence. "Lassiter was a pal of mine, Jensen."

"*Was* is right."

"I'll not let his death go unavenged."

"Then you're a fool. As crazy as Jud Vale." Smoke shoved him toward the batwings. "Get out of here, Blackjack. If you're in my sight ten seconds from now, I'll kill you."

"And stay out of my saloon!" Bendel hollered. "All of you trash that work for the Bar V. I'm tellin' you now—pass the word: I'll kill the first one of you that pass through those batwings. I'm tired of this." He leveled his reloaded double-barrel, sawed-off express gun. "Move, damn you!"

Blackjack moved.

Smoke glanced at Walt. "Supplies loaded?"

"All on the wagon."

"Let's get back to the ranch. I suddenly got a bad feeling about this day."

Jackson took one look at Jud Vale and struggled to contain his laughter. At the same time he was fighting to keep from busting out laughing, he was making up his mind about the Bear Lake Fight, as it was being called by some.

Jackson was switching sides.

Jackson was a gunfighter, and a good one, but he had had a bad taste in his mouth about this fight right from the git-go. He just didn't think it was right to fight women and kids and old men. And now he had heard that Jud Vale and old Walt were really brothers, and that didn't set well with him at all. He didn't have any trouble understanding how brothers could hate each other; he'd seen that many times before. But in this situation, there wasn't any reason for it. Come to think of it, there wasn't any reason for any of this, and there damn sure wasn't even one ounce of reason roaming around in Jud's crazy head.

And where in the hell did Jud come up with that costume he was struttin' around in?

Man looked like the fool he really was.

Time to go, Jackson concluded, just about the time the lone hand came staggering in from the gunfight with Cheyenne and the kid.

Jackson listened, then slowly walked to the bunkhouse to get his kit together. He rode out without being noticed. He headed for the Box T range, but in a very roundabout way, going by the way of the trading post and stopping in for a drink of whiskey.

That longing for a drink of whiskey just about cost him his

life: when he stepped into the saloon he was looking down the barrels of a sawed-off shotgun.

"Whoa!" Jackson said. "I'm friendly, Bendel!"

"Not if you're ridin' for the Bar V, you ain't."

"I quit 'um. Jud Vale is as crazy as a bessy-bug. All the wrappin' done come plumb off him." He grimaced, remembering the sight of Jud all dressed up in that silly-lookin' outfit. "In a manner of speakin', that is. I figured I'd toss my saddle on a Box T horse."

Bendel lowered the express gun. "They need some help, for a fact. Have a whiskey, on the house."

"Don't mind if I do. Smells like gunsmoke in here, Bendel."

Bendel told him what had gone down.

Jackson sipped his whiskey and mulled over that bit of information. He would have enjoyed seeing Blackjack get the snot whipped out of him. If ever a man deserved a good butt-whippin', Morgan did. Him and Lassiter and those others with that grand plan to ambush Jensen. That hadn't set well with Jackson either, but by the time he'd learned of it, it had all blown over.

Jackson thanked Bendel for the whiskey, stepped into the general store for some tobacco and cartridges, then headed out for the Box T.

He was feeling better with every mile he put behind him.

19

"And I seen Jud sendin' men out in all directions." Jackson was wrapping it up for Smoke and Rusty and the others. "Ain't no way we're gonna bust Miss Doreen out of there with just two or three men and a handful of kids. I don't think her life is in no danger. Don't you ladies take this the wrong way now, 'cause I think a man doin' what Jud is gonna do against her will is wrong, but at least she'll be alive."

"And you say Jud has really gone around the bend?" Walt asked.

"Gone around the bend! Man, he is total low. Walks around that big house with a gold crown on his head, all done up in diamonds and rubies and the like. And he wears a robe."

"You mean he's wearing something like a dressing gown?" Smoke asked.

"Hell, no! Excuse me, ladies. I mean one of them ear-mine robes that he had hand-sewn and all made up for him over in Russia."

"Ear-mine?" Alice questioned. "You mean ermine fur?"

"Yes'um. That's it. A white one. Comes all the way down to his ankles. He looks real stupid stompin' around the house in that robe, wearing a crown on his head, and cowboy boots on his feet. I'm tellin' y'all, it's gettin' to be awful weird around that place. Plumb spooky."

"Are the men laughing at him?" Walt asked.

"Not to his face. He's still totin' a gun strapped around his waist. And that makes him look even dumber."

"But still dangerous," Rusty added.

"Even more dangerous," Jackson told them. "'Cause you don't never know what a crazy man is goin' to do."

They all agreed with that.

Walt leaned back and scratched his head. "Well, let's come up with some way to get Doreen out of that nuthouse. Anybody want to start?"

Those seated around the table fell silent as they looked at one another. Smoke finally broke the silence.

"I'll gear up and leave tonight. We've got to know just where in the house she's located and how many men Jud has on guard and where they are. I'll find that out and then we can make some plans. But first we have to bury Cheyenne. Let's do it at sunset. That was his favorite time of day."

They all agreed that was a good suggestion.

"I just wish I knew if Doreen was all right." Alice sighed the words.

"She ain't all right, ma'am," Jackson said, a grim note to his statement. "But she ain't dead either."

They buried Cheyenne just as the sun was going down, with Walt reading from the Good Book. Alice and Susie and Micky cried, and some of the other boys looked like they were having a tough time keeping the tears back. All but Matthew. The boy stood with a grim look on his face. Smoke knew the look well. He could read revenge clearly on the boy's face.

Smoke knew just how Matt felt. He'd been down that rocky path many times in his life.

After the words were read, one by one, they filed past the dark hole and tossed a handful of earth into the pit. The clods rattled against the rough pine box that young Eli had built for Cheyenne that afternoon. Then each one of the other boys had solemnly driven a single nail into the coffin.

Moments after the funeral, Smoke saddled up and rode off into the gathering darkness. There was a hard look on his face. He was getting more than a little weary of Jud Vale and his hired guns.

Deep into the Bar V range, about three miles from the mansion, he guessed, Smoke picketed his horse and slipped into moccasins, leaving his hat and taking his rifle. He had swung wide getting to the location where he had left his horse, taking a route that, if he were in Jud's place, would post the least number of guards.

He worked his way toward the mansion, hoping to find the location of just one of the guards. He wanted to talk to one of Jud's men. Smoke didn't think it would take him long to get what information he needed . . . and it didn't.

The guard woke up with a raging headache from where Smoke had clubbed him on the back of the head. There was a bandana tied over his mouth and he was very cold from the waist down. He couldn't understand that. Then he realized his britches were gone. He cut his eyes and felt even colder fear clutch at his heart as he looked at Smoke Jensen, who was squatting a few feet away, clearly in the moonlight, a big-bladed knife in his hand.

"I'm going to ask you a few questions," Smoke said, in a voice that made the hired gun want to go to the bushes, something fierce, to relieve himself. "And you're going to give me correct answers. You know who I am?"

The man nodded his head.

"You've heard the story about what I did to one of the men who raped my first wife and then killed her and our baby son?"

The hired gun almost came unhinged. *Everybody* knew what Smoke Jensen had done to the gunfighter Canning. He had taken a knife—maybe the same damn knife Smoke was now holding—and turned Canning into a gelding, then cauterized the wound with a hot running iron.

The hired gun nodded his head vigorously.

"You wouldn't want me to do that to you, would you?"

The man made strangling, choking noises behind the bandana.

"I didn't think so." Smoke reached out with the point of the blade and the man almost had heart failure. He breathed a little easier as Smoke cut the gag loose.

"You yell, and it will be the last sound you'll ever make on this earth," Smoke warned him.

The hired gun nodded.

"What's your name?"

"Johns."

"I want the locations of all the guards. Quickly."

Johns told him. Quickly.

"What room is Doreen being held in?"

"Top floor. The room facin' the crick back of the house. The winders is all nailed shut so's she can't get out."

"Has any harm come to her?"

"No, sir. Jud hit her once, but that's all. He ain't messed with her in no way. He says he's savin' all that for when they get hitched up proper."

"And when is that going to be?"

"Don't know. And that's the truth."

"How many men does Jud have on his payroll?"

"I'd have to say close to a hundred now. He's got a regular army. But a lot of them is trash. They ain't gonna stand when it starts gettin' hot. I'd say he's got near'bouts seventy fighters. And hirin' more."

"Jud can't afford to pay that many men."

Johns sighed. "He can afford it. I'll tell you all I know. Then if you'll let me go, I'm gone to see the Pacific Ocean."

"You level with me and you can ride."

Smoke cut his bonds and told him to put his pants back on. And to wash his longhandles the first chance he got. Smoke built a cigarette and tossed Johns the makings. The man lit up and inhaled, then started to talk.

"The ranch is just a front for Jud's other doings. He's into all sorts of things. Got hisself four or five gangs workin' all over two or three states, robbin' trains and stagecoaches and stealin' gold and cattle and you name it. I don't know all that he's got goin' for him, but I do know that he's a rich man, and that he's gone plumb crazy. A lot of his own men—not none of the ones that's been with him for years—is beginning to talk about doin' him in and takin' over. I been thinkin' about driftin'. So far I ain't kilt nobody that wasn't facin' me with a gun, and I ain't never stole much of nothin' in my life. Beef ever' now and then for something to eat, is all."

"Is he going to call his gangs in to help in this range war?"

Johns snubbed out his cigarette. "Smoke, there ain't no way of tellin' what that man is gonna do. He might have done sent for them for all I know. I'm tellin' you the man is crazy as a lizard."

"Anything else you can tell me?"

Johns thought for a moment. Then slowly shook his head. "I reckon not. Except for maybe to warn you to expect anything. Jud Vale has done turned crazy."

After Johns had ridden away, Smoke said, "All right, Clint, you can come in now."

A chuckle from the darkness. "You are very, very good, Mr. Smoke Jensen. But I fear I must decline your kind invitation. I am in one of my moods and there is no telling what I might do."

"Jud has Doreen," Clint said.

"I know. But now is not the time to attempt to mount a rescue. We are too few and Jud has too many. We will have to devise some sort of diversion to pull as many men as possible away from the ranch, and then no more than two or three go in to get her."

"Have you a plan?"

"Unfortunately, no. But I know Doreen very well. She is very, very bright. I am certain she has guessed that the key to her survival lies in her keeping a cool head about her. If Jud Vale wants her to be his queen, to parade about in fine gowns from Paris, France, that's what she'll do if that's what it takes to stay alive."

"Jud's own men—some of them—are talking mutiny. That might turn out bad for Doreen."

"Yes. I thought about that. I think we have a week or so before anything like that happens. Probably longer. It will take that long for Jud to pull in his various and far-flung gangs."

"If that's what he has in mind."

"He does. I've been on these ridges since early afternoon. He's sent riders out in all directions. I'm guessing that some of them are riding for the gangs."

"Then we'd damn well better do something before the odds against us get ridiculous."

"I'll let you know when I have a plan."

Smoke heard a whisper of cloth against brush, and knew that Clint Perkins was gone, slipping into the night.

Smoke sighed and shook his head. This had turned into one great big mess. *The next time you think about a vacation,* he thought sourly, *try riding east instead of west.*

Then he felt guilty for thinking that. His own children would be grown some day, and if they got into a jam that was not of their own doing, he hoped someone would be around to help them.

Someone like Smoke Jensen.

He rose to his moccasins and started back to his horse. This was one of the few times in his life that he felt helpless, and he had a hunch the feeling was going to get much worse until it got better.

If it ever did.

Matthew remained in bed, embarrassed by all the fuss being made over him, but enjoying it nonetheless. There were no signs of infection in his wound, and he seemed to be healing nicely and quickly.

Walt had ordered all the boys to stay close to the ranch.

What cattle remained were bunched in the box canyon with plenty of graze and water and could take care of themselves for a time. The boys worked at turning the ranch compound into a fort.

Everybody knew that an attack, and it would be a big one, was inevitable. It was just a question of when.

Smoke and Rusty and Jackson went over everything they could think of.

"As far as weapons and ammo goes, we got enough to outfit a battalion of army," Jackson pointed out. He grinned. "I recognize a whole lot of them rifles and pistols from the Bar V boys."

"We've filled ever' water barrel we could tote in," Rusty said. "The house and barn and bunkhouse is fortified like none I ever seen. That was a good idea Jamie had about haulin' up big rocks and stackin' them window high around the house and bunkhouse. It'd take a lot of giant powder to do any damage."

Jackson rolled a cigarette, licked, and lit up. He glanced at Smoke. "You in deep thought, Smoke." He passed him the makings.

"Three reasonably young men—that's us. Three old men. Two women. One little boy, and fifteen young boys. That's all that's standing between maybe a hundred or more hired guns, bounty hunters, outlaws, and a crazy man who walks around his mansion in an ermine robe with a jeweled crown on his head proclaiming himself to be king. I've been in some strange situations in my time, but this one has got to take the cake."

"How about ridin' into town and sendin' a wire to the governor?" Rusty suggested.

Smoke shook his head. "I discussed that with Walt. We both agreed we'd be wasting our time. The governor has made it clear that he doesn't have the manpower to do us any good down here. Reading between the lines of that remark, I'd have to say that the governor is not going to get involved. Why, is anybody's guess."

Jackson was thoughtful for a moment. "I know maybe half

a dozen men I could get to come in here. If I could find them, that is."

"Yeah, that's my problem, too," Smoke said. "Louis Longmont would come in here in a flash, but I have no idea where to find him. For all I know, he might be in Europe. I have a hunch that all this is going to be over before any of us could locate and bring people in. Jud's got the jump on us in that respect."

"If we could just get Doreen free of that nuthouse of Jud's, we could sit back here and wait Jud out," Rusty reflected. "I think even if Jud sent all his men over here, we stand a pretty good chance of holding them off."

"Attacking us here will come," Smoke said. "I believe that. But only as a last resort. Jud's got Doreen; that's what he wanted most of all. His main concern now will be in keeping her."

"The thing to do, the way I see it," Jackson said, "is to try to think like Jud. But how in the blue blazes could anyone think like a crazy man?"

"You can't." Smoke nixed that. "I think his moods change, or could change, every day, maybe every hour. I believe he's so far around the bend that he's become totally unpredictable."

Rusty glanced at him, "You're sayin' that even Jud don't know what he's gonna do next?"

"That's right. And if you ever get a chance, look into the eyes of Clint Perkins. His and Jud's eyes are identical. They're both madmen."

"Then it's true that Jud is Clint's father?" Jackson asked.

"Yes. And Clint can be just as whacky as Jud. No telling what he'll do next. He doesn't even know."

"You think he still cares for Doreen?"

Smoke shrugged. "In a way, I suppose. But I think he's driven more out of hate for Jud than concern for Doreen. And that could get Doreen in trouble if Clint tries something on his own."

"How about contactin' the Army and seein' if they'll do something?" Rusty grabbed at straws.

Smoke shook his head. "There again, we'd have to go

through the governor to get them. And for some reason, the governor, or, more likely, someone in his office, is blocking all requests for help."

"Nearest Army unit is stationed up near that little ol' town some folks have taken to callin' Pocatello," Jackson said. "And there ain't no more than a handful of soldier boys garrisoned there."

"We seem to be just goin' around in circles," Rusty said bitterly. "Gettin' nowheres in a hurry."

Jackson allowed as to how that was the truth.

"Did you know that Matthew has Cheyenne's old Colt?" Rusty asked Smoke.

"No, I didn't. But it doesn't surprise me. The boy loved that old man. And every time I look into his eyes I see revenge."

"I do know that feelin'," Jackson said. "The boy's a natural gunhand, Smoke. And there ain't nothin' none of us can do to slow him down. I knowed that the first time I seen him. I don't have to tell you that it's in the walk, the bearing, the eyes. He's gonna be hell on wheels, you mark my words."

Smoke slowly nodded his head. "I know. I saw it, too. It was like looking into a mirror and seeing myself years ago."

"I do know that feelin' myself," Jackson said drily. "I sometimes wish my daddy had taken the gun away from me and beat me over the head with it when I was a young'un. But it wouldn't have done no good. I had a fortune teller read my palm once. She told me I was a gunfighter. I was fourteen years old at the time. Rememberin' that still spooks me." Jackson touched the butts of his guns. "I think, Smoke, that when it's all said and done, we're gonna have to go in and fetch Miss Doreen."

"So do I, Jackson. But for now, all we can do is wait."

Rusty looked toward the direction of the Bar V range. "I sure miss that girl. I surely do. I reckon I been smitten, and she feels the same way." He looked into the eyes of Smoke Jensen. "And I ain't waitin' very long."

20

Jud pounded the end of his staff on the floor and bellowed at his "subjects," as he had recently begun calling the assorted riffraff he had on his payroll.

"Bring the queen to my side!" he squalled.

Several of his bodyguards—he now had a dozen around him at all times—went upstairs to fetch the most unwilling Queen Doreen.

Jud had ordered all the furniture removed from one downstairs room in the mansion. All the furniture except for two huge padded chairs that were placed in the center of the room: his throne and Doreen's slightly smaller throne. Jud's "staff" was a thick piece of oak, about four feet long and weighing about twenty pounds, long enough and stout enough to fell a buffalo. Jud had read several books about how royalty dressed and behaved. Since he didn't have a goblet from which to drink his wine—wine being something royalty drank—he had found a quart jar, so he used that in place of a jewel-encrusted goblet. It was kind of hard to hold, but it was either that or a bucket, and a bucket wasn't very dignified. Jud had also stopped shaving and was growing a beard; that was something else that all male royalty of the time did. Or so he had read.

He had been informed that the sole survivor of the gunfight with Cheyenne, Matthew, and Rusty had died of his wounds. Jud waved that off by muttering about serfs and the like. Since the gun slick who delivered the message had no idea what a serf was he couldn't take umbrage. He did think his boss looked like a plumb idiot; but as long as the good money kept coming, the gunhand didn't really care how Jud dressed. But he did figure that damn fur coat Jud wore was kind of hot for this time of the year.

Doreen was ushered in, all silks and satins and fancy shoes, with a jeweled crown on her head.

Jud pounded his staff on the floor and bellowed, "All rise for Queen Doreen!"

Since there weren't any chairs in the room except for the two thrones, that was an unnecessary command, but Jud thought it sounded regal so he did it anyway.

Highpockets left the "Crown Room" and walked up to Gimpy Bonner on the front porch. "The son of a bitch is crazy, Gimp!"

"I allow as to how you're right, Highpockets. But as long as the money keeps comin', I don't care if he walks around barebutt nekkid and rides a camel."

"Now that would be a sight to see!"

King Jud and Queen Doreen held court for a few minutes, but since there was nobody with any complaints for Jud to hear and rule on, it got sort of boring after a few moments.

"Would you like to stroll about the estate, my queen?" Jud asked.

"But of course," Doreen said with a smile. *I might find a chance to cut and run away from you, you ninny!* she was thinking behind her smile.

It was quite a sight to see. Jud, in his cowboy boots and spurs, his six guns belted around his middle, wore an ankle-length ermine robe and toted his twenty-pound staff. Doreen had on a gown that would have been the envy of the Queen of England. As they strolled around the "estate," both were careful not to step in the many piles of horse droppings that littered the grounds.

"I wish you would do something about this . . . unpleasantness," Doreen said, pointing to a fresh pile of road apples.

"You're absolutely right, my queen." Jud told one of his bodyguards to order the mess cleaned up and to keep it clean.

It did not take Doreen long to conclude that while Jud

certainly was as crazy as a road lizard, he wasn't stupid. The bodyguards flanked them as they strolled, and there were guards in the front of them and in the back. Jud summed it all up with a strange smile on his face.

"There is no way you are going to escape, my queen. So put it out of your pretty head and just enjoy all the privileges you are being accorded. This is your home, for now and for always."

"Very well." Doreen spoke through tight lips. "I want my room redone and I want it done immediately. I hate the colors!"

"Uh . . . yes, dear."

"And I want satin or silk sheets. Those cotton sheets are just so shabby!"

"Right, my queen."

"I want my breakfast served to me in bed."

"Uh . . . of course, dear." Jud was beginning to wonder if having a woman around on a permanent basis was going to be worth all the trouble. He wondered if other kings had the same problem.

"And I want a party."

"A party!"

"Yes. A great big fancy ball." She was doing some fast thinking and hoping it would work. "And I want everybody in southeastern Idaho invited. We'll announce our engagement there."

Jud fell to his knees; unfortunately, one knee landed squarely in a fresh pile of horse manure, but Jud appeared not to notice. "Oh, Doreen—do you really mean that?"

"Of course, I do. I'll start working on the invitation list immediately."

Jud kissed her hand. "I'm so happy, my queen!"

You won't be so happy when you see the guest list, Doreen thought. *And on the night the ball is held, that's when I turn back into a pumpkin and get the hell away from you and this nuthouse!*

"Bar V rider comin'," Jackson said, "And he's comin' up holdin' a white flag."

Jud had reluctantly agreed to invite Walt and Alice and Smoke and Rusty. He had done so after Doreen had pointed out that he had a hundred or so men on the ranch—what could Smoke do with all those guns around him?

Scott Johnson, the Arizona gunhand, handed Smoke several envelopes. "You lose, Jensen," he said with a nasty grin. "Miss Doreen and Jud is gonna announce their weddin' plans at this here shindig. And she said to tell you that that Shakyspear feller said it best when he was talkin' about friends, Romans, and countrymen. Whatever the hell that means."

Scott turned his horse and rode off.

Smoke smiled, thankful that he had wintered that time with Preacher and all those books. He remembered the line well. "I come to bury Caesar, not to praise him!"

"Wipe that hound dog look off your face, Rusty," he told the man. "She's telling us to get her out of there and giving us a way to do it."

"Damned if I see how."

"Jud'll probably have men at the door friskin' certain people before they enter the mansion," Jackson said. "We won't be able to carry guns inside." He paused. "We, hell, I wasn't even invited!"

"You'll be going, though," Smoke told him. "At least part of the way." He looked at the date on the invitation. "We've got a week to plan things out. First thing I've got to do is see who all was invited and who is planning to attend. I'm going to send Jamie and Leroy to poke around some." He looked at Rusty's long face. "Relax, Rusty. We'll get your sweetie back."

The governor was invited to the party. He sent word that he would not be able to attend. So did the general in charge of all federal troops in Idaho Territory. But Sheriff Brady said he wouldn't miss it for the world. And the young reporter from the Montpelier newspaper would attend. Most of the ranchers and a few of the farmers—Doreen had insisted the nesters be invited—agreed to attend the party.

Smoke had decided he would go in unarmed. When the time

came to grab Doreen, he would bust a guard over the noggin with something—maybe the punch bowl if it came to that—take his guns and really liven up the party.

Smoke was going to stay close to the ranch until the night of the big event. He didn't want to put Doreen's rescue in jeopardy by running into any of the bounty hunters who were out looking for him. That could come later.

At the Bar V, Doreen had everybody there, from the cooks to the cowboys, running around the lower half of the territory, driving them about half-crazy, picking up this, that, and the other thing for the ball. She wanted them to be so tired, come the night of the event, that all they would want to do is lie down and sleep and to hell with the party. She didn't know if that would be the case, but it was worth a try.

Jud had ordered cases of champagne sent in, and as many different types of "finger foods," as Doreen called them, as could be found within three days' ride of the Bar V. Since no one in their right mind would work for Jud Vale, he was forced to use some of his own hired guns and cowboys to act as waiters. He bought them all brand new black suits, with white shirts and black string ties, and low quarter shoes and white gloves. There was a lot of bitching going on about that, but Jud told them either do it or haul their ashes.

Doreen had insisted upon a band, so Jud managed to round up a guitar player, a fiddle player, and someone to toot on a bugle. It was the best he could do on such short notice.

Jud was undecided as to what to wear to the gala event. Doreen said she would clean up his ermine robe—it had a few food and wine spots on it—and he could polish his crown and shine his boots and spurs. He would look so nice.

She wanted him to look like the fool he was so everyone there could see the real Jud Vale.

"Can I wear my guns, Doreen?" Jud asked.

"Oh, but of course, darling!" She had overheard him telling his men to frisk everyone. She hoped Smoke and Rusty would be able to arm themselves, once inside the nuthouse.

Time was running out.

* * *

Smoke laid down the ground rules.

"Walt, when you get the signal from me, you take Alice and get gone from Jud's place. I'll wait about forty-five minutes before making my play. That'll give you time to get Alice to the west side of the creek. You wait there."

The rancher nodded his head in agreement.

"Jackson, you and Dolittle and Harrison will be stationed at the creek, our side of it, with rifles. Just as soon as we drop Doreen off, Alice and Doreen can take the buggy and hightail for the ranch. We'll hold off the men Jud is sure to send after us."

"Sounds good to me," Dolittle said. "I been cravin' some action."

"Yeah, me, too," Harrison agreed. "I may not be good for too much else, but I can damn sure still pull a trigger."

"And you can bet that Jud will have everybody that can ride a horse after you," Jackson warned. "He'll be killin' mad."

"We'll have a good fifteen to thirty minutes' start on him, though," Smoke said. "After Doreen makes her little speech about being kidnapped, and me with a Colt stuck up Jud's nose, the sheriff will have to make some noises about law and order and all that. Of course, once I turn Jud loose and he hoofs it back to the mansion, he'll ignore anything the sheriff might have to say and come fogging after us."

"We might get some more people on our side by doing this," Walt mused aloud. "Maybe this will give some of the smaller ranchers and farmers the backbone to join us in fighting my brother."

"If this don't, nothing will," Rusty added. He looked at Smoke. "You got another plan if this one don't work?"

"No," Smoke admitted. "But I'm thinking this will work because it's so simple and it's something that Jud won't even suspect any of us trying. For a handful of us to kidnap the man right in front of all his men, at his very own engagement party, is something that has to be unthinkable to him. At least that's what I'm hoping."

"I have to tell you, Smoke," Walt said. "Matthew says he's going to be a part of the action, come the night of the party, whether we want him to be, or not."

Smoke took that news without even so much as a blink. "It doesn't surprise me, Walt. The boy has shed his youth and left it behind him. We've both seen it happen out here many times. It's a hard time in a hard land that's filled up with hard men. I was only about a year older than Matthew when I teamed up with Preacher. About two years older than him when I killed my first man, with a pistol that Jesse James gave me back on that hard-scrabble farm in Missouri. Matthew will make it, and I'd not be a bit leery of him standing alongside me in any gunfight."

"I wanted you to know." The rancher closed the subject.

Smoke nodded his head. "Stash fully loaded rifles and pistols in the buggy, Walt. Cover them with a blanket. We're not going to have time for reloading, once the fight gets to the creek."

"We have enough weapons, for sure," Walt said with a grin, his eyes twinkling. Then he sobered. "I'm going to lay the rules down to the boys. They are to remain on this ranch, come the night of the party. Anyone who disobeys that order loses his job."

"Good. I think they'll stay put." Smoke met the eyes of the men. "We're only going to have one chance at pulling this off, people. So let's do it right the first time. That's it."

21

"My, my, what a grand place," Rusty remarked, as the huge mansion of Jud Vale came into view. "Looks like a palace for sure."

Smoke's Colts were hanging from his saddle horn, as were Rusty's guns. Both men felt naked without the weight of the pistols. The buggy was loaded with rifles and pistols, the arms covered with a blanket.

"Well, we're certainly not the first to arrive," Alice pointed out. "Even though it is early."

Susie had stayed at the Box T to look after Micky and the boys.

Smoke looked at Walt and saw that the old rancher's eyes were sad.

"My brother had it all," Walt said. "But he couldn't stay away from crime. And now he's as crazy as a loon, surrounded by men on his own payroll who plot to kill him. It's tragic."

Smoke disagreed with that summation, but then, it wasn't his brother in question. He kneed Dagger forward, moving toward the mansion.

They were conscious of many eyes on them as they entered the ranch grounds. Hostile, murderous eyes—everyone thinking about that ten thousand dollars on the head of Smoke, and wishing that Jud hadn't lifted it for this event.

Smoke swung down from the saddle and looped the reins around a hitch rail, with Rusty doing the same, and looked up at the sky. He read the sun at about half-past five. The invitation had said from six to ten. Smoke figured to start his own party at seven.

"Mr. Vale said that all hosses was to be put in the corral," a surly puncher told Smoke.

Smoke turned and grinned at the man. "His name is Dagger. He killed the last man who tried to do anything with him. But you're welcome to try."

The Bar V hand eyeballed the walleyed stallion. Dagger showed the man his big teeth and the puncher made up his mind.

"Hell with that hoss." He looked at Rusty. "What about yourn?"

"They're brothers," Rusty told him.

"Hell with him, too!" The puncher walked off.

Walt and Alice were already climbing up the steps to the porch. Shorty DePaul was there, standing by the door, collecting invitations, looking very uncomfortable in his stiff new black suit.

Smoke grinned at him. "You do look awfully cute, Shorty."

Shorty told Smoke where to go, how to get there, and what to do with his comment along the way.

"Feller's plumb testy, ain't he?" Rusty said.

Shorty had a few words for Rusty, too.

Smoke and Rusty followed Walt and Alice inside the mansion.

It was a grand place, Smoke noted, no doubt at all about that. Imported chandeliers and French furniture and all sorts of knickknacks and assorted gewgaws scattered all over the place.

"What's all this stuff good for anyways?" Rusty questioned.

"For people to look at and admire," Smoke told him.

"Looks junky and sissy to me."

Smoke grinned at him. "Your mind will change after you're married." Rusty blushed at the thought.

The punk gunfighter who called himself the Pecos Kid walked up, carrying a tray of little crackers and a bowl of dark-looking stuff. "Gentlemen," he said, speaking the word as if it hurt his mouth. "Some whore-derves?"

"What the hell is a whore-derve!" Rusty said, leaning over to take a sniff.

"That is Russian caviar," Smoke told him. "Louis Longmont used to keep some on hand at all times. Try it, it's good."

"How do you eat it?"

"Take a cracker and use that little spoon to dab some caviar on the cracker."

Rusty spooned a glob on a cracker. "Well, ain't I the fancy one, though? My, my." Rusty took a nibble and grimaced. "You got any ket-chup, Pecos?"

Smoke thought Rusty and Pecos were going to tie up right then and there, and if they had, Rusty would have shoved that whole bowl of caviar up the nose of the Pecos Kid. He pulled Rusty away and told him to behave himself; they had a more important mission that came first.

One of the ranchers, who had been in the trading post when Matthew shot it out with Smith, walked up to him. His face was ashen.

"What's the matter with you?" Smoke asked.

"Have you seen Jud?"

"No."

"He's walking around with a crown on his head and all dressed in a fur robe. He's carryin' a stick that looks like a good-sized saplin'. The man is insane!"

"That's what some folks have been trying to tell you people for months. Don't you people even care that he took Doreen by force and is holding her here against her will?"

"I heard that but I didn't believe it." He sighed. "All right, gunfighter. I believed it. But what could I have done?"

"Join in the fight against Jud?"

But the man shook his head. "No. He has too many hired guns on the payroll. He'd roll over us like stepping on a bug."

There was contempt in his eyes and scorn in his voice when Smoke replied. "Do you look under the bed at night for ghosts and goblins before you blow out the lamp?"

The rancher flushed but wisely contained his sudden anger and kept his mouth closed.

Smoke turned his back to the man and then stopped short when he spotted Jud. Rusty was standing with his mouth open, staring at the man as if he was sure his eyes were deceiving him.

Jud was quite a sight. He looked to Smoke like he'd just stepped out of a Russian opera. Jud cut his eyes to Smoke and hate filled them. He snarled at Smoke and walked away.

"You seen Doreen, Smoke?" Rusty said.

"No. I expect she'll be making her entrance just a tad after six. That's the way the fashionable ladies do it, so I been told."

"Why? Hell, she can tell time, cain't she? She ain't stupid."

"No. I mean, yes, she can tell time. No, she isn't stupid. Ladies do that so all the people will be present to look at them when they make their entrance."

"I shore don't know much about wimmen."

"Rusty, after you've been married for five or six years, you'll discover something."

"What?"

"That you don't know any more about women after all those years than you did when you got married."

"Well, ain't that just something to look forward to?"

Smoke laughed at him and moved on, walking through the lower part of the mansion. He spoke to several of the farmers that he knew. Ralph's father took his arm.

"I don't know what you got planned in the way of gettin' Miss Doreen out of this place, Smoke. But I'm with you all the way. Me, and about a half dozen other men."

Smoke started to tell him to stay out of it, then changed his mind. Somebody had to be the first ones to stand up to Jud and his army of hired guns. If the cattlemen in the area wouldn't, then maybe the farmers would shame them into joining them.

"All right, Chester. Here's what you do: when you see Walt and Alice leave, you and the others follow them. I'll tell Walt that you boys are with us."

Chester smiled. "I put rifles in the wagon. The wife can shoot nearabouts as good as I can."

"Good man!" Smoke gripped his arm and walked on. They stood a chance if he could just get Doreen out.

Smoke declined a glass of champagne being offered by the German gunfighter, Jaeger, who was minus the top part of an ear, thanks to Smoke. The German glared pure hate at Smoke.

"I ought to take off the other ear, Jaeger," Smoke told him. "So you'd have a matched set. But then you'd have a hell of a time wearing a hat, wouldn't you?"

Jaeger growled something at Smoke in German and moved on, toting his tray of drinks.

Smoke moved over to stand by Sheriff Brady's side. The sheriff gave him a curious look.

"Have you decided whether this is in your county, or not, Sheriff?"

"I don't know. I didn't come here to arrest anyone. I didn't bring any men with me. Why? Are you planning on starting something?"

"Me?" Smoke managed a shocked look. "Heavens no, Sheriff. I'm just here to have a good time."

"Right." The lawman's reply was drily given. "Sure, you are."

"Have you seen Jud, Sheriff?"

A pained look passed over the sheriff's face. "Yes, unfortunately. But there is no law against a man wearing a fur robe and a jeweled crown."

"Oh, I never said there was, Sheriff. But it might make a person question Jud's sanity—right?"

"Like I said, Jensen: I'm not here in any official capacity."

"Enjoy yourself, Sheriff." Smoke moved on, snaking his way through the growing crowd. Somewhere in the house, a clock chimed six o'clock.

He caught the eyes of several farmers; they gave him a

slight nod and a wink. Chester had done his part; the men were with him. Smoke returned the nods and found a place next to a wall. Rusty soon joined him and with their backs to the wall, they waited.

At ten after the hour, the bugler started tooting, the guitar player started strumming, and the fiddler started sawing.

"Sounds like a catfight to me," Rusty said.

Then Doreen made her entrance, and the crowd oohhed and aahhed. She was dressed to the nines, all done up in silks and satins. She was playing her part to the hilt, acting like a queen as she moved through the crowd, smiling and offering her hand to the folks.

Jud stood to one side, a big grin on his big face. He looked like a damned idiot.

Walt and Alice offered their congratulations to Doreen and then Walt glanced at Smoke. Smoke nodded his head. The old rancher and his wife slipped out the front door unnoticed and climbed into their buggy, heading back toward Box T range.

In pairs, the farmers and their wives began slipping out of the mansion. At a quarter to the hour, all those who were on Smoke's side had left. Smoke found Rusty.

"Start staying close to the Pecos Kid, Rusty. When I make my move, you grab his guns and watch my back."

The cowboy nodded and moved off into the milling crowds.

The band was doing their best to play a tune that Smoke could but vaguely recognize. Sounded to him like they were all in different keys.

Smoke moved over to a table near the hallway, where the grandfather clock was located, and took a glass of champagne just as the chimes donged out seven o'clock. He finished the glass, then walked up to Jud and Doreen, jerked both Jud's guns out of leather and placed the muzzle of one in the man's ear. Jud's bodyguards froze, not knowing what to do.

The band stopped playing; the milling crowds were still as the word spread throughout the ground floor of the mansion. Rusty had clobbered the Pecos Kid with a silver platter of fried chicken and grabbed his guns. The Kid lay on the floor, his head on a pile of chicken.

Smoke said, "Tell your men to start tossing their guns out the windows, Jud. If just one of them tries anything, I'll kill you where you stand."

"See that they do it, Jason." Jud managed the words out of his fricasseed brain and past his anger.

Six guns began sailing out the open windows.

"Get horses out front for Doreen and King Vale," Smoke ordered.

Jason nodded at one of the bodyguards.

"Make your speech, Doreen," Smoke told her.

Doreen spun around to face the crowd. "Jud Vale kidnapped me and brought me here against my will. I've been a prisoner in this house." She looked straight at Sheriff Brady. "Do you hear me, Sheriff?"

"I hear you, girl."

"I hate this man," Doreen said, pointing to Jud. "I would sooner marry a grizzly bear. I planned this whole party so's Smoke and the man I really love, Rusty, would come and rescue me."

Rusty was grinning and blushing. He looked like a lit railroad lantern.

"I'm ashamed of you people!" Doreen yelled at the crowd of men and women. "Not a one of you would help Walt and Alice or Smoke and Rusty stand up to this nitwit!" She glared at Jud, standing with his crown tilted to one side of his big head. "To hell with you all!" Doreen shouted.

"Let's go!" Smoke said, shoving Jud toward the door.

Outside, Doreen hiked up her expensive gown and showed Rusty bare legs as she stepped into the stirrup and mounted up. The cowboy did his best to look away, but the sight was just too tempting. One eye was going one way and the other was on a shapely leg.

"Settle down, Rusty," Doreen whispered. "Your time is coming. I promise."

"Have mercy!" Rusty said.

Smoke prodded Jud into the saddle. Jud hiked up his robe and showed some leg, too; but it was definitely not a scintillating experience for anyone. Especially the horse, who swung his head and tried to figure out what was on his back.

Smoke stepped into the saddle. "Jud dies if anyone follows," he warned the crowd. "Tell them, King Vale," Smoke said sarcastically.

Some lucidity had returned to Jud. Having the muzzle of a .44 laid against one's ear can do that. He twisted in the saddle. "Stay back. Our time will come. Just stay back."

"Let's go, King," Smoke said. "Your royal procession is about to parade."

The Pecos Kid woke up with a chicken leg stuck in one ear, wondering why the band had stopped playing.

22

"You'll die hard for this," Jud warned them all, as they clip-clopped along, Jud's crown bouncing from one side of his head to the other. "Especially you, Doreen. I'll turn you over to my men and let them have their way with you. And that's a promise."

Doreen turned in the saddle, balled her right hand into a fist, and busted Jud square on the nose. His crown flew off his head as the blood began to trickle, leaking down into his beard.

"You can pick your crown up on the way back," Smoke told him.

Jud cursed them all.

Smoke turned at the sounds of a single horse coming up fast behind them. It was the young reporter from the paper at Montpelier.

"I'm on my way to get this story written," he shouted at them. "I'll see that this is printed all over the state."

He galloped on past and then cut north, toward the town.

"He's dead, too," Jud growled.

"Give it up, Jud," Smoke advised the man. "Send your gun-hands packing, break up your outlaw gangs, and settle down."

Jud mouthed a few choice words at Smoke, none of them the least bit complimentary.

Smoke rode on for another mile and then twisted in the

saddle and knocked Jud sprawling, on his butt, in the road. Smoke grabbed the reins of the riderless horse and shouted, "Let's go, people!"

Jud sat in the dirt and squalled at them, shaking his fists and cussing.

"They'll be coming after us now!" Doreen yelled over the pounding of hooves.

"We'll make the crick," Rusty told her.

Jud jumped to his feet and began loping up the road, back to his ranch. He reached the spot where his crown lay in the dust, the jewels twinkling under the starry light. Jud plopped his crown back on his head and stomped on, his anger and hate growing with each dusty step. A mile farther on, he met a large force of his men, hanging back a couple of miles.

"They're heading for the creek!" Jud shouted, pointing. "Get them. Kill them! Kill them all."

Jason rode up, leading a horse. "I figured they'd set you afoot, Boss." He handed Jud a brace of six guns.

Jud swung into the saddle. "Somebody give me a piece of rawhide," he ordered.

A piece of thin rawhide was found and handed to him.

Jud made a chin strap for his crown, tying it tightly under his square jaw. He rode to the head of the group and paused, looking back. At least sixty riders. He lifted his hand into the air. "Forward!" he shouted. "Slay the infidels!"

"What the hell's an in-fidel?" Gimpy asked.

"Beats me," Jake Hube told him. "Must be something like a Injun, maybe."

The riders surged forward, with King Vale in the lead waving a six gun and shouting curses.

But many of the smarter gunfighters had either stayed back at the ranch or were bringing up the rear of the force. They were too wise in the ways of Smoke Jensen to think Smoke would not have a backup plan in Doreen's escape. Probably he had set up an ambush.

John Wills—who had been wrapped up in poison ivy by Smoke—and his buddies, Dave and Shorty and Lefty, trailed a good mile behind the main force. Jaeger and Chato Di Peso and Hammer, along with Blackjack and Highpockets and DePaul and about a dozen others, had not even left the ranch area. They sat on the long front porch of the mansion, eating fried chicken dunked in caviar and drinking champagne. All of them had a very strong hunch that many of those chasing after Smoke this starry night would not come back at all. The rest would come straggling back in, all shot to hell and gone.

But that would be all right with them. They were professionals in this business, and hardened to the ways of their chosen profession. This night would probably see the end of many of the punks and two-bit gunslingers who had hired on, looking for a cheap and fast buck and a few quick thrills to take back home and boast about. What they would get is a shallow grave. If they were lucky.

The crowds had quickly departed after Smoke had made his move. All but the bugler; he was now drunk as a cooter and blowing cavalry calls into the night. Some of the gunslingers had dumped him, bugle and all, into a horse trough. But that had only slowed him down for a few moments. He had shaken the water out of his bugle and kept right on tooting.

Jaeger spread some caviar on a cracker and nibbled. "Only ting de damn Russians ever did dat vas any gut was make caviar," he growled.

"What's this stuff made of anyways?" Pike asked.

"Vish eggs."

"What the hell's a vish?" Highpockets paused in the lifting of a caviar-spread cracker to his mouth.

"A vish is a vish. Swim in wassar."

About half of the men threw the caviar to the porch floor and stayed with the fried chicken.

"Here they come," Jackson announced.

Smoke, Rusty, and Doreen had just made the creek in time to dismount and take positions. Alice and Doreen had told Walt and the others they were staying and to shut up about it. They had taken rifles and squatted down behind logs with the other farmer women.

Matthew stood by a cottonwood, Cheyenne's long-barreled Colt in his right hand. The boy was calm as death, and his hand was steady.

Smoke eared back the hammer on his Winchester; he heard the sounds of others doing the same. As the charging riders came into range, Smoke lifted his rifle and took aim at Jud's crown. He squeezed off a round and drilled the arch of the crown, blowing off the arms and the dangling pearls.

"Huugghh!" Jud croaked, as the chin strap momentarily tightened, cutting off air due to the force of the impacting slug.

Those on the Box T side of the creek began filling the night air with hot lead. The first volley cleared half a dozen saddles and wounded that many more.

Spooked horses began bucking and jumping, sending another half-dozen riders to the hard ground. One gunslinger, afoot, his hands filled with Colts, tried to ford the creek. Young Matt took careful aim and squeezed the trigger, dead-centering the man, putting the slug right between his eyes. The gunny pitched face-forward into the creek.

Rusty shot the punk Glen Regan just as the kid was turning. The rifle slug went right through both cheeks of Glen's buttocks. Glen dropped, squalling and crying, to the creek bank, losing his guns, both hands holding on to his injured backside.

"Fall back, men!" Jud yelled. "Regroup but don't lose courage. They are but riffraff and swine who face us. You have the power of royalty on your side."

Jackson put another dent in Jud's crown, knocking it down to one side of the man's head, giving the man a thunderous headache. Jud's horse spooked and tossed him into a thorn bush and royalty's bare legs and backside took the full brunt of long thorns.

"Yowee!" Jud hollered, jumping to his feet. Holding his ermine robe waist high, he beat a hasty retreat up the bank and jumped over the crest.

"Let's get gone from here!" Cisco Webster shouted, just as Walt put a slug into the man's saddlehorn, tearing the horn from the saddle and knocking it spinning. Cisco's horse panicked and went snorting and racing into the night. Unfortunately for Cisco, the horse stampeded the wrong way, taking him right across the creek. "Whoa, goddammit!" Cisco yelled.

Rusty reversed his Winchester and knocked Cisco slap out of the saddle, the butt of the rifle catching the man on the jaw. Cisco was unconscious before he hit the ground, landing amid what was left of his broken teeth.

The fight was gone from Jud and his men. Jud screamed in pain as he was lifted into a saddle. He was still yelling and cussing and waving his arms as what was left of his army rode back toward the mansion.

The night fell quietly, broken only by the moaning of the wounded.

"What do we do with them?" Alice asked, listening to the pleadings for help.

"Leave them!" Chester's wife said, bitterness making her voice hard. "Would they help us if the situation was the other way around?"

Smoke booted his Winchester and swung into the saddle. He turned his horse's head toward the Box T ranch house and his back to the wounded bounty hunters.

That ended any further discussion as to the fate of those who chose to take fighting wages from Jud Vale.

Smoke stepped out of his room the next morning and stood in the pre-dawn quiet, drinking his first cup of coffee. He had an odd feeling, a premonition, that matters would be coming to a head very soon. Why that jumped into his mind, he didn't know—only that he felt it to be true.

Jackson walked out of the bunkhouse, a mug of coffee in his hand. He joined Smoke on the bench by the side of the barn and built him a cigarette, passing the makings to Smoke.

"I got a funny feelin'," Jackson said. "Come on me sudden-like; woke me up."

"That Jud Vale is going to bring this war to a head real soon?"

"Huh? You been readin' my mind. Yeah. Reckon why we both come up with that?"

"We've made a fool out of him too many times, Jackson. Last night was probably that much-talked-about straw that broke the camel's back. Now he knows that people are laughing at him. With his ego, he won't be able to tolerate that. He'll have to do something to reinstill the fear that people once had for him."

"By killing us." Jackson's words were offered in a flat tone.

"That's it. Or part of it, at least."

"He ain't gonna get it done."

"I believe that. I just don't want to see the women or the kids get hurt."

They drank coffee and smoked their cigarettes in silence for a time. "What are you gonna do when this mess is over?" Jackson asked.

"Head south. My wife and kids are down in Arizona. The youngest took a lung infection. Had to go there for health reasons. You?"

Jackson took a moment before replying. "Walt's asked me to stay on. Says he'll give me a working interest in the ranch if I do. And . . . well, me and Susie been eyeballin' each other. I might do it. I backed into gunfightin' like a lot of other men. Never set out to hunt me no reputation. It just come on me. One day I looked up—I'd been punchin' cows for a man over in Nevada Territory—and these two men 'bout my age come into the saloon where I was havin' a beer and braced me. Said they was gonna kill me. I asked them why. They said 'cause of who I was. Surprised the hell out of me that I was anyone special. They grabbed for iron and I was faster. The boss said he didn't want no gunslicks on his payroll and paid me off the next day. I drifted. Hooked up with some men headin' for Utah to draw fightin' wages. I reckon the rest is history."

Rusty had walked up, to stand quietly and listen. When Jackson fell silent, Rusty said, "You ought to stay, Jackson. Me and Doreen is gonna get hitched up soon as the trouble is over. The ranch is damn sure big enough for the both of us."

"I been thinkin' on it for sure."

"Light's on in the kitchen," Smoke said. "Breakfast pretty soon."

"Dolittle's up. He'll wake the boys," Rusty told him. "What's up for today?"

"Going over every inch of this ranch compound and making sure we can stand off a heavy attack. It's got to come. Jackson, I want you to take some of the boys and start clearing off all the brush from the hills and ridges around this place. Make damn sure we can't be burnt out. That'll also cut down on the risk of any riflemen slipping in on us."

"Good move," Jackson agreed.

"I'm hungry," Rusty said, one eye on the light coming from the kitchen window.

"I've never seen you when you weren't," Smoke said with a smile. "When you and Doreen get married, you best plant a big garden."

"You do know how to use a hoe, don't you?" Jackson kidded him.

"I 'spect, the way you and Susie is calf-eyin' each other, you'll be hoein' right along 'side me," Rusty fired back.

Jackson laughed. "Yeah, if it all works out. Be a welcome relief from gunfightin'."

"Don't ever pack those guns too far out of sight, Jackson," Smoke warned him. "It doesn't work. I know. I changed my name and tried it for a time. You'll always have to keep a sharp eye on your backtrail."

"I know." Jackson's words came after a sigh. "But I do wish that some of us could get that message through to young Matt."

"Could anybody tell you anything when you were his age?"

Jackson smiled ruefully. "Nope. I heard all the words, but they never sunk in."

"Matt will have to find his own way," Smoke said, standing up from the bench. "Just like we did. But I think old Cheyenne—in the time he had to spend with him—taught Matt a thing or two."

"Walt is talkin' about hirin' the boy on as a full-time puncher," Rusty said. "Matt says he's through with schoolin'."

"That's a good idea. I imagine Matt will stay for a year or two. Then he'll get ants in his pants and drift. All we can do is wish him well."

Rusty looked toward the ranch house and the lighted kitchen window. "Damn, I'm hungry!"

23

Jud Vale lay on his belly in bed, while a doctor from Montpelier probed and dug and pulled out thorns, some of them more than three inches long. Jud hollered and squalled and carried on all through the procedure.

But the pain seemed to have done one thing: it had cleared Jud's mind, at least for the moment. His ermine robe and crown had been tossed to the floor. He was still as nutty as a pecan pie but some lucidity had crept through the madness.

Through the open window of his bedroom, Jud could see men digging graves to bury the recently dead. He cursed Smoke Jensen, his brother, his bastard son, and everyone else he could think of.

Especially Doreen. He cussed Doreen for playing him for a fool until he was breathless. Long after the doctor had left, doing his best to hide a grin, Jud was still cussing.

Jason came to his room and waited until his boss and longtime partner in murder, rape, and robbery had calmed down some. "What do you want me to do with them royal duds and that bent crown?"

"Put them in the closet. I might decide to wear them again."

"Jesus, I hope not!"

"I lost it for a while, didn't I, Jas?"

"You were off your trolley for a fact. I thought I was

going to have to shoot you there for a time. You was becomin' unbearable."

"Was I that bad?"

"You turned into a plumb idiot."

"It's so hazy. I don't remember much of it."

"Be thankful for that." Jason pulled out a chair and sat down. "You think you're all right now?"

"Yes. For a time. But I don't know when I might go off again. Or for how long. It's frightening, Jas. It really scares me."

"You want me to bring one of them newfangled head doctors in to take a look at you? I could have it done on the sly."

Jud thought about that. It was tempting. Finally he shook his head. "No. Let's see if I can't lick this thing on my own. Did Luddy and his boys come in?"

"Early this mornin'. Phil and Perry and Rim is on the way. Be about thirty more men."

"How many did we lose last night?"

"Six dead. A dozen wounded. A couple of them ain't gonna make it." Jason was beginning to feel better; Jud was starting to talk like he had good sense.

"How many quit us?"

"That's surprisin'. Nobody. Yet."

"I figure it's gonna be a week before I can sit a saddle. Then we're going to wipe out the Box T. We're going to kill everyone there, bury the bodies deep, and burn all the buildings. Scatter the ashes with rakes; carry off the stones. Level the well and fill it up with rocks, cover that with dirt. Plant some trees and bushes. Not a sign is to remain that anyone ever lived there. I am Walt's only living relative. And I can prove that in a court of law. Everything will go to me. The land, cattle, money, and all that gold that's over there."

"Sounds good to me." He grinned at Jud. "Good to have you back, Boss."

"It's good to be back, Jas." He moved and grimaced, his southern exposure throbbing with pain. "Pass me that bottle of laudanum."

* * *

The hills and ridges around the ranch complex of the Box T were cleared of brush for a half mile in any direction. In heavily timbered areas, the timber was thinned and cut up for firewood. Wagons were put into use to haul dirt from far out in the Box T range, the dirt used to fill up any depressions in the earth for five hundred yards from the complex. It kept the boys busy and Smoke and the others close to the ranch.

But when the week was drawing to near a close, Smoke was told by Walt they had to make another supply run to the post for food.

"Let's do it," Smoke told him. "We have time to do it now and get back before dark. I'll tell Jackson to stay here at the ranch. We'll take Rusty. If we run into any of Jud's men, they might try to prod Jackson into a fight for changing sides."

"And you don't think they'll prod you, Smoke?"

"They'll die if they do," he replied simply.

"Any trouble?" Smoke asked Bendel.

The owner of the trading post shook his head. "I ain't seen hide nor hair of any Bar V hand all week and I have been expectin' them. I got the word that they was gonna come in and bust up my place." He smiled. "But I understand King Jud Vale is havin' to sleep on his stomach of late."

"Oh?"

"Yeah. Seems like his horse throwed him and he landed in a thorn bush. He was wearin' that silly-lookin' robe. Doc Evans from over Montpelier way spread the tale, to use his words."

Smoke and Rusty and Walt—the rancher was having a rare drink of whiskey while the shopkeeper filled the order—all had a good laugh, at Jud's expense.

Walt wiped his eyes with a bandana and smiled. "I guess any feeling I might have been carrying around for Jud has finally left me. God might punish me for the way I feel, but I can't feel anything except contempt for the man now."

"He doesn't deserve anything else, Mr. Burden," Bendel told him. "He's made life miserable for everyone around here for years."

Rusty had taken his beer to the batwings. "Riders pullin' up outside," he announced. "'Bout a half dozen of them. I don't know none of these old boys. Don't look like I'd really care to get to know them all that good, neither. Damn, but they is *ugly!*"

Smoke walked to the batwings. "The Almond Brothers. Killers. Call themselves bounty hunters. Barry, that's the oldest, he's got a few brains. The rest of them are close to being morons." Smoke finished his beer and set the mug on the plank. "I'm going outside. No point in having your place shot up."

Rusty stepped back into the store, exited that way, and pulled a rifle from his saddle boot, jacking in a round. At the sound of the cartridge being shucked into the chamber, Barry Almond looked over the saddle at him.

"You huntin' trouble, cowboy?" the bounty hunter asked.

"Naw," Rusty told him. "I just seen me five big rats. I like to shoot rats."

"Rats? Where'd you see five rats?"

"I'm lookin' at one of them," Rusty told him, just as Smoke pushed open the batwings and stepped out on the porch. Walt was right behind him, holding Bendel's double-barreled express gun.

Barry smiled, a slight cruel movement of his lips. His eyes did not leave Smoke. "I seen you work once, Jensen. You're fast, all right. I'll give you that much. So I reckon some of us, including me, will probably take some lead. But they's five of us ag'in you, that ugly redhead, and one stove-up old man."

"Ugly!" Rusty blurted. "Me! Why, you so ugly you ought to wear a sack over your head! And I ain't real sure them brothers of yours is even human. I've seen bears that was better lookin' than them."

"I'm a-gonna kill that freckle-faced puncher, Barry," an Almond brother said.

"You can sure have him, Race," Barry said. "But Jensen is all mine."

Smoke had stepped off the porch to stand in the street. He didn't want Dagger to catch a bullet. And there was something else: the stallion was alert to trouble, and he had sensed the situation building. If Cal Almond, who was standing next to the big horse, put a hand on him, Dagger was going to kick him into the next county.

Cal shoved roughly at Dagger. "Git the hale outta the way, horse!" he said, stepping around to Dagger's rear.

Dagger let him have it. Both rear hooves lashed out, one steel-shod hoof catching the killer in the groin, the other in the belly. Cal went sailing out into the middle of the street, screaming in agony.

"One down," Walt said.

Leo drew on the old man. But Leo never really knew the mettle of the men who came to the West when it was really raw. And he had failed to notice that Walt had eared back both hammers of the 12-gauge.

Walt shot the bounty hunter in the belly. Really, he shot him all over the place as rusty nails and ball bearings and other assorted bits of hand-loaded metal tore his body apart.

Rusty stepped out and leveled the Winchester just as Max turned, drawing. Max caught a slug in the belly that bent him double and spun him around. Max pulled the trigger and shot himself in the knee. He tumbled to the street, screaming rage and hate and pain.

Smoke palmed both Colts and began putting lead into Barry and Race. The .44 slugs dotted the trail-dusty dusters, pocking them with blood as the slugs tore into flesh.

Race went down first, sinking to his knees in the dirt, dropping his guns as life left him.

Smoke felt a bullet tear his cheek and another slug rip a narrow gouge on the outside of his left thigh. Smoke and Barry Almond faced each other, guns belching fire and death.

Smoke had known that Barry was going to be hard to put down, and the bounty hunter was living up to his reputation.

As the fourth slug from Smoke's .44's hit Barry, the man went down to one knee, cursing as he slumped to the dusty and rutted road. Using all his strength, he lifted his left-hand .44.

Smoke shot him between the eyes just as Cal managed to work his way past his terrible pain to lift his guns. Smoke turned and fired twice just as Rusty's Winchester barked and Walt's express gun roared. The last of the Almond Brothers died on his belly in the dirt, having been torn to bloody bits by the three guns.

The silence was shatteringly loud for a moment. Then Smoke broke the stillness as he ejected empty brass and began reloading. The spent brass tinkled as it struck small rocks in the road. Loaded up, Smoke holstered his Colts and turned to face Walt, still standing on the porch of the trading post.

"Thanks, Walt."

"Felt good," the old rancher said. "In more ways than one. I knew that night back at the crick, I'd misplaced my backbone for too long."

Max groaned and cursed as he lay in the dirt, his blood staining the earth under him.

Rusty walked over to the killer and kicked his guns out of the dying man's reach. "He ain't got long," the puncher said, glancing at Smoke.

Max looked up at him and cussed the redhead.

"If I was a-goin' where you're goin', partner," Rusty told him, "I believe I'd try to clean up my mouth some."

The last words to pass the bounty hunter's lips were curses.

"You boys put them down," Bendel said, coming out of his saloon with several shovels. "You can damn well help me plant them."

They looked up at the sounds of hooves clip-clopping up the road. Several gunhands from the Bar V were riding out, bedrolls tied behind the saddle and their saddlebags bulging full.

"We ain't huntin' no trouble," one told Smoke, eyeballing the carnage sprawled in the dirt. "We're pullin' out."

Smoke knew the man and knew he was no coward. Something had happened at the Bar V. "What's the problem, Jake?"

"The mainest thing is you, Smoke. This here poker game has done got too rich for my blood. I'll hire my guns out to whoever pays the price, and you know that. But I ain't no thief. I ain't never stole nothin' in my life." That curious moral streak that hit so many men who lived by the gun surfaced in Jake. "That damn Luddy Morgan and his bunch of no-goods come in. Rim Reynolds and Perry Simmons and that crazy Phil What's-His-Name is due in anytime. I ain't havin' no truck with that trash."

"If we're lucky, Jake, we'll never see each other again," Smoke told him.

"You're gonna have to ride clear over to Oregon if you want to see me, Smoke. And since I ain't on Vale's payroll no more, I can tell you this much without be-trayin' no confidence: Jud's gonna attack the Box T—I don't know when or I'd tell you. He's gonna burn the place to the ground, kill ever'body there, and then bury the bodies deep . . ."

Walt's lips tightened at that.

"He's gonna remove all sign that there was ever a building on the place," Jake continued, "and he ain't prancin' around wearin' that stupid robe and crown no more, neither. He's come to his senses . . . for a while, at least. But the fool is liable to go off agin any time. He's worser than any cow who ever et loco weed when he drops off the deep end."

A hired gun pulling out with Jake spat a stream of tobacco juice into the dirt and said, "Them ol' boys that's comin' in is all bad, Smoke. And the ones that's stayin' is just as bad. Jud's gonna take this here fight right down to the killin' end." He noted the thin trickle of blood oozing down Smoke's cheek. "You lucked out agin, Smoke. An inch over and somebody would be plantin' petunias on your grave."

Smoke nodded in agreement. His leg hurt but he knew it was not a serious wound. He'd had enough lead dug out of him to fill a good-sized gunnysack. "How many men does Jud have?"

"I'd say nearabouts a hundred," Jake told him. "Maybe more. He's promisin' them the moon and the stars and wimmin and apple pie and ever'thang else 'ceptin' his drawers iffen they'll stay with him and see this thing through. I reckon most of them will do that. Me and the boys here just couldn't see to do that. I never did like the idea of fightin' wimmin and kids." He looked at Rusty. "You got yourself a good woman with that Do-reen. She'll stand by a man when the goin' gets rough. Wish I could find one like that. See you boys." He lifted the reins and Jake and his buddies rode on.

"Well," Rusty said. "Let's plant these ol' boys and get back to the ranch. Looks like we're in for some excitement. Lord knows," he added drily, "we been so bored of late."

24

Walt had doubled the supplies and borrowed pack horses to bring the additional staples to the ranch. There, Smoke made a slow walking inspection of the area surrounding the complex. There could be nothing else done to make the place any more secure.

After supper, he called a meeting in the lantern-lit barn.

"Here's the way it's going to be, people. No one leaves this area. No one. Not for any reason. Jud is going to hit us, and he's going to hit us hard. When? Very soon, I'm thinking. He should be able to sit a saddle most anytime." He noticed the smiles at that and had to join them in the rough humor. But his smile faded quickly. "I thought that after the so-called party at the Bar V the other night, and what happened afterward, that Sheriff Brady would do something—anything! But that doesn't appear to be the case. I don't know whether Jud has bought him off, or what. Maybe the sheriff just doesn't want to get involved. Whatever the reason, it looks like we're in this thing all by ourselves. We can handle it. But it's going to get rough and dirty. Any of Jud's hired guns with an ounce of mercy in them have pulled out. What's left is the crud. That's what's going to be hitting us. Be ready for it. That's it."

Smoke looked at the young kids, kids that were growing up fast. Too fast, probably, for he saw no fear in their eyes. Did they really know the danger that faced them, or was this just kid excitement? Probably a combination of both, he thought.

"I'll stand the first watch," Walt said. "Then Smoke and Rusty and Jackson can divide up the rest. We're going to have to do this every night. Three-hour pulls for each of us until it's over."

"Anybody seen or heard anything from Clint?" Alice asked.

No one had.

"The last time I spoke with him," Smoke said, "he said he was having one of his spells—one of his moods is what he called it. He wouldn't come close to me."

"That's probably good for you," Doreen said. "He gets murderous when those things take hold of him. He thinks everybody is his enemy."

There was nothing else to say, so Walt broke up the meeting by telling everyone to go to bed. He got his rifle and took up a position by the corral, taking the first watch.

Smoke slept a few hours and then went out to relieve the rancher. It was one of those Idaho nights that inspire poets to write the loftiest and most eloquent of verses. The heavens were filled with stars that clung so close to earth, one could almost feel they were touchable.

"Quiet," Walt said, standing up and stretching. "Everything is at peace with the other, I reckon. Well, almost. Even the birds stopped calling a few minutes ago."

Smoke tensed. "No birds are calling?"

Walt was silent for only a few seconds, then he cursed himself for being an old fool! "Dammit! What's the matter with me? I'll alert the others." The old rancher took off in a bow-legged lope.

Smoke ran toward the bunkhouse, catching up with Walt and telling him to get to the house and get little Micky into the root cellar; he'd alert the others.

Smoke knew better than to bust into the bunkhouse with everyone on the alert. That would be a good way to catch a bullet. He paused at a window.

"They're here, boys!" he called softly. "Get to your positions and keep the lights out doing it."

He rousted Jackson and Rusty and they ran to preset positions around the compound. None of them saw the youngest of the kids leave the bunkhouse, race across the area, stop by the side of the barn for a moment, and then slip into the darkness of the huge barn.

Chuckie and Clark and Jimmy and Buster grinned at each other. They'd had the very devil of a time getting just the rocks for their slingshots; but they'd finally found some with just the right texture and their weapons were strongly made, their pockets bulging with smooth little stones.

They knelt down in the darkness and waited. They could hear Smoke up in the loft on one end of the barn, talking to Jackson who was up in the loft on the other end.

The boys waited in silence, slingshots in their hands.

Smoke searched the darkness of his perimeter but could see nothing out of the ordinary. If Jud and his men were out there—and that was still iffy—they were on foot and staying very quiet.

Chuckie thought he heard something behind him, at the far end of the barn. He looked at the others. Their eyes were wide; they had heard it, too. Then the very faint sound came again, but this time it was closer.

Someone was in the barn with them, and it wasn't anyone from the Box T. The boys knew all the positions of those friendly.

Chuckie slipped a rock into the pocket of his slingshot and ever so slightly shifted positions. Then he saw the clearly outlined figure of a man. And the shape of the hat told him it was no one from the Box T. Chuckie lifted his slingshot, pulled the rubber taut, and took aim. He let the rock fly and his aim was true. The rock struck the man in the center of his forehead and knocked him off his boots. The man made one grunt of pain as the rock hit him and then lay still on the barn floor.

Smoke was down the loft ladder in seconds. He looked at the slingshot-armed boys and sighed. It was too late to send them back to the house. But he couldn't help but feel proud of them. They were a gutsy bunch.

Smoke moved to the fallen man. He didn't know him.

"What's goin' on down there?" Jackson whispered from the hayloft.

"One of Jud's men." Smoke returned the whisper. "The boys dropped him with a slingshot."

Jackson chuckled softly.

"That means they've infiltrated us. Look sharp, Jackson."

Smoke cut several lengths of binder twine and securely tied the hired gun. He stuck the man's guns behind his belt and took his rifle. He looked at the boys looking at him. "I ought to spank you," he whispered. "But I feel too proud of you to do that. Now, dammit, boys, stay down and out of sight! This is not a game."

"Yes, sir," Buster said, as Smoke headed for the ladder.

Smoke had just cleared the landing when Rusty's rifle barked from his position in the bunkhouse. A man cried out in pain as the bullet struck true. Smoke ran to the hay door as gunfire began pouring in from all sides of the ranch complex.

Below him, the boys readied their slingshots as they crouched down behind bales of hay.

Jackson sighted a running figure, fired, missed, and fired again. The second slug dusted the man and sent him sprawling to the ground, side-shot and out of it.

Then the compound was filled with running men as they left their positions on the near-barren hills and ridges around the ranch and charged. Smoke could hear, over the gunfire, the sounds of horses coming hard.

The first wave of running men were cut down by the savage fire from the house, the barn, and the bunkhouse. Their bodies lay sprawled under the starry sky. One man, only slightly wounded, tried to make the barn. He was knocked to his knees by slingshot-propelled rocks and then knocked unconscious as a rock fired by Buster hit him on the side of the head and dropped him to the ground.

The boys grinned at each other.

Doreen sighted in a man and pulled the trigger, the Winchester slamming her shoulder. The slug caught the hired gun in the chest and ended his career.

Susie turned one around with a rifle shot and Alice finished him with a pistol. The rancher's wife was calm and steady, this being nothing new to her. She'd fought Indians for years before this.

One of Jud's men reached the outside bunkhouse wall. Jamie shot him between the eyes as he carelessly poked his head up just a tad too far.

Then the hard-running horses came into view, the riders carrying burning torches. The first half-dozen to reach the compound were blown out of their saddles by rifle fire. The boys in the lower level of the barn then went to work, sending rocks which impacted with horses' butts.

One man was knocked out of the saddle as a rock struck him on the jaw. He fell on his torch and quickly became a living firebrand. He rose screaming to his feet, his clothing ignited, and tried to run. Walt ended his agony with a bullet to the head.

The horses went into a panic as the rocks pelted them, stinging and confusing and angering them. The horses began bucking and jumping, trying to escape the hurting stones. Riders were tossed to the ground and shot down by rifle and pistol fire.

One managed to reach the house and jumped in through a window. Doreen picked up a pot of coffee from the stove and tossed the contents on the man, the scalding coffee catching him flush in the face. He dropped his guns and began screaming in agony, running around the room, crashing into furniture in his frantic rush to get away from the awful pain.

Alice shot him in the head and permanently ended the wailing.

A bounty hunter ran into the barn as rocks from slingshots pelted him, stinging but not stopping his charge for cover.

Little Chuckie grabbed up a pitchfork, tines out, and braced himself against the impact. The gunhand ran right into the pitchfork, knocking Chuckie down as the tines tore into his belly. Screaming in pain, the gunny ran toward the other end of the barn. The handle of the pitchfork, sticking several feet out of his belly, hit a wall and stuck there. The gunny screamed his life away, unable to pull the handle from the crack in the stable wall or free himself of the tines.

Chuckie got sick.

A torch hit the roof of the bunkhouse and lodged there, soon catching the roof on fire.

Smoke lit the fuse on a stick of dynamite and tossed the bomb into the milling and panicked scene below him. The explosion knocked several horses to the ground, busting a couple of riders' legs and creating even more confusion in the fire-lanced night.

Smoke began tossing stick after stick of dynamite from the loft to the ground, as his eyes spotted Rusty and the boys running from the bunkhouse to a storage shed. A Bar V rider turned his horse as he spotted the boys, lifting his pistol. Smoke shot him out of the saddle. His boot hung in the stirrup and the frightened horse took off at a gallop, dragging the screaming, flopping, and helpless man.

All the steam seemed to leave the Bar V men at once. Those still mounted wheeled and raced from the fire-lit ranch. Those on foot ran away into the darkness.

"Cease firing!" Smoke yelled. "Hold your positions!"

The crackling flames from the bunkhouse became the only sounds in the bloody night.

"I'm gonna let it burn itself out!" Walt yelled from the house.

"You all right, Jackson?" Smoke called.

"I'm okay. How about the boys down below?"

"We're all right," one called. "Chuckie got sick, is all."

Smoke climbed down the ladder. He stopped as his eyes saw the pitchfork-impaled gunhand, the man's hands still gripping the handle in death.

"I had to do it, Mr. Smoke," Chuckie said. "I didn't have no choice."

"You did fine, Chuckie," Smoke assured him. "You boys stay down behind those bales of hay."

Smoke found a sack and then eased his way out of the barn. Staying close to whatever cover he could find, he began working his way to the storage shed. On the way, he passed men who were moaning and twisting in pain. He took their guns from them and dropped them into the sack. Rusty saw what he was doing and stepped out to begin calming and corralling the milling Bar V horses. Jackson stayed where he was, keeping a sharp eye out for any return raiders.

But Jud's hired guns had apparently had enough for one night. No more hostile fire came.

Susie and Doreen rolled the dead man out of the living room and off the porch. A couple of the boys dragged the man out of the front yard.

"Rusty, at first light, I want you to ride for Montpelier and get that reporter and then find Sheriff Brady. Bring them both here. If Sheriff Brady won't come, send a wire to the governor's office and one to the Army up at Fort Hall. But I think Brady will come."

"Right. What do we do with the bodies?"

"Lay them over by the side of the barn and cover them with whatever you can find. Use their own bedrolls and ground sheets if they were carrying any. We'll put the wounded in the barn."

Walt walked up. "I count twenty dead and twelve wounded. Some of them ain't gonna make it."

"I guess you better bring Doctor . . . what's his name, Walt?"

"Evans. He's a good man. He'll come." Walt looked up at the sky. "I hope they come quick. It's gonna be a warm day and these bodies'll start to bloat in a hurry. Flies will be awful."

25

Sheriff Brady took one look at the lined-up bodies and paled under his tan. Doctor Evans and his assistant began working on the wounded.

"I'm filing charges against all these men," Walt told the sheriff. "And I'm filing charges against Jud Vale. They worked for him, they acted under his orders."

"Can you prove that in a court of law?" Brady challenged. "And I ain't tryin' to be a horse's butt about it, Walt. Just askin' what the judge will ask."

"I understand. We can prove it if some of these men will talk."

"Fat chance of that," Brady said. "But we'll give it a try. Walt, I'm going to call in the U.S. Marshals. It'll take them about two days to get in here by train. I just don't have the men to handle this by myself."

"Then why not deputize all the farmers and such around here?" the rancher suggested. "Form a posse. We'll go in and arrest Jud and his men."

"First I got to find a judge to sign them papers authorizing such a move. I think it's best if we let the marshals handle it. And I ain't tryin' to back out of my duty, neither."

"I understand. All right, Sheriff. We'll play it your way."

Brady looked around him at the carnage, the burned-out bunkhouse. "This has got to end. I just ain't gonna tolerate it no more. I'll be back with the marshals, Walt. And that's a promise." He looked at the doctor. "You need some help with these wounded, Doc?"

"A few of them can sit a saddle. Walt's lending us a wagon to transport the rest. Help me load them up and we'll be on our way."

The wounded bounty hunters and hired guns were loaded into a wagon, and not too gently either. With Sheriff Brady leading the way, the wagon rolled out; those sitting saddles were doing so with their hands tied to the saddle horn. Smoke didn't hold out hope of any of the hired guns talking.

And as for the U.S. Marshals coming in . . . Smoke didn't think they'd be coming in anytime soon, although he believed that Sheriff Brady would certainly try to get them in. The U.S. Marshals' force was a small one, with a lot to do. They would probably look at the sheriff's request as just another flare-up between ranchers over water or graze, and promptly forget it.

The reporter had indeed written his story about the kidnapping of Doreen and her rescue, but nothing had come of that report. This was still the raw West, with lawmen few and far between. Communities were still expected to handle their own problems without crying for outside help.

Smoke said as much to Walt and the others.

Jackson was the first to agree. "I've seen this happen time and again. In the end, it's all gonna boil down to men facin' men with guns. That's the way it's always been, and that's the way it's gonna be . . . for a while yet."

"I'll cling to a small hope that the marshals will come in," Walt said.

"Cling to a gun with your other hand," Smoke told him.

Chuckie and other smaller boys went down to the creek, looking for more small stones for their slingshots. None of them had ever seen a U.S. Marshal and didn't expect to see one anytime soon.

* * *

Jud Vale took his afternoon coffee on the front porch of his mansion. He was feeling much better—physically and mentally. But he had enough sense to know that his mind could flip him back into madness at any moment, without warning.

He sucked at his coffee cup, with some of the hot brew trickling out of his mouth and dribbling onto his shirt front. Jud didn't pay it any attention. He hadn't gone on the past night's raid against his brother; Blackjack and Molino had assured him they could handle it. They handled it, all right. Came straggling back in with half their men either dead or wounded and captured, talking about kids with slingshots—*slingshots,* for Christ's sake—and dynamite and all kinds of other excuses for having failed.

Jud shook his big head. Slingshots!

He mentally laid aside his burning hate for his brother and forced himself to think rationally.

A frontal attack, a mass attack of the Box T, had failed for the second time, so Jud had to discard any further thoughts along that line. He knew that at one time, and not that long ago, a couple of weeks back, maybe a month, he'd had several plans in mind. Now he couldn't think of a single one, and that scared him. Was he losing his marbles again?

He thought hard; sweat broke out on his forehead. Then it came to him. Burn the damn nesters out. Yeah, that had been one of them. There had been other plans, but the burning out of the nesters was the only one he could think of at the moment. Pretty good plan. Instead of striking at the head of the beast, the head being his brother and Smoke Jensen, start chopping away at the arms and legs.

He called for Jason and told him of the plan. Jason thought that it might work.

"No one will be expecting any trouble this soon after the raid on the ranch. Send some boys out this afternoon. Start with that damn interferin' Chester and his old woman. He was one of them at the creek, wasn't he?"

"Sure was."

"Kill them and burn them out."

"We won't even have to send any of the top guns to do this," Jason pointed out. "I'll send them three punks that come in on the train with some of Perry's bunch."

"Sounds good. Do it."

The six hired guns were in good spirits as they rode out of the Bar V range, heading for Chester's farm. This was going to be good fun. And maybe the nester had a good-lookin' daughter . . . that would be even more fun. They'd hogtie the farmer and his old woman and make them watch while they had their way with the girl.

The punk kid who called himself Tucson Bob vocalized his plan.

The outlaw known as Cline grinned, exposing a mouthful of rotted teeth. "I like that idea, Tucson. You all right." Then he sobered. "But what if they ain't no young girl?"

"Then we'll hang the nester slow; make it last and watch him kick and choke."

"I'd druther have me a young girl who don't want to give it up, but the second idea is a right good one. How far did Jud say this pig farm was?"

"It's just up ahead. Do we ride through the garden first and tear it up?"

"Might as well. They'll get 'em so scared they won't know what to do."

The six hired guns hit the small farm at a gallop, whooping and hollering and firing into the house, riding right through the neat garden.

Chester's wife stuck a shotgun out of a window and blew the would-be gunfighter called Randy out of the saddle just as Chester came out of the barn with a Winchester and emptied another saddle, ending the life and career of the outlaw called Fox. The farmer's wife let loose with the other side of the double-barrel and the punk who should have stayed home and learned his father's dairy business back in Wisconsin hit the ground, landing hard amid the green beans and cabbage, half of his left arm torn off from the buckshot.

Cline leveled his pistol at Chester just as the farmer pulled the trigger. Cline felt a hard blow to his chest and slipped from the saddle, his world dimming just as neighbors galloped up, all armed.

"Don't shoot!" Tucson Bob yelled, his eyes wild with fear.

A neighbor knocked him out of the saddle with the butt of his shotgun just as a gunhand tried to jump the fence and get away.

A half-dozen guns barked and the outlaw hit the ground, right into the pigpen. The hogs moved toward him.

Chester walked up, his eyes hard and his face grim. He stood over the scared punk. "Somebody shoo them hogs away from the body 'fore they eat him. And then get a rope," Chester added.

Tucson Bob started screaming.

"Where'd you hang him?" Walt asked.

Chester and a few of his neighbors had ridden over to the Box T with the news of the attack, after they had returned from the creek.

"Down at the line separating your range from Jud's. Right at the crick so's he can be found. We dumped all the bodies there, too."

"Kinda bothered me hangin' that kid," a farmer said. "He sure blubbered and hollered and begged, callin' for his ma. But then I had to think about what he told us they was gonna do if Chester's girl had been found. Then it didn't bother me so bad."

"How about the kid with his arm shot off?" Jackson asked.

"He didn't make it to the crick 'fore he died."

"After he died," Chester said, "the other kid started talkin' his head off, tellin' us 'bout what they had in mind to do with any girl they found at farmers' homes they was plannin' to raid. He said that's what Jud's men was goin' to do from now on out. I guess he thought by tellin' us ever'thing he knew we would spare him from the rope. He thought wrong."

Walt told the men about Sheriff Brady's try to get U.S. Marshals in.

Chester shook his head negatively. "You been out of touch too long, Walt. And I ain't sayin' that it's all your fault. Brady is a good man, and he'll make his request for help. But it ain't gonna come in. Somebody higher up will block it. We done tried to do what you're tryin' early last year. We sent Jim Martin to see the governor. He didn't get in to see him and was ambushed on his way back home."

"I remember," Walt said, shaking his head. "Another good idea shot all to hell."

Smoke cut his eyes to Jackson, remembering the gunfighter's words: "In the end, it's all gonna boil down to men facin' men with guns. That's the way it's always been, and that's the way it's gonna be . . . for a while yet."

Smoke couldn't agree more.

Several days drifted by, and it was as Chester had predicted: nothing was heard from Sheriff Brady. One week after the night raid by the gunmen, Brady rode slowly up to the Box T. He looked like a man with the weight of the world on his shoulders.

Walt waved him onto the porch, where the rancher was sitting with Smoke, Jackson, and Rusty. Brady took a chair and the cup of coffee that Susie brought out to him.

"You look like a man whose best horse just died," the rancher remarked. "What's the matter, Sheriff?"

"It's worse than that, I'm here to tell you. There ain't gonna be any help comin' in from the government, Walt. And that's just the beginning of it." He sighed and took a sip of coffee. "I been ridin' all over this county. I can't find a judge who'll sign papers against Jud. One of them outright laughed at me. And I had to turn all them gunhands loose. Judge's orders. He says that since you didn't personal come in and swear to the truth of the raid, I can't hold them."

"Judge Monroe?" Walt asked.

"You got it."

"I always knew he was takin' money from my brother."

"I don't think it would have made a whit of difference if you had come in and signed them papers," the sheriff said. "I've had to open my eyes these past few days and look at things I guess I been avoiding over the years." He sighed. "The mainest thing being that Jud Vale's got a lot of people with their hands in his pockets . . . and some of them hands has been there for a long time. I'm finding out, really finding out, what it means to butt your head up against a stone wall."

"I hate to be the one to ask you this, Sheriff," Walt said, "but how about your deputies?"

"Can they be trusted? Yes. They been with me for a long time and they'll stand. I've bet my life on that too many times not to be totally sure of them." He looked at Smoke and Rusty and Jackson. "You boys want a badge?"

Smoke shook his head. "Not me. Too many restrictions go with a badge."

Rusty and Jackson also declined the offer of being deputized.

Brady said, "I'm about to do something that I ain't never done in all my years of totin' a star around." He was thoughtful for a moment, then drained his coffee and stood up, hitching at his gun belt. "You boys handle this any way you see fit. I won't interfere in no way. If Jud starts squallin' for the law to come in, I'll tell him I'll get to it as soon as possible. Then I'll toss his complaint into the trash can. If the judges get on me about my foot-draggin', I'll tell them the people elected me, not them, and if the people don't like the way I'm doin' things, then come election time, they can vote me out of office as easy as they voted me in."

Brady stepped off the porch and walked to his horse. After swinging into the saddle, he looked at the men on the porch.

"Good luck, boys. If you need help, holler, and I'll come a-foggin'."

Brady turned his horse and rode out of the ranch without looking back.

Smoke took out the Colts, one at a time, and filled up the empty chambers under the hammer. Rusty and Jackson did the same. Walt rose from his chair and walked into the house. When he returned, he had his gun belt in one hand and a box of .44's in the other. He sat down and began filling up the loops in the belt.

"I fought for this land," the old rancher spoke. "Fought hard for it. But until you boys come along, I reckon I'd misplaced my backbone. I'd turned into a scared old man. That scared old man ain't no more. Maybe it takes me a little longer to get goin' in the mornings, but there ain't nothin' wrong with my eyes nor my trigger finger. And I made up my mind about something else: my brother can go right straight to Hell! And if it has to be me who sends him there, so be it."

26

Days after the disastrous attack against the nesters, Jud was still having trouble accepting the fact that most people, from the territorial line west to the Little Malad River, were no longer going to bow and scrape for him. Jud had not only lost his power base, but now he felt his mind going again. He struggled to maintain control. He managed to hold on, but it was becoming increasingly difficult to make rational thoughts work their way through the fog that clouded his brain.

Jason was talking to him, but Jud was having a hard time understanding the words.

"Jud!" Jason shouted at him.

Jud turned his head. Blinked his eyes. "Yes, Jas. I hear you."

"Can you understand me, Jud?"

"Yes. Now, I can. What were you saying?"

"It's time to pull in our horns. We got enough money to last us ten lifetimes. It's time to quit. Break up the gangs and send them packing. Stick with ranchin'. The people has turned ag'in us. It can't do nothin' 'cept get worser."

Jud didn't believe the words he was hearing. This wasn't like Jas. Jas had been his strong friend and supporter for years—long, bloody, murderous, and savage years. Together they had raped and murdered and stolen and savaged from

Illinois to Idaho. Now the man was telling him it all had to come to an end. Jud shook his head. "No way, Jas. It's too late for that." Lucidity was returning to Jud's darkened brain. "Far too late. We are what we are. We can't change. The people won't let us. We've got to stay strong, and we've got to show the people that we're still the kingpins of this area."

"For God's sake, Jud—how? You haven't ridden around the area like I have. Every move I make, they's anywhere from five to fifteen guns on me. The people have had it, Jud. We've come to the end of our string."

Jud looked at the man. "You want to ride, Jas?"

"You mean leave?"

Jud nodded.

"No. You know me better than that. We been together since we was young bucks, full of piss and vinegar. If you say we're gonna stand and fight this out, then I'll be right beside you."

"How many men are still on the payroll, drawing fighting wages?"

"Seventy."

Jud's eyes were hard and savage. "Then tell them to start earning it."

The riders struck at night, wearing masks and dusters. They struck a small farmhouse near the Wyoming line and burned it to the ground, killing the farmer and abusing his wife and oldest daughter before tying them naked to a tree and leaving them. Then they vanished into the night, scattering, leaving no trail that Sheriff Brady and his men could follow. The raiders did the same thing the next night, miles away from the first scene of horror and degradation.

The third night the raiders struck, Sheriff Brady and his men were at the extreme south end of the county while the raiders were working the northern tip of the county. It was the same operation: a farm was burned, the man was killed, the women abused.

But what Jud didn't know was that after the first raid,

Smoke had been absent from the Box T, roaming mostly at night, looking for tracks, and holed up during the day. Just before dawn on the morning of the fourth day, he watched the raiders return to the Bar V, still wearing their dusters. He waited until he was certain that all who were coming in were in, then began slowly and carefully backtracking the trail.

By eight o'clock, he had found where all the raiders came together after scattering. It was on the Bear River Range, but he wasn't certain it was on Bar V holdings. He felt this might be a public range.

He began following the main body of the raiders, finally discovering where they had built a hidden corral to keep their spare horses. Smoke backed off a good half-mile, rubbed down Dagger, and cooked himself a meal. He stretched out on the ground to sleep for a few hours. This night, the raiders would be in for a surprise when they came for their horses. A very deadly surprise.

When he opened his eyes, he guessed the time to be about four o'clock. Smoke built a small fire and made coffee, frying some bacon to go with the last of his bread. After eating, he leaned back against his saddle and rolled a cigarette, enjoying his coffee and the peace and quiet. Come the night, it would not be a bit peaceful, and it sure as hell wouldn't be quiet.

Before dusk settled over the land, Smoke put out his small fire and saddled up, moving closer to the hidden corral. He dismounted and carefully picketed Dagger, hopefully out of the line of fire. Taking his rifle, he moved to well within throwing distance of the corral and found himself a good position. He chambered a round and eased the hammer down; then Smoke settled in to wait for the first of the raiders to arrive.

He didn't think they would come all in a bunch, but instead come drifting in by twos and threes. The first bunch of outlaws would wait until the last had arrived, then take off to do their dirty work.

But Smoke had some dirty work of his own in mind, and

he was confident that the number of raiders who rode out would be considerably less than the number who rode in this night.

The first bunch rode in almost carelessly, certain that no unfriendly eyes were upon them.

Smoke waited and watched through the gathering gloom as the assorted scum on Jud's payroll checked the corral to see if their spare mounts were still there. One man busied himself building a fire and making coffee.

Then the damning evidence showed itself as the men began unrolling white dusters from behind their saddles and shaking out the black bandanas they would use to cover the lower half of their faces.

More men began drifting in until the number had reached twenty. They drank coffee and began slipping into their dusters. The talk was rough as the conversation drifted to where Smoke lay hidden. The Bar V hired guns laughed as they casually talked of murder, rape, and torture. Another man tossed more wood on the fire.

Smoke had carefully gauged the distance between his location and the main body of men. With a grim smile on his lips, he lit the fuses and tossed two sticks of giant powder into the group.

It took a couple of seconds for the men to react, and a couple of seconds was all that was needed for the short fuses to burn down. When the dynamite blew, the din was enormous in the night.

Outlaws were hurled off their boots, some landing hard and breaking bones, others with the wind knocked from them. Horses reared up, screaming their panic, breaking loose and galloping off into the darkness. Those hired guns who were still on their feet were stumbling around, cursing and disoriented and momentarily deafened from the huge explosion.

Smoke knocked half a dozen men sprawling with fast but well-placed rifle shots, then shifted locations, reloading as he made his way toward the corral. The outlaws began pouring lead into the area Smoke had just vacated.

Smoke jerked the rawhide string holding the gate to the post and fired into the air, stampeding the remuda. The frightened horses ran right into and through the milling gunhands, knocking a few screaming to the earth before the steel-shod hooves mangled flesh and broke bones.

Smoke took that time of painful confusion to run back to where he had picketed Dagger and swing into the saddle. Smoke got himself gone from that area, feeling very confident that the raiders would not strike against women and children this night.

He did not head for the Box T, instead pointing Dagger's nose toward the Bar V. He had not gone a mile before a horseman rode onto the trail and waved at him.

Clint Perkins. Smoke reined up and looked at the man.

"Heading for the Bar V to do some mischief, Smoke?"

"That was my plan."

"I'll ride along with you."

"Your funeral."

Clint laughed in the night. "Oh, not just yet, Smoke. Oh, my, no! I have that auspicious but final event all worked out in my mind. And the time is close, but not this night."

"Whatever you say."

"Your plan for the Bar V?"

"Lay up on the ridges and put about a hundred rounds into the house and bunkhouse. Just let Jud know that I haven't forgotten him."

Clint laughed. "Let's ride!"

They rode hard for a couple of miles, then slowed to a walk, sparing their horses but still covering the distance swiftly. They did not talk until they were about two miles from the mansion.

"I'll take this side, Clint," Smoke told him. "The other side is all yours."

"That's fair. How long do we keep it up?"

"Oh, ten or fifteen minutes. We'll wait about half an hour before we start. That'll give our horses time to catch their breath and for some of those behind us to make the ranch and spread the news. There'll be lots of lanterns and lamps lit when they return. That'll give us better targets."

Clint smiled. "See you around, Smoke Jensen." Then he was gone into the night.

Smoke angled off into the timber and carefully made his way to a ridge overlooking the great mansion. He picketed Dagger and settled in behind a tree, just at the crest of the hill.

The minutes ticked by, turning into half an hour. What was left of Jud's raiders began trickling back to the ranch complex, about half of them belly-down over a saddle, tied in place. Smoke brought his Winchester to his shoulder, compensated for the downhill shooting, and sighted in a man, squeezing the trigger.

The slug went high and knocked the man's hat from his head, sending the hired gun to the ground. Smoke's second shot was true. The gunhand tried to rise up on one elbow, then fell face-forward, neck-shot.

From across the way, Clint opened up, the outlaws clearly visible under the light of the moon and the starry night. Smoke joined in, concentrating his fire into the mansion.

Jud, Jason, and the bodyguards hit the floor as .44 slugs began tearing through the walls and windows of the mansion.

A slug shattered the knee of a bodyguard, bringing a howl of pain. Clint was pouring rifle fire into the running men in the yard. He quickly punched more cartridges into his rifle and began peppering the bunkhouse. Smoke shifted the muzzle of his rifle and put two fast rounds into one of the newly built outhouses. A man came rushing out, trying to run while holding his britches up with one hand. One knee caught in his dangling suspenders and sent him sprawling to the ground.

Smoke tried for a lamp in the mansion, his third shot finally striking true, sending coal oil and flames worming across the floor like a flaming snake. Jud and Jason and the bodyguards began stomping at the flames before they caught and burned the place down.

There was little the men around the mansion could do

except curse the birth of Smoke Jensen; they knew it was Smoke on one of the ridges. And probably Clint on the other ridge.

Smoke decided he'd pressed his luck to the maximum for this night, and began working his way back to Dagger. It would take Clint only a couple of minutes to understand that Smoke was gone.

Inside the mansion, hopping mad, jumping around like a huge frog, his eyes bugged out, cursing at the top of his lungs, and just barely hanging on to what little sanity was left him, Jud began screaming orders to get Smoke Jensen, declare war on everybody, burn down Montpelier, assassinate President Arthur; do whatever needs to be done . . . just kill that damned Smoke Jensen!

Clint fired one more round before he pulled out, putting his shot into the living room and plugging a suit of armor Jud had imported from England.

"Another day, Father," Clint muttered, slipping back to where he'd tied his horse. "Soon."

Smoke slept soundly the remainder of that night, in his room in the barn at the Box T. He had stopped at several small farms, telling the people what had gone down and also that he doubted Jud's raiders would be out doing their dirty work that night. But he told them to keep a guard posted just in case.

He slept late; it was nearly six o'clock when he awakened and put on his hat, then his pants and boots and shirt, slinging his gun belt around his waist, and stepping outside.

"What went down last night?" Jackson asked, handing him a cup of coffee.

Smoke took a sip of coffee before replying. Jackson was smiling when Smoke finished.

"Wish you had invited me along," he said wistfully.

"I didn't know what I was going to do until the last minute. But it will be interesting to see what Jud does next."

"Interesting is one way of puttin' it, for sure."

27

"Jud's sellin' his herds," the farmer said, dismounting in front of the ranch house. Walt led him to the porch and offered the man coffee, as Smoke and Jackson and Rusty joined them.

It was just past dawn and three days after Smoke and Clint had assaulted the mansion.

"He's pulling out?" Walt asked, a hopeful note to the question.

"No," Smoke said. "I'd say he's gearing up for a long and expensive war. Putting his hands on as much hard cash as possible." He glanced at the farmer. "When did you find out about this?"

"Late yesterday evenin'. My neighbor, Jim Morris, had been up to Montpelier. Stopped in for a drink and heard cattle buyers talkin' about it. Them buyers done sent men in to move the cattle."

"Knowing we wouldn't harm any innocent party," Smoke mused aloud. "Good move on Jud's part. Then they've begun moving the cattle out?"

"Oh, yeah. Job's might be near half done, I reckon." He cut his eyes to Smoke. "Them bounty hunters—Wills is one of them?"

Smoke nodded. "I know them."

"I heard some talk, Mr. Jensen; heard it this mornin'. Word

is they're pullin' out on Jud's orders. Goin' down to Arizony, lookin' for your wife and family."

"It would be something Jud would do," Walt said. "That would be one way to get you away from here."

Smoke stepped from the porch, his face tight and his eyes hard. He walked to the barn and saddled Dagger. The road by the trading post would be the one they would be most likely to take. Smoke would be waiting for them. It was time to bring this boil to a head. Crazy or not, when Jud Vale started threatening Smoke's wife and family, Jud Vale was a dead man.

Doreen had a poke of food waiting for him when he rode up to the ranch house. Smoke stowed it in his saddlebags. There was a gunnysack filled with dynamite tied onto the saddle horn. One side of his saddlebags was stuffed with ammunition and spare pistols. Smoke looked at Rusty and Jackson.

"Jud may be doing this trying to pull us all away from the Box T. Well, it isn't going to work that way. You boys stay here. This is my show. I'll be back."

The farmer grabbed hold of the reins. "No, sir," he said firmly. "That ain't the way it is and it ain't the way it's gonna be. This is *our* show. They's men comin' here right now. Farmers and hired hands and shopkeepers and such from all over; as far away as Montpelier. Sheriff Brady and his men is comin' in, too."

"Riders comin' for a fact," Rusty said. "Horses and wagons. Looks like a regular parade."

Smoke cut his eyes. It did look like a parade. He picked out Chester and his wife, and a dozen other farmers and families. He smiled as he saw Doc Evans's buggy. Right behind it was the editor of the Montpelier paper, Mr. Argood. Coming up to intersect the line of horses and wagons and buggies was Sheriff Brady and his men. Chester whoaed his team and stepped down, helping his wife to the ground.

The farmer had a gun belt around his waist and his wife carried a rifle. He walked to Smoke and looked up at him.

"We ain't no good as gunfighters, Mr. Smoke. But we can damn sure defend this ranch while you boys is gone."

"I can't interfere or condone this, Smoke," Sheriff Brady said. "But I can stay right here and then sort out the pieces when it's over."

"And I'll be here to patch up the wounded," Doc Evans told him.

"I'll get my guns." Walt turned toward the house.

"Walt!" Alice said.

"Hush, woman," the old rancher told her. "A man's got to do what he's got to do. You just keep the coffee hot. I'll be back."

Rusty and Jackson were walking toward the barn to saddle up.

Matt walked his horse toward Smoke. There was a grim look on Smoke's face as he noticed the way the boy was wearing his guns. He carried his Peacemaker on his right side, and Cheyenne's old Colt on his left side, butt-forward for a cross draw.

It was like looking into a mirror that reflected years back. Like looking at himself as a boy.

"I'll be comin' with you," Matt told him.

"I can't stop you."

"That is correct, sir," Matt said politely.

They waited and watched for a few moments, as the farmers took up positions around the ranch and the women gathered on the porch. Rusty and Jackson rode up, leading Walt's horse. The rancher stepped out of his house, kissed Alice on the cheek, and swung into the saddle, booting his Winchester. The four men and the boy headed out, Smoke in the lead.

It was to be the start of the bloodiest day in that part of Idaho Territory.

They reached the trading post, coming in from the back of the long building, dismounting and tying their horses at the rear of the store. Jackson had pointed out the bounty hunters' horses in front of the saloon.

"Jackson and me will handle this," Smoke said. "The rest of you stay here."

The shopkeeper's wife rushed out the back door. "They got my husband and Bendel all trussed up like hogs," she whispered hoarsely. "They're waitin' on you, Mr. Jensen. And there's eight or ten more gunhands just over that ridge," she said, pointing.

"Thank you. Hunt some cover, ma'am." He looked at Jackson. "First things first," he said, then pushed open the back door and stepped into the gloom of the storage room.

Smoke had made up his mind that this battle and as many others as he could arrange would not be a case of stand up, face, and draw. The odds were just too high.

He had both hands full of Colts, hammers back, when he kicked in the door to the saloon and went in shooting, Jackson right behind him, doing the same.

Lefty went down with the front of his shirt stained with blood and smoking holes. Smoke dropped to one knee, partly to give Jackson better shooting room and partly to show a smaller target, and put two slugs into the head of Shorty Watson. Jackson had knocked John Wills and Dave Bennett spinning. Bennett went down to the floor, blood leaking from his mouth; he was dying and cursing as Wills staggered out the batwings and fell off the porch, landing on his back.

Smoke stepped outside just as Wills was lifting his guns. Smoke shot him between the eyes just as the sounds of galloping horses reached him.

Walt, Rusty, and Matt stepped around the corner of the building, rifles in their hands, and emptied some saddles. The charging gunhands did not slack up.

Smoke lifted his Colts and let the hammers down just as a hired gun galloped past the trading post. The .44's knocked the man from the saddle. Jackson was beside him on the porch, guns blazing. The badman turned good man emptied two more saddles.

The early morning became eerily quiet as Smoke and Jackson began punching out empties and reloading. The shopkeeper's wife untied her husband and Bendel. The saloonkeeper was furious as he joined Smoke on the porch.

"By God, I've had it!" he yelled. "I'll not tolerate any more of Jud Vale's highhandedness."

"Nor will I," the shopkeeper said, taking the shotgun his

wife offered him. "From now on, I see a Bar V brand, I blow the rider out of the saddle."

"That goes double for me," Bendel said, stripping the guns from Wills and loading them full.

Matt led the horses around to the front.

"Let's ride!" Walt said.

Three miles from the trading post, Smoke and his little force rode right into a group of Bar V riders. There was nothing gentlemanly or honorable about the fight. Smoke just dragged iron and started shooting, Walt and the others doing the same.

They looked up from the body-littered road as Clint Perkins rode up, a wild glint in his eyes. 'It is time, is it?" he called. "Very well. I recall an Indian saying: "It is a good day to die.'" He turned his horse's head and rode off toward the Bar V.

"I didn't know we was just gonna ride up to Jud's front door and start shootin'," Rusty said.

"I didn't either," Smoke said. "But maybe that's the way it's got to be." He put Dagger into a gallop and the others followed, leaving the bodies in the road without a second glance.

One hired gun groaned and rolled over in the road. Finally he sat up, his head bloody and throbbing. He gingerly touched the wound and winced. It was painful, but not serious. He got to his boots, found his horse, and crawled into the saddle.

"Hell with this!" he said. "It's gone sour." He reined up when the trading post came into view, and watched Bendel and the shopkeeper and his wife digging holes in the back. The gunhand wisely changed his mind about having a drink and carefully skirted the trading post. He thought California ought to be a real good spot to head for.

He knew there had been four or five men at the trading post, about ten more lying in ambush out from the post, and five with him. That was twenty men dead or dying at the hands of Smoke and the others, all in one morning—and the morning wasn't even half over! Yeah, California sounded real good.

"Move, horse. Jud Vale's number is comin' up this day, I'm thinkin'."

Cisco Webster, the Texas gunhand whose teeth had been

knocked out by Rusty back at the crick, looked up at the road, just at the point where it crested the hill. He felt a touch of fear clutch at his belly.

Six men sat their saddles, looking down at the mansion, and Cisco didn't need a crystal ball to know who they were.

Highpockets noticed the direction the man's eyes were taking and he looked up. Like Cisco, the gunfighter felt a slight lash of dread touch him at this sighting.

The yard was crowded with bounty hunters and gun-slingers, all looking at the crest of the hill.

Smoke urged Dagger forward, riding with the reins in his teeth and his hands filled with Colts.

"What the hell are they goin' to do?" Hammer asked.

"It's over," Buck Wall told him. "I woke up with a bad feelin' about this day."

"You quittin'?" Chato Di Peso asked.

"I shore am." Buck walked toward the bunkhouse just as Jud appeared on the front porch.

"Where the hell do you think you're going?" Jud yelled at him.

"I'm quittin'," Buck called over his shoulder. "Like right now."

Jason had appeared on the porch beside his boss. "The hell you are!" he said, and shot Buck in the back.

The gunfighter pitched forward, dead before he hit the ground.

Smoke picked that time to charge. They split up, with Smoke and Clint riding right into the front yard, the reins in their teeth and hands full of Colts.

Matt and Walt went to the right, Jackson and Rusty to the left.

Hammer grabbed for his guns. Smoke shot him down, the slug taking him in the chest. Hammer died sitting on his butt in the road, his hands by his sides. After a few seconds, he slowly toppled over.

Shorty DePaul came out of the bunkhouse just as Walt and Matt were galloping past. Shorty sighted in Walt. Matt's gun crashed and Shorty felt the sledgehammer blow take him in the belly, about an inch above his belt. Matt fired again, his second slug striking the gunfighter in the chest and knocking him down.

"Kilt by a punk kid," were Shorty's last words.

Rusty and Jackson rode right into a knot of startled gunslicks. Pike and Becket went down under bullets fired at almost point-blank range. Molino stepped out of the barn and put a slug into Rusty's shoulder. Rusty border-rolled his Colt and shot the man in the throat. Molino hit the ground, coughing and gurgling.

Jaeger and Chato Di Peso saw the outcome of the fight very quickly and slipped through the dust and confusion to the bunkhouse, quickly gathering up their possessions. They grabbed horses—neither one of them giving a damn whose horse it was—and pulled out.

Cisco Webster watched as Smoke jumped from the saddle, and ran behind a building, reloading as he ran. Dagger trotted to the corral and began harassing the mares.

Cisco ran to the storage shed, flattening out against a wall. He stuck his head around the corner just in time to catch a bullet right between the eyes. He sank to the ground, a very curious expression on his dead face.

Clint, out of the saddle and down on one knee, doubled over the Colorado gunhand, Barstow, with two .44 rounds to the belly, then shifted his Colt and ended the career of Highpockets.

Jackson had helped Rusty out of the saddle and left him behind good cover with half a dozen Colts taken from the dead and dying. Jackson went headhunting. He walked right up to Rim Reynolds and several of his men and began shooting as fast as he could cock and fire. Rim went down screaming in pain with two slugs in his belly. Jackson was burned on one arm and took the loss of part of one ear but he was still standing when the others were down. He calmly and swiftly reloaded, shook the blood from his face and stepped back out into the fracas.

Walt and Matt were standing side by side, the old and the young, their guns taking a terrible toll. Crazy Phil was down on his knees, with four of his men on the ground with him. Old Walt winked at young Matt as they reloaded.

Clint was working his way closer to the house. He had but one thought in his demented mind.

The Pecos Kid and Glen Regan—Glen was walking slow due to the gunshot wounds in his butt from back at the creek—tried to make the corral and get away. Rusty dropped them both midway.

Blackjack Morgan stood with his legs spread wide, his hands over the butts of his guns, facing Smoke, who still held his Colts in his hands. "I'm faster, Jensen!" he called over the din of battle.

"No. You're just dead," Smoke told him. He lifted his right hand and shot the gunfighter. There was a time for discretion and a time for valor, but at no time was there a moment to be wasted on fools.

Smoke stepped over the dying man and walked on.

A searing pain in Smoke's left leg turned him around and slammed him up against a wall. Gimpy Bonner and Scott Johnson faced him. Smoke lifted his Colts and let them bang. When the dust and gunsmoke cleared, Smoke was bloody but still standing.

Smoke reloaded, checked his wounds, and bound a bandana around the leg wound. He walked on as the sounds of galloping horses came to him over the shooting. About a dozen men were hauling their ashes away from the ranch. Smoke lifted his right-hand Colt and ended life for Ben Lewis, who had lined up Jackson with a rifle. Ben danced for a moment, his spurs jingling his death chant; then he slumped to the ground.

"Jensen!" the voice turned Smoke around to face Luddy.

Smoke didn't hesitate. Just lifted both guns and began firing and walking toward the man. He stood over the bloody outlaw, their eyes meeting.

"I thought you'd give me a fair chance, Jensen!" Luddy gasped.

"Did you ever give anyone a fair chance, Luddy?"

Luddy laughed humorlessly. "Can't say that I ever did,

come to think of it." He shivered once. "Cold. Mighty cold all of a sudden." He closed his eyes and died.

Smoke turned away.

The gunfire had all but faded away. The grounds around the great mansion were littered with bodies. Jason was sitting on the steps, his shirt front bloody, but he was holding on to life long enough to see the outcome of what was about to take place in front of him.

Clint and Jud faced each other, both of them with the same wild light in their eyes.

"Hello, Daddy!" Clint said sarcastically.

"You son of a bitch!" Jud snarled at him.

"You sure got that right," the son told the father, then grabbed iron.

Father and son stood ten feet apart and put lead in each other. Both went to the ground on their knees at the same time. Both continued firing. Jud toppled over and Clint was only about one second behind him.

Walt walked up, one arm dangling uselessly from a .45 slug. He looked at the scene in front of him, then lifted his eyes to Jason.

"I reckon it's over and done, ain't it, Walt?" the man gasped.

"I reckon it is, Jason."

"I reckon Jud just tried to toss too big a loop. Is that the way you see it?"

"Why did you and Jud kill my son?"

Jason laughed, a nasty bark of dark humor. "'Cause we wanted to, you old bastard!" Jason closed his eyes as the pale rider came closer.

Walt lifted his Colt and eared the hammer back. Then he slowly lowered the weapon as Jason tumbled down the steps to lie on the ground.

"Ride for Doc Evans and the sheriff, Matt," Smoke told the boy.

"They're comin' up the road now, Smoke," Matt told him, pointing. "And it looks like the Army is with them."

28

Smoke had to hang around for the hearings—both state and federal government, since the Army had finally gotten involved—but that was all right, his wounds needed the time to heal. He watched as Rusty and Doreen, then Jackson and Susie got married. Since Walt was Jud's sole living survivor, Walt took possession of the Bar V. He signed over the Box T to Rusty and Doreen and gave the Bar V to Jackson and Susie. Matt stayed on as a hand for Rusty. Walt and Alice were going to build a little place on Bear Lake and retire.

Jackson was having the great mansion torn down on the day Smoke rode out. The couple planned to build a smaller, much more practical ranch house.

Smoke stopped by the trading post for a beer and to say good-bye to Bendel.

He was halfway through his beer when Jaeger and Di Peso pushed open the batwings. Smoke sighed and set the mug down.

"Your time to die, Jensen," Di Peso told him.

"I don't think so," Smoke replied, turning and drawing both guns.

Smoke stepped over the bodies and walked to Dagger, swinging into the saddle and pointing Dagger's head south, toward Arizona and Sally and the kids. Bendel's voice stopped him.

"Smoke!"

He twisted in the saddle.

"If you ever plan a return visit, do me a favor, will you?" Bendel yelled.

"What's that?"

"Please bring a damn shovel!"